Masks

Books by
E. M. Prazeman

THE LORD JESTER'S LEGACY

Masks

Confidante

Innocence and Silence

Coming soon:

THE KILHELLION

Masks

BOOK ONE OF THE LORD JESTER'S LEGACY

E. M. Prazeman

Cover design by Ravven
    http://www.ravven.com
Iinterior book design by Kamila Miller
    http://wyrdgoat.com/Cover_Art.html

ISBN-13: 978-1482050028
ISBN-10: 1482050021

Reprint, November 2014
Also available as an ebook from Smashwords, Amazon, Barnes and Noble
and other retailers. This book and other fiction and non-fiction books can
be purchased from the Wyrd Goat Press website.

Please support producers of art and content by taking freely only that
which is offered for free, and fairly compensating for that work which the
artists of the world create and ask for pay in exchange for the hours and
years of love and training and toil they've put into it.

If you find the cover stripped off of this or any other book, it may have been
reported as destroyed and the publisher and author have not been paid for it.

To Lisa, Steve, David, Dale, R.R. and all my other friends
who might not want to be named even in this very anonymous manner
because there's still fear, and hate, and politics.
Dale ... you're still missed even after all the years gone by.

And to my tribe, some of whom don't mention their religious beliefs
because there's still fear, and hate, and politics.

Politics will always dog us, but maybe someday the fear and hate will be directed
only at those who actually earned it through selfish acts of predation, violence and
destruction against the young, the good, the hard-working and the innocent.
It's a silly dream, I know, but sometimes dreams come true.

Sometimes it's even the good dreams that come true.

Chapter One

Mark guarded the moneybox at a small table beside his mother's shrouded body. Butlers in dark overcoats, rich merchant's sons dressed like lacy nobles and other regular patrons of his mother's wine shop sorted through estate wares. Gray light outlined the shadowed people as they came in from the spring morning's chill. Some perused the selection in the barrel room. Some touched Mark on the top of his head as they passed and whispered, "*allolai* protect you." They stole bits of his composure and mussed his hair.

A tall, heavy-shouldered man came in. Mark looked hopefully, only to be disappointed.

His father had been missing for a whole day now.

Mark wormed his hand into the winding sheet and held his mother's icy hand. Squeezed it. It didn't feel like her anymore. More like raw poultry in a glove.

Thomas, one of the regulars, came over with his battered purse. "How about two gules for the two barrels of burgundy you have left." His sweaty, dark-bearded face mounded into a smile.

Mark opened his mother's ledger. She'd purchased the burgundy for two gules a barrel. The familiar lines of her tidy handwriting threatened to make his eyes tear up. He shut the ledger. "No."

The smile smoothed away and Thomas leaned closer. "Come on, boy. That's more than you've seen all day."

Thomas' forceful manner made his cheeks burn. Mark owned a certain fondness for him, but it felt too much like Thomas wanted to take advantage. "Make a better offer or leave off."

"Here now," Thomas said, reddening. "Your mother never treated a paying customer so! I wouldn't cheat you. We've always been friendly, haven't we, Mark?"

Thomas' smile failed to disguise a glint of cold anticipation in his dark eyes. What did he really want? "They're worth thrice more. And I can sell it by the carafe if I want." His fears of losing everything his parents had worked for churned back up, though it wasn't as bad as—

His mother had still been alive when he found her soaked in blood, gasping, unable to speak. He saw terror and pain in her eyes—

The bastard laughed. "By the carafe? The landlord won't lease this place to a song boy. You have a day at most to make your money and run."

Mark's heart skipped. "Lord Jorbeth knows I helped keep the books. I'm old enough." Older than the baker's ten year old son, and that illiterate bully managed the store while his father slept all day. Mark's face warmed as his temper rose. "And my father will turn up soon."

"Take the money you have and run while you can." The nastiness had left Thomas' voice and his eyes widened with earnest. "I mean it, boy." Was that real concern in his eyes? Thomas opened the purse and picked out two gules from a jumble of argen, cupru and bits. "Find me later. I know a place you can stay."

A man like Thomas oughtn't have that much coin.

"I can't run," Mark told him. "My father has an indenture and the only way I can pay on it is if I have the shop."

"Never mind the indenture. I can protect you from the Church."

Mark's heart jumped. No one, well, maybe someone from the islands could protect him from the Church. But what did Thomas want with him, and why would Mark need protection?

The doors swung open and two priests strode in. Half red, half white robes billowed around them. Their absurd, black-winged hats were unexpectedly intimidating as the men towered over him. The younger priest carried two ledger books bound in black. He swept cork pullers and flatware off a table and opened his books to places marked by red ribbon. Dust billowed out from the pages.

The estate patrons shrank back into the shop corners to watch.

Lord Jorbeth followed the priests in. He looked anxious, his clean-shaven face pale against a black velvet coat and vest. Another lord came in after Jorbeth, a large, blond man that looked like he did more sailing than lording judging by his weathered face, braided hair and thick beard, though he wore finely-tailored clothes.

"This sale is closed," the elder priest announced. "All funds and remaining property are being held by the Church."

What? Heat rose up through Mark's body, and then chill poured down.

Everyone set aside whatever they held and fled, snaking around the unmoving priests and lords. The elder priest watched carefully, like he expected thievery.

The coins dropped back into Thomas' purse and he grabbed Mark by the arm. "Come along son." He hurried toward the door with the others. The priest grabbed Mark by the other arm.

"What are you doing?" the priest asked sharply.

Thomas released Mark's arm and smiled. "Taking the boy home." He looked unafraid, even defiant.

The priest looked between them. "I think not." His gaze settled on Mark, cold and ancient. "You are the heir?"

Thomas twitched his head, hinting at negation.

Mark stole courage from he didn't know where. He'd rather tell the truth and make it on his own than trust Thomas, who probably had something other than charity in mind. "Yes." His heart fluttered and he caught his breath as the priest's grip tightened.

"Hand them over," the priest said, shifting his gaze to Thomas.

"What, Your Wisdom?" Thomas' tone made the words sound more sarcastic than respectful.

"The gules you offered the boy. Hand them over."

"But I haven't bought anything," Thomas protested with a laugh.

"It's true sir." Mark realized his mistake in address when the priest lifted his chin with affront. "Your Wisdom. He offered but I didn't—"

"You dare lie to me?" The priest glared at Mark.

"I'm not," Mark protested.

The priest turned his attention back to Thomas. "The gules. Or do I need to speak with your lord on this matter?"

Lord? Perhaps he shouldn't have been surprised that Thomas worked for a noble, considering his regular visits to buy good wine, but the fact that the priest seemed to know Thomas and was willing to take such a large sum from him without a qualm shocked him.

Thomas bowed his head and, much to Mark's surprise, handed over the coin with a bold and unpleasant smile. "I'll come back for my barrel of wine, and the rest of what's mine." Thomas surreptitiously looked back at Mark. He didn't look upset, only like he wanted to make sure Mark understood that he should have left before the priests came. How had he known that they were coming?

Thomas went out into the street with purposeful haste. It seemed darker outside, as if a storm were coming.

The priest released Mark and pointed to a stool. Mark sat, feeling as if he'd been robbed. He didn't know how to get whatever it was he'd lost back again. He supposed it was kind of Thomas to lay claim to only one barrel of burgundy when he could have at least attempted to lay claim to two and, thanks to the priest's lack of regard, would have probably gotten it.

The priest raised his hands and spoke foreign words. He sounded bored. He lowered his hands and walked over to Mark, looming over him. "You are their sole child?"

"Yes, Your Wisdom. Mark Seaton." Mark didn't know his place with a priest. He didn't know the priest's place here, either, unless it had to do with his indenture. Maybe he was a mavson, here to investigate. "Someone murdered my mother and my father is missing," Mark told him. "The guard said—"

"When the murderer is caught he'll be executed," the priest said. "What should concern you now is your indenture."

The words shouldn't have made him afraid, but cold filled his belly just the same. "My father kept his indenture in good order, and until it's proven that—" His father couldn't be dead. "He could arrive at any time."

"The mavson assigned to this case doubts that anyone will see your father again."

"But it's only been a day—"

"Perhaps if you were older you could manage on your own, but since you're still a child the Church will manage this matter for you." The priest turned his attention to Lord Jorbeth. "You said the table and chairs are part of your property."

"Yes," Jorbeth said. Too much white showed in his eyes. Mark's stomach clenched up tight. "And the household furniture."

The furniture? *No.*

"Show me," the priest said.

They went upstairs. Mark gaped for a heartbeat before he followed after them. "My lord," he protested, fighting back rage that choked his chest and throat, "my father still might come home and these are our things, you know they're our things, things my father—"

"Hush. You don't know the first thing about what your parents did and didn't own. I do." Lord Jorbeth leaned close. His breath smelled like cloves and sour wine. "I'm trying to save a few things for you, Mark," he whispered. "Trust me. Now go downstairs and be silent."

Mark stayed on the stairs while the landlord continued up. The priest moved heavily around their private rooms, his footfalls knocking dust from the ceiling. Trembling, Mark went back downstairs to his mother and took her cold hand again. He wished he dared look at her again, but the last time he'd pulled back the winding sheets her face had looked like a mask, cold and comfortless.

The other lord quietly watched Mark. He was a powerfully built and unhandsome man. "Your insolence will earn you a beating," he said.

Mark lowered his gaze, his heart thundering in his ears.

The priest returned with Lord Jorbeth. The younger priest continued to write busily. "We will inventory the landlord's possessions, and then we will sell the remainder to pay against the indenture, Lord Gillvrey," the elder priest said.

Mark knew that name well. The thundering in Mark's ears grew louder. He wished he mattered to this man that worked alongside his father.

Lord Gillvrey surveyed the room with disinterest. His gaze returned to Mark. "How much would the navy pay for the boy's indenture?"

Mark blinked, not sure he'd heard right. The navy had lost so many ships in the war. Dozens had sailed from this very port, and not all of them returned. Did he want to send Mark to his death? "I can sail for you," Mark promised. Everyone assumed he was too small, even his father, but he knew he could be a great sailor if someone just gave him a chance. "I would work hard for you, just as my father did. Please."

"How old is he?" the older priest asked the younger one.

"Eleven," Mark said, but the priest didn't listen to him. Maybe eleven would be too young to get shot, or stabbed, too young to drown or be blown apart by cannons. He'd always wanted to sail, but not to war.

The younger priest paged back in one of the ledger books and peered down his nose through his glasses. "Eleven years, five months."

The priest spared Mark a glance. "Looks younger. Still, old enough to serve in the navy."

Lord Jorbeth cleared his throat. He looked at Mark, half-appraising, half-apologetic. "I'll pay thirty gules."

Thirty gules. He never thought to be worth so much, and at the same time it seemed a mean amount for a person's life.

Gillvrey sniffed again. "I'm certain the king pays more than that."

Anger and terror mixed him up inside, but Mark managed to open his mouth and the words escaped. "If I'm dead I'm not worth anything. Or is a corpse worth something, my lord?"

"The last figure I heard was fifty gules for a sailor of less than fourteen years," the priest said, ignoring Mark. The priest writing at the table lifted his pen and nodded in agreement before he set to writing again. "The boy could do well more than fifty gules worth of work for you in his lifetime, Lord Gillvrey. It might be a better bargain to keep him than sell him to the navy."

"He's frail boy." Lord Gillvrey shifted his attention to stare at Mark. "Trade shipping is for strong men."

Mark found his voice, and his mind again. "I read, write, and I know enough arithmetic to keep books. And I am my father's son. I'll grow into my height in time." He couldn't believe he was trying to sell himself. "My lord, why am I being sold? My father held this indenture for longer than I've been alive and has never missed a payment. Can't you wait until the end of the month at least?"

"Your family owes two hundred fifty gules before it earns out for the *Swift-by*, so don't pretend the ship has anything to do with you aside from a distant dream," Lord Gillvrey said. "What matters now is that you wouldn't manage on that ship, and I have no use for you on land."

"That doesn't erase my father's payments." Mark looked to the priests. "If he's trying to buy the ship then what my family earned is owed back." He'd dreamed of owning the *Swift-by*, but if he couldn't, at least he wouldn't see it stolen through political conniving.

The priest crossed his arms, annoyed. "Lord Gillvrey is not in fact buying the ship, nor is such a thing possible while you live. He merely holds the trust for your family's indenture. Since he has no use for you and you are too young to carry an indenture by yourself, the Church is taking legal guardianship and will assign the most profitable work we can find for you until you come of age, at which point the indenture might be renegotiated if you so demand. I understand if you're afraid to go to war, young man, but bear in mind that you might distinguish yourself, and that you might win a share of a prize that will earn out the indenture in entire. Then you'll have a ship of your own."

As if he would survive to see it. "Why can't I work here?"

"Because you won't be able to turn a profit here. No one will do serious business with you. You couldn't keep up the lease payments, never mind pay against your indenture."

Mark's chest contracted. "So you intend to send me to the navy? Who gets the indenture if I die? The Church?"

The priest's eyes flashed with anger. "You dare imply that the Church would deliberately profit from your death?"

Mark lowered his gaze and his voice. "Please, I just want to understand."

The priest relented. "If you default and have no near relatives who wish to claim it, the balance of the indenture goes to auction, a thing that I'm sure Lord Gillvrey wishes to avoid since I doubt he would compete well in an auction. Ships are in high demand at the moment. The guarantor will indeed be the Church, with a certain amount going to the Crown. There are other details related to the hull fund—it's complicated."

"So complicated that you haven't the time, or is it that you don't have the ability to explain it?" Mark's voice shook and his face burned with anger and his hands trembled and there was nothing he could do.

"You ought to be glad that the Church will protect you. Bankers of a more sinful constitution could arrange to take advantage of a default just as you suggest."

Default. He made death sound like a hatch mark on a piece of paper. "I would rather auction off the indenture now than to be sold like a slave to the navy."

The priest looked over his glasses at Mark. "That would be very foolish. Anyway, you're too young to decide for yourself."

Mark wanted to scream the words but his voice choked them into a broken protest. "I thought slavery was a sin, your wisdom, but it seems it isn't if the Church oversees the selling."

"Stupid boy," the priest spat. "The Church is your only ally now. Best you be silent and thankful the Church is looking after you through me."

Lord Gillvrey crossed his arms and smiled smugly. "Is there anyone else who might be interested in offering the boy gainful employment?"

Lord Jorbeth leaned against the bar and put his head in his hand like it hurt. Mark looked toward the door and wondered if he ought to run, and if he ran, if he could find Thomas before the sacred guardsmen caught up with him.

"The Church—" The priest paused as a carriage, pulled by many horses, rattled up the street. Mark expected it to keep going, but it stopped. "The Church can set a modest wage and put the boy to work at civic duties until there is a more satisfactory offer, but if those who know him don't want him, it's unlikely a stranger will make a better offer."

The door opened and yet another lord came in, a wrinkled man of average height, gray hair cut short and bound into a short tail in a lush velvet ribbon. Silks and brocades shone under a mink cloak lined with velvet. He had small eyes, a small nose and a large mouth that made Mark think of a fish. Behind him, a jester leaned casually in the doorway.

Mark's gaze locked on the jester. He wore a black porcelain demi-mask covered in a complex gold design enhanced with sapphires and blue diamonds. The jester's black clothes sparkled with sapphires as well. He had weight to him but he balanced with terrible grace, his hand resting on a glittering rapier. An elegant dueling pistol rested on his other hip in easy reach.

His clothes alone could have bought Mark's indenture several times over.

The priests straightened, chins lifting, and the priest doing the writing bared his teeth at the jester. For a moment they all stood in poses like a tableau for a tragedy.

The old lord's gaze fell on Mark with expectation that seemed braced for disappointment. He looked Mark over, and his expression lightened. "Interesting find."

"My Lord Argenwain," the priest said tightly, "we are in the midst of a legal proceeding."

The name nearly stopped Mark's heart. Argenwain, head patron of Seven Churches and a great personal friend to His Royal Majesty King Michael. Which meant the jester was Gutter, favorite of the king.

"My lord my lord." Gutter laughed, moving past Mark's mother to sidle around the priest. "We are here for the sale. The boy is for sale, isn't he? And I've brought a buyer."

"He's not a slave," the priest informed Gutter. "He is renegotiating a contractual indenture—"

Gutter chuckled. "Does that increase or decrease the price?"

"I had no idea Lord Argenwain was interested in carrying a contractual indenture for an insignificant commoner," the priest said again, his tongue cutting the words into tight syllables.

Gutter turned his attention to Lord Argenwain. "You can trust me about his voice, my lord. At the moment he probably couldn't hold a note if I put it in his hand, poor boy, shook up by all this legal rape, otherwise I'd have him sing us some cheer."

At any other time, Mark might have blushed with shy pride, but instead a fearful cold grabbed his spine in its teeth.

Lord Argenwain looked Mark over again. "What is the rate?"

"A sol and I'll give him up," Lord Gillvrey said.

The amount stole Mark's breath. Only the highest nobility traded in sols, the equivalent of one hundred gules. He wanted to run, to hit something, to hide. Instead he lifted his chin and swallowed his fear. "Maybe you should have asked for double. Then they'd be doubly sure not to take it."

Gutter circled Lord Gillvrey like a lady circling her partner in a dance, an uncomfortably sensual and predatory movement that made Mark blush and shiver at the same time. "One sol. Is that all?" Gutter asked.

"A sol is nothing to sniff at." Lord Gillvrey's shoulders jogged briefly. "But I suppose the sum means little to you. He's yours, if you want him."

Mark had to sit. Lord Jester Gutter, the most notorious jester in the three kingdoms, was in his mother's wine shop to buy him. His romantic daydreams about clever, playful jesters shattered into a reality that filled him with awe, like watching a storm toy with the huge ships in the harbor.

He wished he had that kind of power, even though he quaked in its presence.

Lord Jester Gutter approached the priest. "What would it take to hold the boy's indenture outright?"

The priest glanced at Gillvrey, who shook his head. Jorbeth watched all this with an expression of quiet horror. "Two hundred forty seven gules buys the boy's indenture and use of the *Swift-by*, a large trade ship," the priest said. Gillvrey's mouth opened in protest, but he didn't make a sound and shut it again.

Almost two and a half sol. Mother and father together could have eventually paid it, but by myself ....

You are worth more than this. The strange voices that had haunted his mind since his earliest memories, sometimes friendly, sometimes disturbing, spoke in a foreign language but he'd always been able to understand them.

This one, the one Mark called Ruby, had spoken directly to him when his mother died too. Both times Ruby had failed to comfort him.

Meanwhile Lord Argenwain's eyes had brightened and he looked to his jester with a bemused expression. "Trade ship? I've always been interested in ships."

Maybe all they'd wanted was the ship all along, but they'd called Mark a find.

"I don't intend to sell the whole indenture," Gillvrey protested. "I inherited it from my father and I won't give it up."

Lord Jester Gutter's eyes smiled behind the mask. "And why would you? Except." Gutter's hand caressed the swept hilt of his rapier. "I think it would be a mistake to hold your remaining interest in the ship, my lord. Trade is such a volatile thing during war. The risks are so much higher than in peacetime. If something happened to that ship, wouldn't you have rather sold the use of it while you could?"

Gillvrey looked down at the jester's jeweled boot buckles. "I'm willing to take on that risk. My family always has. We are in shipping, after all."

"And I imagine it's a good, fast ship," Lord Jester Gutter said. He stepped precisely heel toe, heel toe, making staccato beats on the worn floor. "Something the military might be interested in commandeering, especially after their recent naval disaster."

"It's unsuitable for naval action."

"I think a certain commander I'm acquainted with would disagree. But even if he decides it isn't worthy for naval action, as you say, I think you'll have trouble hiring cargo. Merchant lords, fearing pirates, are hearing from knowledgeable sources that it's better to send as much of their wares overland as possible, for the time being."

"Those who deal with me trust my judgment." Gillvrey hissed, his breath coming hard.

Gutter leaned against the bar beside Gillvrey. "If that ship isn't suitable to employ in a war as you say, it's highly unlikely anyone would be willing to ship cargo on such a defenseless vessel."

Gillvrey made a sad attempt to compose himself. Every movement Gutter made reminded Mark of theater, and Gillvrey appeared to be doomed to tragedy. "Are you threatening to undermine my business?" Gillvrey asked.

Lord Argenwain chuckled. The papery sound made Mark shiver. "No, no, of course not. I would never condone such a thing." Gutter laughed as if his lord had made a joke.

Lord Gillvrey looked to the priest. "You must do something. My interests are at stake here. This is my property."

No, thought Mark. *It's mine.* "If my parents were safe, you'd still have it, too. I guess this is your tragedy as well as mine, my lord." Mark willed every word to stab, wished he could see the lord bleed for it.

"They're not doing anything illegal," the priest said. His gaze met Lord Argenwain's, and it looked like the two of them had just made a silent pact.

"Why are you doing this?" Gillvrey demanded.

"Because my master wants it." Lord Jester Gutter's eyes behind the mask became darker and seemed to open into deep places, terrifying in their chill. Mark didn't want to be at his mercy, but better to be in his service than dying at sea. "What was your name again, my lord?" Gutter asked. "If you choose to keep the ship I certainly will put in a word with merchants in every friendly country. I'll encourage them to do the right thing by you, and I'm sure they'll listen carefully to my advice."

Gillvrey's shoulders sank. Lord Jester Gutter's eyes smiled again and he faced the priests. "Sold, for two hundred forty seven gules."

"Less the sale price of the wine shop's contents," the eldest priest said. "As those are technically part of the boy's inheritance."

The jester glanced around the room. "I'll send the butler to purchase the best of it tomorrow. Can we take the boy tonight?"

"His contract must be completed first," the scribbling priest protested from his table.

"And in the meantime he has to stay in a cell at the church?" Gutter scoffed. "Ridiculous. Let us feed and shelter him and spare the Church the trouble and expense."

Food and shelter. Those things seemed unimportant compared to his mother's body growing colder and thinner every moment.

His father might arrive at any time, and Mark would not be here.

The old priest gave Mark a look that might have been gentle on a younger, less stern face. "Take him, then, and beware the wrath of *morbai* for your wicked ways, jester."

Gutter laughed even as Mark shuddered. He walked to Mark and gestured toward the door. "It's all right, Mark. You'll have a better life this way. And someday, you might own that ship."

Earn out that mighty sum before his life ran out? Mark looked back at the tables where his mother lay. He noticed a stain on the white winding sheet, dark reddish brown, in her body's shadow. That rich, ugly color reached across the room like a disgusting odor, making him gag. "But what if my father comes back?" Mark asked. The priests just stared at him coldly, so Mark turned to Gutter. "My lord jester, please, my father might come back any moment."

"Then the matter will go to court." In that moment, Gutter's voice sounded very kind, and gentle, and apologetic. Mark thirsted for that compassion almost as much as his mother's love.

"Can't we wait?" he pleaded.

"Such things are best handled promptly," the older priest said.

"I'm sorry." Gutter's voice hushed down to a whisper.

He wanted to run up to his room, hide in his bed among his things and wait for his parents to come back somehow. No matter how good this chance, all he really wanted was to be home. "Will someone tell my father where I am, should he come home? And what will happen to the indenture if he does?"

Lord Jester Gutter crouched before him, earnest eyes peering through the mask. "Mark, you should have listened before. You have a second chance to listen to me now. Walk away from your old life, and never look back. I know it hurts, but I promise things will get better." He pulled out a battered purse. Thomas's battered purse. It was filled with gold. "You will make handsome wages as a servant in my lord's house, more than your parents together. And I'm sure Lord Argenwain will make some fair arrangement with your father in regard to the indenture. With the Church's oversight, of course."

Thomas—it couldn't be. A jester had been coming to his mother's shop for years. Why? To buy wine and to trade oranges and chocolates for a song from her son?

It makes no sense.

"You've been watching me," Mark said.

The jester smiled. "You're a smart boy." Thomas, Lord Jester Gutter, straightened. "It's time to begin a life that will employ your intelligence and talent to its full."

Lord Argenwain got a wistful, almost sad look. "He's so young."

"He'll grow, my lord." Gutter's voice, though gentle, also held a sad note in it.

Lord Argenwain held out his hand. Though Mark had never dreamt of jewels and sleeping in soft rooms, those images tumbled into his mind. The old lord watched him with guileless eyes, gentle and inviting. An instinct he couldn't name warned him that something was wrong, but better to face that unknown than war.

Under the priests' sharp gazes Mark walked to Lord Argenwain and took his hand. Like his mother's hand it was cold, but it squeezed and held him, and led him to the golden carriage waiting outside.

Chapter Two

Mark's lip stung as he dabbed the paste into the blood. His hands shook but he managed to work quickly. He tried not to look at himself in the mirror. The lace, the pale blue velvet, the diamond buttons—he didn't own any of it, not even himself.

I should have let them sell me to the navy ....

A conclusion drawn eight years too late.

He wrapped a neckerchief over the fresh bruises around his throat. White gloves covered his red knuckles and the rug burns on his palms.

The gold clock chimed once—it was a quarter after.

Mark's heart punched high in his chest. He dashed out into the long hallway and hurried down the marble stairs.

Professor Vinkin stalked out of the lower east hall, his bulky valise bouncing against coarse linen trousers. His brown coat, of a loose fashion from a decade before, matched a floppy brown hat. Most of his slick black hair had pulled free of a single limp ribbon.

"Professor Vinkin—"

"We'll have to reschedule." The professor's bunched-up shoulders and the tight disappointment in his voice hurt worse than the lost history lesson. Mark darted in front of him and predictably the professor stopped well before there was any danger of physical contact. Vinkin had plenty of room to step around and get to the front door, but he didn't move. His shoulders rose closer to his ears.

Mark didn't know if the professor was that way around everyone, or just him, but he felt guilty either way for trapping him with it.

"Stand aside, please." Vinkin looked shabby but his voice carried more refinement than Lord Argenwain's. The marble entry made him sound even more grand.

"Please. I'm sorry. You can charge for the full hour—"

"That would be unethical."

"—or half. Just stay. Please."

The professor focused on a delicate wall sconce where a carved, gilded candle waited to be lit. "By the time I arrange my materials again you won't have time for even half a lesson. Now please, stand aside."

"I'll pay you double." It would set his indenture back a bit, but it seemed like a small sacrifice.

The professor hesitated. "You can't bribe time." His shoulders bunched up even higher and he hurried past, brushing the wall to get as far from Mark as possible.

No.

"If you leave, Gutter won't be happy with either of us."

The professor went rigid beside the door.

Mark didn't expect that much fear. He stammered onward. "And Lord Argenwain won't like it either." Still a threat, but softer, he hoped. Shit, the professor might never come back after this. "I'm so sorry. I didn't mean—" What had he meant to do? "It's just that—" The professor made him happy.

The professor set down his valise before Mark could think of another tack. Hope, warm and vibrant, rushed through Mark's tangled guts and he took a full breath.

Professor Vinkin's shoulders lowered as he turned. "I know they're hurting you."

Mark's breath shortened as the professor's gaze slid around, touching everything but him. "It's not them." It didn't matter. "If there isn't enough time for a lesson, then just sit with me." He almost offered to pay again, but he hesitated in time. Why did the professor have to be so complicated? Everyone else Mark knew, except Gutter of course, was so simple. As long as they benefited in some way, they were happy to spend time with him.

The professor's gaze stopped on the alabaster statue of a half-dressed boy reclining with a fawn in his arms. It seemed innocent at first glance. The grace and softness in the composition distracted from the crass symbolism, assuming the viewer knew terms like staghorn and supple and 'the depth of one's lean.' A nearly prone male would accept almost any attention a man might wish to visit on him. The fawn implied even more.

Mark hated that statue. It didn't just flaunt Lord Argenwain's preferences for boys. Everyone assumed Mark leaned just as far as the boy in the statue, and that it had begun when he first came here eight years ago.

He'd been a fawn, but he'd never leaned *over.*

Kneeling wasn't so bad.

The professor gestured back down the hall where the study lay and Mark's heart leapt. Mark led the way, opened the door but the professor gestured for Mark to go first.

The professor shut the door behind them. He'd never done that before. Mark's joy took a dark turn. "Can—" *Deep breath.* "I order some chocolate for you?"

The professor gestured to a chair and Mark sat, his obedience now an act of will instead of flowing from his gratitude. But he'd do whatever he needed to keep this man in his life.

As he'd always done to survive among the men in his life.

"Take off the scarf and gloves." The professor's voice had a soft quality that made Mark uneasy.

Mark slipped off the gloves, one finger at a time and then a tug. He'd undressed for Argenwain many times, but he hadn't felt so naked in the unveiling of so little for a very long time.

Mark unknotted the neckerchief and unwound it. The lace-edged silk slid and flowed over his hands.

The professor finally looked at him. "Did Lord Argenwain do that?" The soft voice didn't hide the professor's disgust. Mark couldn't tell if his revulsion was unwisely directed at the most powerful man in the city, or Mark, or the entire household.

"No."

"Don't lie to me, Mark, or I will leave."

Irritation crowded out the guilt and embarrassment. "You teach history, but I've learned more about politics from you than anyone else. I would think that you'd understand the danger you're putting yourself in. Besides, what would the truth get you?"

"So it is him."

"No! It's—" Maybe the truth would help. "Lord Argenwain is impatient with the new valet." Cruel should have been the word, but Mark didn't dare say that even though nearly every room at the manor was perfectly private. Not because he feared Lord Argenwain. He feared for the professor if he should repeat something he shouldn't. "And Bainswell takes it out on me. Because I'm short and slender," *and I lean,* "and I'm Lord Argenwain's pet."

"And Lord Argenwain does nothing?"

"It's beneath him to notice." And from Gutter when Mark wrote to him—nothing. He fought down a gut-clenching feeling of betrayal.

"He doesn't have to notice. He could evict that degenerate and be done."

Mark cringed. "I know."

"So Lord Jester Gutter enters into this."

Mark hated to admit it, but it had to be true. "I haven't been told anything. I just have a feeling that Bainswell is another sort of tutor."

"To teach you what? How to conceal bruises? Which, by the way, I feel I shouldn't applaud you in this matter but most of the time I don't see anything." A shudder went through the professor, but it didn't look like horror. More like hot rage.

Mark pressed his lips together to firm the paste over the cut. "I'm learning to be wary. Unfortunately he caught me after fencing practice, and I was tired—"

"You should have skewered the bastard!"

Mark wanted to shove him. "You think it's that easy? You do it. Ram a long length of steel into a human being—" He barely kept the memory of his mother's death behind him. Her last moments pressed close, her dying breaths more vivid than what he remembered of maternal love.

Murder. How could the professor suggest it?

"It's what he wants you to do, isn't it?"

"There are other ways to deal with men like him." *I've let this go too far.* "But enough about that. We shouldn't be talking about it."

"I believe it's long past time to talk about this. Why do you tolerate it? This isn't how jesters are trained."

"He's not training me to be a jester. It would be useless. I'm—" He didn't want to say it. His dreams felt too fragile. "Even if he was training me wrongly, then maybe you can tell me how *you* train liars, thieves and killers at university." Mark's temper had him now but he didn't care. The heat felt good. "You're very quick to advise me to kill a man because he bruised me. It seems to me that your opinions need a new accountant."

"I thought you invited me for a discussion, but you subject me to a lecture instead." Arms crossed and hunched, the professor watched Mark from somewhere high and immovable.

The heat bled away, and with it most of Mark's passion. His favorite tutor turned out to be made of books rather than flesh. Mark longed for him to be wise and to reveal the answers that would make the years before his freedom more bearable. "I'm sorry." *I thought you'd be a friend to me.*

"I teach history," the professor murmured. "What you want is theology. I was never very good with religion. I don't care about *morbai* or *allolai*. I care about people. History is a study of *human* victory and error. I fear the choices you'll make without those history lessons in your heart. I see a young man being run through a maze. And I'm afraid of what you'll find at the end."

"I know where I'll end up." He couldn't remember how his father looked anymore, but he remembered the creak of ropes and wood in a strong wind, the stormy color of deep water, and the shadows that masts and rigging made on sunlit sails.

"Mark?"

Mark reluctantly lifted his gaze from the past to his teacher's face.

The professor uncrossed his arms and braced his hands on a chair. "Have you considered going to the Church for protection? Lord Argenwain is absolved of wrongdoing if Gutter provides for him, but that doesn't mean you as the provided object can't protect yourself from harm from both of them. If you're not willing—"

"You mean leave because I don't want to lick an old man anymore? To what? Sit in a cell for my own protection, earning nothing toward my future, knowing that anyone of means would be insane to have anything to do with me, assuming that they didn't hate me because I'm a staghorn and a traitor to my lord. No one would give enough of a shit about me to flick a cupru onto the street for me to pick up." He wasn't even angry, just tired of looking at the layers of filth covering his life.

Everything always felt so ugly and grim when Gutter was away. Mark hadn't seen him all winter, and he dreaded how much worse things might get as the weeks reluctantly slogged toward spring. Gutter wouldn't cross the mountains until then.

Professor Vinkin pressed himself away from the chair. He went to the door. "I would find a position for you at the university, if you decide you've had enough of bruises and terror and being a repository for forgiven sins."

Mark blushed, dark with anger and hot with shame.

"As I said, I'm not well versed in religious matters, but I do believe in the hells, and I hate to see someone I've grown to care about very much live in a hell made for him in life." Professor Vinkin went out and shut the door.

As if the University could shelter Mark from two men second in power only to the King himself.

That admission made him feel like he'd been filled with cold molten gold. He was too heavy to move, trapped by wealth and power.

In the quiet the old study clock gently tocked. It never chimed on the hour like the other clocks in the manor. Gutter said Lord Argenwain needed a room where time passed softly.

Gutter had said it with such affection. Mark had felt a surge of jealousy at the time. It seemed peculiar that Gutter's love for his lord never treaded anywhere near even a chaste kiss. In fact, though Gutter inspired intense feelings in everyone, he behaved as if he had no sexual passion for anyone.

Mark didn't dare linger in case Bainswell came looking for him. That bastard—Mark had never met anyone like him. The first time Mark fought back, Bainswell had laughed. He'd enjoyed the brutality more.

Mark set off for his room, every sense hunting for the slightest hint of ambush. He would never run, and he'd never hide, but that thin, watery courage had led to some nasty beatings.

A knock startled him. Someone had arrived at the front door just as Mark crossed the foyer. Heart still tapping fast and light, Mark opened the door. "Lord Argenwain's residence. May I help you?"

Obsidian stood out in the snow about a dozen feet from the manor's entrance. The wind threw aside any protection his cloak might offer and savaged his silks and lace, turning the young jester into a beautiful yet seemingly ragged thing. He wasn't wearing his mask, but he had makeup on his lips and eyes. He gripped a silk purse with a heavy brass clasp in his left hand while his right rested on his rapier. He faced the gate for a long moment before he trotted lightly up the granite walkway to the door. "Mark—is Gutter here?"

"No." The way Obsidian's breath came so sharply and the fearful glances he cast into the manor and back out made Mark's skin prickle.

The peace ties on Obsidian's pistol and rapier fluttered loose in the wind.

Mark opened the door a little wider, not sure if he should invite the jester in. "He's been gone all winter and we don't expect him for at least a month."

Obsidian closed his eyes and nodded. "Good."

Chapter Three

Obsidian sucked in a deep, shuddering breath and then opened his eyes. They looked wide and wild, enhanced by the dark makeup he wore around them and the dark frame of his hair that curled like exotic ruffles. "May I speak with you a moment?"

"Me?" Mark took a step back. He'd always liked Obsidian, and for a while he'd concealed more than fondness for the young man from Hasla, but that had been from afar. He hadn't actually traded more than niceties with him before. "What about?"

Obsidian stood there, waiting.

Obsidian had only just graduated from the university and he didn't have a lord yet, and Gutter hadn't warned Mark against him, but still.

Mark ducked farther back from the doorway and gestured belatedly. "Come in."

"Do you mind if we meet in your room?"

Several unlikely fantasies raced through the back of Mark's eyes before he managed to respond. "This way." He hurried ahead of Obsidian, caught up in the jester's nervous energy.

Mark worried at how everything must look—fine enough for any lord but of course none of it was his, or even furnished at his choosing. It all seemed overly thick and gaudy, drawing attention to the rich gifts that were supposed to compensate for the sins Mark had to carry for Lord Argenwain.

Obsidian didn't notice any of it, and for the second time in one day Mark had a man he admired shut him into a room for privacy.

Obsidian braced his back against the door. The light had begun to fade outside, but even in the dim lighting Obsidian's dusky skin looked pale. His gloves were dirty and his dark hair looked tattered on one side, like some had been ripped from his head. His ruffled shirt was a bit askew and ballooned out from under the short front of his waistcoat. The lacing on his waistcoat was out of proper tension as well, and one of his stockings sagged at the ankle.

"Are you all right?" Mark asked him.

"Is this room safe from spies?" Obsidian asked.

"Almost every room in this house is safe from spying, especially mine. The doors are thick and they're all carved." No one could seal a glass against them to listen. "They're lined in velvet, and there's a rug to muffle the space under."

"And secret doorways? Spyholes?"

"Not in the bedrooms, the study, or the offices. Not to my knowledge anyway, and the servants won't know of them. Only Gutter, maybe my lord, if they exist." He knew these things because they'd been pointed out in his lessons when matters of spying came up, but he hadn't needed them for himself before.

"And the servant's entrance?"

"Closed off in all the private rooms. Mine is behind that armoire."

Obsidian's fingers worked nervously on the seams of the purse. "I need you to take care of something for me, and I don't trust anyone else." He worried the purse a little longer, then offered it.

Mark accepted it reluctantly. He started to open it, but Obsidian gripped his hand, pinning it to the clasp.

"Leave it. Best not to look at it." Obsidian relaxed his hold but his fingers lingered on Mark's hand. "If I don't come back to claim it by tomorrow, I need you to deliver it personally to a Mister Rohn Evan in Perida."

Everything stopped, and then Mark's heart started again in a big kawoomp that made him gasp. "I can't do that."

Obsidian gripped his wrist. "Please—"

"And what's this about you not coming back for whatever this is?" Never mind that Mark couldn't even leave the house without permission— Obsidian's not-so-veiled suggestion sank in and kept sinking deeper. "Are you going to duel?"

"No. This is too important for a duel." Obsidian finally let go and backed away.

"You're going to murder someone?" Everything familiar fell into darkness. He could barely see Obsidian through the ghostly sight and scent of his mother bleeding and gasping for life in his arms. "Get out."

"Mark—"

"You have choices, and this is the choice you made? Have you made it before? Is that why you're doing it, because it works and it's easy?"

"No, no I haven't and it isn't easy but if I don't do this, there's going to be a war, or worse. You're too young to understand."

"Oh, I'm too young." Mark's whole body shook. "I would have been shipped off to fight in the Island War if Gutter hadn't saved me, but I'm too young to understand the threat of war?"

"My brother died in that war."

"My mother was murdered, my father disappeared and I don't even know why. All I know is that when someone tells me that they're going to go spill blood it's not a tactic or intrigue or a—a—I smell the blood. I smell it now. And the thing of it is, is that it didn't smell like any blood. It smelled like her." He had to stop to catch his breath, and only then he realized what Obsidian had said.

Mark wanted to shove the purse at him and order him out. He wanted to ask how his brother had died, if Obsidian had been there, wanted to compare the scars in their hearts and ... what? Nothing either of them did now would make anything right.

Obsidian just stood there, waiting. For an apology? Mark could give him that. "I'm sorry. I want to help."

"Then help me."

"Is there something I can do to change your course?"

"You don't even know what it is," Obsidian shot back.

"How did you think this would turn out? You'd just drop this by, expect me to leap nimbly onto the nearest ship if you died and sail to one of the most dangerous cities in the world and give it to a stranger. This is your plan? Or did some lord promise to wed your soul to his if you did this for him?"

"You think this is my choice? Gutter drove me to do this. The only part I get to choose is whether or not he finds out about what's happened, and I don't want him to know."

"And so you come to me?" Was it stupidity or blind desperation?

"Yes. Because if I fail, and you fail, Gutter is the one that must salvage the situation. He forced me into this, Mark. I'm just fighting to keep everything from exploding apart."

"You should ask him for help when he comes home." Mark held the purse out, though part of him wanted very much to have Obsidian's courage. He wished he dared to stop being the household toy, even for a brief moment.

"You think he'll wave his hand and make the world obey." Obsidian walked to the vanity mirror and gazed into it. "And he would. Sometimes I wonder if he doesn't rule the kingdom in more ways than the King. When I was your age—"

"I'm nineteen, not twelve. And you're what, twenty five?"

"Sorry." Obsidian put his back to the mirror and braced on the chair. "I feel old. I look at you and I miss the university. I miss trusting people. I miss having a thousand bright futures to choose from." He shrugged. "Anything Gutter asks of me, I will do. But I'll never trust him again. Not willingly."

Those last words connected sharp and hard to Bainswell's presence in the house. Other things related to Gutter and death threatened to connect to those words, but Mark pushed it all away. "Gutter saved my life." Saying the words a second time weakened them somehow.

"I trust you more than I trust him, especially in this matter. I don't know you well, but I know enough. He trusts you too, and that is rare. I didn't choose you because I had no other choice. I chose you because you are the best fit for this, if you dare. I know you're capable. I just hope you have the courage to match."

That warmed his pride, but he knew that was dangerous. No doubt Obsidian only intended to manipulate him. "Hope? I would think you'd be wiser than to take a risk on me. Maybe there's another way to do this, whatever this is."

"Even if I got it back, he would know it existed, and he would connect it to me. Right now he doesn't know what he has or how important it is, so that has kept things safe, but that won't last long. I have to get it back before he shows it around or does something stupid with it, and then ...." He bit his lip.

"You say you know he doesn't know how important it is." Mark realized that his hands were worrying the seam between the silk and the clasp, and that it might tear. He set it aside on his stocking dresser, where it seemed to tug at his attention.

Obsidian seemed to keep part of his attention on the purse as well, though Mark doubted he could have blinked without Obsidian noticing. "He wouldn't believe I'd have anything important, even if I told him it was. That's my one hope."

"So buy it back and then in time he'll forget about it. What are his chances, realistically, of seeing something related to this again and connecting it to you?"

"I'd thought of that. Small, but not zero."

"Is it worth murder to assure zero, even if zero possibility is achievable? For all you know he's shown it around to a dozen people by now."

"He hasn't had time." Obsidian didn't sound like he believed his own words.

"Just try. Find out what he has or hasn't done before you kill him. I'll do what you ask. Just consider, at least, that it will be less dangerous for you to talk than to fight."

Obsidian looked sidelong at him with a strange, unearthly calm that made Mark's skin prickle. "You argue well. Maybe I should send you as a go-between. Are you willing to go that far to save a stranger's life, and perhaps mine?"

"I don't know enough to answer you." Easier to ask for details than to answer. He wanted to say yes, but he had a horrible feeling that serving Obsidian's purpose would end very, very badly.

"He's a classmate of mine." Obsidian's voice deepened and tightened. "He has the heart of a bully, though he plays at being friends with everyone. In this case that works to my advantage. I'm hoping he won't tell anyone what he's done until he's sure that it will dress him up. Money might sway him, but I think it will please him more if I act like I've cooled down and want to be friends. Maybe you can charm him and praise him on my behalf and then offer him the money as if he's won a bet."

"It might sound more convincing if you talk to him yourself."

"He's still trained as a jester, like me. I'd have a hard time convincing him that it wasn't a mask."

"I don't see why he'd believe me any more than you."

Obsidian's hands chopped the air. "Fine! Tell me your brilliant plan that will allow me to achieve my ends without bloodshed."

Feign a robbery? The jester would likely see through the ruse and attack one or both of them as soon as Mark appeared rather than allow them to coordinate an attack against him.

"I don't have much time."

Strangely, Mark's mind returned to his first fear—a duel. "What about challenging him to a duel? Not to the death, but first blood."

"Then he'd know the importance of the item in question. If I lose, he'll be sure to investigate why I want it so badly."

"Approach indirectly. Ask him to meet you. Make an offer of money if it will get him there. But when he arrives, confuse him. Tell him that you both know why you're really there, and hand him something outrageous. Love of a woman he's never met, but insist you're sure he's seduced her. Put him in a position where he's defending himself from a false accusation for which you're willing to take his life and risk yours to resolve. My hope is that he won't want to fight for a woman he's never met. Then all you have to do is let him talk you out of the challenge."

"But how will I get the ring?" Obsidian flinched.

Mark kept talking as if he hadn't heard the slip. "Tell him you both know why he took the item. Let him guess. His mind will come up with its own most convincing argument. I expect he'll believe that she gave it to you. He may even offer it to you. That would be best. If you dare, you might even refuse it on first offer, and claim that it's gone too far. That might distract him from the item's importance."

Obsidian shook his head. "I don't know."

"Are you a better duelist than him?"

"I know he's won a duel, and I've never fought in one. At University our instructors were very careful not to expose how skilled we are at arms to each other. That, and a strict rule against dueling kept most of us from trying to impress a potential patron lord."

"Does he have a patron lord?"

"No."

That made Mark feel a little better about the situation. As long as he didn't have one, he didn't have to preserve an image or reputation in his lord's name.

"I think this is an acceptable plan, but I have to think about it," Obsidian said. "I still prefer the odds in an ambush much better, but I fear I'll fail to surprise him and it will come down to a bloody brawl. Or he won't have the item with him, and it will be impossible to find it if I kill him. The sort of challenge you're talking about, I would have a chance to learn if it's on his person when we meet."

Mark didn't want to leave too long a silence. "I'll guard the purse with my life." Offering any smaller assurance might have been a deadly oversight. Hopefully Obsidian wouldn't dwell too long on the fact that Mark knew there was a ring. "Let me know if there's anything else I can do to help."

Obsidian cocked his head and seemed to reconsider. "I'll be at the Rythan Gardens tonight about eight o'clock. If you really want to help me, meet me by the swan bridge. Do you know where that is?"

Mark nodded. Lord Argenwain often roamed the gardens in summer, but instead of taking a fine lady or a fashionable dog he took Mark. "Don't depend on me. Lord Argenwain rarely allows me to leave the house on my own."

"It is as it is." Obsidian paced a bit before he settled by the door. "If Lord Jester Gutter comes home, please don't mention any of this. Don't even tell him I was here. If he finds out, tell him we had a little tryst."

Heat rushed to Mark's cheeks and burned his ears and throat.

Obsidian gave him an apologetic smile. "I have to go and prepare. Be careful with that purse. Hide it somewhere safe, and whatever you do, don't bring it to the Gardens if you decide to meet me. And remember Mr. Rohn Evan. Perida."

Thanks to his training he'd remember the whole conversation to the last word, but Mark nodded dutifully.

Obsidian bowed a short little bow, hand on his heart, and went out.

If Obsidian was willing to kill to get the ring back, what would he do to Mark to keep the secret of its existence? Sure, Gutter knew about the ring already, and Mark was Gutter's creature—

I will sail from him someday

—but Obsidian had his own concerns about Gutter, and his own secrets.

As much as Mark loved Gutter, his skin tightened at the thought of what might happen if he complicated one of Gutter's intrigues, and Mark had far more reason than Obsidian to trust that Gutter would be merciful.

Would Obsidian really kill me?

His gaze settled on the purse. As long as he had it, it would afford him some safety. Just as he had with the ring, Obsidian would hesitate to do anything to Mark until he was fairly certain he could retrieve the purse.

The purse might have even been a layered show of trust, not just toward Mark, but toward Gutter should things unravel.

Mark rubbed his face, trying to smooth out the rumpled feelings in his crowded mind. If he'd ever considered becoming a jester, he would rethink that path now. He wished he were at sea, with his father's old mates on *Mairi*, sailing for the islands or the southern sands in Vyenne, or even to the north and mysterious Melssa with its fanatic priests. He could visit all the places he longed to see, and move on before that place became too dear, or too dull, or too dangerous ....

And he could trust his father's men.

Do they even remember me?

Lord Argenwain didn't allow him to go to the docks. Mark had begged how many times?

Lately, hardly at all.

But they'd gone to the lighthouse rock for picnics and to enjoy the view of vast Hullundy Bay, a body of water so large that no one could see all the way across it, making it appear to be a sea. Mark would try to guess which of the three-masted trade ships in Seven Churches' port was *Mairi*. She was tall, and white, with buff sails. He remembered that much, and a red line at the waterline, and the androgynous figurehead at the bow with wing-like flows of feathery whorls from its arms meant to represent an *allolai* spirit

He heard a faint bell ring for the upstairs maid. The clock pointed to four. He had an hour before dinner, and an hour before sunset. The days grew longer, but it felt like it would be winter forever.

Something blocky made a straight edge even through the purse's thick padding. It might be a small, thick book, or a large stamp ....

Part of him didn't want to look in case it might change his life for the worse, but he knew realistically it had already changed everything. He started to reach for it, but thought better of it. If he broke a seal inside or left tatters of threads that had been sewn in a specific pattern, Gutter might not protect him from what happened next.

Would Gutter let Obsidian kill me?

Would Gutter kill me himself?

If only the answer were no in all cases.

Gutter might do terrible things if he believed Mark would leave him, and that's exactly what Mark hoped to do in about three years.

Throughout history, intrigue had enslaved countless men to causes they hated because of one spilled secret. If Mark opened that purse, he might not just cut off his future but his own head, and he might force Gutter to be the executioner.

His curiosity burned like never before. He picked up the purse, refusing to allow his fingers to probe the firm shape cushioned inside, and looked around for somewhere to hide it.

He is ready for all this and more, a voice whispered. It startled him, because not only did it not feel like his own thoughts, but he hadn't heard the voice in his mind in a long time. The words sounded close to Hasle, if it were sung ...

Ruby?

He didn't care to listen to the voices when he heard them—they were often cruel—but this time the words encouraged him.

I shouldn't listen to them. They're probably just my imagination anyway.

Sometimes he feared he might be insane, or worse ....

What are you doing? another voice whispered. It sounded farther away.

The bell at the door jangled and he nearly dropped the purse in shock. It might be one of Lord Argenwain's fawners, but he had a feeling it had to do with the purse.

Shit shit shit—

He suppressed a frightened laugh when he came up with the best temporary hiding place after discarding the usual under-clothing-in-a-drawer between-the-mattresses inside-a-boot ideas. He uncovered his chamber pot, confirmed that the maid had already cleaned it that morning, and covered it back up. He had second thoughts a moment later, but he had no time to find a better place. He had to see who it might be. Mark made certain his clothes were tidy and walked quickly to the top of the stairs.

Bainswell, that thick but somehow elegant brute, opened the door and a large but graceful man in a heavy black cloak strode in. Mark's heart leapt and then shrank as his joy drowned in fear.

Gutter swept the snow-dusted cloak off and dropped it into Bainswell's arms, revealing a coat and waistcoat glimmering darkly with subtle embroidery. He pulled off his feathered, jeweled hat as well and set it on the valet's head. The black porcelain demi-mask stared up at Mark, and Gutter smiled. That warm expression was far more precious than the sapphires and gilding and opal inlay that transformed the rather plain, old-form mask into a creature of strange charm and uncertain beauty.

The greatest jester in the world had come home.

Chapter Four

Mark measured his way down the stairs, and tried to express his pleasure through the formal bow he delivered without giving away his alarm. *He's going to notice.*

"Is our lord in and awake?" Gutter's deep voice made Mark's toes curl inside his shoes.

"He's in, but whether he's awake, I couldn't say." *Did I sound nervous?* Gutter glanced toward Bainswell.

"I couldn't say, lord jester." Bainswell looked like he wanted to crawl away, but he stood there holding the cloak in his arms as if it weighed nothing. After a beat he noticed the heavy satchel Gutter carried. "May I take that for you, lord jester?"

Gutter's gloved hand tightened on the strap. "Hang those things and let him know I'm here." The flat voice Gutter used on Bainswell cut gently and without effort, like a very sharp knife.

"Yes, lord jester." Bainswell hurried out of the foyer.

"You didn't come through the pass, did you?" It seemed so unlikely as to be impossible, but then, Gutter seemed capable of anything.

"No. I traveled 'round Vyenne." Gutter set a hand on Mark's shoulder. It seemed to weigh more than usual. "I'm surprised Bainswell is still here," Gutter said.

Surprised that he hasn't been dismissed or that he isn't dead?

Mark didn't want to gamble on the answer to his own question, much less talk about it. "I'm surprised you're here. I'm glad, but ... I hope everything is all right?" He wondered if Gutter's arrival had anything to do with Obsidian.

"If everything were all right, nobles wouldn't need jesters and commoners wouldn't need patrons. But I am here on urgent business." Gutter hugged him briefly and Mark relaxed. He followed the weight of Gutter's hand toward the stairs. "You seem nervous."

Mark tried not to tense up, but he couldn't help it.

He hasn't asked about your studies—the tutor. Vinkin would make a good excuse for Mark's unease.

"I—had an argument with Professor Vinkin, and I'm not sure he's coming back." He realized a heartbeat later that his ploy might turn the knife's point toward the professor. "I wasn't going to mention it because I wanted to try to smooth things over with him on my own."

Gutter pursed his lips in a comical, thoughtful expression. "Then I won't interfere. I think that might teach you something more valuable than history."

"I tried when he was leaving but I was clumsy. I think I'll just have to apologize or something."

"You're quite adept at manipulation, though you may not realize it. Your status may be getting in the way. But that will change, maybe sooner than you expect." Gutter walked with Mark up the stairs. "How have things been while I've been away?"

He didn't want to talk about it, especially since his complaints in his letter had gone unanswered, but it was better than leaving an opening for questions that might lead to Obsidian. "The usual. Our lord—"

"The usual? Really."

Mark didn't want to talk about Bainswell, but apparently Gutter wouldn't let it go as long as he sensed Mark's unease. He'd probably noticed the bruises, new and old, and the small split in his lip. "You're too kind. You've only just come home and you're willing to listen to brandy chatter without even a glass to warm you."

Gutter's eyes sharpened. "You're learning," he murmured. The approving tone sent a ripple of pleasure through Mark. "Trust your intelligence, and mine. Tell me. Right here." He stopped at the top of the stairs.

"I've been practicing my fencing. I've developed a technique to react quickly to the slightest sounds and glimpses, but I think I need a new teacher. Doing this on my own isn't working very well. Have you found a new *secontefoil* for me?"

"You're too much for a *secontefoil*. I don't think you need a *pointefoil*, or any other fencing master. Not anymore. Working on your own seems to be working quite well. I'll test you before I leave tomorrow." Gutter's hand settled back on Mark's shoulder and urged him toward Mark's room.

Not my room.

It wasn't just the purse hiding there. The ominous mention of a test involving Bainswell shrank his guts. "Why are you doing this? Why all the effort and expense? In three years—" He shouldn't have asked, and especially he shouldn't have pointed out that he was due to leave.

"But we'll still be friends long after you have left this house."

We're friends?

Questioning it aloud would sound too ungrateful, though the suggestion of friendship made his heart race. "Of course we'll be friends. I'm honored. I just—I'm not worthy of all this. And the training—"

Gutter's hand slipped from Mark's shoulder. "The world is very dangerous, especially now. I want you to live a long and happy life. Part of that happiness will arise from knowledge of history, art, music ... how is your music coming along?"

He always asked, and Mark at least could be honest about that. "I still haven't found my voice. My instructor says I'm his best student, but I don't *feel* the music like I used to. I wonder if he's just flattering me to please Lord Argenwain."

"That's my fault," he said softly.

"That he flatters me?"

Gutter smiled and a little more tension eased. Mark felt his shoulders glide down.

"I think I'm just overly aware of what I'm doing. Before my parents died, I didn't really pay attention," Mark admitted.

"I don't think it's just your parents. We both know what our lord is, Mark."

Mark wanted to get through this as quickly and shallowly as possible. "He didn't force me to do anything. It's all been willing. Truly." The forcing part was absolutely true, and the willingness had to be true because otherwise life in the manor would be unbearable. "I do remember being able to sing with heart after I came here, but ... anyway, I think it will change in time." He almost said, *when my indenture has paid out,* but he caught himself before the words escaped.

"I'll miss you terribly when you do leave us." Gutter spoke softly, with a hint of sadness that made Mark believe he really might let him go. He took a few steps toward Mark's room. "Come. I have something I'd like to give you. A present. I've been looking for a long time, and I've finally found one that I think will work." Something like a boyish nervousness made Gutter's voice sound breathy.

I just have to remember not to look toward the bed too much, or avoid looking at it. I'll just sit on it, and it'll be all right. He'd hesitated too long as it was. "Is it a puppy?"

Gutter chuckled and waited for Mark to let him into the room. He'd always been kind that way, treating Mark's room as his private space, and thankfully Lord Argenwain followed his jester's lead. "Guess again."

"A peacock?"

"That's closer."

Mark's curiosity burned hot. "Really?"

"One more guess. A real one this time."

Mark considered the size of the satchel and measured it against Gutter's eagerness. "I'm afraid of making you feel like you've fallen short somehow. You know, you've always been very good to me." His frustrations and fears fell away and he wished he could express his real gratitude. Maybe it was inspired by Gutter calling him a friend. He'd never done that before.

Gutter's smile warmed. "If you guess it's a crown I won't care. Make a guess."

Mark took a deep breath. "I think it's a jeweled collar." Gutter had just come from Saphir, famous not only for its many unusual religious sects, masked theaters, bathhouses, and the Eshku Fasemasq—Mark had heard it translated variously but thought of it as the Masked University—but for the oft-copied Hemirzi collars.

"A reasonable guess, but this is a little more exotic." Gutter set his satchel on the bed and slowly opened it. The hairs stood up at the nape of Mark's neck. Gutter reached in like someone trying to pick up a living thing without waking it up. As he drew out a bundle of glittering silk, Gutter let out something between a sigh and a coo. He offered it to Mark.

Mark's skin crawled.

This is the second time today I'm being offered something I won't want to bear.

He didn't know where the thought had come from. He didn't even know what this thing was.

Perfect, the voice-thought murmured in sweet, low notes.

His skin prickled into gooseflesh and his breath ran short.

Gutter had a strange look in his eyes that his mask only emphasized. He waited eagerly but with a terrible patience, while his hands held the silk package with a kind of yielding possessiveness.

The daylight outside had begun to fail, and with a start Mark remembered Obsidian's peril. He stopped himself from glancing toward his bed's feet.

He's not leaving until I take it.

Mark didn't want Gutter to leave any more than he wanted to take that thing inside the silk. But if he refused to even touch it—what would that do to the friendship Gutter had only just admitted today?

Mark settled his hands and his heart sank as he felt the edges of the mask through the silk. It felt lighter than he'd expected. Gutter let it go as if it weighed like gold.

Mark's hands started to shake, and that shaking went into his belly.

"It might not fit," Gutter said. His deep voice soothed Mark, but the trembling only spread into Mark's spine. Gutter seemed to fade back, though he didn't move. "And you may not suit each other. But I have a feeling this one ... I think it will work for you. If not, well, it's very fine, very valuable, and might prove to be a useful gift someday." Gutter's breath caught. "Never sell." The words fell hard though the tone was soft. "You'll know which ones aren't to be sold. They aren't slaves. They have to come and go willingly."

Please don't be a death mask please don't be a death mask
I can't accept this.

He tried to say the words again, but they didn't come out.

He couldn't help but glance toward the window. It had started to snow. Maybe that accounted for the lowering light—but he knew it was getting late.

Mark pulled the silk free of its tucked edges and wadded it in one hand.

Tear tracks. Slate gray but opalescent, perhaps made of black pearls somehow, pooled under the eye holes and trickled down to points where the jaws would be. The right side—he realized that he was already thinking in terms of left and right as if he wore it instead of relative to looking at it—had fewer trails than the left. The eyes smiled, complete with crow's feet wrinkles fashioned from a delicate material that looked like human skin, except that it was an inhuman, eerie metallic bronze with the creases stained for emphasis. The lower points of the mask that covered the cheeks weren't symmetrical. The left was more substantial than the right side. It blushed around the cheeks.

But it had no mouth. It was just a demi-mask. Not all full masks were death masks, but no death mask exposed the mouth. At least, none he'd been taught about.

He had to remind himself that Gutter was still there, but the knowledge didn't hold. The mask had absorbed all of his attention. Mark turned it over to see the inside, and started to put it on. He barely managed to stop himself. His heart started to pound and his breath came in short, uneven gasps. He looked to Gutter, but it was as if Gutter wasn't there.

Gutter had taken off his own mask. Underneath he had another mask painted on his warm-toned skin in pastels brushed over red and black and silver and green. It was one of the most famous patterns in the world, that mask Gutter painted on his face and revealed to so few. They called it the Gutter Rose, but it only could be called a rose in the most abstract way. His humanity gave way to that pattern of petal, leaf and thorn around his eyes. Gutter looked far more like a human being when he wore his porcelain mask than he did when he revealed that painted skin.

Gutter stood there, watching.

"I'm not a jester. This belongs to a jester." Mark started to set the mask aside, but his hands refused the work.

"Jesters aren't the only ones who wear masks." The Gutter Rose sounded reasonable, calm, instructive. "Nobles wear them sometimes, when they go out in disguise. Criminals wear them. Commoners wear them for festivals. Even priests wear them."

That last revelation shocked him, though not enough to distract him from his own fears. "But those masks aren't like this one. This one—" He couldn't put words to the feeling.

"It's alive. I know. You know too. You can tell the difference between a young lady wearing makeup for the first time, and a woman who becomes a lady of quality by the care and polish of her visage. And you also know when a mask is inhabiting the wearer." He made a bridging gesture. "—but this mask isn't one of those that takes you completely over. You'll remember everything you do and say. Perfectly. At least, that's the way it's worked before. You two might not get along." He lifted his chin and his weight sank back like a king settling into his throne. "There's only one way to find out."

"Maybe later?" He wanted to provide an excuse, but nothing came to mind.

Mark expected the Gutter Rose to express disappointment. Instead, Gutter put his porcelain mask back on and his left shoulder twitched up briefly before he quickly fastened the silk ties. Those ties were the only threadbare thing on him. Even the gray in his dark hair seemed a sign of strength rather than age. "You and I are going on a journey."

"We are?" He'd dreamed of it as a child, going off with Gutter to see the world, but dread squirmed in his belly.

"I'll be gone only three days. Then I'll be back and you and I are going … somewhere. Together. To meet someone." He said it as if he'd invited Mark to a casual game of cards without bothering to conceal the daunting stakes. "I have a bag packed for you. You'll want to pack a few of your own things. Favorite clothes, perfume, makeup—but nothing boyish. On this journey you'll be a man. You are a man, but no one in this house has treated you like one, not really. It's time for that. Past time." He turned to pick up his satchel and murmured, "but we mustn't rush things." He went to the door empty-handed and opened it. "You'll be gone at least a month. I'll leave it to you to inform all of your tutors. It should add new weight to your negotiations with your Professor Vinkin." Gutter left the door open and strode down the hall, past the stairs, toward Lord Argenwain's suite.

"Gutter!" Mark took a few steps into the hall. He'd meant to demand an answer, but he didn't have the right question yet, and it occurred to him that he'd forgotten two important words. "Thank you."

Gutter stopped and stepped back to expose his profile. "You have my thanks as well."

Mark knew better than to ask why without thinking for himself first. His emotions stretched between the sailor he wanted to be and the future Gutter seemed to offer.

That's the question.

"Could I become a jester?" Mark halted within easy reach.

Gutter's eyes smiled, but his mouth remained soft and neutral. "Do you want to?"

The mask, still in his hand, felt warm and light. It was not him. That life ... he didn't want it. "No."

Gutter's eyes flinched down.

Mark wished he had another answer, but any other would have been a dangerous lie. "I want to travel with you. I want to see all the cities around Hullundy Bay and the Royal Court and Hasla, especially Saphir, and perhaps even tour Vyenne and the islands. Most of the time I love this life with the clothes and the rich food and the music. Especially the music. But I can't." Right then he knew exactly what it was he couldn't do, one thing among many things that jesters did for their lords so that their noble souls remained unstained by evil. "I can't kill him." He couldn't speak those words above a whisper, much less kill Bainswell.

Gutter walked back to him. He slipped off his gloves and took Mark's hand, hot, bare skin on bare skin. "I'd hoped you wouldn't."

"Then why the fuck—"

"Shhh." Gutter led him back a few steps to the sitting room. The door opened to blinding light. Even as dusk approached, the huge wall of tall windows exposed them to the crystalline whiteness of winter reflected and brightened by the white and silver décor in the room. Gutter released Mark's hand and shut the door. "Have a seat."

"No." He tried to set the mask aside, but that felt like too much rejection when all he wanted was that friendship between them to become something real. Betrayal twisted his gut again though he tried to ignore it. "Gutter—"

"Don't bow your head. Look at me."

Mark took in a tattered breath and forced himself to look up. His height matched that of many of the city's mid-to-short adult men, but he still felt like a child. Gutter's broad chest, full belly and masterful height made Mark feel even more slender and short.

"Do you know what the difference is between a jester and every other man that kills?"

Mark shook his head.

"A jester must do it for *good*. Not his own good, often not even for his lord's good, but for a higher good. He must decide for himself what is right and do it, no matter how unpleasant the task, and he can't pretend he's following orders given by men who will bear the true responsibility. A lord would endanger his soul if he even hinted that a sinful act might prevent disaster."

The words sounded like they came from a deeper place than the university Gutter studied at so long ago.

"I had to know that you would learn to defend yourself. I also needed to know what you would do on your own. I especially needed to know what you might think I'd want you to do, and whether you would do it. Now I know. You feared that I wanted you to kill him, and you followed your own heart. Mark, you have no idea how important that is to me."

All those months of suffering—and Mark didn't even care what had happened to him, only that Gutter could do such a thing to anyone.

"I know it was cruel. I'm sorry. But I'm also so proud of you. I'd always believed, from the first day I saw you, that you are one of the kindest, sweetest, *good* people I've ever met. Now it is proved, a thing far more valuable than belief, no matter how strong that belief might be."

The praise didn't soften Mark's unbearable confusion.

"I rarely dare to speak of the sacred. It's time now, just a little. A small sacrifice, though it may be that we're safe here." Gutter slowly measured his way to Mark's side and touched the mask. Mark tried to give it to him, but Gutter only guided it toward Mark's face.

Mark pulled it back down to his side. "I want to be a sailor. Please."

Gutter let out a sigh. His hand cupped Mark's face, and he kissed Mark's forehead. "Keep the mask. We'll talk more about this on our journey. I promise I won't spend the entire way trying to convince you of anything. We'll just talk, as friends. Because I do count you as a friend. One of my few, true ones. I'm just afraid that once I start telling you all I want to tell you, you won't want to be my friend anymore."

Mark's throat tightened. He wanted to say I love you, but it was too confusing. Gutter had been a father, a divine spirit, and a mystery, and too often while he was away, the subject of endless daydreamt adventures that sometimes verged into intimate fantasy. The word love came too close to admitting how much Mark's life relied on Gutter's existence, and how thin and dark the rest of the world felt. "You're the one who always leaves me. I've always waited faithfully for you. And you know, all you ever have to do is send for me and I'll speed away to find you. No matter what I become or where I go, I'm yours." *Whether I want to be or not.*

Gutter's hand tightened on Mark's face and the jester kissed Mark's forehead again. This time Mark wanted to flinch back, but he held his ground.

Whatever darkness had passed through Gutter didn't show when he stepped back. "When I return, we'll discuss what to do with the situation here. I'll let you decide, once you hear the entirety. All right?" Gutter opened the door.

Mark nodded, and the jester slipped away.

The sitting room's silver and porcelain clock tick, tick, ticked. Mark had little more than an hour to decide what to do.

He took the mask back to his room and set it on the bed. Gutter had left his satchel behind.

Look inside.

No.

He didn't want to find out what else was in there. It would only draw him in deeper. He went to his window but he didn't look out. He closed his eyes and let the snowy light soften the darkness through his eyelids. He imagined himself in an oilskin coat and heavy boots and rough trousers. He imagined the sea spray, and a floppy hat on his head, and the rush of water all around, and the wind and the gulls and the men singing. Excitement and joy shuddered through him and he sang roughly, stumbling over the long-forgotten words. "Owah may, long away, 'cross the gray sea ...." His father was there. Time had blurred the memory of his face, but the long, blond ponytail, lean body, short beard and thick arms remained. He had his black captain's coat and the black tricorn captain's hat, all faded at the shoulders and peaks by sun and salt.

The first dinner bell rang. Mark had to help serve, which meant he had to check his appearance before he went down. Maybe Gutter would invite him to sit with them. He sometimes did that, but this time Mark didn't want to. Mark hurried to his room, checked his appearance in his mirror—

His hand traced along his hair. Blond his like father's, with darker hair underneath and behind his ears like his mother's.

The last time he'd seen her, her hair was muddy with blood.

He pulled his hair back from his face, tied it quickly with a ribbon, and went toward the stairs.

Gutter emerged from Lord Argenwain's bedroom. He couldn't have had time to share more than a few words with their lord. "Mark."

"Is something wrong?"

Gutter tossed him a small pouch. "If you hurry, you'll make it back in time to sit with our lord at dinner."

It took Mark a moment to realize what he had. It weighed far more than usual. "I'm paying in advance?"

"Two months."

That made the journey feel too real. He doubted it would be a grand adventure. If anything, he feared Gutter was right. He wouldn't want to be friends when he heard the truth. "Thank you." But Gutter had said 'sit with our lord', not 'sit with us.' "You aren't leaving tonight, are you?"

"No, but I have to visit someone in town. I'll have dinner there." Gutter hesitated. "Out of curiosity, what gave me away?"

"What do you mean?" Maybe Gutter wondered why Mark thought something was wrong. Was some of the rose smudged? It was hard to tell. Perhaps the mask had rubbed it off a little.

"I just came out to give you that, but you had the impression I was leaving."

"Oh. I just—you said I'd have a chance to sit at dinner with Lord Argenwain, and usually when you're with him, you say we and us and our." He realized that Gutter had always included Mark in 'our' when he said 'our lord.' He included Mark in service to Lord Argenwain with him, as if they worked at the same level. Did he do that with the other servants? Mark didn't think so, but eight years was a long time to go over, and his memory wasn't perfect, just trained well.

Gutter stood a little taller. "I hadn't realized I'd been doing that. Interesting." He let out a short laugh. "Very interesting, that it's so reliable. So little else about me is." For a moment Mark felt as if he could see through all the masks and glimpse the person underneath, the person he really loved. Self-deprecating, gentle, kind, and generous not just with his wealth but with his acceptance of who people were, no matter how repulsive others might find them.

"Thank you, many times again." Mark bowed in the friendliest way he could, hurried downstairs, grabbed his thickest greatcoat and cloak, shoved on his best pair of winter boots and let himself out into the snow.

Chapter Five

The gardener spent a great deal of time keeping the driveway smooth and packed well for Lord Argenwain's sleigh. It had several loose inches on top, and walls of snow as high as Mark's shoulders on either side with the frosted dark green of ancient holly hedges rising out of them. Beyond those hedges lay a garden beyond most people's imaginings. Gutter's design.

Mark wondered if, despite the obvious benefits of position and money and nearness to the king, Lord Argenwain had had trouble finding a worthy jester because of his sexual bend. In that regard Gutter may have been too understanding, and Mark tried not to dwell on that too much.

I'm always trying to ignore and forget things. I have to get out of this house.

He always imagined freedom better once he passed the garden gates and walked along the sidewalk in front of the great manor. When he was alone out here, he could pretend to be a passer-by astonished by Pickwelling Manor and the massive property it commanded at the top center of the hill in the center of the city. The situation had only one flaw: no view of the bay, a strange deficiency for a great house in a coastal town on Hullundy Bay. It wasn't just the angle against Cathret's famous one hundred mile cliffs. The cliffs were actually quite low in this area, less than forty feet high at the port itself. The main problem was that Pickwelling stood uphill from the university, once an enormous castle. Those high walls, covered in ivy, and the fat corner towers, barred all but glimpses of the great bay at the horizon on either side.

Gutter once told Mark that people feared, when Lord Argenwain settled here, that he would have the university moved, stone by stone if necessary, to a new place. They had nothing to worry about. The only views Argenwain cared to enjoy were in private salons, in his garden, and in his own bedroom. The old man was probably too near-sighted to see any farther anyway. Mark allowed that he must have been different as a younger man, but the fact remained that Argenwain didn't do any harm to the university, and that people then and now still believed he was capable of doing whatever he wanted politically and monetarily.

Mark had to walk in the road where street sweeps kept the way more or less clear for sleighs and carriages. He passed a whole row of grand houses lined up across the street from Argenwain's, too grand for Mark to own even in his imagination. They looked like ample portions of dessert lined up in front of a wedding cake.

It took Mark twenty minutes to reach the edge of the property. Just before he crossed the intersection, he noticed a pair of priests walking uphill through the snow. His heart jumped and fluttered wildly inside him but he couldn't move. Their ridiculous winged hats made them look unnaturally tall, and their half red, half white robes made their left sides appear larger than their right. Absurd, but monstrous. The wings on the white hats had slits through which red peered out, like they were wounded. Were they coming to the house? Mark wanted to dash back to his room, but he couldn't move.

One looked up at him. All the wild fear inside him went still, but noise rose in his ears instead, roaring and rushing.

The priest, hair traditionally hidden by the hat, beardless, could have been just about any age but he looked old and gray. His companion seemed younger, and he seemed to struggle with his emotions as much as his footing. The older priest's gaze slipped from Mark to a fine house painted yellow and white—the violin house, as Mark called it because the eldest daughter practiced violin every day.

Please not that house.

He'd grown up with her music. In winter he seldom heard her but in summer she practiced with her windows open and Mark lingered near the wall in that part of the garden so he could hear her better.

The priests stepped onto the dry stone where the servants had swept, walked relentlessly up the stairs and knocked on the door.

The priests that had come to settle Mark's father's indenture hadn't knocked. They'd just walked into his mother's wine shop and claimed everything a grieving boy had ever known. For his own good, of course. Because he was too young to understand, they'd said. He'd needed protection from his father's guarantor.

Which would have been ideal, except nothing they did protected him from anything. Worst of all they, who were supposed to hold justice higher than anything, didn't care about who murdered his mother. They gave only a token platitude when Mark begged them to wait until someone found out one way or another if his father was dead or captive or if he'd ...

He wouldn't have abandoned us.

Over the years his childish certainty, born from pain, had faded. Fortunately logic remained to bolster him.

His father wouldn't have abandoned his men and the ship he loved, especially not before his son reached his age of majority. The decisions the Church made 'in trust' suited no one but the Church itself.

Until Gutter got in their way.

The door to the violin house opened, emitting a beam of cheerful light that widened slowly.

Who had died? Maybe the priests had some other reason to visit that house, but Mark couldn't think past the feeling that the music he loved had been silenced.

The priests entered, the door closed, and he was alone.

It was getting dark. Obsidian ....

Obsidian didn't know Gutter was in the city. That knowledge might change everything.

Mark hurried toward the Church. He could tell Lord Argenwain he'd been delayed in delivering his payment and have time to meet Obsidian at the swan bridge, hopefully before the other jester arrived. If the other jester was already there, he'd be forced to wait, and hopefully not too long, until the two parted ways.

But what if Obsidian was hurt or killed?

Obsidian falling in a duel conjured terrifying images in his mind that tangled with his mother's death, but he would rather be there tending to Obsidian's wounds and calling for help than to imagine him dying alone in the snow.

The Church grounds neighbored Argenwain's. They didn't look as stately, but only because so many buildings crowded the property. Looming beside the road, the barracks for the sacred guard had all the fine qualities of a large manor house aside from the blocky utilitarian design. Two large three-level wings attached to a central tower where the sacred guard held their group meals, functions and practices. Even now a group of them had begun to sit down for a meal. Their uniforms matched the red plaster walls and white trim on the windows. Hidden behind the barracks, a horse nickered to his companions other in the stables.

A small garden, sheltered behind a large gate, gave a bit of breathing room between the barracks and the Church itself. Mark slowed. People like him weren't allowed inside. Only nobles and their jesters could enter the great domed hall. Sometimes he could hear the most exquisite music, but tonight the Church was silent.

The architecture sang for itself in the place of a human choir. The rounded shoulders on the dome's support perfectly echoed the dome's curve, gracefully connecting it to the linear façades beneath it. Icicles hung from feathery embellishments and formed crystalline bars in front of arched panels. Carved leaves and blossoms of no living design embellished the panels, layers on layers that seemed to hide something within them.

Four vaulted galleries attached to the dome structure, the ones behind taller than the ones in front like long mountain ridges fronted by foothills with the great peak in the middle. Walls and arcades enclosed the way toward the entrance—double doors set deep under a lofted gallery. The lines carried his gaze ever higher in bounds and leaps to the lantern at the top of the dome. Light always glowed there—either sunlight fragmenting against the leaded glass, or lamplight burning bright from within.

He'd halted without meaning to, as he often did, to stare. Mark tugged his gaze away and trotted, skidding on the packed snow, to the Court.

The Court always reminded him of a graveyard. The flat of its roof stood on a level with the Church's ground. Conical lanterns laced with filigree allowed air to exchange with the spaces below, but little if any light managed to work its way inside. That silver filigree was the only variation from black on the building's exterior. Iron railing ran between the lanterns closest to the roof's edge. Many of the ten-pace sections of railing had made their long-dead makers famous for their beauty. Most had strange, somewhat floral motifs, but a few had martial or legal themes.

The central lanterns clustered together like a close copse of trees, the centermost reaching high enough to provide a deadly fall if someone managed to climb to its sharp peak.

Those lanterns weren't silent. The wind made hollow, lonely noises in them. Steam rose from a few, creating fragile ice sculptures around the iron.

An iron grill, from which hung icicles, alternated with covered arches to shade the broad stairway down inside the Court. The last of the evening light began to fail in a narrow stripe behind him as he paused before the open doors. Just inside, four guards in black uniforms stood with death-like patience, seldom blinking.

Mark impatiently waited a few moments to let his eyes adjust before he hurried past them into the vast atrium. His shoes clicked on the dull marble floor, the sound bouncing close to his ear off the marble walls and ceiling. Arched pockets within the ceiling seemed to hide unpleasant things. The cold made him clutch his arms, and even in the faint light cast by tiny lamps set in the walls, he could see his breath go white and vanish almost instantly as it did on only the coldest days above. Though others roamed or waited in the Court, he felt isolated and alone.

The echoing emptiness softened as he passed into the clerk hall where a priest, the younger of the two that had visited him after his mother's death, had managed his ledger for the past six years.

Doors and benches provided the only embellishment down this lonely hall. Two people waited ahead of him at the third door; a young woman with unbound hair in a plain but well-made dress and coat with a matching wool hat, and a poorly-dressed servant with ginger hair that suggested a Nuech ancestor somewhere in his lineage. Judging by his shoes, he worked in a stable. He probably smelled of one too, but Mark's nose had gone numb already.

The poor man had to be freezing, especially sitting on the iron bench. He had only a coarse shirt, thick breeches, and the holes in his shoes revealed holes in his stockings too.

Mark could only stand to watch him hunch there, white-lipped, for a moment. "Sir—would you like to borrow my cloak?"

The man gave him a long look over.

Mark peeled his cloak off. The chill immediately seeped past his great coat, but he'd felt worse. "Here." He held it out.

The man stared at him.

The young woman tipped her head toward them but kept her gaze down-turned.

The cloak started to get heavy. Mark pushed it toward him. The man flinched up and backed away. "Keep away from me." He walked a pair of paces and kept his back turned.

Especially when he walked with Lord Argenwain, he'd gotten some pretty dark looks, but this ... and how did the man know? Or did he know? Revulsion, pity, disdain, mockery all came with being an old man's boy, especially from those who considered their own sins as ordinary and forgivable by comparison. But this was more like fear. Maybe he thought Mark was a jester, but it seemed too disrespectful a fear to be that.

"What about you?" Mark wasn't sure the young woman had heard him. He didn't lend much voice to the idea. But then she nodded, and her pale cheeks turned a bit pink. Mark settled the cloak on her shoulders and sat a few feet away from her.

The door opened and a clerk in crisp brown and white scuttled out. The coarse man strode in. He didn't stay long enough for Mark to strike up a conversation with the young lady. She slipped out of Mark's cloak and went in, though she spared him a glance from the door before she shut it.

Would his father's crew reject him, now that he was whatever he'd become?

The sea would wash it all away.

He just hadn't met the right lady yet, was all.

Except the men who'd impressed him and made his face warm and his heart skip hadn't needed an introduction. All they had to do was walk by. He'd never known a woman to do that to him.

He couldn't blame Lord Argenwain, though he wanted to. Lord Argenwain hadn't yet invited him into his rooms for intimate conversation the first time Mark noticed a certain soldier. Mark only saw him once, but he dreamed about him so many times since then ....

He loved that dream.

The cold started to get to him. Mark wrapped himself back up in the cloak. What could she be doing in there so long? A few unworthy thoughts crossed his mind. At first it struck him as funny, but then not so much. She shouldn't have to go to a man in that way and trade that sweetness he'd sensed from her for a payment on indenture.

Not that priests were supposed to do such things, but he didn't carry much faith in their supposed purity.

At last the door opened and the lady slipped out. She left the door open and gave Mark a curtsey and a smile before she went on her way. To his relief, she didn't seem upset or ashamed or tousled. He leaned up to his feet, stiffened by the wait more than the cold.

A guard came running. Mark stopped in the doorway, uncertain. Warm air from the priest's porcelain stove drifted out, caressing the bare skin on Mark's face.

"Come in," the priest called.

The guard yanked open the first door in the hall. "We must close the building. There's a fire at the docks."

Chapter Six

"Are you coming in or not?" The priest's sharp voice cut through Mark's shock. "You're letting the cold in."

Mark walked, and then ran down the hall. As he hurried through the atrium and up the stairs, Mark's heart pounded a frantic beat. All he could think about was the last time he'd stood on the deck beside his father. Mark had given him an apple, and his father had smiled and taken a big bite out of it before he kissed Mark's mother goodbye. He'd kissed Mark too, on the top of the head, and told him to take care of his mother.

Was *Mairi* in port?

The street was quiet, as it had been when he'd arrived. He thought he tasted strange smoke in the air, but it could have come from someone burning something unpleasant in one of tens of thousands of hearths in the city.

A small group of guards on horses went by, walking their horses carefully on the treacherous ground. So that was it. They wanted to close the building so that all the available guards could go to the docks and help.

Maybe it hadn't spread very far.

Except he knew in his heart that *Mairi* was in the middle of it.

Gutter. Please, no, don't let this be about me.

Mark started to trot toward the docks, slipping often in the snow. He hadn't gone more than a half dozen blocks before he passed a group of boys with sooty faces. Their wide eyes looked strangely clean and bright. They weren't in naval uniforms, but their rough-soled boots and oiled coats marked them as sailors.

"No." He couldn't bring himself to ask them anything. He just pushed himself harder. His breath came hard and he tasted sharp blood.

The closer he got to the docks, the more people he saw moving uphill in groups—mostly children, women and ancients. They coughed or wheezed or gasped, some of them quite winded from their haste, but otherwise most of them were strangely quiet. Bells began to clang in the distance, and a rushing sound rose above the winter's usual gusts of wind.

His first taste of smoke that differed from hearth fire came not from the sky but from a man so burned he had hardly any clothing. His exposed skin was black, and cracks revealed a terrible, beautiful pink. Two men carried him uphill on litter stained with soot and blood. The image kept shocking back into his mind long after he'd passed them, and that smell ....

People are made of meat.

Mark coughed and hurried on. Now people watched from windows, or packed their things into carts. A few hurried toward the docks with buckets. It started to snow again.

No, it was ashes falling from the sky.

A harsh, hot smoke blew all around him from the sea. Mark pulled his neckerchief off and wrapped it around his nose and mouth, but the smoke still choked him. An instant later it cleared, only to blow back in his face. His eyes burned.

The fancy stone and brick houses all stood behind him now, replaced by ancient townhouses with plaster walls, some in better repair than others. The streets narrowed and ran off in odd directions, creating wedge blocks and alleys overhung by signposts. He followed several guards past a familiar landmark, and his heart jerked back to his childhood.

The Bracken Watertower.

Dusk and smoke created a darkness much harder to see into than the shadows usually cast by the gas lamplights, but the water tower stood out clear and bright. Its whitewashed stone walls shone as if they emitted their own light, and the smallest, longest of the city aqueducts made a dark beam like a sword thrust into its side. Icicles hung from the aqueduct's arched supports, and liquid water gurgled beneath the wide iron grates all around its base.

The faint roaring he'd heard in his ears all along now overshadowed the alarmed voices and the clanging bells.

Mark brushed his hand along its side as he ran around the water tower. Then something split through the air, not a sound or color or scent, but something powerful that cleaved Mark's mind as if an axe had split him open like wood.

There's nothing we can do. Ruby's voice stung his mind's wound.

He clutched his ears in pain, and gasped with relief as the pain faded. He forced himself to move onward, unsteady at first but then faster and faster toward the docks.

Turn him back, a strange voice said in his mind.

No!

Mark gritted his teeth. "Leave me alone." He had no idea if the voices would respond to his plea.

A few blocks later he finally trotted on wood planking, and his gaze flinched back from the hell before him.

Flames turned the boiling clouds of smoke ochre and umber and burnt crimson. Masts exploded and split and cracked, blackened and warped by the heat. Men cut lines with axes and ran buckets of sea water from the fire pumps where sweating men worked desperately to keep the flow going. All the while the fire chugged and growled and surged with a voice like thousands of soldiers shouting all at once on a charge to war.

Mark threw off his cloak and joined the men at the pumps first. He forced his weight down against the bar in rhythm with the men on the opposite side. Tears streamed from his smoke-stung eyes. The wind gusted with swirls of smoke, clear cold air, and bursts of hot ashes. Where was *Mairi*?

Red line at the waterline.

He fled the pump for his burning ship and joined a group of sailors and guards throwing buckets on her deck. If they worked hard enough they could save her.

They had to save her.

He sweltered inside his winter clothes, but he knew that was better than the raw heat that seared the exposed parts of his face worse than a sunburn. He didn't care if he blistered. The flames surrounded him, flashing in from above and all sides. The men around him fought as heedlessly as he did, shouting encouragement to each other. With every bucket his muscles cried and burned with exhaustion. Steam mingled with the smoke. Just one more bucket, and one more, and one more.

They were winning.

Mark dashed up the gangplank onto the deck itself and two men followed. Sailors tossed him buckets and he caught them in the air. A sailor doused him in seawater. "So you don't catch fire!"

"Save the cabin. If the insides catch it'll spread below and we're done for," Mark told him. They moved the bucket chain forward into the heat. The blackened deck seared his boots. He poured a little water into each one and kept moving. He managed to clear enough around one of the hatches to quickly open it—the handle singed his hand—and peeked below. No fire. He quickly shut the hatch. "Leave this closed. It's safe below."

"Leave the hatches shut!" called the man beside him, and they spread the word. All at once the fire retreated into smoke and steam and he was surrounded by sailors.

"I think we've saved her, boys!" a sailor cheered.

Mark couldn't cheer—the smoke had all but choked him to death—but he felt lighter as he threw bucket after bucket across her decks to cool the coals.

Someone began calling orders and the sailors began working the ropes. "Get these masts down in the water!" the older sailor barked.

It had been six years, but he should have recognized someone by now. "Where is Jennison?" No one heard him at first. Mark grabbed an elder sailor. "Where is Rob Jennison?"

"Who?"

"Jennison?" Horror rushed through him. "Isn't this *Mairi*?"

"No, m'lord. *Mairi's* where it all started. She couldn't be saved. They rowed her out." He gestured into the bay.

Mark clutched the hot rail to keep from falling over and looked.

What remained of *Mairi* burned in half-sunken pieces that floated well over a mile out in the vast bay. So beautiful, and dark, and bright, the bones formed a moving architecture of flame and glowing coals that reflected in the water all around her. No one could hear the screams from the small boy he'd once been, the one that had played on the staircase pretending to sail through storms and battles and into the clouds among the stars ....

Mairi's death outshone those dreams, ending them forever.

"They tried to save her figurehead, but no one could get to it." The sailor's voice choked with emotion. "Midge saw it but we couldn't get any sense out of him about it."

Mark knew he ought to feel something more than awe as the ship lit the waves with glorious light.

The charred figurehead pointed unnaturally toward the sky. Mark remembered singing one afternoon long ago while one of the men laid a loving coat of fresh paint over the figurehead's flowing hair, black like the feathery designs draped from its arms. He remembered suddenly that the figurehead had a compass in one hand, and a fierce but friendly smile on its mouth. His father told him the figurehead loved to explore, like it was its own person. It had a favorite song, he'd said.

For love of sea we go, we go
For love of wind and love of foam
She don't love us, she loves to roll
She loves our toil and trials, oh

He didn't realize he'd been singing it until he started coughing. The coughing turned to crushing sobs. He gripped the rail hard until the pressure brought him back. He turned away to help. Nothing else mattered anymore.

The sailor who'd told him about *Mairi* began to work alongside him again. "Midge said they were inside shut in tight and he said something about a *morbai* dancing across the deck. Sad to say we can't trust but a bit of what he says, but he saw something for sure."

"He's a madman?" The world itself seemed mad.

"Mostly not. Captain thinks he's a Seer, but who can say who's a Seer and who's conkers, you know?"

"I understand too well." Where were his voices now?

"I'm sorry, m'lord. I'm sure not a man survived who wasn't ashore with his sweetheart."

He couldn't think of anything to say. "Thank you." Mark left him there, left the ship and started helping another bucket line. By this time most of the fires had been put out, but they still had work to do and so he worked until his hands were bloody and he couldn't stand anymore. He sat by an idle pump in the slushy, dirty snow and rested his head on his knees.

Hard, gloved hands pulled him up. A sacred guard. For a moment Mark thought he'd be dragged back to Argenwain's, but the guard helped him to settle on a bench beside the harbormaster's office. "Where are your men, my lord?" the guard asked.

It took Mark a moment to gather his meaning. He didn't want to lie. "I'm all right. I just need to rest a moment. Thank you for your help."

"You're hurt and drenched and sooty. Forgive me but you're in no way all right. I'll send for a coach."

"I can't pay." Actually, he realized he could. He had two months advance on his indenture ....

He drew the pouch from his vest. At some point he must have tucked it in. He didn't remember doing it.

The money felt heavy in his hand.

He'd have to pay out the indenture even though *Mairi*—

She had a hull fund, but even if that fund had enough to begin the building of a new ship, that wouldn't bring back the dead men, or the ship he loved, or his father. And if he decided to build a new ship from what remained of that fund after the death dues were paid, the balance would fold into a larger indenture.

The pouch was so heavy.

"Starker!" The guard had crouched but now he stood up. "Is there any hope of a coach?"

A guard came over. "That's Lord Argenwain's boy. Keep a good watch over him. I'll find someone to take him home."

Mark forced himself up. "No. Thank you both, but I have business to attend to." Mark shoved the purse back into his vest. "Thank you for your help."

"Are you sure?" The words barely grazed Mark's back as he hunted for his cloak. He found it near one of the pumps, a mashed pile of dirty, soaked wool that had once been soft and fine. He twisted it a few times, looped it around the bar on the pump and pulled to wring it out before he slung it over his shoulders. Bent like an old man, Mark made his way off the docks and up the hill.

An old memory came back to him, this time not of his father but of Gutter. Mark had just been settled into his new room and he sat and everything felt heavy and dark around him. Gutter had taken his hand and just held it for what seemed like forever until Mark gripped back and then Mark had surged into Gutter's arms and Gutter held him close.

He wanted nothing more in the whole world than to be in Gutter's arms, but Gutter was gone. He'd gone—

—on an errand.

No.

Someone like Gutter, if he wanted that done would have paid someone to do it after they'd left on the journey Gutter had promised to take him on.

But then that person would have a secret against Gutter—

"Shut up." He stopped and squeezed his itching, burning eyes shut and told himself that something evil had invaded his mind to lie to him.

Except he knew that the voices hadn't spoken. The thought had come from his own mind.

What would Gutter do to keep me? What did he do to have me in the first place?

"Shut up! I'm nothing!" He'd startled a woman on the street but he didn't care. Everything reeked of smoke, and his thoughts staggered through a burning maze of ruined ships.

I have to go home.

Mark slogged through trampled, icy snow made gray and rough by fallen ash and focused on his pain so that he didn't have room to think.

A boy darted out from an alley and stopped him. "Please, m'lord. You've come from the docks? Have you seen my father?"

Mark's heart stopped for a painfully long moment. He'd gone rushing around like that too at this boy's age, moments after his mother had died.

Those long moments on the longest night of his life.

Mark didn't have to crouch like that one tall sailor had long ago to address him. The twelve year old was only a bit shorter than him. "Who's your father, boy?"

"Kris Wrest."

"I'm sorry. I don't know him." *I don't know anyone at the docks. That life is as dead as*—"Go home. Go home. It's dangerous and your mother will miss you. Go on. He'll be on home soon. The fire's almost out." Mark set his hand on the boy's shoulder and steered him back up the hill. "Run! Run home."

The boy sprang from Mark's push and sprinted back into the alley, arms and legs pumping in awkward disarray.

The alarms stopped clanging one at a time, until one last chime sounded and fell away. In the following quiet he could hear a woman wailing a long way down a street behind him. Had she lost a son, a father, a husband? Was it someone from *Mairi?*

He had no right to mourn his father's men. He no longer knew them. He had no right to mourn the ship either. He hated his own pain and grief he'd lost the least of any of these people. His loss was just a dream built of memories, and he'd wept over those memories a long time ago. He should do something to ease the pain of the widows and orphans made today instead of drowning in pity with his lost hopes in the bay.

He had trouble seeing in the grim darkness. Smoke muddied what little light came through windows, and cloaked the stars with red and orange-tinged haze overhead. The grand clock at the Messenger's Hall rang out the hour of relief—eight o'clock, the end of the unlucky 7th hour after noon.

Eight.

His memory jolted him.

Obsidian.

Obsidian had to be at the gardens right now—

Obsidian might know if and how everything connected. The fire. The ring. Gutter's unexpected arrival in Seven Churches by the Sea. It shouldn't have mattered anymore, but it did. In fact, it was the only thing that mattered. All else had died.

Mark ran a pair of blocks before he slipped on ice and packed snow. It took all his strength to keep from taking a hard fall on the street. His breath felt sharp and rough as he tried to pace himself between a walk and a trot. The gas lamps hadn't been lit in these parts. The only light came through windows to reflect like gold on the clean snow left untouched and piled in drifts against the tenements. A few of the interior lights were gas, but most in this older neighborhood burned oil or candles.

He bent eastward and ended up on the unfamiliar downhill side of the University. Young jesters-in-training laughed and chatted behind the high stone walls. Unlike the streetlamps near the docks, the huge gas lamps curving out from those walls had been lit.

A coach. The slender, one-handed driver stood grooming the shaggy winter coat of his bay horse.

Mark hurried toward it. "Please! Take me to the gardens." The driver opened the door and Mark climbed in. "To the Fall Entrance."

"Thank you, my lord." The coach barely rocked on its springs as the driver climbed up. He released the brake and the horse began to pull its load at a plodding, careful pace. Mark wished he could hurry them, but he knew that in this weather and light, it was the best the horse could do safely. He didn't think he could do much better, if he could even make it to the gardens at all on foot. His feet had gone numb. He pulled his boots off, opened the door, and spilled the seawater out of them. His stockings felt heavy and muddy. He squeezed them out as best he could. His hands felt hot and the very air abraded the ragged edges of skin like sandpaper on his raw flesh.

He ought to go home before the chill overtook him, but all the things he'd witnessed clawed behind his eyes. He needed Obsidian to tell him something, anything about Gutter's presence here. Maybe the truth, or a too-convincing lie, would help Mark find his way home. Because he couldn't go home like this, not-knowing if Gutter had killed those men and destroyed his dreams, not-knowing if Obsidian was alive or dead, not-knowing if what happened tonight would be the least of what he'd have to live with for the rest of his life.

Besides, he still might beat the other jester there and let Obsidian know Gutter was back. He couldn't be sure if that would make things better or worse, but Obsidian needed that information. Obsidian's own future might shatter into darkness if Mark failed him now.

Mark pulled his boots back on. He couldn't just show up and try to stop them from dueling. If they were both there his arrival might spark an attack, and he might get himself shot on top of everything else. He had to approach quietly ....

He could try to involve the guards, but he had a feeling he wouldn't find any. They'd be at the docks.

Why tonight of all nights?

Because Gutter is here?

He had to admit that he had another reason to go to the gardens tonight. Obsidian had known Gutter in far different circumstances than Mark, and Mark had to know.

What am I to Gutter, really?

Would he do something like this to me ... and why? He couldn't seriously believe that losing *Mairi would make me want to stay with him. He had to know I'd suspect him.*

Or maybe he's testing my trust.

Or my stupidity. My loyalty.

My friendship.

My love.

That little flicker in Gutter's eyes when Mark told him that he didn't want to be a jester ... Mark huddled over his knees and wished he hadn't seen that. He wished they hadn't spoken of it at all. If he'd lied, would *Mairi* still be safely floating in the bay?

The horse warmed to his task and they made it to the Fall Entrance sooner than Mark expected, but later than he'd hoped. Mark climbed out before the driver could help him and paid out of his advance. "Wait here," Mark told him. "Just wait a half hour and I'll pay you double."

"It's pitch black in there. Will you need one of my lamps?" the driver asked.

"No. I'll find my way."

"My lord?"

Mark wished the driver would stop talking. It was hard enough to walk into that garden without someone stretching his last nerve.

The driver also looked like he hung from his last nerve too, but a kindness in his voice and his expression won through. "My lord, the gardens aren't safe at night. I'll stay if you ask, but perhaps it might be better if I found an armed escort for you." His voice tripped over a shiver. "Or, or I might provide. I have a pistol." He began to rise from his seat.

"No, thank you."

The driver sat back heavily with a pained sigh. "As pleases you, my lord."

Mark winced. He couldn't let the driver mislead himself anymore, not when things could go badly and he might stay for fear that he'd be accused of abandoning someone of importance. "I'm not a lord, or a jester. I'm just a boy." That last bit came out without him meaning to. He'd been called Argenwain's boy for so long—he didn't realize he'd declare himself that to a stranger when indentured servant would have served as well, if not better. "I'm on an errand. I have to go. Wait if you can, but if—just go if you have to."

"Good luck." He seemed more at ease, though he looked around the streets and to the garden gate with more obvious concern.

"Thank you." Mark steeled himself with a few hard breaths, and then forced himself to hurry past gates of stone and iron.

Chapter Seven

The Rythan Gardens looked vastly different than they did by day. The paths seemed narrower, walled and overhung by dark hedges and black trees with limbs lit by ice. The snow on the ground helped him a little. The snow took what little light his eyes could perceive and made it glow blue against the black depths where shadows and branches and leaves seemed like solid masses of darkness. Even so the paths between the black weren't as clear as he'd hoped. At least someone had lit the old-fashioned oil lamps. Bulbous and copper-turned-verdigris, they had leaded glass panes that cast short swaths of diamond light.

It helped that the paths were perfectly level. Mark walked near the center where a few travelers had left rounded, weathered footprints in the snow. He wished he'd brought something, even a dagger, so he could defend himself if he had to. Until the driver had mentioned it, it hadn't occurred to him that someone other than Obsidian and his bully would be here. In daylight with Lord Argenwain, the gardens had seemed as tame as a clipped hedge.

His heart kicked hard against his ribs as he neared the swan bridge. He heard nothing, not even a whisper, and he couldn't see beyond the lights focused on the stone swans.

The two massive swan statues connected by the top of their heads. The path began as a slope up the first swan's tail, broadened on the back between the wings, and became stairs on the curved neck that led to a platform on top. Stairs led back down to the second swan's back and onto an island.

Mark chose to cross the frozen pond alongside the bridge rather than expose himself on the bridge itself. He hoped that Obsidian was there, alone, but he didn't dare call out his name. Maybe they'd both already left, or maybe he might interrupt at a critical moment, or get himself shot—

I'm going to get myself killed.

The idea of going back home, perhaps to face Gutter's sympathy or explanation or whatever Gutter had planned, seemed worse. Mark had to know the truth.

What if they all died because of me?

The cold penetrated past the skin and made his bones ache, especially in his hands and feet. He kept walking, though he slowed, listening for the slightest hint of human life ahead.

The snow on the ice lay perfectly flat. A cat had walked across as well, long enough ago that its prints had rounded at the edges and snow had filled the pads.

The distinctive sharp sound of a rapier leaving its sheath raked through the air. A pistol going off slammed into Mark's chest. He froze in place, certain he'd been shot, but the pain never came. Then he heard a moan. The moan turned into a rising cry that made every hair on his body stand on end.

Was it?

Obsidian.

Mark wanted to run to him, but he crouched down and crawled toward the island. Every muscle burned to hurry, but he forced himself to creep. His breath came in little gasps that stirred the snow near his face.

Two figures lay on the ground up a short slope. A lit fountain of swans taking flight amid curtains of water frozen by winter loomed beside them. The light softly touched on the black silk and wool Obsidian wore, and on crimson spreading in the snow, turning it garish colors of red and pink. Obsidian writhed and wept, clawing at the hideous mask on his face. The figure in blue lay terribly still, a rapier obscenely stuck in his chest. A pistol lay in the snow near the dead man's hand. Just beyond the pistol a blue velvet cloak embroidered with silver and white sparkled in the golden light.

"Obsidian." Mark's voice cracked with cold horror. He crawled to Obsidian. Blood boiled from Obsidian's thigh. Obsidian held his leg with one hand, but not over the wound. Didn't he know he had to press the wound? Mark set his hands over the wound and pushed down, pinning the leg against the snow.

Obsidian screamed. "No!" He finally pulled the mask free from his face. He gasped in shock.

"I'm sorry." It was stupid thing to say.

Obsidian had washed the makeup he usually wore under his mask from his face, leaving only a thin outline of black around his eyes.

He didn't wear his usual mask here.

Obsidian's cheeks were gaunt with pain.

"I have to get you a physician." *No, I can't leave him this way.* "Take off your belt. We'll tie it over the wound."

Obsidian's breathing tightened and hitched. He pried at his belt buckle, bloody fingers slipping on the metal. Finally he worked it open. He couldn't pull it free.

Mark risked helping him with one hand. Blood pulsed up between Mark's fingers while he yanked on the belt. It took forever but he pulled the belt free and pushed the leather over the wound. It didn't cover enough. "Shit." Mark knelt on the wound. Obsidian hissed. Mark unwound his neckerchief and wadded it up. He rolled it onto the wound when he pulled his knee off. It seemed to help. Mark worked the belt around Obsidian's leg twice and buckled it on. "I'm going to get a physician."

"Don't leave me." His breath came in gulping heaves.

"I have to. I'll be right back."

Obsidian grabbed Mark's coat. "No! No. Don't go."

Leave him. It's too late. The foreign whisper slipped unwelcome into his mind.

"I hear them whispering," Obsidian gasped.

The hair on Mark's neck prickled. "Try to stay calm." He couldn't carry him and dragging him would make things worse. "I'll get the driver to fetch a physician."

"Don't bring anyone. Get the ring from Lake. Take it and take the book to the islands. If Gutter finds out you were here and that you know about the book and the ring, I don't know what he might do."

"He won't find out and you won't die and I won't know anything if you stop telling me. Just wait." Mark tried to pry Obsidian's fingers loose from his coat.

"Please don't leave me alone. I'm a jester without a patron, and I killed a man. Please. Please help me. Chant, or sing. Something."

"You wore a death mask. Your soul should be safe. You can talk, so you can breathe. You're strong. You're strong enough to live."

"Please. I see them. I see them."

Mark stripped off his cloak and coat. Obsidian's own black and gold cloak lay nearby in the snow. Mark covered him with that as well to help keep him warm. "I'll be back." He ran down the slope, across the pond, down the path. He knew this would happen. They both knew this would happen but all Obsidian cared about was that stupid ring. All that blood and pain for intrigues—

—all that fire—

Gutter orbited both catastrophes. Mark couldn't reconcile the man who'd saved him and cared for him with the Lord Jester that everyone dreaded.

Mark staggered onto the street beyond the gate. No driver. Fresh tracks skidded off westward up the snowy street.

He wasted a few precious seconds staring. He shouldn't have been surprised that the shot had frightened the driver away. Part of him wasn't surprised, though it felt like Obsidian had fallen into the sea and the ship had sailed away, leaving him to drown.

Mark ran back. He slipped several times, clumsy from exhaustion. He didn't care if Obsidian could answer his questions or not. He just wanted him to live.

Obsidian moved strangely in the snow, his body flexing in a way that would have seemed sinuous and beautiful if it wasn't so odd. Mark grabbed him up under the arms and started to drag him. Obsidian had no other hope.

Obsidian's arms worked unevenly, making it hard for Mark to hold onto him. Mark's back whined in protest and he couldn't catch his breath, but he refused to give up.

His heel caught and Mark slid. Obsidian fell onto his legs. Mark grabbed him hard around the chest and tried to position himself to stand up again.

Obsidian's head lolled against Mark's face. That's when Mark realized that Obsidian hadn't uttered a single protest, or grunt, or anything. Mark laid him down gently. Obsidian's eyes stared, unblinking, toward a distant lamp. The dull, reflected light revealed the ugly fact that his eyes had begun to dry and cloud and freeze.

Mark sat heavily in the snow. Obsidian's living expression flashed through Mark's memory. Obsidian's dead, ashen face snuffed that memory out. The living memory tried to return, but the reality of those black-rimmed eyes cut it down over and over again until the living memory faded to nothing and only death remained.

Obsidian had begged him not to leave. He died alone and afraid. "I'm so sorry." But sorry wouldn't make it right.

I failed him.

He wanted Gutter. Gutter would make it all better.

Gutter did this.

I don't know that.

But taking this to Gutter would be another betrayal and a failure. Obsidian had his reasons for keeping Gutter out of this, whatever this was. To keep Mark safe? He'd said as much, but who should Mark believe, a young jester or the man who'd—

Who'd put me in the hands of a man like Lord Argenwain? Who may have burned up my future in order to impose his own?

"You tell me to leave a man to die, but when I need to know where my father is, who killed my mother, when I need to know the truth about Gutter, you're silent." The snow deadened his voice, and no answer whispered inside his mind. He touched Obsidian's face. "If you're *allolai*, I hope you take him into your care, and if you're *morbai* ...." He couldn't make threats or demands of whatever spoke to him. He didn't even know if what he heard was real.

The bloody smears he left on Obsidian's face were real.

Why had Gutter returned home so soon at the risk of his life, whether it was by sail past the Sefrenne Talon or travel overland on treacherous Vyenne's bandit baron controlled roads?

He couldn't make himself hate Gutter, but he no longer trusted him. Maybe he hadn't trusted him in a long time, but before this he'd had little need to care whether he trusted him or not. Now he had to choose between Obsidian's last request and Gutter's plans for him.

For the first time in his life, Mark hated that he loved Gutter.

He was done with lessons and the future Gutter wanted for him. He refused to go back to that damned house where everything existed to keep Lord Argenwain happy and in the king's favor. The cursed ring and book made as good an excuse to leave as any. Perida wasn't his first choice, but it was the best destination for an escaped indentured servant.

Except.

Mark had to go back for one thing.

Could he sneak inside and get it without anyone noticing?

No. Argenwain had too many servants, and no secret ways in that Mark was privy to.

He could leave—

Am I seriously going to leave?

—without Obsidian's book.

If he didn't have both the ring and the book, he might wind up on the islands without enough to get him an audience with Rohn Evan, the man who hopefully had more answers than Mark had questions at this point.

Fuck them all. Why not just leave it all behind?

And go where and do what? Either way he'd have the Church after him for default on his indenture, and Gutter, and Lord Argenwain and who knew who else had dealings with Gutter or Obsidian in this matter. He wouldn't find safety anywhere on the mainland. He had to go to the islands, and if he had to go to the islands anyway, he'd go to see Rohn Evan with everything he needed in hand. That would honor Obsidian's trust in him, and Mark would be far enough from Gutter's reach—

He'd be completely alone.

No. From there he could write Gutter, and this time he expected Gutter would write him back. Whether they'd exchange lies or truths, he would still have a connection to the world he'd always known. Maybe he'd find out what friendship with Gutter really meant.

It still felt like a leap off a high mast, but through his fear and grief he felt a rare moment of hope. And at least he'd be at sea, where he'd always wanted to belong.

But he couldn't sail from Seven Churches by the Sea. Lord Argenwain, Gutter and the Church all had the power to stop shipping traffic while they hunted for him, and all three would want him back.

He needed a plan.

Mark stood on shaky legs and walked to where Obsidian's bully lay curled in the snow.

The homely man with the friendly face and long, unbound brown hair wore one ring, an unusual ring. It had to be the ring that Obsidian mentioned, because jesters didn't wear rings like this one.

It was a signet ring. Only lords used them. In theory, noble lords had little to hide in their correspondence and so a wax seal pressed with their signet ring was considered perfectly adequate security. A jester had to employ more crafty means to secure a letter against being read by the wrong person.

The ring easily slid free of the jester's hand, already cold and shrunken by the snow. Mark couldn't make out much of the design. Between the insufficient light and his shaking hands, all he could make out were a few intertwined lines.

He rolled the ring between his fingers, and then gripped it hard in his fist. He'd had enough. The thought of three more years of this with little hope of a ship awaiting him at the end sickened him. He should have left a long time ago. It was long past time to start a new life, and it would begin tonight.

A downstairs maid hurried to the door when Mark opened it. The entire downstairs remained lit up as if for a party, but darkness shrouded the upstairs above and behind her. "Mark! Everyone is looking for you."

"Shhh." Mark slipped inside and shut the door behind him. "Is Lord Argenwain asleep?"

"Is that blood?"

"It's all right. It's not mine." He'd managed to keep his composure so far, but it started to crumble. He tightened his hands and took a slow breath in. "The fire—people died."

"I'm so sorry." She sucked in a gasp. "Your ship—"

He shook his head. He couldn't talk about it, or even lie about it. "Is Lord Argenwain asleep?"

"Yes. He was so worried it gave him a headache. He had three brandies and went to bed." She winced. "You're going to catch it tomorrow."

"I think they'll understand. Besides, what are a few months more of indenture? Even if it's a year more. I don't care." He realized that he sounded insane. He softened his voice. "Besides, this is my home. It always has been."

"You aren't afraid they'll throw you out, sell your indenture—Mark, Lord Argenwain—I've never seen him so angry."

That gave him a little chill, but he shook it off. He had so much more than Lord Argenwain to worry about now. "I'm going to wash up and go to bed." He had to ask, though he feared the answer. "Is Gutter home?"

"No. Lord Jester Gutter told us not to wait up for him. He said he knew where you were and that he'd bring you home safe."

That made Mark wonder, but he nodded without thinking it through and headed up the stairs. "I doubt I'll get any sleep tonight, so if you like I'll answer the bell for you."

Her shoulders sagged and she let out a sigh. "Are you sure?"

He nodded. "Good night."

"Do you want a lamp?"

"No thank you."

"Good night again, then. And thank you." She put out most of the lights before she left.

He didn't dare spare the time to light his hearth fire or to run downstairs and heat some water for washing. He shuddered as much from lingering images of burning ships and dying men in his mind as he did from the chill in his room as he washed himself with a scant amount of cold water leftover in his drinking pitcher. He bandaged his hands in handkerchiefs, then dressed warmly before he emptied out his large art bag back from when he used to take lessons in plein air painting. He filled it with extra stockings and warm shirts, a spare vest and breeches, the money pouch, a stationary case with a small ink vial and quill tips, a shaving kit, and ...

He remembered that Gutter had left his satchel here. It was gone now. He looked toward his vanity. The mask sat there next to its silk wrapping. Two sealed and puzzle-tied leather cases lay beside it.

He took the mask Gutter had given him and held it near his bedside lamp. The black pearl tear tracks looked wet.

Gutter believed that this mask wouldn't take Mark over and make him forget himself, though Gutter suggested that he wasn't sure about how the mask would react to Mark. That admission of uncertainty suggested a certain amount of honesty.

He wouldn't use it, but he wouldn't leave it behind, either. If he took it with him, then Gutter might hope that things would work out between them somehow. And maybe they would.

But Gutter better have a brilliant explanation for all that had happened.

Either way, it would help keep Gutter guessing, and confusion would be his ally tonight.

Mark tucked it away, and put the letter cases in his bag. He might need makeup too, so that he could dress himself up respectably. That made him wonder how exactly he was supposed to present himself, not just to the islanders, but to carriage drivers and ship captains and anyone else he might have to deal with.

Lord Argenwain had people looking for him, but they wouldn't be looking for a jester.

He could also hire carriages and a ship more easily as a jester. The money he carried wouldn't seem so odd, and most people wouldn't ask a jester too many questions.

He wouldn't wear the mask, though. He didn't trust the mask, not without knowing what he would do from within it.

Or what it would do with me.

The more he thought about running away the more he wanted to leave and be on a ship, any ship bound for anywhere.

He grabbed a deck of cards, a ring, another pair of stockings, and several neckerchiefs. He barely noticed what he shoved into his bag anymore. When it bulged past full he tucked the signet ring and pouch securely inside his vest, covered the top of his bag with a plain white neckerchief, put on his best feathered hat and cracked his door open.

Only a few lights still burned downstairs, oil ones. Lord Argenwain didn't care to have gas lights in his house, though he approved of them as streetlights. He claimed to dislike the expense, but Mark knew the old man was a little afraid of them.

Mark crept to the servant's stairs at the back of the hall. Any moment Gutter might come home. It wouldn't take him long to learn that Mark had been here and left. Mark didn't want to be in the house or anywhere nearby on the streets when that happened.

He'd take one of the carriage horses. He wasn't a very good rider, but he'd learned upon the eldest of the six horses Argenwain kept in town and she didn't mind a saddle and bridle.

So now I'm a horse thief on top of everything else.

He'd forgotten a coat and cloak but he didn't dare go back now. He went out the back door to the stable, following in the path formed by the stablemaster's footsteps. They'd filled with snow since the last time he'd walked out here. He had a proper bed in the house and would be fast asleep. The stableboy, though, would be asleep in the little room in the back beside the tack room.

Mark set his bag beside the eldest mare's outer door and snuck to the tack room, groping in the dark. One of the horses murmured. He didn't dare try to soothe it—he'd be just as likely to cause a stir and wake the others as to calm it down, and it would waste more time. He opened the tack room door, lit a lamp, and carefully lifted first the mare's saddle, dusty from disuse, and her bridle. He left the door open and the lamp lit. There'd be little use in covering his escape. His best friend would be speed.

He crept back and opened the mare's door. She swung her head up from where she lay and heaved up to her feet, snuffling. He let her nose the bridle and saddle. "What a good girl, Neatbye," he murmured. "Remember me?" She pressed her nose into his hand and he stroked her face. Her ears switched and she kept pushing her nose into the wrappings on his hands—perhaps she didn't like the smell of blood.

He'd forgotten a blanket. He thought about saddling her without one, then realized if he hurt her he'd not only hate himself but she might not get far even with his light weight on her. Mark set her tack down and went back to the tack room. The horse from before grumbled more insistently.

The stableboy's door opened and Mark leapt back, stifling a gasp. "Jessen? I didn't mean to wake you."

Jessen rubbed his eyes with his thick fists. "Mark?"

"Can you help me saddle Neatbye?"

Jessen combed his hands through his short bristly hair and went into the tack room. He lumbered as if he still slept while walking. Mark tried to stay calm. Jessen lit the lamp in Neatbye's stall. Mark had no reasonable lie to offer in objection.

Jessen saddled and bridled her quickly, then led her out.

Mark held out his bag to Jessen to hold while he mounted up. His heart pounded and fear muffled his ears.

The ground felt like a long way away. Mark settled the shoulder strap so the bag would rest behind him. "Let's hope *morbai* aren't meddling tonight."

"Where are you going?" Jessen asked. He yawned.

Mark didn't dare hesitate too long. "Back to the docks. *Mairi*—my ship, was lost and ..." He didn't have to pretend his pain. "I'm delivering a little comfort to those left behind." It would throw Gutter off.

Assuming he got away before Gutter spotted him.

"Will you manage the side gate for me?" Mark asked.

Jessen led the way and the mare followed him more than Mark's rusty instructions to her. He feared she wouldn't go out, but she seemed to trust the streetlamps just fine for her footing and let him nudge her into the night.

He needed a heavy greatcoat or a cloak or something. He felt warm enough now, but he expected that it would take at least two days travel up or down the bay shore to the nearest port, assuming he could travel that fast in winter. He had no idea if people even ventured out on the land routes this time of year. Perhaps Gutter had just come through overland from the south, or he might have taken a ship from northern Vyenne. Hard to say.

It didn't matter. Mark had to try.

His gut lurched when he remembered. He knew exactly where he could find cloaks fine enough to present himself as a jester if he had to. He had his own coat there too.

What if the guards had already come to the gardens? The driver might have called them in.

He had to take a chance at it or he might freeze to death. He'd heard of frozen soldiers found in the spring thaw and farm families discovered dead in their cottages after a brutal storm. That knowledge now breathed into his face with intimate and deadly promise.

Mark guided Neatbye to the Fall Gate. The only fresh tracks were his and the ones that came from the driver and carriage. Mark rode her into the gardens.

Obsidian still lay there, lips turning a delicate pale blue-gray. Mark forced in a breath through his nose, lips tight to keep them from trembling, and dismounted. He gathered up the bully's cloak, Obsidian's cloak, and his own filthy cloak. He almost left his bloody and sooty coat there, but he realized that it might get back to Gutter and then Gutter would know he'd been here and he might guess about the ring and everything.

Assuming he knew anything about the ring and book at all.

The idea that Gutter wouldn't know about any of it seemed ridiculous.

Mark folded all the cloaks up into a roll and draped it over the mare's hindquarters.

The pistol still lay in the snow.

He'd need weapons.

Gingerly, he removed Obsidian's pistol from its holster and checked it. It was loaded and sealed so it could be carried in weather. He didn't want to remove Obsidian's rapier from Lake's chest, but the scabbard already lay free on the snow from when they'd removed Obsidian's belt and it would be easier to manage than wrestling with Lake's body to get at his rapier and scabbard. Mark placed his hand on the hilt and pulled. It stuck at first, but then began to slide. The sensitive steel spoke to his skin as it dragged past bone and through meat and skin and cloth, each layer separate and distinct, until it came free in the cold air. Mark cleaned it with snow and Lake's coat before he sheathed it. Perhaps the cold and dark protected him, or maybe everything else had numbed him. Either way he didn't feel sick or horrified like he thought he ought to. He tried not to think about it while he took Obsidian's loading kit, and almost as an afterthought, both men's purses, powderhorns and Obsidian's ammunition bag.

He didn't want Obsidian's mask. He didn't even want to touch it. The hesitation came from the strange feeling that abandoning it here to whoever might come across it would be the same as leaving a wounded man in a ditch to fend for himself. He walked over to where it lay face down in the snow. It had writing on the inside—the masker's signature, and its name. Too Mon. Mark didn't recognize it. He turned it over with his boot.

The hideous thing was a full face mask of heavy black leather. The eyeholes were more ample than necessary for human eyes, and the nose dropped into a bulb like a crookneck squash. The mouth, in contrast, smiled pleasantly with lips that looked supple enough to kiss. Black hair—it might have been Obsidian's own—formed a thin mane of dark ringlets.

It smiled at Mark, askew and dotted with snow.

Mark had never seen a death mask before. Strange shudders rippled through his chest and gut and he didn't dare look away from it in case it—

What?

—came alive.

The more he stared the more friendly it seemed, but that didn't reassure him. Mark bent down and touched it. It flinched—it couldn't have; he didn't see it do anything—but it did and he flinched too. With all the will he could muster, Mark picked it up.

An eerie image came to him of Obsidian drawing it out at the same time as he drew his rapier and holding it to his face, of Lake drawing his pistol and firing ....

Mark rode back the way he'd come, too afraid to leave by a different gate in case worse things lay deeper in the Rythan Gardens than two dead jesters.

Less than an hour later he rode southward out of the city. Daylight would come soon, and with it a widening search for the runaway indentured servant boy who might have been a jester, or a sailor on *Mairi*.

Or maybe both of those had always been false promises.

Maybe what he'd find ahead of him would be the first real future he could call his own since his mother's death, the first future Gutter hadn't planned and manipulated him into, a future that until now Mark hadn't wanted or chosen for himself.

He hoped his flight would take him to a future worth fighting for.

Chapter Eight

White sky, fog, snowfall, snow and ice. Only the trees had more than just white to them, in shades of gray and slate and grim green in the lees and undersides of the pines. He slogged in knee-deep snow, his shoulders and back aching from carrying the bag or dragging it through the snow, whichever seemed better at a given time. The strap dug into his shoulders even through the thickness of two cloaks. When he dragged it, the strap hurt his wounded hands and wrenched his already weary back. The cloaks dragged him down as well, but he didn't dare leave them or he'd soon freeze to death. And no matter how many times the wind blew his hat off, he forced himself to pick it up again. The wind through his sweat-damp hair chilled him too quickly without it. Compared to all that, the rapier scabbard dragging in the snow seemed insignificant.

Less than a half hour outside the city, Neatbye had halted and refused to go forward. He'd dismounted and tried to lead her, and she followed for a while, but then he slipped and dropped the reins and she didn't let him catch her again. As a final statement of defiance she'd kicked her hind legs in the air at him. Luckily she dislodged the roll of cloaks and his bag in the process. Without that, he would have been forced to follow her back to Seven Churches.

He'd wanted to keep all three cloaks, but after a few miles he found he couldn't bear the weight of his water-soaked one, so he buried it on the side of the road.

Road—ha. Stone markers, some ancient and some new, some ten feet tall or more, kept him on the road but it gave him little advantage. The road proved to be barely more passable than the drifts and gullies on both sides. He tried to follow the furrows made from sleighs that had passed through, but it appeared that none had gone by in days if not longer and his boots broke through the crusts they made as often as not anyway. At least the road had fewer deep spots, but it still had them. The last deep stretch he'd traversed lasted over a hundred yards and he crawled much of the way to avoid what happened too often despite his efforts—sinking up to his knees in loose snow. The frequent incursion of snow into his boots had made his stockings wet. He didn't dare stop long enough to change them.

He wished he had gloves. Covering his face helped. Though his neckerchief stank and was wet and damp and cold, it wasn't as bad as the fresh air slicing down his throat. He kept his hands in his coat sleeves. The bones in his fingers ached and every step on his half-frozen feet stabbed all the way up to his knees.

Neatbye had the right idea.

He wished he'd thought of bribing a small boat fisherman in Seven Churches. He fantasized about it. He could have found his way to the road after being let off on a beach somewhere and walked not nearly so far to his destination—the port town of Reffiel.

He also imagined a sleigh coming along and the passengers insisting that he join them. They'd coo and fuss ...

... and turn him in to the authorities because he was obviously a runaway indentured servant with things stolen from dead men.

He'd read about the wilderness and winter travel and how soldiers suffered and died in the cold, but that didn't prepare him for the real cold, and real misery, and the real wilderness. He wasn't even in the deep wilderness, just the uninhabited stretch along Hullundy Bay's long shore between Seven Churches by the Sea and Reffiel. It didn't matter that it wasn't deep wilderness. The pines surrounded him, relentlessly empty.

Empty, but not silent. The wind made the heavy branches shift just a trace, enough to occasionally jostle loose snow that made thick, luffing sounds as it traveled down in an uneven staircase fashion to the soft ground. Branches cracked and broke, shattering smaller limbs as they crashed down. The snow made thin, sizzling sounds as it blew across icy crusts. And the cries of gulls and rasping of crows sounded harsh and threatening with no city to dwarf them.

It was, as Trevole had written, inhuman desolation. Mark had thought it a spiritual statement. Scholars had made it seem so. But here it eloquently described the utter lack of human love, compassion, and civilization. Even disdain and hate was better than the knowledge that if he fell and died here, he'd be covered over in an hour and everything would once again be nothing but cold white and ice.

He hadn't brought any food, but thirst bothered him more. His throat was raw from the cold air. Normally he'd yearn for hot brandy but all he wanted was water. He remembered from history books how soldiers who ate snow died faster, so he just let the thirst rake him until he couldn't stand it anymore. Then he balled up a little snow until it felt like ice and let it slowly melt over his tongue.

His shirt was damp with sweat but he didn't dare change it for a dry one. He just end up with two damp shirts, not to mention baring his skin to the weather could lose him more warmth than he might gain. It seemed impossible to be so cold with so many heavy layers of clothing, but he was, especially his hands and arms and feet and legs. His belly and chest were so warm in contrast it made his guts squirm, and the clammy shirt made him shiver.

When it started to get dark he tried walking faster, but it exhausted him and he ended up plodding forward at an even slower pace. Then the hour that he'd dreaded crept up on him. A fog moved in from the sea. He couldn't see or hear the bay, but he smelled salt in the air. The sea still held much of his fate in its grasp. As the bay's night breath spread all around him with the twilight, he couldn't tell road from drift or marker from tree, and he had to stop.

At first he thought to leave the road to avoid the people hunting for him, but he feared he'd get lost, so he settled in the lee of a large road marker. There he dug himself a hole. He used Obsidian and Lake's purses for protection for his hands after he emptied the contents onto the snow. He didn't bother to keep their things separate, and just scraped them all into one purse afterward. He was afraid of getting buried should the snow start to fall heavily, so he only made the hole a couple of feet deep, and rolled himself up in the cloaks.

The darkness closed in. His breath warmed the inside of his nest. Surrounded by wool, no longer burdened with the hateful bag, his body eased a little at a time until all at once he relaxed. His hands hurt and his back and his shoulders ached but he wasn't fighting to make step after step anymore. He felt safe enough to wad up a little more snow for water.

The little bit of packed snow eased his thirst enough that at last he could sleep.

Mark woke to darkness, all but smothered in wool, and thrashed free. Cold air slapped his face. Thin daylight and heavy snowfall surrounded him. Snow, helped by a bully wind, had covered him and filled his tracks such that he had to look hard to see which way he'd come from. He hoped that he remembered correctly that he'd sheltered at a marker on the left side, or he might end up doubling back toward Seven Churches, or worse, stray off the road altogether.

His belly growled and twisted up tight with hunger. He ate a little snow, then wrapped himself in the cloaks and waited until he felt good and warm again before he began to gather his things. Everything ached, especially his back and shoulders and knees, but he felt stronger than he'd been at the end the night before. He just wished he knew how far he'd come, and how much farther he had left to go. Another whole day? Two? Three?

This time he didn't want his feet to get so cold. After he changed his stockings he tied neckerchiefs around the tops of his boots so that snow would have a harder time getting inside. He wrapped another one around his face and over the top of his head.

He went through his bag with a more critical eye this time. He rid himself of the stationary case, and a deck of cards he didn't remember taking. He tossed them and they fluttered away across the snow like leaves in the wind.

He cut off the ends of the damp pair of stockings from the day before to use as long mittens. He also changed his shirt and left the damp one in his nest. The brief cold from changing only made the bliss of warm, dry clothing that much more wonderful. He used the damp neckerchief, the silk now frozen, to tie his hat on his head like women sometimes did with diaphanous scarves when they went riding. He didn't care. No one would see him and even if someone did, embarrassment wouldn't be his highest concern.

Mark's hands traced over the mask he kept tucked in his jacket, and then the signet ring and book tucked in his waistcoat. All safe.

He willed himself to begin his march across even deeper snow than the day before. The strength he'd gained from rest quickly ran out. He guessed he'd walked less than an hour before his legs gave out and refused to lift him again. He knelt awkwardly in the snow until his knees began to burn, then shifted to sit more comfortably. His throat was so dry he couldn't swallow.

Mark ate a little snow and drew the purse with the book from his waistcoat. He carefully removed the ring from his inside waistcoat pocket as well and cleaned the blood out of the design. If Professor Vinkin had presented him with something like this, he would have been eager to decipher their importance. Now he only felt a weary need to understand before they got him or someone else killed.

The script on the signet ring seemed to form letters. He turned it around several times before he settled on a direction and decided they must read RT in Hasle. It was in the royal script, which had no equivalent in the Cathretan alphabet, sort of a capital letter but only used for the first letters in a noble's names or in place names. He'd hated reading certain translations from Hasle in Cathretan because the translators often used a doubled capital letter to signify the usage, and it popped up in strange and seemingly incorrect ways.

In any case, the ring could be a noble's initials, or a household signet, or even a city official's mark. Regardless, it would have belonged to a nobleman.

Or woman, he reminded himself.

Obsidian shouldn't have had it. Had Gutter given it to him?

A powerful anger boiled up from nowhere. It shocked him, but it gave him new strength. Obsidian's death and all the other deaths and harm that came from the fire and the signet ring—if Gutter was really to blame, Mark could never forgive him. Yesterday his mind had been so wild with confusion and fear and so dulled by exhaustion that he didn't know what to think. He still didn't want to believe, but the possibility that Gutter had caused so much suffering overshadowed everything else.

And if Gutter had set the fire, had he also killed the woman for which the ship had been named? And what might have he done with her captain?

Alone, surrounded by winter, the answer seemed far more clear than it had in all the years he'd spent in Pickwelling Manor. Mark knew he didn't have the truth of all of it. He might still have most of it wrong. But at least, after years of lying to himself and hoping and believing Gutter was his savior first and foremost, he could be honest and accept the possibility that the mighty lord jester deserved his fearsome reputation. That acceptance gave him strength, and a desire he hadn't felt since he'd held his mother in his arms for the last time.

He wanted justice. Not the way the Church performed it, but the way the Church promised to fight for it, the way it was supposed to.

To have justice, he first had to find the truth.

He placed the ring back inside his waistcoat pocket and then opened the clasp on the purse.

The purse held a small, square book covered in leather with flapped edges to protect the pages from the weather. The crisp and bright paper had a smooth texture, and the ink had the distinct, clean edges and sharp scent of something recently written and not yet exposed to years of alternating damp and dry. The writer used good, dark ink, something a noble could afford for everyday use.

It described a code, a particularly devious code that employed single symbols not just for letters but for common words, and some of those common words and letters had more than one symbol designated for them. It also had single symbols for several common letter combinations—tor, ing, ed, man, old. A letter written in such a code would be practically indecipherable, especially if the writer additionally wrote backwards or some such.

Its main fragility revolved around the difficulty of memorizing the code, which required either an exceptional memory or copies of the code book for everyone who needed one. The more copies, the more vulnerable the code. Its second fragility lay in the fact that anyone who put their hands on a document written in it would immediately recognize that he or she had something of secret importance. That usually inspired an investigation that could expose that secret regardless of whether or not the code was deciphered.

So who was using it? Gutter? If so, then why would Obsidian care if Gutter had this particular copy of the book or not?

Maybe Obsidian didn't care as much as he cared about losing the ring, if even for a little while, and what Lake might unwittingly reveal by showing it around. That would explain why Obsidian felt safe leaving the book with Mark. But then why ship the book to Perida instead of asking Mark to give it to Gutter if something happened, as something awful had?

Mark put the book back in the purse, noticing that he had in fact broken threads when he'd opened it. Those broken threads might matter to Mr. Rohn Evan, but Mark had no need to worry about that until got to Perida.

If he got to Perida.

And if he was taken by the Church before then?

He'd better get rid of the book and the ring in that case. Hopefully he'd see the riders coming in time to surreptitiously shove the book and the ring in the snow. If he pretended to fall while running away, they wouldn't know to look for anything there. The ring would survive but he doubted anyone would find it. Weather would destroy the book and keep its secrets safe.

Mark worked his way back up to his feet, covered his hands in the cut stockings, and slung the bag onto his shoulder. Even through two cloaks, a coat, waistcoat and shirt, it bit into the bruise from carrying it the day before. His back cramped up. At least it wasn't unbearable, and it weighed a bit less. His clothes weighed him down more, but he rejected the idea of parting with any of them. He'd need them tonight, especially if the snowfall and wind kept up.

At first he sang softly under his breath to keep his spirits up and keep himself company, but he soon grew too breathless to sing. Cold and exhaustion reduced him to a mindless thing that shuffled from marker to marker because it didn't remember how to stop. His body worked so hard he tasted blood, and his lungs burned even worse than his legs. Often the snow would start to fall so hard he couldn't see even a few steps ahead. He'd allow himself a rest until the snow eased, and then force himself onward. Sometimes he thought he heard his father's voice, talking about the islands. The islands were always warm, and green, and the sea was green too and warm and alive, full of stone forests and colorful fish that flocked from copse to copse as if they were birds in the scrublands.

He hadn't even seen scrublands, but he could imagine those too, and the mountains that sheltered Saphir City—all the places he'd never been. If he could just take one more step, and another, and another, they could all be his.

Maybe he could even go back to Gutter someday, if Gutter turned out to be innocent of everything Mark feared he'd done. Though Mark missed his father, that man was only a faint memory. Gutter was real, and strong, and he would never vanish and leave Mark alone as his own father had. And if Gutter was good ...

A jester must do it for good. Not his own good, often not even for his lord's good, but for a higher good. He must decide for himself what is right and do it, no matter how unpleasant the task ....

The words gave Mark strength to go onward. He didn't have to be a jester to trust in the sentiment. Yes, he was running from his lord and risked defaulting on his indenture. Yes he'd stolen a horse, and had even taken things off of dead men, but he believed this would all work for something good in the end. He swore to himself that if he lost that sense of higher good, he would stop.

As he dragged himself onward, too often he saw Obsidian dying, and he remembered what the steel told his hand as he pulled it free of Lake's body. The memory of the shot that had killed Obsidian rang out so clearly that sometimes it startled him mid-step and he'd turn to look. The emptiness would close in then, reminding him how alone he was, showing him with buried trees and barely exposed road markers how quickly he'd disappear once his legs gave out for the last time.

Mark thought his eyesight had begun to fade from weariness, but he looked up and realized dusk had darkened the sky. He labored up a long rise, stockings wet and icy up to his knees. What he saw at the top woke him from his daze.

The road dwindled into a path cut into a cliff. Hundreds of feet below the cliff curved, inviting Hullundy Bay deeper inland before it joined with the last broad stretch of the Trossmare River. Countless dark projections intruded into the water, docks and ships made tiny by distance. A lighthouse flashed on a large but barely definable island that twinkled with tiny gas lights. Lines of lights on the mainland suggested roads.

He'd reached Reffiel, but he had no idea how to get to it.

The path down the cliff didn't look continuous. It couldn't possibly be the way down. "This is insane," he gasped. "This can't be right." *I must have strayed from the road.* He dropped the bag with a small cry of pain and turned in place, looking for somewhere that the road might fork and veer away to circumvent the cliffs, but he saw no markers to the east, nor anything that distinguished itself from the steep fields and rugged forest that lay in all directions.

The path that seemed to present itself could easily be ridges of ice clinging to the cliff that could give way when he tried to walk on them.

He started to walk into the woods, hoping to find a way farther south, but quickly sank up to his thighs in a snow drift. He didn't see any more road markers. Mark stared in place at nothing for a moment before he forced himself to slog back to the cliff's edge. This top portion at least didn't seem so bad. It was wide enough to accommodate a sizable coach, though barely. Mark took a few steps down, then a few more.

He had little choice. He'd go as far as he dared. He could always turn back if he had to.

The snow reflected enough light to glow in sharp contrast to the dark, ice-coated rocks, but as the dirty, faded sunset dimmed he felt in constant danger of misjudging the slope and plummeting to his death.

The snow gave way and he began to slide. One of the mittens slid off his hand and he gripped with a clawed hand, scrambling with his feet over ice—

He stopped short of the cliff's edge. He'd traveled forty feet closer to Reffiel.

Very slowly he reached for his rapier and drew it as far as he could, and then put his hand on the bare steel and drew it out the rest of the way. He turned it about and gripped the hilt.

If this doesn't work I'll slide over the edge.

He lifted it and brought it down hard on the ice-covered snow. The pointed flare on the crossguard broke through and held.

He needed another tool, but he didn't have a dagger with him. The cloak pins were too narrow, as was his hat pin.

His body flattened on the slope had stopped on its own. He had to trust that if he stayed low, he wouldn't simply slide off the path.

He didn't want to trust anything.

I can't stay here all night like this.

Very carefully, moving one limb at a time, he edged away from the cliff's edge toward the thin security of the path's inside line. When he couldn't go any farther without moving the rapier, he lifted it.

He didn't slide.

Mark sat up, teeth chattering more from fear than cold. Inch by inch he moved over until he could put his hands on the icy rocks on the path's safe side. Hanging on with one bare hand and one still in a mitten, he stood.

Behind him, the mitten he'd lost was just a few steps away, but it seemed impossibly out of reach. He didn't want to go back up, and he didn't dare walk down.

The rapier.

He sheathed the rapier, un-strapped it from his belt, and used the sheath as a walking stick with one hand on the rocks. He let the bag drag behind him. It served as a kind of anchor until it began to slide. Mark could do nothing to save himself when it hit his feet except fall into the rocks.

He banged his knees scrabbling for purchase, but he held on. Twenty more feet closer to Reffiel.

Mark minced his way down as close to the cliff's wall as he could manage, and grabbed for purchase in the ice and snow with his bare hands every time he slipped on the steep slope. The ice cut his skin and turned it white.

The ground grew icier and more brittle farther down. He sat and slid on his bottom, using the crossguard on the rapier to slow his descent. At any moment he could lose control. He clenched his teeth so tight he thought they'd break, and fresh blood made his bare hand slippery.

The road turned around a peak and dropped precipitously toward the port, or what he assumed was the port, since all he saw in the deepening dark was cast in black silhouette. Rocks and distant buildings, trees and ship masts weren't readily distinguishable from each other. The snow didn't cling to the road in this portion, with the wind veering this way and that. Ice coated bare stone, a deadly glitter under the bleak, cloudy, twilight sky. The road hung treacherously over the cliffs, with an awful view of the black sea and even blacker rocks. The wind blew more fiercely and froze his face.

Mark sat and rested before he allowed himself to contemplate traversing this next stretch. He couldn't feel his feet anymore.

Loose rock littered the path. Rough rock. He gripped a piece that fit neatly in his hand and rubbed it on the ice. It bit in.

He found another piece for his other hand and continued downward, sliding on his ass. Darkness surrounded him, and he seemed to move along only by inches, uncertain of where the cliff's edge might be. All he could do was trust that as long as he had a rock wall near his shoulder, he had to be away from the deadly fall that waited for him on the other side.

At last he made it to a stretch of soft, dry snow. He stood unsteadily and limped on the slanted shoulder nearest the cliff, touching the rock wall when it was in easy reach to assure himself he wouldn't wander off the road. Hints of shadows and the blue glow of snow served as his only visible guides.

The ocean sounded closer.

The road leveled out and broadened. Snowy roofs shone ahead. His spirits lifted, but he couldn't hurry any more than he could fly. Once among the colorful houses he saw an occasional light in a window, not in this area but ahead, and the steady light of gas lamps at street corners. This was a modest neighborhood. He guessed that the occupants saved their oil and candles by going to bed early every night.

The houses improved in size and quality and he staggered into a town square, where a sacred guard armed with a heavy sword and a large pistol paced on his watch past a gas lamppost. He wore a crimson greatcoat trimmed in blazing white, thick white trousers, tall, blood-red boots and a steel helmet padded in white fur. Fur-lined gauntlets covered his hands. Mark stopped, amazed to see a human being. A moment later his cold-numbed mind thought guard, bad.

The guard saw him and approached. "Milord?"

"I want a coach." A shudder went through him, the closest his body had managed to a shiver in hours.

"Immediately, milord." The sacred guard hurried back to the square and around the corner out of sight. He seemed to be gone a long time, but finally he re-emerged and hurried back. "What happened to you?"

Mark stared at him. He thought maybe he should come up with a clever story, but the words wouldn't come. The cold had stolen his mind.

"I'll send for the mavson."

Mark's shoulders tightened with alarm. "No. No. I need to get warm first."

The guard, who'd started to leave again, walked back to him. "Of course, milord."

Now that he wasn't moving, he slid deeper into misery and cold.

If I don't move I might never move again. Mark started walking.

The guard caught up with him and put a hand on Mark's arm. "Milord, you should wait here. A coach will arrive shortly."

"Isn't there anyone here who might let me in?"

"By the time I get someone to answer a knock the coach will be here." The guard drew a flask from his side. "Here, have some brandy."

He doubted he could swallow it. "Do you have water? Warm water." The thought of warm water inspired him to take a few more steps. He could think of no finer luxury.

"Please, milord. The coach won't be long. May I help you unburden yourself?" He held out a hand.

Mark shrugged off the bag. It fell gracelessly onto the snowy ground. The guard picked it up for him as if it weighed nothing. "Thank you," Mark told him.

"Did you come from the east?" A shrill edge of disbelief sharpened his question.

It seemed unwise to lie. He didn't know the town well enough to offer an alternate explanation.

"Are you hurt?" the guard asked.

Mark had to think about it, though the answer was obvious. "Just my hands, I think."

"Where are the others in your party?"

Of course someone like a lord wouldn't travel alone and on foot. He couldn't reasonably claim that he'd traveled alone, though it happened to be the truth, without telling the guard that he was a jester. He didn't like the footing that would put them on.

Obsidian and Lake rushed forward in his mind, along with the horror. Grief came too. Two days ago, though he'd staunched the flow of Obsidian's blood with his own hands, he felt little sorrow, just panic and raw pain. Now grief rushed him and stole his breath and choked him. "Dead. Killed." Mark struggled to steady his breath. He squeezed his palms against his eyes.

"I'm   sorry,   milord."   He   sounded   more   uncomfortable   than compassionate.

The coach finally arrived with another sacred guard riding on the back. They helped Mark step up. He sank gratefully onto a plush bench. He didn't care what it cost, as long as he didn't have to walk or stand in the cold anymore. The first guard placed the bag at Mark's feet. They shut the door and the coach began to move.

He must have dozed off despite the sway and rattle of the coach, for the next thing he knew the coachman had woken him and taken up the bag. His feet felt like they'd been cut apart, sewn back together by a palsied drunkard and set on fire.

The coachman offered his hand and helped Mark down out of the coach. "I'll fetch the proprietor," the coachman told him and hurried off.

Mark waited by the coach, not certain he could walk without help. A hairy, short man arrived in haste not long later.

Though it was a weary hour, the hairy man looked awake and eager, dressed in a delicate brocade coat with matching waistcoat and breeches and proper white stockings. His cravat had plenty of lace. "My lord, my lord! What have they done to you? My goodness, come in." The coachman and the proprietor supported him by the elbows, but even the slight weight on his feet agonized him. They helped him up white steps. He had only a vague impression of overdone architecture like a ridiculously frosted cake. They ushered him into a red and gold entryway. He thought he'd been taken accidentally into a lord's mansion, a lord with very poor taste. He saw no sign of servants, so perhaps this wasn't a lord's house.

"Is this a hotel?"

"Yes, my lord, the finest in Reffiel."

He saw no other patrons in either of two well-furnished side rooms where the hearths had been banked for the night.

"Perhaps a hot bath, my lord?" the proprietor offered.

Anything to get warm quickly. "Yes. And hot water to drink. And hot brandy."

"Immediately my lord." Servants had begun to emerge and responded to the proprietor's hand signals to them with haste.

"What do I owe you, coachman?" Mark asked.

"Oh, we shall pay for you, my lord, no need to fuss with a mere coachman's fee," the proprietor protested.

The coachman and the proprietor helped Mark up a short, broad flight of stairs. Ahead of them, a young woman in a white maid's uniform hastened to light gas lanterns on the wall. "Do you have hot food available at this hour?" Mark managed to ask.

"Of course." Another hand signal and a servant dashed away.

Maybe a priest would come to investigate. He wasn't sure if they kept late hours of if something unusual like this would wait until morning. "I don't want to be disturbed during the night."

"Never!" the man protested in shock. "I will have any servant who dares disturb you whipped to the bone."

Mark quieted at the reality behind those words, though it looked like the man had exaggerated. "Allow me to decide if it's a whipping offense."

"Of course, of course. I only meant to display my devotion to your comfort, my lord."

"I just need to rest and recover in peace."

"I will turn any visitors away," the man assured him. "But perhaps I can send for a doctor?"

"I will ring for help if I need it."

There weren't many doors down the short hallway at the top of the stairs. They took him to the first door and the coachman held him up while the proprietor opened the door.

It reminded him of Argenwain's rooms, except that the suite smelled of gardenia rather than an old, sometimes incontinent man and his favorite perfumes. Doors led off everywhere. A servant worked at building a healthy fire in the hearth, and he heard water pouring near the rear of the suite.

"Thank you," Mark told them as they settled him into a chair. "I want privacy as soon as the bath is poured."

"Yes my lord," the proprietor said, showing his first sign of hesitance. "But would not my lord prefer some assistance? Clearly you have had a trial of some sort."

"I have." Maybe it was the warmth in the room or growing dread, but his mind was starting to work a little better. "I'll discuss the particulars of my adventure with a mavson when I'm ready. In the meantime I want to eat and sleep." He'd sounded more curt than he'd intended. "If you're worried about payment, I can give you an advance."

"Payment? No, my lord, my concern is for you," the proprietor assured him.

"Thank you."

"Immediately, my lord." He clapped his hands and the servants left, including the one from the bathroom. A waft of rose scent and warm bread and ham followed in her wake.

As soon as the door shut he bent to the ground and crawled to the fire. He knelt there, worshipping the heat on his bandaged hands, though it burned his wounds and the tips of his fingers relentlessly. A moment later his strength drained away and his eyes closed ....

Chapter Nine

Teeth bit into him and Mark woke with a gasp in a soft bed in a dark, unfamiliar room. The feeling of teeth faded. A bad dream, brought on by countless aches and pains. He didn't remember undressing or getting into bed, but an untidy trail of clothing suggested that he hadn't been helped by a servant. He eased out of bed and padded to the window. The street lights in the fog made it seem light outside, but he assumed it wasn't yet dawn.

In the bathroom he found the brandy, now cold, and a full plate of dinner. He ate and drank his fill, gorging like a starving dog.

He had to leave, and quickly, before guards—or worse, a priest—came to ask more questions about his dead companions and how he got here.

For all he knew, riders from Seven Churches would be here any moment, or had already arrived. He wasn't sure when or how Lord Argenwain and Gutter would begin their search, but by that first morning light they would have done something extreme. If they didn't enlist the Church for aid, then they'd hire an army of people skilled in finding runaways. They might even harness both and more to get him back.

He wasn't sure how much a room like this would cost for the night. He guessed perhaps a pair of ar. He remembered that Obsidian had a great deal of coin in his purse and Lake had some too, though when he'd dumped them out he hadn't cared enough to notice how much. All the coin in the world wouldn't have bought him a stick of kindling back there.

He didn't want to waste time counting it, but he had to know how much he had available to buy his way to the islands. His bruised and cut fingers spread the coins on a small table near the bed.

It amounted to a fortune. Combined with his advance, he could buy just about anything he could imagine. In addition to the twenty two ar and a good handful of cupru, he had two golden sol, and that was in addition to the thirty ar Gutter had given him for his advance. None of it was money that Lord Argenwain would notice—he'd lost more in a night of casual card play—but it could buy a great deal among commoners.

It had been a long time since he'd worked in his mother's wine shop, but not so long that he'd forgotten that two cupru would buy a nice pastry and an ar could purchase a round of the finest brandy for a dozen men. Flashing a sol would buy a fancy carriage with four decent carriage horses, and the other could buy a pretty cottage to park it by.

Maybe he could buy a cottage in Perida, pay his landlord rent for a share of land to—

What? Grow his own food? What would he do for a living? Sing? Suck dick? The reality of what he'd done set his heart pounding. He saw *Mairi* burning in the bay, and Obsidian's blood pouring from between his fingers.

Gutter was coming for him.

His fleeing to the islands might stop the Church. It might even daunt Lord Argenwain.

It wouldn't stop Gutter.

I'm panicking I have to stop panicking.

He had to stop panicking but he also had to leave. He didn't dare ring a servant and ask how much he owed. He left two ar on a stand by the door, washed in a hurry, and dressed in the least fine of his clothing so he hopefully wouldn't call as much attention to himself. One last check for the ring's security before he tucked away his purse. He stuffed the other purses in his bag. Anyone who searched his bag might assume he was a thief, of course, but at that point he'd have worse troubles than worrying about what he appeared to be. He wore one cloak. The other he rolled up with his damp clothes and blooded coat wadded inside.

The snowy, foggy streets rambled at odd angles in every direction, leaving some blocks with only enough room for one or two buildings. He listened for the ocean, but it was hard to say from the echoes which direction the sounds came from. He limped down a slight slope until he found Fisher Street. It would make sense for Fisher Street to connect to the water, but he wasn't sure. He turned onto it and continued downhill.

A guard dozed on his feet a few blocks later. Mark walked by trying not to look nervous. Just then his face started to itch. He hadn't made time to shave in days and the unaccustomed growth had started to annoy him even more than his bruised and aching body. He rubbed it, too aware that it looked like a nervous gesture.

The guard didn't wake.

After what seemed like an hour he saw a mast, and hurried to the docks. To his relief, the fishermen appeared to only just now be leaving. Maybe others would leave with the tide as well, ships that might travel all the way to the islands.

Daylight began to glow in the fog. The port didn't have as many large ships as Seven Churches by the Sea, and he didn't notice more than two naval vessels, but there were enough ships to hope that at least one would be leaving in short order.

The first few ships had only idle men on board, and when he asked if they sailed today they all said no. The next was bound for Seven Churches. Another was heading south in the evening—perhaps he could take it to a larger port nearer to the open ocean. He hurried back toward shore and down toward the end of another pier when he noticed a group of five guards, faint but distinct with their helmeted heads, through the fog. He laughed.

The laugh surprised him, and scared him. Maybe a secret part of him felt relief, to be caught before he'd committed himself to sailing to Perida. Maybe desperation, exhaustion, and fear had twisted his mind.

They hadn't noticed him yet. There was enough activity around the docks that Mark didn't particularly stand out.

He skipped the next ship because the one after was pulling up the gangplanks. Mark dashed up the last gangplank onto the deck.

The sailors all drew away like he might hurt them. One sprinted away.

"You there." A tall, very dark man with straight hair flying wild, perhaps an Osian, wearing what might be considered a sort of uniform—broad feathered hat, blue greatcoat with gold embroidery near the sleeve ends and a proper buff waistcoat with breeches—approached. He stood in stark contrast to the pale-skinned, fair and brown-haired Cathretan sailors in their oilskin trousers, knit hats and awkward wool coats. "You can't be aboard this ship. We're not accepting passengers."

"Please—"

"Get off before I throw you off." Judging by his fierce expression, he meant to literally toss Mark over the side. It was a long fall to the dock.

Another tall, dark man joined him. He wore similar clothes, black with gold, but he kept his hair shoulder-length and tied back in a ribbon in

Cathretan fashion. The first man stepped aside deferentially. "Sir, this boy just charged on board—"

"Please. I can pay." Mark tried but failed to disguise his urgency. "My father is a sailor, a captain. He's missing. My mother's dead. I need to find him before the Church does. Please." He didn't know why he'd told them those things. The words kept coming as if an embodiment of desperation drew them out by a sharp thread. "Is this ship bound for the islands?"

The man in the black coat—he had to be the captain—looked into Mark's eyes. His eyes were cruel and strange, a deep blue edged in brown, and he seemed as unfeeling as the wilderness Mark had left behind. "Which island?"

"I don't know. I don't really care at the moment."

The first mate glanced at his captain with a pleading look. The captain smiled. "If you don't care, you're in luck. Johns, let's set sail."

Johns looked to argue, but he nodded. The captain glanced past Mark and scowled.

The guards were coming in a hurry, dividing themselves among the ships along the pier. "Get below," the captain said, and made his way toward the bow.

Mark rushed toward one of the hatches, then changed his mind and darted into the main cabin. He stripped off his cloak, coat and waistcoat as he went. *I'm too small and unweathered to be a sailor.* He turned into what appeared to be the navigator's tiny room, stuffed with charts, and pulled off the ribbon that bound his hair. He yanked off his weapons, boots, hat and stockings and stuffed them under the bed. He started to take off the handkerchiefs protecting his hands, then thought better of it. A new sailor might have rope burns on his hands and he wouldn't just leave them to rot.

Trousers peeked out of a drawer.

He stripped off his breeches and pulled the trousers on. They were far too large. He used the belt from his breeches and cinched it tight, then cuffed the legs. The cold air bit him. He pulled a blanket over his shoulders and spread his hands over the map stretched on the lone table in the room.

It was a pretty good map of the Cathretan coast.

I can read ocean maps. I can fake this.

The captain was arguing with someone, and they were coming closer.

Mark found some ink, stained his fingers a bit, and then washed his hands so it wouldn't look quite so deliberate. He also ran his hand along a shelf and rubbed the dust on his cheek, forehead and near his chin, then faded the marks with a little rubbing. His skin turned pink, but the cold quickly faded the color. His short but annoying beard itched like mad and it took all his will to keep from scratching it. He pressed the skin with the backs of his hands instead.

"So now you feel compelled to invade my private quarters," the captain growled.

I'm a new navigator grateful for this chance to prove myself. Mark closed his eyes and took in a breath before he opened them again.

The captain and a guard came in. Mark nodded to the captain and went out. The guard gave him a glance—

—and let him pass.

The first mate rang a bell. As the guard turned away, the captain twitched his head in the direction of the main deck. Mark heard the captain and the guard follow not far behind.

All the sailors gathered by the main mast, perhaps forty men altogether. The men didn't speak, or look about. They just formed four loose lines and waited with their hands held behind their backs. Mark imitated them. No one gave him a second look or appeared in the least way curious.

The captain went below with the guard. After a few minutes several more men came from below and formed up with the rest.

I'm a young navigator. He breathed it, and believed it the way that he made himself believe that pleasing Argenwain wasn't demeaning and unpleasant. And it hadn't been every time. More than once, Mark had gone to him unbidden, if for no other reason than to hold the old man in his arms afterward. On those rare nights, neither of them had to be alone.

Now, though, he had to be a sailor. He'd barely allowed himself to dream about it, and now he had to make the guards believe he was one. He noticed the impatience in the men, but they were bored too, and thinking about things. Maybe they had sweethearts ashore. Maybe they wanted another drink, or maybe they were hungry. They all had lives beyond standing here, and so he had to have one too.

Someone he loved, waiting for him on the islands. He imagined ....

He couldn't make it a woman and really yearn for it. He imagined the soldier, and blushed, but he longed to see him again and that longing made the world he needed outside the ship real enough to believe in.

He wished it was real. The soldier didn't even have to notice him. Mark just wanted one more glance to carry with him for another three years.

Please don't let me be a staghorn for life.

Even with all of Argenwain's power and wealth, Mark could see that Argenwain would never enjoy the same life that other men took for granted, where they could walk down the street hand in hand or kiss their sweetheart under a parasol or joyously declare an engagement. Lord Argenwain had children, but for obvious reasons they didn't stay in the same house with their father and they never brought his grandchildren to visit.

Mark didn't know how many men had a trace of lean to them, but he doubted there were very many. There would be few chances to meet someone. The odds that he'd find someone to love and live with the way Mark longed to love and live with someone someday ...

... like his parents had lived together with him.

He didn't even know if that was real. Maybe they had staged that love for his sake.

If they did, then no one really loved anyone. He didn't remember much anymore, but he remembered how happy his mother had been when she'd heard that his father's ship had docked and he was on his way home.

As Mark would be happy coming home to someone like that soldier, to be welcomed and safe and loved. Argenwain had never met someone to be with like that, at least as far as Mark knew. He had his friends, but it wasn't the same, just as having a servant service him would never be like having a lover.

The captain came back topside with the guard, who glanced over all of them. Mark thought about the soldier and wished he was with him.

"Someday, I will catch you at it," the guard told the captain. "It'd be better for you if you just stopped coming here. You're not wanted. None of your men are."

"If I truly wasn't wanted, I wouldn't come," the captain told him. "But I do good trade here. As long as there's good trade, I'll keep coming back."

The guard started to leave, but then he hesitated. "That little one. I don't remember him."

"My new navigator? I would think you'd have recognized him from other ships. I know I've seen him around Hullundy Bay a few times before, usually in someone's shadow."

"You're short a few. Where are they?"

"Dead. My old navigator with them. Sickness at sea a month ago."

Shit I'm on a sick ship and I'm wearing a dead man's clothes. He knew it wasn't rational. After a month, assuming the captain told the truth, the sickness would be gone. Most likely anyway. It still made him shiver.

The guard grunted and left. As soon as he'd passed the bow of the ship behind them, the captain started walking. "Johns, get this ship out of here. You, come with me." The captain led Mark to the cabin and sat in the narrow space beside a table big enough for a small dinner party. "You went to my navigator's room. Why?"

"Because I'm obviously not a regular sailor. I'm too short, too thin, too pale. And I can read maps."

"Charts, like this?" He stabbed his finger at the map.

"Not well, but I understand a few of these symbols, and I can read very well. Shallows, here. Those look like ocean currents. That looks like ... seasonal winds?"

"Who was your father?"

Mark hesitated.

"That's long enough to concoct a lie."

"No. No. It's just ... he disappeared."

"So you said."

"The same day my mother was murdered."

The captain's eyelid twitched. "Did he kill her?"

"No!" The fact that he'd feared it made him want to cry out the denial again, scream it, force it to be true beyond any doubt. Better to believe that Gutter had killed her than his own father. "I don't even know why I told you those things in the first place."

The captain lifted his chin. Outside the sails raised and men began calling out to each other. "It's *Dainty*. I've grown to trust her when she brings someone to me. But I'll still want more from you. Your father's name, for starters."

The ship had brought him? He'd heard of sailors believing strange things about their ships, but this made him uneasy. "What are you talking about?"

The captain's expression hardened. "I'll have your father's name. Now."

"Erril Seaton." He didn't realize how that name would make his eyes tear up. "Of the—"

"Swiftly-By?"

"*Swift-By*, sir." He blinked several times to clear his eyes and focused his thoughts on the fact that he'd just jumped onto a ship that sacred guards disapproved of. These could be some very bad men.

"I've actually heard of them, but that doesn't do you much good, does it. He disappeared years ago. The way you spoke of it, I was under the impression that it happened recently."

"I can't say any more about it without explaining more than you'd be willing to hear, sir. I hope you will simply accept that the last few days have been unsettled."

"Even if you are his son, a lot can happen to a man's son when he's on his own. His good name earns you nothing on this ship."

"I didn't expect it would." The fact that his father's name carried weight with a stranger, and that the captain remembered *Swift-By*, weakened him somehow. It was as if the strength he'd needed to remember it started to collapse into another's knowledge and sleep. "Did you know him?"

"No. Just of him." The captain smoothed his hands over the table top. "I'll help you. I'll help you because you offered payment, which I'll accept, and because I'd rather trust *Dainty* than turn away a young man in trouble due to my prejudicial distrust of all things related to continental nobility. Having said that, if you disappoint me in any way, you'll be cast off the ship along with our old dinner bones and our laundry water."

Mark wondered what the captain might do if he found the masks, the book, and the signet ring. He wished he had somewhere to hide it all. "Thank you, sir."

The captain nodded.

Mark bowed. "Am I excused?"

"One more thing." He stood, the chair scraping hard against the unpolished floor. "Do you believe that islanders protect those who flee from unpaid indentures?"

"I've heard the same as everyone, that indentures are forgiven and that they protect men loyal to the islands regardless of their circumstances. But that's not why I'm going there."

"Good. Because that was a wartime arrangement, and we're no longer at war, Mr. Seaton."

He'd said 'we.' "I take it that you're an islander, sir?"

The captain's expression warmed. He eased past Mark and Mark followed him out on deck. "I'm a free man. Nationality is of no importance unless war comes again. If we ever meet at war you'll know my home, because I'll be there defending her."

Chapter Ten

Mark feared he might be one of those men who sailed sickly, but after sitting quietly through dinner with Captain Shuller, his first mate Johns and a few others, he slept through the night and well past morning without even a dark dream to trouble him. In the morning, after checking to see if they were clean, he asked permission to, alter, mend and wear the navigator's clothes, and then for the first time after the longest stretch without, Mark shaved his face and washed his hair.

He felt a lot less desperate as he walked the deck and leaned against the rail. He didn't know what to do. He wanted to help but he didn't know how. Words came to his mind but he couldn't attach most of them to anything. Shrouds. Capstan. Mizzenmast. For-ra and aft'rer, port and star-way, lee and storm. The sailors on *Dainty* spoke with a slightly different accent than his father. He'd already heard star-way as star-eye, unless that meant something else. He didn't dare ask.

The men seemed tense, and not just because of the hard, cold wind. Maybe they feared a naval vessel would come chasing after him. Maybe they thought he was a jester and might rope them into an intrigue.

Both of those things might be true, at least in part.

He fidgeted with the handkerchiefs twisted around his hands.

The captain joined him at the icy rail. "Holt told me they were looking for a runaway indentured servant. Said he'd stolen a horse, and money. A lot of money."

"How much do you want?" Mark asked.

He expected the captain to ask how much he had, but the man shrugged. "I think it's wrong for men to steal. I think it's wrong for men to flee their indenture. People owe each other. I owe my men wages. I can't stop paying them because I decide one day that they're holding my freedom hostage. But I do have a little trouble with the way the Church manages inherited indentures. A child doesn't choose to enslave himself in hopes of earning out for something his father dreamed of owning someday. I don't think that's fair. I also object to the way the Church sells indentured children like cattle."

Mark held his silence. He had no idea whether the captain planned to threaten him, embrace him, throw him overboard or offer him something.

He had nowhere to run. He didn't even have the Church to protect him here. He never thought he'd miss that sort of protection. He'd always hated the idea of asking for it, but it had been there for him nonetheless.

"You would have been, what, nine years old when your father went missing?"

"Eleven, sir."

The captain nodded.

"I wanted her. The ship." Mark had to stop right there or his heart and guts would break apart and bleed inside him. He shouldn't have said anything. He didn't know why he kept telling this man such private things.

"But something happened."

Mark twisted the handkerchiefs tighter.

"Holt also said that this servant killed two men during his escape."

Mark's head felt as if it would float away and his body seemed to disappear. His mouth dried out and he thought he might be sick.

"How did you hurt your hands?"

Mark unwrapped one of them. "On buckets." The sharp air quickly numbed his hand.

"Buckets?"

"Buckets of water. And I cut them on ice and rocks trying to get here. I have soft hands." Mark wrapped the wounds back up. The pain helped keep him focused on the words in the conversation and away from the memories that tried to force their way into his mind.

"Did you kill a man or two recently, Mr. Seaton?"

"You'll know I'll deny it whether it's true or not."

"Who were they?"

"Jesters. I didn't kill them. They killed each other in a duel." He must have left something behind with them, or maybe because it was Obsidian, Gutter might have guessed Mark had been involved, or maybe it was just an excuse someone used to widen the search. Hells, the Church might have just decided he must have done it so that the mavson wouldn't have to go to the trouble of an actual investigation. Regardless, if the guards had mentioned it, that meant his name was irrevocably associated with Obsidian and Lake's deaths.

"You knew them?"

"One of them."

"You were there?"

"Captain Shuller, I know I'm at your mercy. And I know you won't believe anything I tell you. I don't understand why you're asking me all these things unless you need justification to throw me overboard or you're bored or you have some cause you're trying to recruit me to. I wish you would just tell me what you want from me."

"Actually, I've believed almost everything you've told me. I do have my doubts, but the story you're not telling me ... I want to know why you're going to the islands. The real reason."

Mark's heart started to pound, but at least his head felt attached to his body again. He wanted to ask who Rohn Evan was. He wanted to trust this man enough to tell him that though he had something he needed to do for a dead man, what he really wanted more than anything was to drop off the signet ring and the code book and sail away until he didn't remember anything of his old life at all. Not even his mother.

Damned little is left of her anyway. Just her death. Her death is always there inside me.

"Normally I charge ten ar for your sort," the captain told him. "I'll settle for eight. Lucky number and all. If you have it. If not, then you'd better get to work. My first mate could use some help in the kitchen. You may have noticed we're a bit short-handed."

"I'll pay you eight and I'll help too, if you teach me a bit about sailing."

"Fair enough. Help with cooking first, and when your hands heal up, my men will show you the ropes." The captain tapped the rail and let him be.

Mark stared at his retreat for a while, then his face curved and warmed, like spring sunshine had woken him from a bad dream. A moment later that sick feeling of dread returned, but it wasn't as dark as before.

He just hoped he could keep his possessions stored away where no one would snoop into them.

Then again, he'd just neatly given the captain the truth. Would the masks and everything else seem all that damning?

He'd get rid of it all soon enough and then ...

He would be free.

Mark opened one of the letter cases, reading by lamplight while the sea drummed on the hull and rocked the creaky ship in its sleep. The letter still smelled sharply of fresh ink. He unrolled it.

Schooled in the style of Tells and Keener, Lark's grace, beauty and quiet wit will serve with seductive elegance. His innocent façade works as a political stiletto, his unusual tastes opening paths to hidden rooms. As an entertainer, his voice is unequaled in all the realms. As a companion, his loyalty is unbreakable. As an adornment, he will be the envy of any court. His only flaw is gentleness, a flaw that like water seeps into old wood to shatter the tree in winter. It has been a pleasure to have him in my household. If only men lived forever. I would see this one come into his full.
Lord Merrin Argenwain

Mark's face burned with a feeling somewhere between pleasure and embarrassment. He reread the letter several times. He had no idea who Tells and Keener were, but he suspected his lack of university training had something to do with a style of training that they, perhaps two jesters, or two lords or some combination thereof, had begun. It didn't say specifically that Mark was a jester, but it implied it heavily. The lack of surname, the double meaning name, the political bent to the stating of his skills—political stiletto? He shuddered just remembering how it felt to draw a rapier free of a dead man.

Seductive elegance. Every compliment in there implied the work Mark would do. His soul would be stained the colors of corruption from it. The *morbai* would hunt his soul down before his body had grown cold and joyfully feast on his spiritual scars and character flaws unless a noble protected him.

He put the letter away. The two letters had identical puzzle knots, so he assumed that they'd have identical contents. Not that it mattered. He wouldn't use either letter, or his mask, unless he had no choice. With any luck he'd deliver Obsidian's things without incident, and then ....

He sat quietly and closed his eyes. The ship swayed slowly, gracefully, rocking him. The sailors' boots drummed on the decks, light and fast compared to the heavy, deep surge of the waves, and their voices sounded so cheerful. The air had a clean, heavy scent very different from the coast, a purity that eased his heart. That living, salty air mingled with the heady scent of clean sweat, fragrant wood and golden oils spiced with resin. He'd never breathed in a more beautiful perfume. Below it would be far different of course, with the bilge water and so many men living in close proximity with only limited access to water, but he could get used to that, would gladly live in far worse conditions if it meant he could stay.

I could live like this forever, in peace.

He had to find a way.

His time at sea rushed by too quickly. Every day the air grew warmer, and the sea turned brighter, until one day he woke to clear blue skies and warmth he hadn't felt since last summer. The ship's rapid, pounding rush through the waters eased to a sluggish roll as the winds relaxed and worked against the sails with the uneven attention of a sleepy lady occasionally stirring to fan her face. The sailors shed all their clothes save their trousers and a scarf for their heads or a ribbon to hold back their hair. Mark blushed at all the bare skin at first, but then he had to try it himself. He badly scalded his skin by midday. It took several long days to heal. The sailors promised him it wouldn't hurt so badly the next time, but Mark only bared his back for an hour at most after that.

He climbed around like a wild animal as they all worked to keep the sails in the best possible trim, and learned knots, and polished brass. The captain showed him how to measure their way across a chart, and how they gauged their speed and distance on a given day, and how to reconcile their course so that compass, the stars and sun roughly agreed with each other. They had to work a great deal with triangles that had odd sides. The captain seemed pleased that Mark knew how to solve distances by sides and angles and that he could estimate the numbers in his head before he applied the problem to paper. All those measurements mattered all the more because for reasons of wind and current, the captain seldom sailed the ship along the shortest line toward their destination. Often he would stare at the horizon for a long time, seeing things in the clouds and smelling hints in the air that made him veer away from what he'd determined to be the best course only hours before.

As much as Mark thirsted to read sacred poetry someday, he wanted to learn to see the wind like that even more.

The only thing Mark didn't like was the food after the first few days. It got progressively worse, but at least it didn't make him sick. The captain provided plenty of wine to wash it down with, which helped. He felt a little sticky from bathing in seawater, but he got used to that.

The captain gave him some salve to use on his hands to help them heal. It worked so well on his skin he used it on his arms and face and throat as well.

All these things made him feel alive. He didn't feel like a smudged and dented toy anymore. He felt ... free.

Best of all, his music came back. At first he sang under his breath along with anyone else that picked up a tune, but then something relaxed inside and he started singing on his own. As he'd hoped, no one made a fuss about his singing except to request a song, or to teach them lyrics he'd made up. Maybe it was the work. It felt more natural to work and sing than to stand at attention in front of an audience and perform. He suspected that making his own choices and choosing his own time to sing had a lot to do with it as well. He didn't care why, as long as the joy of it stayed with him.

Before he knew it he'd fallen in love, not just with music and the sea and the ship's seductive rhythm, but with the men. They never hurt him. They bickered and some sneered at him, but no worse than the guests and sometimes even the help at Pickwelling Manor when they thought they wouldn't be overheard. For quite a few days after he made Mr. Gerren's acquaintance, Mark expected the midshipman to beat him senseless somewhere belowdecks when no one who might care was around to notice, but neither that rough, unpleasant man nor any sailor at all ventured to raise a hand against him. Most likely it was because he was a paying passenger, but he liked to think that the men on *Dainty* simply weren't that sort.

And they touched him so freely. At first he thought they might be making unschooled advances, but he quickly learned that a tug on the shoulder or quick clap on the back or cuffing someone's crown was a form of communication. He envied the ease with which they spoke that silent way. The closest thing he'd seen to it he'd learned in fencing. A tap on the facemask, a slap on the thigh, a glancing touch on the wrist—the sailors touched in the same precise but friendly way as a *secontefoil* corrected his students. And like fencing, the touch never lasted, except in certain situations such as that strange game they called arm wrestling. He didn't dare try it. They'd probably snap his arm in two before they realized his fragility. Anyway, he learned to respond, or rather, not over-respond when someone took his hand to change his grip on a rope or touched his arm with a smile when he did something right.

"We've had excellent weather," the captain remarked at dinner just after their third week at sea. "Chances are slim you'll see a storm or a becalming before we land, so you have the luxury of dreaming about life on the sea as it should be."

"We'll miss you," Johns said, and raised his glass.

Everyone drank, except Mark. Mark set down his wine. "Captain, I'd like to stay on, if you'll have me."

Captain Shuller lost that hint of smile he sometimes got in the evening after a day of decent winds. "Excuse us, everyone. I'd like to speak with Mr. Seaton in private."

They bustled out all at once, and shut the door behind them. Mark's shoulders sank. He waited for the captain to speak first, but the man just sat there, a hand on his glass, his gaze fixed on Mark's face.

Mark focused on his hand on his glass. The glass might have been a pretty thing once, but scratches made it look dull. "Thank you for sparing me the humiliation, but you didn't need to send them out to tell me no. I know I'm not of much to use to you."

"On the contrary. You're good with figures. I've never seen anyone calculate difficult numbers in their head so quickly. It's useful in navigation, and it would also be useful to me as far as the ship's books. I have inventory, payroll and taxes to figure, and they often change depending on the country, the port, the circumstances and deaths and such. I could use a man like you in a number of ways."

"But you're still saying no."

The silence made Mark look up. The captain was still staring at him. "Why did you want to go to the islands?"

"If I tell you can I stay?"

The captain glanced aside impatiently. "I won't make a promise like that."

The captain had many fine qualities, but Mark liked his honesty best, especially when so many men would agree to satisfy their curiosity and then later look for an excuse to break their promise. "I should thank you."

"For what?" The captain finished his wine and set the glass aside in the glass tray. No one on the ship left things sitting loose for long. Everything had a snug home.

His father ran his ship like that. Tight. Clean.

Shipshape. The words were coming back.

"I'll have an answer from you, Mr. Seaton, to one question or the other."

He couldn't say anything about either the book or the signet ring or the captain might demand to see them. So far, at least as far as he knew, no one had ventured into the navigator's quarters to look through his things. At least nothing had been noticeably shifted and nothing had gone missing. His privacy might vanish if he hinted that he had something dangerous and more valuable than gold on board. "I have a message to deliver."

"It must be an important message."

"I have it memorized." That was true—he'd memorized the code book during quiet times. The only other things to read on board were related to sailing and the captain hadn't let him touch them.

"It's something dangerous, isn't it."

Mark nodded.

"Was your story about looking for your father a lie?"

"No, sir." He set the unfinished glass of wine in the tray. "But I don't think I'll find him alive. I'm hoping to learn something about what happened to him."

"And that relates to the message ... how?"

"The message will introduce me to someone who may know something. Maybe I won't find anything. I don't think it matters anymore. Whether I learn the truth or not, it won't change what I want. What I've always wanted. What my father did all his life, and what he wanted for me. I want to sail." He tried to ignore a growing queasiness at the thought of returning to the mainland with *Dainty*, even as a legitimate crewmember. It would be dangerous, and not just for him.

"Quite a few of my passengers have wanted to stay, passionately. Then they remember how proper food tastes, and fresh water. Some of them come back for a leg or two. It's rare, but it happens. And then they sail their first storm, or someone is lost overboard, or a sickness travels through the ship, or we're attacked by pirates ...." He shook his head. "I doubt you'll come back, Mr. Seaton, but if you're still willing when we're ready to set sail we'll try another leg and see what happens. We're short-handed, and you're not a burden. Far from it. But please, consider carefully. I won't think less of you if you choose another path."

"Thank you, sir." Mark stood, and bowed, and retreated to his room. He didn't want the captain to see how irrationally, stupidly happy he was, nor notice the fear Mark tried to ignore underneath his joy.

Chapter Eleven

Porpoises played in the wake off *Dainty's* bow. The wash made sizzling sounds and sent spray into humid air scented of sweet spices. Gulls dogged the ship, and ahead of them, gray and ivory sea birds with short wings dove under the water, leaving trails of bubbles. The heat made him sweat, but pleasantly, like fencing in the garden in summertime.

Mark couldn't see much of Perida City despite the cerulean daylight. Mostly he saw mop-topped trees and rocky hills piled behind a bay crowded with ships and timber buildings.

Meridua Island was larger than he expected. From this close, a few miles from the bay, he could have mistaken it for a piece of the mainland.

He felt half-undressed in the filmy, bloused shirt and thin silk stockings he'd bought on the previous island, but if he'd worn proper linen he couldn't have worn his waistcoat without passing out. He didn't mind looking effeminate, but fainting was a bit much even for him. The captain assured him that fashion on the island allowed a proper young man to walk about without a coat over his waistcoat. Good thing, but he still felt underdressed for walking about in public.

He'd gone barefoot long enough that it felt odd to belt on shoes over proper slippers again. It didn't help that the slippers were new and hadn't shaped to his feet yet. The few days of wear he'd put into the shoes hadn't softened the straps, either, and they cut into the tops of his feet.

Mark leaned against the rail, sipped red wine from a silver cup, and tried not to worry. He'd felt private and at home on *Dainty*. He'd suffer through delivering the book and ring as quickly as he could, and then he intended to come back and stay with her forever. Finally at sea, after so many years of confusion and loss ... he didn't want to leave the ship at all.

The captain settled beside him. "Best be careful until you get to the parks."

"Parks?"

"The neighborhood surrounding city hall. The rest of the city, and the docks in particular, can be dangerous. Men who fought in the war lost their fear of lords and jesters after killing their fair share of them. They won't grant much respect to a stranger just because he wears fine clothes."

Mark lost interest in finishing the wine. "Thank you for the warning." His stomach churned uneasily.

The captain nodded.

"I hope I'll be back tonight."

That made the captain laugh. "No rush, Mr. Seaton. We'll be here at least two weeks if not longer. We've had hardly two days in a given port with no time for leisure all along the Hullundy coast in cold weather. We're all ready for some sunlight and fresh food. I'm hoping to reserve some time for the old lady at the cleaning yards, and most of my men will be spending some well-deserved time ashore with their sweethearts."

I swear not a man survived who wasn't ashore with his sweetheart.

That night when *Mairi* burned rushed back to him. He smelled smoke and in his mind he imagined a dark figure dancing across *Mairi's* deck while the men inside screamed—

The sailors had told a lot of stories, and more than one about figureheads that screamed when they died. He wondered if that strange, painful thing he experienced at the Bracken Watertower had been *Mairi's* death cry.

"Are you all right?"

The captain's voice steadied him. "Yes, sir." He still smelled smoke, but it faded. He realized his hands hurt from gripping the rail. Mark forced himself to relax.

"There is one thing I feel compelled to mention before you go ashore," the captain said. "It's clear to me you're in a great deal of trouble. I like you. My men like you. But as long as you keep secrets I won't be inclined to help you. And if you bring trouble to my ship, my lack of desire to help or protect you will be the least of your worries."

Mark drew in a shaky breath. "I'd rather go back to Cathret bound in chains than let anything happen to *Dainty*." He doubted the captain believed him, especially since it sounded so over-played, but he meant it with a passion that frightened him. "Anyway, I don't see how anything regarding this matter would come back to you. I'll be cautious on your behalf just the same."

The captain grimaced. "I would be reassured, Mr. Seaton, if you shared your situation more openly with me."

"I hope to do just that very soon." Soon he'd have no use for secrets. Maybe he'd even get the chance to uncover a few about his father's disappearance and his mother's death.

The captain drummed on the rail. "Time to get back to work." He pushed off the rail. "It might be best if you stand out of the way somewhere. You wouldn't want to ruin your clothes, and anyway, this will be a little more tricky than anything you've learned."

"I won't get in the way."

The captain nodded and headed off.

The play between muscle and sail, rope and bone still remained a mystery, but he recognized the steps to the dance if not how it worked with the wind as they orchestrated an approach. The ship passed two large floating statues of half-naked women with long, wild hair while the men furled the sails to slow the ship on their way to the docks. The men waved to the statues and blew kisses at them as if they were alive.

Mark had never seen so many ships, and Seven Churches by the Sea had more than its fair share. There had to be—he counted by fives for a bit— well over a hundred war-ready ships with respectable cannon and countless trade vessels that could be converted to fight in a pinch.

Dainty slowed even further until she came to a near halt with all sails furled. The men lowered longboats into the quiet bay waters and rowed her in the rest of the way. After quite a bit of maneuvering that included some help from sailors on ships they passed, Mark started to wonder where they'd find space to berth. They ended up tying up to a larger ship, whose captain cordially allowed Mark, Captain Shuller and Mr. Johns passage across his ship to the docks. "The harbormaster will give us a better place once we've paid for our berth," the captain told Mark. "So don't come looking for us here. Ask at the harbormaster's quarters."

"Yes, sir."

"Good luck." He held out his hand.

Mark hesitated only a moment before he shook. The captain's hand felt warm, but dry, his grip solid and comforting. Mark had seen the men shake on various things over the course of the sail, but he hadn't actually done it himself. He'd understood it meant some sort of pact, but this felt more like goodbye. "Thank you, sir."

The captain nodded, and they parted ways.

Mark resisted the urge to make sure the book and ring were in place. He checked his pistol to make certain it was in order, then made his way through the maze of wooden walkways toward land, his art bag slung on his shoulder. Before he was truly ready for it, he set foot for the first time in Perida among people of so many colors and forms his mind couldn't place them all. He was forced to think of them only as islanders, nationals of the newly-formed Meridua, once known possessively as the Cathretan Isles.

The people smiled openly, and laughed heartily, and cursed freely. He blushed more than once at profanity he barely understood, and the obscenities weren't even directed at him.

It saddened him that at least one in every dozen, or perhaps even one in ten men had visible scars or missing limbs from the war. One man he saw sat on a low platform with wheels. He had no legs. How could a man survive the loss of both legs? It spoke of his strength. His friends that crouched beside him had no pity in their eyes. Just respect.

It felt as if the land rolled like the sea as Mark walked. He thought the sensation would pass quickly, but after several minutes it hadn't faded. Perhaps that explained the distinctive gait that some of the older sailors had on shore. He hoped one day to earn the shadow of it in his stride.

White sand roads traveled unevenly between crowded buildings of driftwood and thick beams that likely came from wrecked ships. Many of the buildings had rooms with at least one side open to the road, and few had glass windows—just screens or shutters, often braced or barred wide open. Some of the buildings were huge, the largest being among the shipyards where massive hoists loomed and rows of ships being repaired or built in dry dock lay in frames or awkwardly on their sides, their disassembled masts stacked beside them.

The masses of people had few carts and next to no horses to impede their casual business. No one seemed to be in a hurry. Dogs roamed freely, sometimes at heel, often with no sign of an owner. Many of the animals were massive in size—some tall and lean, wolfhounds or a bastard cross, others heavy and shaggy, usually white with a ginger mask or purest black and in the company of sailors. Large dogs usually made him nervous, but none of the beasts paid any attention to him.

Fashionable men and women both seemed to prefer scarves on their heads rather than hats, though they sometimes wore both. Some of the straw hats were woven in amazing designs as delicate as lace. Those of means still wore the familiar coats, waistcoats and hats Mark was familiar with, but they seldom wore velvet or linen, preferring silk far above any other material. They seemed to wear cloaks mainly for embellishment or shade, usually lighter colors and light, sometimes translucent fabric or even lace. Some of the ladies had hats that seemed to be made entirely of feathers and dried flowers. Others wore fresh flowers in their hair. They all seemed very innocent and carefree, except that every male above the age of majority carried weapons. Especially those that had just turned fourteen seemed too young for such responsibility. They looked so young and small, even compared to him. They wore either a large dagger, or a sword with ostentatious pride. Some even carried pistols. Women often carried daggers or pistols as well, and a few carried rapiers.

Most of the streets ran in shadows, either covered by awnings or shaded from the glaring sun by tall buildings on both sides. Some of the buildings were four stories, all timber built. It looked dangerously unstable.

And children—they ran wild everywhere. He'd never seen so many.

Yes I have, in my old neighborhood in summertime.

The children dashed around playing indecipherable chasing games, sometimes with dogs running among them. The adults worked or traveled in groups in the shade, talking, rarely sparing him a glance. Those brief glances, though, spoke to him. They knew he didn't belong here. Was it the clothing, or his barely-tanned skin, or did they somehow recognize the curve of his spine?

He hoped they were more wary than unfriendly toward strangers.

A man selling what he called juice freshes seemed kind, so Mark approached him. "Excuse me, I'm looking for someone." He hoped Rohn Evan was a person of importance. If not he'd have to try to get his hands on a directory. "Do you know of a Rohn Evan?"

The man grinned. "Sure I do. Ev'ry'n knows him."

Mark didn't realize how straight and tight he'd held his spine until it eased. "Where might I find him?"

The man made an exaggerated nod. "It's a long walk on the Black Shore Road. Easy goin' from the parks, due west, on the windy side of the isle."

"And how do I get to the parks?"

The man's grin broadened. "Up there at the dontist turn north and then west at Main and you'll see 'em right ahead. Isn't more than two mile."

"The dontist?"

"You know, the dontist. Makes teeth?"

Mark nodded. "Thank you." He paid him a bit, shouldered the bag so it sat close under his arm even though it blocked the draw for his pistol, and made his way in the direction the man had gestured. He didn't see any signs for a dental business, so he kept going straight.

The streets narrowed and quieted. He would have felt a little more at ease without the crowds, except the buildings here looked rough and the few people about seemed overly accommodating toward each other. It felt like an act, like snakes pretending friendship and ease while watching for a moment of weakness. They stared at him lazily, measuring him.

There weren't any children here. A lone dog growled at him from beneath a slanted, half-rotten porch.

The hairs on his neck prickled up. A group of drunk men about his age rounded a corner. They looked him over, openly predatory, but moved on.

I need to get out of here.

Mark didn't want to back out or turn around, so he aimed for a narrow alley that looked like it would go through to the next street over. He heard someone whistle. His attention switched that way.

Just in time he heard a whisper of a foot in sand and turned.

Sharp pain shot like red lightning through his head. Bainswell—he spun with an infuriated cry and shoved.

Metal flashed to his right. Mark threw himself back from the sword attack in shock. Not Bainswell. He ran, piecing together that he was in a fight for his life. His head throbbed and he couldn't see beyond flashes and blurs. Heavy steps and heavy breathing ran close after him. He fought for air. The man behind him wasn't losing ground. A sickening horror suffused him as he realized he couldn't run fast enough to escape.

Mark pivoted and swung the bag. The impact slammed through his arms.

The swordsman grunted and fell. The euphoria from his small success died as a second man charged in. Tight with terror, Mark retreated to a wall, prepared to surrender.

Which would give these men all the power.

His body more than his mind remembered his training. He dropped his bag, drew his rapier and the pistol. The second man, tall and bearded with drink-reddened eyes and a rusty rapier, slowed.

"Give me the bag," the rapier man snapped.

Mark's head screamed with pain and he couldn't see straight. He nudged the bag toward them, but not very far.

The man raised his rapier slowly. "Good. And now your purse." He had scars on him, and he looked confident.

"It's in the bag." Mark managed to keep his voice steady, but the pistol wavered all over. He would have pulled the trigger if he thought he had a chance of hitting something.

The first attacker stood and slapped his hands against his pants, leaving smears of pale sand on dark clothes that may have been the remnants of a military uniform. He picked up his sword. He had a broad chest and a thick scar on his arm. "Give over your rapier." The swordsman drew a dagger.

The look in the man's eyes made Mark's balls creep up. Mark knew but he couldn't explain how he knew that the man intended to kill him.

Gutter had taught him to never give up a means of defense without the promise of better. Sound advice he found more difficult to follow than he'd expected now that he faced a competent swordsman with cold death in his eyes.

"You can have the bag. Just let me go." Mark couldn't let them have it— it had the masks—but he didn't want them to know he'd fight for it given the chance.

"Give me the rapier!"

Mark's heart skipped and his breath staggered. His hands shook. No matter how hard he gripped the rapier it felt loose in his hand. Gutter's voice intruded. *Don't grip. Loose, just not so loose they can knock it out of your hand.*

"Someone help me!" Mark cried. As if in answer, a door rattled shut somewhere up the street.

"No one gives a shit about you," the rapier man said.

"Let's just kill him," the swordsman said.

"We should wait for Jonas and Bates."

"He's just a boy," the swordsman said. "Should be easy."

Fire, Mark. Gutter's voice sounded clear as a morning songbird in his mind. Mark's pistol instructor held the target, and if Mark missed, he might hit the man.

Don't close your eyes when you pull the trigger.

Mark's pistol hand steadied and he aimed for the glint of a button on the swordsman's chest. He cocked the mechanism.

Both men rushed him.

Do it!

Mark fired the pistol. Time seemed to slow. A tiny bit of blood sprayed red where the bullet struck the center of the swordsman's chest. Mark slapped him across the face with the pistol and lunged past the thrust from the rapier man. No pain yet. Mark's rapier pierced the swordsman's soft belly and he whipped it out before the blade might be trapped.

Time sped up again. He tasted blood on his lips.

Mark charged and the rapier man retreated. A man started screaming. Mark chased the rapier man as if this was a practice bout before his fear checked him. Two more men came running into the street, a new broadswordsman, the other with a machete and a pistol. Mark retreated to the wall again. The rapier man hung back, watching. Mark tried not to let himself be distracted but the downed swordsman made weepy, animal sounds where he gasped against the ground.

It was three men on one. Mark's fear spiked and he couldn't catch his breath.

Don't let the enemy choose his time, and never give a man with a pistol time to aim, cock and fire.

Mark charged the pistol man. The man's eyes widened. The pistol report felt like a punch to his gut. The rapier point, just off-line, sliced him—ice-fire-hot-pain—across his arm as he closed. He shouldered the rapier man, shoved, and snapped his point across the rapier man's face. His blade cut the shallow meat and skipped on skull bone. The broadswordsman slashed. Mark deflected the blade toward the rapier man, who backed away. Mark crowded the broadswordsman. He was too close to bring his point to the target so he punched with his edge along the throat as hard as he could and sliced hard. To his surprise the blade's edge opened the broadswordman's neck.

Pain flared from Mark's thigh. He staggered back, too breathless to scream, unable to straighten his leg all the way. The broadswordsman fell with a grunt, blood blooming from his throat. Blood and unwashed bodies cloyed the air.

The man with the machete stared at him. He started to approach, but then a huge man in a floppy hat arrived, Mark couldn't say from where. The machete man lowered his weapon. The man with the rapier retreated to him and the two ran.

Mark's heart battered his chest and he couldn't catch his breath. He limped backed until he was braced on the now-familiar wall, on the verge of retching.

Still alive.

The broadswordsman lay on his side, dying hard, kicking and choking from his throat wound. His hands clasped tightly over his own neck. Mark forced himself to look away and focused on the big man coming closer every moment.

The big man stopped a few paces away, a pistol held low in one hand, a crude, heavy short sword in the other. Mark clenched his teeth. He couldn't stop shaking. His fingers were glued tight around his rapier. He forced his fingers to relax, though they weren't nearly soft enough to be quick anymore, his sword on guard. His injured leg supported him, but it stubbornly would not straighten. He had to rest its weight on the ball of his foot.

"You all right, milord?" the big man asked.

Mark blinked up at him. "Who are you?"

The big man sheathed his sword and holstered the pistol. "Grant Roadman, milord." He took his hat off. "Look, if you need me to send for someone, I can do that." His words swung in an easy accent Mark had never heard before.

Mark took the offer as a good sign and let himself really breathe. Big mistake. The wall kept him from buckling, but his guard dropped. Grant stepped closer and Mark forced himself back on guard, hissing from the pain.

"Whoa!" Grant stepped back, putting up a hand. "Easy. I'm not gonna hurt you."

Mark wanted to believe him. The man had a kind look to him, though Mark wasn't sure he could trust a kind look. For all he knew, the man selling the juice had sent him up here to die. "Thank you for saving my life." Any moment he'd catch his breath again. Any time now.

"I did nothing valiant, milord. Just came out to see what the noise was all about." Grant looked down at the dead man still bleeding into the sand. The sight made Mark queasy. The other body's hands had fallen from the throat and existed as an unmoving dark blotch in his peripheral vision.

My fault he's dead.

The dying man, the first one he'd skewered, wouldn't stop moving.

He's suffering. I should put him out of his misery.

Slitting his throat, and the added pain that would give him, seemed just as horrible as letting him die. No good options. Those glazed eyes didn't seem to harbor a soul in them. Perhaps he felt nothing anymore, and his body kept twitching and shifting because it had nothing within to tell it that life was over.

"You need help, milord?" the big man asked.

Mark forced himself to look away again. "I'm in your debt." Maybe that's why this Grant person still lingered; he wanted to get paid. Just as well. Mark needed him. "I don't suppose there's a doctor nearby."

"Um, sure, toward the parade."

"What about a coach?"

"Aren't no coaches for hire on the island, milord. Y'either own a carriage or you don't."

"Well I don't at the moment." His breathing had eased, though the air burned his throat. "Would you mind leading the way to the doctor?"

Grant looked about. "I could fetch a friend or two from the Rum House to watch you and go get her while you wait."

More strangers to contend with? "No thank you." His mind then locked on the fact that he thought Grant had said her. A woman doctor?

"All right. We should get going, then, if you're rested up. There's more of them, you know."

"More of who?"

"The Morbai's Kiss. They got a taste for killing mainlanders and do it when they think they can get away with it. You shouldn't've come here. It's their place an' everyone knows it." Grant walked over to where Mark's bag lay and picked it up. "Have to say, I haven't seen fighting like that since the war. Damned good, damned brave."

A dead man lay nearby, still twitching. A man he'd killed. Another corpse lay with sand sticking to sweaty and bloody skin. He didn't feel brave. He felt sick.

He realized he still stood on guard. Mark finally let his arms rest. More strength slipped from him, and that frightened him. Mark started to sheath his sword before he remembered he'd need to clean it first. At some point he'd dropped the pistol. "Do you see my sidearm anywhere?"

Grant looked about a moment before he walked and picked up the pistol. Mark limped after him. "It's this way," Grant told him, and started walking uphill past the curve. Mark clenched his teeth and set the best pace he could manage after him.

One leg burned and stung, the other felt disjointed and insubstantial. His body felt as if it were a broken doll's rather than his own. The first block went on forever, and the next one ahead seemed even longer and steeper. "How much farther?" Mark asked.

"Not much. Need to rest?"

"No." He wanted to get as far away from the blood as possible.

"You're not looking good," Grant told him.

"I'm fine." Red splotches spattered his vision, and the skin on his forehead crawled. He was having trouble catching his breath again.

"Look, my place is right over here," Grant told him. "Maybe you should wait in there and I'll get the doctor to come over."

"No, I'll make it." The sunlight dimmed, and the air felt hot and somehow that made him feel cold.

"Sure, if you like."

He crossed another intersection. The buildings here looked slightly better, a neighborhood of tall tenements with brightly-painted plaster walls and elegant if somewhat rust-stained ironwork balconies. "How much farther?"

"Not much."

Mark staggered but didn't fall. The effort of keeping his feet stopped him dead. Sweat stung his eyes but he felt colder than ever. He willed himself to take a step, but his body didn't obey.

Grant had gotten ahead of him, but he stopped and came back. "You've lost a lot of blood."

Mark looked down. Thick crimson streaked with darker wine colors stained his breeches and stocking. His shoe squelched. It had filled with blood. He looked back the way he'd traveled and saw bloody splotches and drips in the sand.

"Why don't you sit down in the shade and I'll get the doctor."

Where he'd be helpless.

He couldn't go on. The realization forced him to accept that he would be at someone's mercy very soon. Grant had saved his life, and he hadn't run off with the bag or finished him off or taken any other of many advantages he had available. The next person who stumbled on Mark bleeding in the shade might not be as noble-minded. "Where is your ... place?"

"Right here, at the top of these steps." Grant gestured with the bag toward steep plank stairs leading up between sections of a faded orange tenement building.

Mark steeled himself. He'd endured beatings, hours of fencing practice, perverse exercises meant to strengthen him and make him more flexible. He could manage a few stairs. He lurched toward them and started up.

The stairs seemed to go on for hours, an agonizing succession of lift-pain-step-pain-rest with only his sheathed rapier to help balance him. He stopped briefly to retch, but he managed not to vomit. Finally Grant stopped by the door at the top, unlocked it, and Mark shuffled into a long, narrow room with the barest of amenities. Grant set down the pistol and dropped the bag by a table with two chairs. The front area doubled as a kitchen and sitting room. The large bed cordoned off by a dresser at the far end had thin, tattered blankets. A lone closet made of crude but heavy oak had a stout lock on it. Grant had an empty armor stand and a modest cabinet with some dishes, food and wine, but besides that there wasn't much. "Lay down on the bed," Grant said. "I'll be back quick."

"Thank you." Mark sat on the bed, his wounds burning and biting. His head hurt so badly he couldn't see in focus. He peeled off his waistcoat, wincing as fresh pain from his arm wound burned and stung.

Grant went out and shut the door behind him.

The room had no windows, just a small rear doorway covered in fine netting that led out to a balcony, but the tropical sunlight and glare from the white sand street gave Mark more than enough light to check his injuries. He found a long cut on his right arm, and a fleshy slice on his thigh that seared every time he moved. Other than those and some bruises that had already puffed into rigid lumps, he seemed all right. He pressed his hands over the leg cut again. It hurt like nothing he'd ever felt before, ice and fire and a constant gnawing far worse than he'd felt when he'd damaged his hands on the bucket. The nearest thing he'd felt to it was when a practice weapon broke and sliced his skin. That was shallow, though, and it didn't bleed or make him feel weak like this.

Crap, his clothes. They were ruined.

Maybe not. Maybe this would wash out and stitch back together.

Am I really worried about my clothes? Really?

Mark's eyes closed. Gutter had saved his life again, without even being there. His voice had told him what to do, and would never leave him. An unexpected feeling of peace settled in. The scent of his own blood mingled with the warm, enticing scent of Grant's bed. He laid back, wincing at the sharp stretching and opening of cuts. Nice, soft bed, quiet, his heavy and poorly-hinged weight supported at last .... He knew he shouldn't relax in a stranger's bed, but somewhere between the pain and exhaustion, he forgot to care.

Chapter Twelve

Mark woke on a hard bed to pain and the musky scent of an unfamiliar man faintly tinged by fish. A filmy shirt covered him to his knees and he was draped in a light blanket. He sat up. A flash of sharp pain in his head, arm and leg reminded him of the fight.

Grant.

Shit, the book and the ring! He groped for his waistcoat. Gone.

His bag sat by the bed. He grabbed it up into his lap, ignoring the hot stab in his bandaged arm, and opened the top flap, panicking—

The ring sat on top of his personal effects with the book tucked in on one side.

Had Grant looked at it? Did it matter?

At least he had them. Tension rushed out of him in several panting breaths, leaving him dizzy and confused. Even if someone had taken his money, it didn't matter. He'd be on *Dainty* as soon as he got rid of the damned things.

Someone shifted on the floor at the foot of the bed and sighed.

Mark's heart fluttered up into his throat. "Who's there?"

"Just me." Grant sat up. Mark's breath caught.

Golden hair, a tidy beard and eyes the color of tropical green water graced his benefactor's strong face. A scar across Grant's nose didn't detract from a gentle gaze and the sublime harmony that only the most handsome men owned. If he didn't know better Mark would have sworn he'd met an *allolai*. His heart hammered hard and heat blushed in his belly.

"Something wrong?" Grant's green eyes narrowed.

"No." Mark bowed his head and focused on the bed. His head throbbed worse and he tried tipping it back instead. Still hurt. He settled for keeping his head bowed. "I—thought I recognized you. Never mind."

"Maybe you've met one of my cousins. I've got dozens."

"That's probably it." Mark forced a smile.

"Hey, dozens and cousins rhymes." Grant chuckled, but then his ears and cheeks blushed deep pink. "Never mind."

"It was cute." Mark smiled. Obvious, but cute.

Grant stood up and stretched. He had a body like artwork, a few picturesque scars like rivers on a muscular landscape. Warmth and tension spread between Mark's legs despite his aching head and sliced skin. The last thing he wanted was to be aroused. He wasn't hard for the man, but it wouldn't take much encouragement to get that way.

Grant stretched again. "Hungry?"

Hollow belly, weakness, a little nausea, and he did find hunger in there as well. "Yes." Mark gingerly set his feet on the ground. When he moved the pain had jagged edges that made him grind his teeth. Someone had wrapped his leg and arm wounds. It held his wounds tightly closed, but he didn't feel sure enough to stand yet.

"I got bread, butter, cheese, and wine."

"It all sounds good. Thank you." Mark's rapier, pistol and dagger were on an armor stand. They looked like they'd been cleaned. They rested among well-maintained martial equipment that he was pretty sure hadn't been there when he first came in.

Grant owned a heavy canvas and hardened leather jacket that could serve as armor, as well as a sword and a pistol fitted with a crude wooden handle. All of the equipment had seen action. The short sword was little more than a sharpened bar with a wooden hilt wrapped in rawhide. His boots didn't fit the armor. Black, knee-high, oiled and with sharkskin soles—a naval sailor's boots.

Grant unwrapped food from oily paper and began to pare thin slices from a small wheel of hard, dry cheese.

Mark had no idea what to say to Grant. "I want to thank you. For helping me." The words sounded so trite.

"You did a good service." Reluctance in Grant's words suggested that he wanted to say no more. "So what brings you to the islands?"

Grant was an honest man. He'd want honesty back, but Mark couldn't give it to him, except in the form of a lie with all the right words put in to reassure him. "I couldn't find honest work on the mainland. I have hopes that things are better here. If not, I've already had an offer to crew on a ship."

Grant shrugged. "Sailing's mostly honest work most of the time."

Mark had to reward him somehow. "What do I owe you?"

Grant sliced up some bread. "For?"

"Taking me in and finding a doctor in time to save my life." *Not stealing my extremely valuable things, slitting my throat and dumping my body in the ocean.*

Grant poured a couple of mugs of wine, then braced on the counter. "Don't worry about that."

"I'll have to insist when I know you better."

That won a smile that made Mark warm.

He couldn't let himself get distracted. "I need to find a man named Rohn Evan. Do you know of him?"

"Colonel Evan? Everyone knows him. Why?" Grant still had that casual sway that sweetened his words with poetic music, but Mark heard a warning tone behind the question.

"I have a message for him."

"He don't like jesters."

Grant had seen the masks. Protesting his innocence probably wouldn't work, especially since Grant probably thought Mark had already lied to him about the sailing business. "I'm not in service to anyone."

"He's not lookin' for a jester, neither."

"I'm not looking for a master. I don't want to work as a jester, here or anywhere. I just want to deliver this message and go."

"Well, I'd take you but I got business with the Church."

He couldn't mean as a witness to the fight, could he? Mark tried to gauge his expression, but he found nothing helpful there. Grant's face carried such a pervasive look of kindness, it was hard to tell what the man thought of him. "You didn't do anything," Mark told him. "And I ...." If he posed as a jester, the Church would have no reason to interfere unless a lord or another jester came forward and accused Mark of a crime. The temptation to lay claim to Lark rose up inside him.

No.

"It was self-defense," Mark reminded him. "And you didn't attack anyone."

Grant pared some mold off a wedge of cheese. "I know. I got a duty, as a witness."

Everyone did, but Mark had never known a commoner to willingly admit it, never mind do his duty. "Then I suppose I'll have to go too." He might have to pose as a jester after all.

What would the captain think if that got back to him?

"Not very jesterly of you." Grant peeled uneven pieces of cheese onto an old wooden platter.

"Look, if I explain everything to the constabulary priests, then you don't have to get tangled up in it."

"I gotta go to trial either way."

"Trial? There's no reason for a trial."

"Men are dead."

Mark tried to make some sense of it, but he couldn't. "But they're commoners, right?"

"This isn't the mainl'nd. Things are better here. Here, all crimes get trials whether a noble brings complaint or not, and all good men are held to have worthy souls. I figure you don't believe but that don't matter. It's my duty and I'll do it."

As bizarre as it sounded, Mark couldn't dismiss it. Aside from Gutter, he'd never seen anything special in a noble that suggested that they had worthy souls while commoners were merely fodder for *morbai* in the afterlife. The idea that the church here somehow decided that on its own and wrote it into law shook him on a deeper level. The word heresy wasn't a term he dared apply lightly, even in the privacy of his own mind, but what else could he call it?

Grant brought the wine and cheese over to his table, along with a loaf of bread with the end already torn off. He tore fresh pieces off the bread and started eating, washing it down with wine. "Want me to bring you some?"

"I'll come over in a moment." Mark wasn't sure what question he wanted to ask first, so he started in the middle of his thoughts. "Can they counter-accuse?"

"Sure."

Such a simple declaration with huge consequences. "So if I don't support your testimony, you could end up in jail."

"That's about the measure of it." He didn't sound angry, or resigned. The beautiful man with the gentle power of a huge beast ate his breakfast as if nothing special would happen that day.

"I can't let you take that risk alone." And he couldn't let those bastards who tried to kill him win. He'd have to make a statement as a jester and have the case dismissed. He couldn't chance Grant's word as a commoner would measure well against known murderers who'd apparently evaded the law so far.

Grant glanced at him, and Mark thought he saw cautious approval in the green eyes. "You'd really do that?"

Mark had a feeling he was about to step on a hornet's nest. He didn't know enough about the laws here to do this, but he couldn't let Grant face the court alone. Reading about loyalties forged by a saved life failed to convey the strength of powerful gratitude he felt. They also didn't mention how fragile and more precious life seemed after a hard fight. Every breath felt like a gift, all because of Grant. Aptly named Grant, he thought with a pleasant sense of the art in life that poets tried to convey. No, he couldn't let Grant go to court alone any more than Mark could have left his mother to die alone. "What do you know about the Morbai's Kiss?"

Grant shrugged. "They, um, fought on our side, the island side, during the war." He gave Mark a heavy look. "Their reasons for trying to kill you are none of my affair. The war's over. I'll turn myself in and we'll see what's what."

"Do they bother commoners too?" Mark asked.

"Yeah." Grant looked at him askance. "Does that matter to you?"

"If they thought I was a spy I can understand why they'd attack me on sight. Not that I'm going to forgive someone for trying to kill me, but considering I killed two of their friends, it's not like they flew off like birds. But if they're hurting people who have no argument," like his mother, "and they get away with it ...?"

"They do," Grant said softly. "The war, it messed them up."

"Then they need to be stopped. What can I do to help?"

"It works like military law," Grant told him, and suddenly everything became clearer.

"So nobles and jesters are like officers, and commoners are like soldiers."

"Yeah."

"So they can counter-accuse you, and only a noble's or a jester's word will hold stronger weight than number of witnesses." Grant was a brave man to go forward alone. Unless another witness came forward on his side, it would be two on one, and military law was required to give all common soldiers equal word. "Unless someone of more importance than I comes forward to defend them, I can make a statement, you'll walk out of there and we'll be done."

Grant hesitated. "Not exactly. There still has to be a trial."

The court would be busy all day every day if every matter like this came to trial. "You must mean an accounting."

"No, it'll be a trial. I know I said it was like military, but there has to be a trial for everything because just having enough people or some noble type on your side doesn't make you right. A judge has to listen and weigh the facts, and there has to be evidence and stuff."

Though Mark knew intellectually he'd killed in self-defense, the mewling cries of the dying swordsman came back to him. That had been a human being, a mother's son, perhaps a husband and father. "Can they judge me?" He could, maybe even should, be judged but he didn't want to be.

"The priests can't judge nobles or jesters. That hasn't changed yet, if it ever will." Grant delivered breakfast to the table. "The barons come together to hear those things."

"Barons." He was missing something. "A baron is a minor sort of lord, Grant, at least where I come from."

"The only folk who call themselves lords around here are mainlanders come visiting and continental sympathetics. Every islander who owns a house, land and armaments is a baron."

"Everyone? So what do the nobles call themselves?"

"Barons too. For a while no one had any sort of title that wasn't earned in the war, but it didn't work so well to call everyone mister who wasn't an officer so they came up with barons."

It was one thing to wonder what made Lord Argenwain special, and to wonder if *allolai* would save his lord's soul just because he was born noble in the privacy of his own mind. But a cult that tried to remove all sense of rank from the nobility and even removed the separation between a nobleman and an independent commoner—it didn't seem practical or even functionally possible. "Really?"

Grant shrugged. "Freedom, noble-ness and afterliving for all good men or none, I say, and the priests say all. They ought to know. They're the ones who see."

"See what?"

"The visions."

If he hadn't been weak already he'd certainly be weak in the knees now. This islander knew more about the Church than he did after a lifetime of studying history, art, philosophy—everything had been open to him but the Church. "Have you read the sacred poetry, then?"

Grant grinned at that. "I can't read!" He laughed.

Mark shook his head. "It's madness."

Grant straightened up and Mark's belly tensed. He'd forgotten for a moment that he was in a stranger's home, and at his mercy. "I figure you don't understand, so I'm not going to make anything of this, m'lo, that is, m'jeste, but maybe you should remember you're not on the mainland."

Having Grant name him a jester made him even more uneasy than Grant's height and offended glower. "It's just strange to me. I meant no offense." Ancients had visions, not everyday people, or so he'd thought. All this traveled so far outside Mark's experience he couldn't make himself take it seriously anymore. "Have you had a vision?"

"It's not for me. Barons and their jesters, they get them, and priests sometimes too. That's all I know."

"All barons? Even ones that aren't noble—that is, from a sacred lineage?"

"I don't know nothing about that."

"Do you know what's in the visions?" No doubt fancy rooms with leaky roofs and fire and children crying. Everyone had nightmares. Maybe that's what they had begun to call visions now, as if stripping the idea of proper titles had carried over and gave all dreams the same importance as visions.

"I said all I know is that they have 'em." Grant sounded irritated. Mark lowered his gaze. Lust licked down his spine and into his groin, but the potent things Grant had told him quickly smothered it.

A long-forgotten eagerness to see sacred poetry seized him, burning hotter now that he might be given access and learn something that might, what? Give him hope that he might survive in the afterlife? Make sense of these wonderful but frightening and outrageous things Grant talked about as if they were clouds in the sky and dew on the leaves?

Maybe even tell him if the voices he heard might be real rather than madness ....

If what Grant was telling him was true, jesters wouldn't need lords to save them, not if they were good men in their own right. Commoners wouldn't need patrons. Everyone could survive or perish on their own merit.

Gutter had said if all were right with the world, jesters wouldn't need lords and commoners wouldn't need patrons. Had he referenced the Church here in Meridua in that statement?

Mark would have done it anyway to help Grant, but now the idea of doing the right thing held such rich meaning that testifying felt almost ...

Sacred.

Potentially. Assuming he allowed himself to believe even a trace of what Grant talked about. Assuming, again, that Grant wasn't confused, or making things up, or addled from a brain injury or twisted by strange forces in the midst of a battle against nobility.

"When do we have to appear in court?" Mark asked.

Grant blinked at him. "What?"

"I already said I won't let you go there by yourself. If you're going, so will I."

"You're really going to court on my account?" Shock opened his eyes wide, giving him a sweet look. Mark's heart skipped a few beats.

Mark made himself look away. "Not just because you helped me. I'm tired of cruel men winning their way." If they brought a jester or a lord, rather, baron, to their defense, it might get Mark into more trouble than he could handle. But then Grant would need him more than ever.

What about Dainty? *And Rohn Evan?*

A good and honest man's freedom, maybe even his life was at risk.

Grant stood and brought his heels together, a soldierly formality peeking through his gratitude. "I'm glad for your help, m'jeste." He bowed.

"You're welcome. Now, if you would help me up I'll test my feet."

Grant took the two steps required to cross the distance and Mark set his hand on Grant's heavy forearm. The gesture felt uncomfortable, like he'd overstepped his bounds, but his hand tingled with the pleasure of human contact at the same time. As soon as he stood he drew his hand away. His balance felt fine, though the skin on his leg around the wound felt painfully stretched. "Thank you. That should do," Mark told him. Grant took his seat again.

"I suppose I'd better hurry about breakfast," Mark said. "And I should dress." Into what? His clothes, wherever they were, were ruined.

"Fair enough. Can I fetch the rest of your effects?"

"Evidence." Mark bit his lip, on the edge of a thought. He limped over to join Grant at the table. It made him dizzy and he grabbed the chair to steady himself before sitting. "I hope my word will help."

"Of course it will. You're touched by the divine."

"No, I'm really not." Grant might believe, but Mark wasn't ready to, and it felt especially wrong to claim it when he wasn't sure what the letters meant or what Gutter had trained him for. "I'm not a bound jester. I don't know if it'll count for anything, or make things worse—I could always stay out of it if you think it'd be best, but I do want to help you."

Grant stared at him a moment, then looked down. "Things are different here." He tucked his chin and gazed at Mark shyly. "You are a jester, aren't you?"

He couldn't say no anymore. "I don't want to be, but yes."

"Jesters aren't all bad."

"I hope so." Mark raised his mug of wine. "No greater honor to men than justice."

Grant raised his glass as well. "To justice."

Mark sipped and almost choked. He'd had bad wine, but nothing like this: thick and cloying and almost vinegar with oak that may have been used to house something like pickles before they used it to age the wine.

Grant blushed. "Sorry, master jester. Since the war, we haven't been able to get good wine, not without paying more than it's worth. I have a little whiskey if you'd rather have that."

Mark shook his head. He'd heard of whiskey, usually in conjunction with men rotting in gutters. "Here's to improved trade," Mark said, offering another toast.

"To good trade." Grant smiled and took another swig. Mark's second sip wasn't as bad as the first. He killed the flavor with some of the rough rye bread and set to eating the rest of his breakfast. The cheese was past sharp but still edible. It was easily the worst breakfast he'd ever eaten, but he was so hungry he didn't care.

"How far is the court?" Mark asked between mouthfuls.

"Center of town, about thirty blocks."

"I'll need a coach."

"I told you yesterday, there aren't any for hire on the island," Grant said. "But I'll try. Maybe the church will send one."

"Just as long as I don't have to walk." He'd have to get dressed soon. Should he wear his weapons—his heart skipped a beat with a sudden realization. "I forgot to clean my pistol." After practice he'd always cleaned the pistols right away. Had he ruined Lake's beautiful weapon?

"I took care of it. Loaded the pistol after and sealed both your weapons against the salt, too, though the stuff I use probably isn't as nice as what you can afford."

Mark settled. "Thank you very much." He resisted the urge to inspect the pistol. It would be an insult to suggest by even the slightest gesture that Grant hadn't done a good job.

"You're welcome."

A thought he'd had earlier finally completed itself. "Maybe I should wear the damaged clothes. What better way to display evidence than to match the blood to my wounds? Besides, the less time we give them to prepare, the better. Assuming they're caught."

Grant's expression drooped and he nodded. "I have a feeling this time they'll turn themselves in."

Chapter Thirteen

Grant offered Mark a mug of water. It was warm and tasted brackish, but Mark didn't care. Not long after breakfast he began to feel poorly again. By the time Grant had returned from court with a coach, Mark had so overheated in his bloodied waistcoat he wasn't sure he could bear to wear it at all. "I'm not accustomed to the tropics, I suppose," Mark told him. He struggled with the buttons on his waistcoat. "I can button this again when we get there. Do you have a fan?"

Grant blushed prettily. "Fishermen don't have fans and such, m'jeste."

He wondered if he'd packed one and left it in the snow as useless rubbish. The thought made him laugh. Packing a fan in winter was almost as absurd as needing one desperately after pitching it in the snow. "Can you buy me one?"

"I might, but that coach won't wait for me. They'll come in here and haul you off if they have to. Folk are already gathering at the courthouse." Grant let out a huff. "Here, let me help you." He helped unbutton the waistcoat, and then touched Mark's forehead with the back of his hand. "I hate to say it, but I think you got the fever."

Infection from the wounds. It didn't frighten him as much as he expected. All that mattered was relieving the heat.

"We should'a got you some gracian, but I—"

Someone pounded on the door, interrupting Mark's shock and whatever else Grant intended to say.

"That'll be the coachman."

"Let me wet down my hair." Mark stood and narrowly avoided a tumble by grabbing onto Grant as he left to open the door. The room seemed to sway much farther than he moved, as if he walked on a floor that rolled like ocean waves but in all directions.

"Whoa there." Grant propped him back on the bed. "You best sit. Just wait a minute, m'jeste." Grant strode to the door, his footsteps heavy on the bare boards. The sound unnaturally pounded through Mark's chest and skull as if someone was hitting his head with a padded glove. "He's not well," Grant told the men outside. "Just give me a minute, all right?"

"The court is assembling. Can he attend or no?"

"I can," Mark assured them. Compared to his slog through the snow, this would be easy. He had help. And then, after, he'd make them take him to *Dainty* where he'd recover from the fever. He just had to make his case so well that there'd be little argument.

It sounded simple but his eyes ached and felt swollen and his wounds burned and his thoughts kept wandering off to where he lost track of them, leaving him to stare blankly until he realized he ought to be doing something.

Mark started to get the washbowl and pitcher himself, then remembered he couldn't. "Please, Grant—" He gestured. Grant took a moment to figure it out. He tromped over to his little wash area and brought back the bowl and pitcher. He stood in front of Mark and held them helplessly.

Apparently not everyone used his mother's cure for fever. Mark had only a wisp of memory, but the recollection of cold water and her hands in his hair gave him comfort. "I'll hold the bowl. Just pour that slowly over the back of my neck and in my hair." Mark accepted the bowl and leaned over, the sway of the movement making him feel like he'd plant his face in the water. He closed his eyes. The water felt like ice down the back of his neck. Tentative at first, Grant's strong hand began working the water through his hair as he poured. Mark didn't expect his touch to be so supple. He didn't dare hope it was because Grant was practiced at touching men.

"Not sure this is the best idea," Grant murmured. "You might catch a chill on top of everything else."

Mark pawed away some of the water that curved around his face and into his eyes. "People actually catch chills here?" The water stopped. He set the bowl down between his feet and wrung the water out of his hair.

"You bet they do. Here, let me get you something for that." Grant brought him a large rag made from what used to be a heavy linen shirt. The thick cloth implied that the island got cold enough for someone to want to wear such a thing. Hard to imagine with weather like this in winter. Grant's scent softened the rag's dusty smell.

Mark nearly toppled again just reaching for his bag. The room seemed to roll at a steep downward angle every time he moved his head.

"What do you want?" Grant asked, crouching.

"A ribbon. Any ribbon. Please, let me pick one out." He didn't want Grant touching the masks or anything else that might get him hurt. Grant brought the bag close and held it while he found a ribbon and tied his hair back. It took him longer than usual to smooth the ribbon's curls and straighten the tails.

The two men from the carriage strode over and pulled him up. "Hey!" he heard Grant bark, and then things blurred. Shadows rushed by and people spoke in muffled, deep tones. Water seemed to have filled his ears. When he resurfaced he was on the stairs wobbling his way down between the coachmen.

"Grant, my bag." Mark's own voice sounded far away. "Put it somewhere safe. Please."

The men loaded him into a bulky cherrywood contraption that could seat a dozen people. It had beautiful brass fittings and leather cushions and something that looked more like a large umbrella than a roof to serve as shade. He noticed that the coachmen were armed, and he had two additional sacred guards armed with both pistols and long rifles, the sort sharpshooters used.

"Am I being arrested?" Mark asked. He suddenly wished he had his rapier and pistol. The guards' silence worried him. Could word of him have reached Perida ahead of *Dainty*? It didn't seem possible, but they had stopped by a few islands on the way ....

Grant charged down the stairs, his golden hair tied back with an ancient, threadbare ribbon, wearing nothing but a shirt, brown trousers and fisherman's boots. The guards made room for Grant on the footman's step and the carriage began to move. The wheels rolled well and softly on the sand road, but the carriage's sway seemed excessive. He hadn't felt nauseated on *Dainty*, not once, but now he thought the carriage's roll would make him sick. Or maybe it was the wine with breakfast, or the cheese.

He held his head in his hands and took deep breaths, in through the nose, out through the mouth.

What seemed like hours later, the carriage entered a deep shade. Vague impressions of trees and strange carriages and people in fine clothes strolling on tall stone sidewalks flashed by the edges of Mark's vision. Birds with harsh, jay-like voices rasped like small crows and squealed like hawks over the cries of gulls. Beneath that, smaller birds made sounds like dripping water amplified many times, and something gargling rocks, and one whistled more like a person than a bird.

Other sounds whispered, not at the edge of his hearing but inside his mind. Worse than an itch inside his ear, no matter which way he turned his head or focused his mind he couldn't make out what they were saying.

Until—

What is that? Who are you?

We're—The voice faded.

—brother. Please be silent. We—

"Who are you?" Mark whispered to them.

"Huh?" Grant gave him an uneasy sidelong look.

"Nothing." Mark wasn't sure whether it would be worse to know for certain he was going insane, or to know that the voices weren't just absolutely real, but that he could hear what he sometimes feared might be *allolai* and *morbai*. He wasn't ready for the world to be that near to what priests made it to be.

The carriage stopped and the men helped him up. Black and red spots flooded his vision, but he kept his feet moving across the sidewalk, down stairs very similar to the court back home at Seven Churches, and into cool, dark places that soothed his head.

"What is this?" A priest emerged from shadows. He might be a heretic, but he wore the same absurd hat and half-red, half-white robes that the mainland priests wore. He was older, with gray eyes and an unkind mouth whose down-turned edges nearly vanished into jowls. A heavy gold chain around his neck marked him as a constabulary priest.

"The plaintiff, gerson," one of the guards told him.

"You, bring Darren with his bag of medicines, quickly." The priest looked Mark over like he was crawling with maggots. "Is he fit to testify?"

"I am," Mark assured him.

The priest's eyes narrowed. "Who are you? I've had differing accounts but no clear answer."

"My name is Mark Seaton, and ...." What? He wasn't really a crew member on *Dainty*, not yet, anyway, and he didn't want Captain Shuller mixed up in this. "I have a message."

"You're a messenger?"

"All I can lay claim to at the moment is that I carry a message. I have no letters of free passage."

"Is the message private, public or sacred?" He would have only guessed the last if he thought that Mark might be in disguise or had lost his letters of passage and only now felt safe to reveal himself.

Wait, he'd had a plan. He had to be a jester, didn't he? He couldn't remember.

Yes, he did, so that his word could outweigh those men. "I—I'm of Lord Argenwain's house, a pupil of Lord Jester Gutter."

One of the guards flinched back and they both nearly dropped him. He thought he'd been holding himself fairly well but at the loss of their support his knees buckled. Fortunately he didn't fall before they grabbed him up again.

"So you're a jester," the priest growled.

As much as he hated priests, now that he was in court he didn't dare lie. "Not by any standard but my training."

"I suppose you think you're being clever. Bring him to the fellis room. And you—Grant Roadman, correct?" The guards took Mark away as Grant began to formally declare himself.

The guards helped Mark deeper into the Court. The lamp light seemed overly large, as if each flame were a fire in a hearth. Those lights made him feel excessively warm again.

The gerson caught up with them, accompanied by another, younger priest holding a bag. "Quickly now." The guards picked up their pace and took him into a small, shadowy room with one lamp in it. They set him down in one of several chairs circled around a central table. A tall vase of strange flowers stood by a second door from the room, and a coat rack held several black robes. "Why didn't you give me your jester's name?" the gerson demanded.

Mark didn't have a good answer for him, so he kept quiet.

The gerson leaned close. "I'll have it now."

If he didn't do this, Grant might suffer for it. "Lark."

"Lark, I need to know that you're fit to testify. Tell me," he said, his expression cooling to a steady neutral, "what was Ambergen's Trust?"

"A treaty between Saphir City and Duke Ambergen bound by marriage that lasted all of seven months before Saphir's mayor declared the treaty violate on the grounds—"

"That's enough." The priest looked into Mark's eyes. "You have sufficient faculty for a trial."

"I do?"

"I believe so."

The younger priest offered him a smoldering tube of paper rolled around something greenish brown. "A smoke for the pain."

Smoke. One of Lord Argenwain's friends had gone blind from smoking too much. "I don't think I want it."

"Don't be afraid. It will help. Look." The young priest clamped his lips around it and drew in a breath. He held his breath a moment before blowing out a delicate, almost pure white smoke. It smelled pleasantly sweet. He held it out for Mark.

Mark took it gingerly, touched his lips on it and drew in a breath, uncertain. The smoke coated his mouth and tongue in a bitter flavor and then the smoke seared his lungs. He coughed, then gagged. He couldn't breathe—

All at once the tension bled out of him. That's when he really felt the pain, not just in his head like before. His leg and arm throbbed. The slightest twitch and his wounds bit him savagely.

"Try again," the priest said. "Hold the smoke in."

Mark breathed deep and held the smoke. A wash of drunk pleasure and the gradual relief of his pain left him cushioned in warmth.

"Ready?" the younger priest asked.

"I think so." He wasn't in any shape to go dancing but he could sit or stand, whatever they'd need, and talk.

The gerson supported him when he stood back up, and the guard helped him ease on a black robe far too long for his height. A frog at the throat and a belt held the robe shut. A guard pulled up the robe through the belt to shorten it enough so Mark wouldn't trip on it. Mark hummed a few bars of Fenwell's "Night Walk" while a guard cracked the door and murmured something to someone on the other side. Formal voices and controlled laughs carried above the hubbub of rabble on the other side of the door. This very moment he would stand for the first time in front of the island's nobles—barons—whatever—and jesters. It should have unnerved him, but curiosity made him eager to go out.

Was that—he thought he heard softer voices, a whispered song in an uneven chorus, coming from the court room. Was it a real language, or had the addling of his mind made his imagination equal to reality?

He had to focus on what he knew was real. "How many men of note came to court?" Mark asked. It sounded like a theater out there rather than what he'd imagined a court proceeding would be like.

"Quite a lot," the elder priest told him. "I'd like to believe they're showing their support for equal justice, but I suspect they're here hoping to see the mysterious new jester. Despite our efforts to keep speculation about your identity to a minimum, word raced away."

"But I only just told you—"

"No one believed for a moment that you were anything but a jester."

"Why would anyone think I'm a jester?"

"Oh please. A young man in foppish clothing besting four seasoned soldiers? But we of the constabulary orders prefer not to assume."

Mark's thoughts floated around, little fireflies that he could only catch one at a time. He thought he ought to be afraid, or at least concerned, but then he thought about Gutter and whether this would get back to him, and it seemed funny. What would the papers say? It would appear in small, crowded print on a back page because it had little to do with the mainland. *A young jester, Lark by name, appeared in court ....*

In a murder trial.

It no longer entertained him. It made his skin crawl, and that feeling only worsened with the suspicion that Gutter might even approve.

Or worse, Gutter might be horrified and ashamed. Maybe it would be proof that Mark wasn't a good person after all.

Backing out of the trial now wouldn't change the fact that he'd killed two men.

I'm a killer. I've robbed two human beings of life.

The permanence of it all threatened to shatter him. It didn't seem to matter that they would have killed him given the chance. He wished that their hateful determination made him feel better. Why didn't their murderous intentions balance his guilt?

"Have you had more than just the leaf I gave you?" the younger priest asked.

"Leaf?"

"The smoke," the gerson said impatiently.

"Oh. Uh, no. Why?"

The gerson sighed. "This will be a fine circus."

The younger priest took Mark's pulse at his throat. "I don't like it. He came in flushed with fever, and now he's pale." He touched the back of his hand to Mark's cheek. His hand felt icy cold and Mark flinched from it. "I think his fever is getting worse. Have you had gracian, master jester?"

The thought appalled him. "No!"

The door opened. "It's time," the gerson declared, and walked out into the courtroom all but dragging Mark along with him.

"But—" the younger priest protested, as the guard shut the door.

A door for the second balcony on the other side of the crowded, multi-tiered oval chamber opened. A tall, dark-haired gentleman in a clean-cut gray coat and waistcoat with matching breeches and hair ribbon entered in a stately manner just as the elder priest settled Mark into a plush chair. The elegant gentleman sat on the edge of his seat to accommodate his dress sword, well apart from the small coteries of jesters and barons dotted near the rail one level up from the court floor. A group of anxious women and children entered the pit below the court floor's level, weaving through the crushing crowd toward the front. People made way for them and quieted, though only for a moment. Commoners kept trickling in, some singly, some in small packs, until there was no more room to stand. Their talk created a storm of noise. Within that storm, Mark heard an occasional word that wasn't Cathretan or Hasle, but he couldn't figure out where the words came from. He also heard some smooth, elegantly embroidered Osian, and the dexterous tongues of Neuch, and the sinuous drawl of Vyennen.

It wasn't as warm in the room as it was outside, but the unmoving, stifling air battered Mark's sense of balance. Sweat tickled down his face. Ladies in the balconies fluttered gilded feather fans, while paper ones flashed in the pit. He had no idea how the women managed to survive in their floor-length gowns. He roasted in much less.

A guard escorted Grant, dressed in black robes, to a box between the judge's desk and Mark's chair. Grant blanched when he noticed a large, elaborately dressed noble seated beside—was that a female jester?

The sinuous brunette in red wore a gold and red mask painted directly on her skin. She stared at Mark over her fan, pupils wide and deep.

Grant relaxed a little when he saw the stately man Mark had noted.

A badly-scarred herald came in next, glancing to his right at the large man with the female jester. The man nodded. The herald's black wig and black robes emphasized how slender and pale he was. A ragged line beneath his mouth formed a ridge where his chin had been. His head sat askew over ruffles that hid whatever had happened to his neck.

People started to chatter again.

With no trial to entertain them yet, the jesters started commenting. Unfortunately the comments didn't rise above the pit's cacophony. A jester with a whorled, thorny, purple and crimson mask painted on his face laughed loudly, calling attention to himself. Onyx lines edged in silver lined his eyes and sparkled along the lines between his nose and cheeks, making his eyes seem cat-like. The whorled jester's attention was turned toward a slender, older nobleman, but his gaze flicked sideways toward Mark often. The first instant that their gazes met, Mark felt something sharp and yet enticing, like an expert barber's touch, caress his spine.

The judge's door behind the desk finally opened. Everyone quieted, and many leaned about to get a better look.

The judge wore an ample curly black wig that made his head look too large. Black outlined his eyes. He was a handsome, relatively young man with amber eyes and a stern face. Grant gave Mark a stark look, and Mark smiled, hoping it would reassure him.

"This court is now in session," the herald declared in a clear, formal voice unimpeded by his terrible war injury. "Judge Wellman presiding."

"I'm pleased to see that the barons and jesters of the island have taken an interest in court today," the judge said dryly. "Bring in the accused."

A door opened near the rear of the court. The machete man and the man who'd had the rapier, both dressed in white robes, limped in escorted by constabulary priests. The rapier man wore the bright red cut Mark had given him on his face. Their hands were manacled behind their backs, their sleeves draped like furled wings along their sides. Mark's belly tightened and pinpricks danced on his skin. Fortunately the fever smothered and blurred most of the memories of his blade cutting flesh, and the blood, and the cries of the men he'd killed, and the choppy memories of the cutting they'd done on him.

Most, but not all. Flashes of dying moans and blood scent snuck in with the babble and the sweaty, fishy, perfumed stench of the crowd.

The men went up a short flight of stairs to a small, raised area fenced by flowery ironwork. The constabulary priests in their fine uniforms, dress weapons sparkling in the lamp light, helped them sit.

One of the children near the front sat up. "Daddy?"

"Hush." The woman near the child yanked him back down in his seat.

What would it be like to discover that your father did things ... or did he approve of what his father had tried to do?

Maybe his father was a hero in his eyes, as Gutter was a hero in Mark's eyes—sometimes. Like his relationship with Gutter, the boy's relationship with his father might be complicated. Love offset by pain. Dependence and mistrust balanced with devotion and submission.

What would it feel like to see Gutter placed on trial? To see the great man brought so low. Mark couldn't bear the idea. What the boy faced now had to be excruciating.

The herald raised his hand, palm toward the audience. "For those of you who are uninformed as to the stricture of these proceedings, let me instruct you. The accuser shall speak first, then witnesses for the accuser, and then the accused shall put forward their case and witnesses. Rebuttals and counters are allowed, however, they must be brief. At no point will the audience be permitted to speak. Master jester, state your name for the *allolai, morbai* and attendants of the court."

It took Mark a moment to realize the herald had meant him, and another beat to remember his jester's name. "Master Jester Lark." His belly fluttered. He'd now publicly declared himself something that he had no right to, letter of reference of no. It also made him uneasy that the herald invited *allolai* and *morbai* into this in a tone that suggested that they were literally real, could listen, and might even be interested.

Why won't I let myself believe? If they are the voices, then I know they're here.

Because his mother had always promised him that it was all superstition, while his father maintained that *allolai*, *morbai*, masks with souls and ship figureheads who wept and loved really and truly existed. He was still caught between his parents, and he was still loyal to both of them, though they'd long been gone from his life.

"Are you the injured party?"

"I am." The double meaning, both literal and legal of injured, tickled him and he laughed, though it ought to have been too obvious to be funny.

"Please explain how you were wounded."

The sloppiness behind that question irritated and worried him. Didn't these people know how critical a turn of phrase could be? He could be damned with the verbal misstep of a single word. "I was busy at the time, but let me see what I remember. First, a blow to the crown with a bottle, followed by a rapier slash to the arm and I'm pretty sure the broadsword edge cut my leg. It was a little crowded and the blood in my eyes made it hard to see. Or did you mean to ask me what happened? I believe it's the people, not the instruments they used, that are on trial here."

A few chuckles echoed in the room, but a softer sound caught his attention. It was a single intake of breath from where some of the lords and jesters sat. It ought to have been too subtle to hear.

"This is not a matter for amusement, Master Jester Lark," the priest said.

Something near the ceiling glowed like an emerald shadowed in dusky purple clouds, distracting him. Maybe it was a reflection from someone's jewelry.

"Master Jester Lark!"

The herald stood before him. Mark blinked, not sure what had happened.

"This is not a debut. Please refrain from singing."

"I—" Mark hesitated. Had he been singing?

"Do you see the men who assaulted you in this courtroom?" Impatience hardened the herald's voice.

The court seemed darker and he couldn't make out anything but shadows. "I can't say. It's dark."

"Are you saying it was too dark to see them?"

"No. I recognized them the moment they came into the room. They're both right there."

The ones who'd lived.

"How did your meeting with them come to pass?" the herald asked.

"One attacked me from behind after his companion whistled to distract my attention. They pinned me to a wall, and demanded my bag first, and then my purse." Mark remembered charging, and the man with the rapier retreated, teeth bright in a grimace, framed by an innocent blue sky. The machete man had a pistol, and he aimed—had it gone off? Mark couldn't remember. But that was all after. "They argued about waiting for Jonas and Bates." Did he have that in the right order? His memory, usually so quick to answer his mind, now failed him. It seemed like a fitting punishment for his snit about how the herald posed his questions.

Someone or something started moving the lamps, maybe to improve the lighting but they must have been children because they were playing around. Mark rubbed his face. "I'm tired and the lights are dancing."

"He's addled. He doesn't remember a damned thing," one of the accused protested.

"Duly noted," the judge assured them.

Duly noted? His temper flashed red, and for a moment all he could see was the rapier man. "I don't know which of them hit me from behind but I know these are the men who tried to kill me." The rapier man stared back at him, cold, hateful.

"Master jester, do you have proof of injury?"

"Show us! Undress yourself!" someone with a rich baritone called out.

Neither the judge nor the herald voiced an objection, so Mark released the frog and belt. "I'll strip naked if it pleases you. I'm trained to satisfy." He let the robe slide off his shoulders and turned in place.

A woman cried out. "He needs a physician!"

"A brave man's pants," a woman with a purring voice noted.

"Control yourselves," the judge said sharply.

"That's my blood on those clothes," one of the accused said. "He was asking around about Colonel Evan, so I followed him, figuring he was up to mischief at best. I asked him what he wanted the colonel for, and he told me I ought to mind my curiosity. I told him I wasn't afraid of men like him, and I had a mind to call the guard. He starts crying for help and cuts his own arm. Then him and that fisherman attacked, and my friends came in to help. I can show you what they did to us. Put a bullet in my body, cut us all up, and killed my friends. Big brute like that and a trained jester. They was both deep into smoke and drink, just like he is now."

"So you admit to being there," the judge said.

"*Allolai* as my witnesses, we defended ourselves from that mainland whore, and if he was hurt it was because we fought for our lives. They attacked us!"

"You're a liar." Grant gripped the edge of his box.

"Your name, for the court," the herald said.

"Grant Roadman, your holiness. I didn't even get in on the fight. I saw the tail end of it. It was four on one before I even got there."

"So how do you explain us getting so messed up if the odds were so bad?" the accused demanded.

"Because you took me for a child." Mark gripped the rail, his hands close to Grant's, passion keeping him on his feet. "You didn't expect me to put up a fight. You planned to kill me and take what you wanted of my effects. It's true I cried for help. You said, no one gives a shit. That may be true, but the lack of regard for who and what I am doesn't make an attempt to take my life in any way defensible." The dim room started sparkling with blue and green and his skin hummed, especially his lips, which buzzed like bees. Dark splotches blotted out the brilliant colors like clouds billowing among oversized stars. "I told you that you could have my bag if you let me go, but you insisted on having my rapier, and I'm sure you would have asked for my pistol next to make your murder that much easier." Everything started to lean over to the right and then up—

Mark jolted awake on the ground with Grant and the stately gentleman on either side of him.

I fainted.

How stupid and embarrassing. His head pounded.

"He's a spy and an assassin, I know it!" the accused cried. "Tried to come to our island posing as a gentleman, but he's a jester, and he's looking for the man who saved us all from ruin. Take his word or mine as to what happened. It don't matter. You gonna pick him over me, this foppish murderer over a soldier who did good service, who lost his blood and friends to mainl'nd tyranny?"

Mark tried to say something in answer, but before he could catch his breath a guard opened the witness door. "Dr. Berto is here."

"Allow him entry," the judge said. "Let's hear what the physician has to say about the injuries."

A large, hairy, male doctor crouched beside Mark, setting down two large, white bags.

"I'm all right." Mark tried to sit up. His words slurred and he gave in to the hands pressing him down.

The doctor took his pulse and prodded him a bit. "He needs immediate medical attention," Berto said. "These are definitely sword wounds. As for this head wound ...." His fingers probed in Mark's hair and a sharp pain made him wince. "He still has bits of glass in his scalp. What poor excuse for a physician examined this man?"

"Are any of the injuries self-inflicted? The arm in particular."

The doctor checked his arm. "It's possible, but I would expect the front of the wound to go deeper in that case. It's far more likely that this is a sword wound incurred by someone standing in front of him, or a knife wound from a slash given by someone standing at his shoulder."

"Can he continue to attend court?" the judge asked.

"No."

But Grant would be alone. "I can stay. I promise I'll keep my seat and I should be fine." He felt much better, though his head thrummed painfully in time with his heartbeat.

"I will take the physician's judgment over yours," the judge said. "Master Jester Lark, you may submit further testimony or witnesses within twenty four hours if you are inclined to do so. We will proceed with Mister Roadman's testimony, as we've had only a few words from him so far."

The elegant man and the doctor helped Mark up and out through the witness door. After a complicated series of turns, they emerged into bright sunshine dappled by trees and the relief of a fresh, if warm breeze.

Chapter Fourteen

Mark couldn't believe that was a trial. It was so disorderly as to be completely ridiculous. He didn't dare say so aloud for fear that his new benefactor might take offense. But how they expected to find justice with people shouting things out and arguing and guessing ....

It horrified him. Were mainland trials like this too?

"My carriage is over here," the elegant gentleman told Dr. Berto as they hurried Mark along a broad stone sidewalk.

"Wait!" The jester with the whorled design on his face and the cat-lined eyes caught up with them. "My lord and master's daughter would like to extend her household's hospitality to the young man." He had to take long strides to keep up.

"As would I." The large gentleman with the lady jester on his arm pursued them. Mark's benefactors, or perhaps captors, didn't pause and Mark had to crane his neck to catch a glimpse of the pair. "As mayor, I insist," the large gentleman added.

"The young gentleman was looking for me."

Mark's whole body took a short leap of alarm at the elegant gentleman's proclamation. The man firmed his grip on Mark's arm, possibly hard enough to hurt. Mark couldn't tell anymore. He couldn't feel much past the slow drumming someone had started up again inside his head. His vision didn't line up properly with his own body, which tended to slant toward the rising ground.

So this was Rohn Evan, the man Obsidian had sent him to find, the man that Mark's intended murderer had called a colonel. Mark knew he was addled beyond drunk, but he'd caught that hard enough to hang onto it.

"My house isn't far from Hevether Hall," Dr. Berto told them. "It would be convenient so that I may better treat him."

"No offense, Dr. Berto, but Dr. Rowart will do just as well." The mayor huffed a bit trying to catch up with them. "And my house is quite near here. You can't intend to drag the poor lad halfway around the island."

"I think it would be safer." Baron Evan slowed a bit to give his driver time to hop off of a fine, if stark black carriage and open the door. Unlike the other vehicles Mark had seen, this one was fully enclosed and glassed.

"No one would dare—"

"Please." Mark sagged in relief as the colonel finally stopped pressing him to get into the carriage. "I thank all of you for your kind offers of hospitality—"

"Don't." The colonel spoke the word quickly and quietly near Mark's ear. It came out firmly, almost like an order, but it had the unmistakable tone of a plea.

He doesn't even know who I am and what I want, and he wants to protect me?

Or maybe he knows what I bring.

Or maybe he wants to make sure I'm no threat to him.

Regardless, Mark intended to go with him. "But I am here to see the colonel."

"It's settled, then." Colonel Evan climbed into the carriage and held out his hand. Mark took it. Something about the way their grips matched made his belly flutter. Mark let the colonel pull him in with the doctor's help. The driver shut the door, and they were off.

To Hevether Hall.

"Who sent you?" Baron, or rather Colonel—he seemed more like a colonel—Evan watched the passing buildings, and he spoke without inflection.

"Obsidian."

"I assume that's another jester." If the colonel only pretended not to know Obsidian, he was a fine actor.

Mark couldn't allow the conversation to continue in that direction. "I'm not entirely sure ... that is, I have a letter, but until I read that letter I ...." He'd approached things from the wrong direction, but every time he looked for a better one he lost his way.

The doctor took his wrist and measured his pulse. "Try to stay calm."

"I didn't graduate from a university. I didn't even attend one." That seemed the best way to explain. "I have, or had, no intention of becoming a jester. I just had to be one, at least for a little while. But I'm not staying."

"Can you give him something to ease the fever?" Colonel Evan asked the doctor. "He's losing his mind."

"I know it's hard to follow what I'm saying. I'm sorry. The gist of what I'm trying to tell you is that I'm serving as a crude and hastily-appointed messenger. As soon as I've delivered my message, I hope to leave Perida and you in peace."

"You need medical attention before you go anywhere," the doctor told him.

"I can get it on the ship."

"No, you can't. You need a proper doctor, and a clean living situation. None of those things are possible on a ship. Now please, try to keep still and quiet."

Colonel Evan finally looked at Mark, and his gaze cut like twin swords. Mark's heart skipped into his throat. The danger he sensed didn't frighten him nearly as much as the rush of complicated feelings. Admiration, lust and trust warred with a cry of warning that jangled every nerve. "What is Obsidian's message?" Colonel Evan asked.

"I can't give it to you here."

"The doctor—"

"It's not just the doctor, or the driver. There's something I have to show you." He didn't dare say anything more than that.

"It sounds like those bastards might have been right," the doctor murmured. "I think this boy plans to kill you."

Colonel Evan looked away, watching the streets and buildings once more. "No. I don't think so."

Mark admired the lines of the colonel's handsome face. The traditional Cathretan name didn't fit with the delicate, olive-toned skin, and the colonel's dark hair didn't have even a trace of curl to suggest Hasle somewhere in his lineage. He'd heard of noble families in the southeast mountains that touched on both the Vyennen and Hasle borders, but he hadn't been introduced to any. Not that all Cathretan people were fair, far from it, but the noble families had that tendency, and were usually bland in complexion as Mark considered himself to be.

The colonel might also be from a lineage originating somewhere far more exotic, like Bel. The family may have changed its name to something more easily pronounced by the Cathretan majority that had inhabited the Meriduan Islands since their discovery over three centuries ago.

He'd reached the limits of his ability to think. The rest of the journey passed in heat and a confusion of sunlight and shadow. The few times Mark experienced full lucidity he saw a strange bird with golden tails so long it seemed impossible that it could fly, and blossoms in vivid crimson with throats like flame among vines with trunks as thick as trees, and a smooth curve of beach with black sand on which no living thing walked or grew. *Black Shore Road.* The sea roared across that sand, and from that point onward the sea thundered relentlessly. At times it sounded as if the waves raced and rushed and crashed all around them. He couldn't tell if any of it was natural or a dream.

The next thing he knew the doctor had him bent over a large silver bowl held by a young woman with hair already touched by gray. They poured frigid water over the back of Mark's neck and it felt like it stabbed right through the spine. Afterward he felt a little better. He managed to walk mostly by himself to a white bed in a teal and cream room. The doors and windows stood wide open but they were hung with pale mesh more clever and fine than a spider's web to help cut the strong sea breeze. The same gauze hung around the bed in place of drapes. It billowed with the touch of the wind's cooling breaths. The ocean pounded close by, and gulls squawked right outside his window. Mark shivered in the damp, drafty room and remembered how Grant told him that people could in fact catch a chill in the tropics.

Grant. "What's going to happen to Grant Roadman?"

"Nothing, I expect. He's just a witness," the doctor assured him. "No one so far has claimed that he killed anyone."

"He has, at his home, a bag. My bag. I need him to bring it to me." Mark had no one else he could trust with it. He hated drawing Grant further into this mess but he had no choice. He didn't dare ask for a servant to fetch it.

"Mr. Roadman doesn't make friends easily." Colonel Evan spoke from the doorway. Mark hadn't noticed his presence before. Everything was so disjointed and strange—he wanted to return to *Dainty* and curl up on the tiny bunk he'd begun to think of as his own and sleep it all away. "He was a good soldier, and he's a good man. I would be extremely offended if I discovered that you were involving him without his knowledge in some sort of mainland intrigue."

"I know nothing of it," Mark told him. "You're in a far better position than I am to know exactly what's happening."

"Because you're only delivering a message."

He didn't sound like he believed it, and Mark didn't blame him.

"Your default is silence." A hint of approval warmed Colonel Evan's otherwise neutral, even voice. He turned to leave. "I'll have my driver fetch your bag."

"I would rather—I asked Grant to keep it safe, and I would feel terrible if he found it missing or anything out of place and thought it was because of me."

Colonel Evan turned just enough to look at Mark past his own shoulder. The gesture would have been coy if the colonel didn't have such a cold gaze. "Mr. Roadman has far better reason to trust me than he does to trust you, but I will instruct my man to see to it that he is there before anything is removed."

The doctor started removing Mark's clothing. The colonel gave him a nod and left.

Dr. Berto rubbed a salve that stank of something sour and moldy into Mark's wounds, and then measured something syrupy and golden into a bottle. "Have you taken anything for the pain?"

"The priest gave me a smoke." Mark shivered through and through. He grabbed up the sheets and quilts. "And I had wine this morning."

"Do you know what kind of smoke?"

"No. He just called it leaf."

The doctor gritted his teeth into a pained smile. "They might as well have put your head in an oven. Some of their remedies work extremely well, but some are ... they practice medicine based on sacred poetry rather than science, and sacred poetry is far too subject to interpretation." He finished measuring out the syrup and put the bottle away into a large case. "Have you heard of gracian?"

Mark's gut clenched in alarm. "Of course I have."

"If you take this as I direct, you will heal faster."

"I don't want to become an addict. No thank you." Mark trembled not just from fever now, but fear.

"It's very important that you take it. This infection you're struggling with is dangerous not just in its own right. Open wounds invite even more dangerous things, things that don't keep mainlanders awake at night worrying every time they catch their skin on something sharp."

Mark had heard of blood worms from the days when the islands were first colonized, and gorer maggots too. "But as long as the wounds are covered ...."

"You may have already been exposed. We don't know how the eggs get in there. We do know that gracian seems to prevent these things from hatching inside the body, and the quick healing can only do you good. I've measured just enough for a week. That's not terribly long."

"I don't want to be another addict floating in grace."

Dr. Berto smiled. "I think you have little to worry about in that regard. Yes, it happens, but most people don't become dependant on it when they take it for the prescribed time in the prescribed manner."

He was all alone and though part of him trusted these people, he trusted them against his will, without a single rational reason save that they seemed to be trying to help him now. "I'll take my chances with the worms."

"If I were a disinterested party I would let you make this choice and be on my way. Not everyone develops the secondary maladies we all dread. If they did, this would be an island of corpses. However, I told the colonel I would do my best, and my best includes this medicine. Your leg wound in particular is extremely deep, and I don't know how long you were exposed to insects and the like before whoever it was that treated you did their work, or how well they did it. I certainly have my doubts on that score. So I'm afraid we are left with little choice. Besides, I intend to stitch you up properly before I leave. You won't feel it once the gracian does its work, and that's for the best."

Stitches. He would have scars. It shouldn't have mattered, but it did. He'd no longer have perfect skin, or the illusion of youth, or even that little bit of innocence he didn't realize he'd had until he killed those men.

The doctor let out a sigh. "Shall I call for the colonel to help me insist?"

"You say most men don't become addicts?"

"Not if they're properly cared for, and you will be cared for."

"Can I take just one dose?"

The doctor shook his head and let out a grim chuckle. "Two a day for four days. I insist that you rally the courage and have a little faith in yourself. Or if not in yourself, than in the colonel who you have come so far to see."

Mark forced himself to nod.

The doctor measured out a spoonful of the syrup and offered it. Mark took it in his mouth and pulled his lips over the spoon before he could change his mind.

Honey, a bitter tang of something like orange rind, and then all the flavor vanished into a soothing warmth that eased his chills. He didn't feel fevered anymore. His gaze focused past the gauzy curtains for the first time. Gulls glided by. He made his way to the window, vaguely aware of the doctor's protest, and sat on the broad sill. The sea was a deep blue-green here and covered in lace and foam. The waves rose in huge mounds and then exploded into white shards against sharp black rocks. The shards rained down among rainbows into pools linked by waterfalls. It was more magnificent than the most artful fountains he'd ever seen. The sky wasn't just blue. Here it appeared to be brushed with a thin coat of violet over the brightest sapphire, and at the horizon it paled to a hue he'd never seen in nature, as if an emerald and a morning glory blossom had dissolved into ice.

He sang softly to it about *Mairi's* death, and the song healed his fear, and his pain, his anger and even the grief that haunted his memories. The lyrics came to him easily from the air and the sea's rhythm and his own breath, but then he faltered on a rhyme and couldn't remember where the music had been leading him.

The doctor led him back to the bed, and stitched him up, and washed him. The woman who'd been sitting by quietly in a chair helped Mark dress into a nightshirt, and then moved her chair beside the bed.

"What's your name?" Mark asked her.

"Trudy, m'jeste. I'm the housekeeper."

"Isn't this the sort of thing you'd delegate to a chamber maid, Miss Trudy?"

"I hope you will allow me to serve as such. We have no one besides myself, Norbert and Philip, and the men are ill-suited for this sort of work."

It wasn't fair to her—such a large house, and now she had Mark to tend to as well. "I expect I'll need help with the chamberpot eventually, Miss Trudy, so I think it's reasonable to call me by the name my father gave me. I'm Mark, and I'm very pleased to meet you."

"Master jester, I think you'll change your mind when you are well again, but I'll call you what you wish while you're ill. Besides, I don't think it's fair to call you by your given name when you call me Miss."

Mark closed his eyes, and his breath sighed out. When he took his next breath, sleep came with it, and dreams so glorious he hoped he'd never wake.

Mark huddled, drenched in sweat, hot and cold at the same time, shivering and desperately thirsty.

Colonel Evan stalked into the dark room following Trudy, who held a lamp for him. Mark flinched from the light. It wasn't bright so much as it emitted sharp, golden needles that seemed to pierce his eyes.

"Trudy tells me you won't take the gracian."

Mark wanted to, but he knew the beautiful dreams waited, and he remembered how everything was easy and calm and how that illusion broke open when he came to his senses. And those senses didn't return all at once, either. They returned like pockets of terrifying clarity in a heavy fog of bliss. One moment he'd be relaxed and the next he'd remember that he was in a stranger's house and there had been a trial and that men might hang from the neck until dead if judgment was brought against them. He'd sink back into calm, half-fighting it, half-willing himself to drown in that peace again, and then surface into the knowledge that his actions would get back to Captain Shuller who might not let him back on *Dainty*. He might be trapped here, trapped in a jester's life with no patron, no lord master, no connections, and Gutter would come for him with a wrath Mark wasn't sure he could face.

Colonel Evan smoothed his fingers over Mark's bicep and gradually firmed his grip. Something about his touch grounded Mark somewhat, though his breath still rushed around so ragged he thought he'd tear apart inside.

"You need to take seven more doses of gracian or it will do you no good to have taken it at all." Colonel Evan spoke softly, though Mark suspected it was more due to the late hour than any consideration for Mark's nerves. "Given that you have to take those doses, there's no sense whatsoever in delaying to the point of withdrawal sickness."

"So this is what happens at the end of it."

"Yes."

"Does it get worse?"

"No. You're well into the worst of it. Trudy, measure out a spoonful."

"Yes, sir." She existed only as a kind face, the fall of her hair lit gold by candlelight, and graceful arms. Everything else was shadow pierced with those needles of light.

Mark drank in the honeyed evil and it fooled him all over again, and again. He dreamed up such poems and lyrics and music, but could never finish any of it. He couldn't even hold it in his mind enough to write it down, though the memory of its beauty haunted him. Sometimes dangerous thoughts came to him, wondering if he took a little more, or took it more often, if that power of lyric might not linger long enough for him to own it and repeat it for the world.

Colonel Evan visited him only to dose him, and then left him to Trudy's care. Mark had no idea how she managed to keep such a faithful watch over him without fading into exhaustion. She had to leave at times, probably while he slept, because she always had clean clothes and she didn't eat in the room. Twice, or perhaps more, she helped him to a bath filled with warm water scented by exotic blossoms and musk. The cook brought food and Trudy fed him biscuits scented of coconut and oranges and sweet hams and strange smoky meats full of fiery flavor that he could only soothe with what they called cool creams—chilled, milky drinks with hints of various fruit flavors. They served him fruits for which he had no name, and edible flowers some of which tasted like radishes and others like a thick, juicy lettuce and others like thin slices of beets, on and on, and fish with meats of such varying textures that some seemed like a form of rich porridge while others needed slicing like steak. Some of the white flesh opened into fans of firm flakes and some came apart in tender shreds like stew meat.

He felt stronger, but less sane, and he wondered if half of what he remembered of any given hour had really happened.

Colonel Evan came in one morning when it came time for Mark's next dose, but this time he drew a heavily padded chair from a corner of the room and sat. "You may have the remainder of today and all tomorrow off, Trudy," he said. "I will sit with the master jester from here on."

"Yes, sir. Thank you, sir." She curtsied and left.

Mark had already begun to feel uneasy as the gracian's effect had begun to ebb. "That was my last dose last night, wasn't it."

The colonel nodded.

"Good." Mark said it, and meant it, but he was afraid. Perhaps the colonel was here to help him through the withdrawal sickness, or maybe he'd come to offer Mark a chance to continue leading a life of ease ... with a price.

The colonel grew impatient after just a few minutes and stood to pace the room. Mark went to the window sill and settled to watch the ocean surge onto the rocks. The tide had changed.

Dainty.

Mark didn't want to call attention to Captain Shuller, but he feared that the ship would sail on without him, either out of necessity or with a purpose to avoid him, if he didn't send some sort of message.

She might have already left.

"I would like to see the docks again," Mark said. "If it's not too much trouble. I hardly saw anything of them before I was attacked."

"I would think you'd prefer to avoid them."

"Do you think I ought to? I have no idea how many there might be of the Morbai's Kiss or if they will try to avenge their men." He really didn't care what the answer might be. He felt a powerful urge to return to the sea.

"Where did you hear of the Morbai's Kiss?" Colonel Evan sounded alarmed enough to make Mark turn away from the sea for a glance. Colonel Evan averted his gaze and began pacing again. He picked up a book from a small collection on shelves primarily adorned with horse statues. A large painting of a wild white horse loomed beside him.

"Mr. Roadman told me a little about them."

"You're right to be nervous about them, but they aren't stupid. The man who led them to victory is a jester. They'll consult him before they do anything further. Whether he is inclined to dissuade them or not, now that your situation is public, his master will be forced to insist that no harm come to you from that quarter. I believe you're safe, at least for the moment."

His stomach shrank. A jester could easily get around a direct order if he wanted to. All the more reason to get off this island as soon as he could. "If you're sure I'm safe from them, I see no reason to avoid the docks."

"I don't think you'll be fit for travel, master jester."

He almost asked why he had to stop the gracian all at once, and if a small dose might not help things along. He didn't feel as if he craved it with any passion. It was a rational question, or so it seemed. The trouble was that he didn't trust himself to think rationally, anymore than he believed that gracian could help him create the finest music the world had ever heard. "Were there many gracian addicts created by the war?"

"More corpses than addicts, but yes. They usually don't live long. Once they start stealing and murdering to get themselves more gracian, we hang them." Colonel Evan paged through a book, his eyes flicking quickly from top to bottom on certain pages. "Only the wealthy manage to cling to life while enthralled to that mistress, and the jesters lay bets as to whether their health or their wealth will fail first. Health or wealth is a particularly cruel taunt that they began, and it has carried into the populace."

That implied that gracian was more expensive than he'd guessed.

He owed the money in that purse to the church in Cathret. Did he really intend to default without Gutter's protection?

The Church never forgave and never gave up.

"You'd better lie down and have some water."

"I'm all right." His thoughts had fallen into a dangerous well. Lord Argenwain could pay off the indenture with the wave of a pen, but it wasn't Lord Argenwain's to pay. It was Mark's. And if Gutter truly had burned *Mairi*, his crime went a small but important step beyond the scars he'd have on his soul for the horrific deaths inflicted on the crew and the destruction of a beautiful ship with many promising years left ahead of her.

If Gutter was found guilty of such a thing, not only would he owe the worth of the ship, but Lord Argenwain might feel duty-bound as a noble to have him executed. It would be a horrific thing in its own right, not just for Gutter, but for Lord Argenwain. They'd been bonded for more than four decades.

Am I willing to face the consequences should I discover that's the truth?

If he killed them, if Gutter killed my mother ....

While Mark had been lost in thought, the colonel had taken a pair of steps closer. "You're trembling. I've seen men fire pistols into their ears trying to escape the fearful things gracian told them would be worse than death. I don't expect that after this short time you would be that desperate. Nonetheless, I insist that you retire."

For the first time Mark noticed it was a considerable fall from the window to the rocks below.

"The fall wouldn't kill you," Colonel Evan told him.

"I don't want to die." Fear didn't course through him, but rage. He'd almost left it behind, soothed by *Dainty's* sweetness. Anger returned to him now with all the force of his grief behind it. Mark moved from the window. "What do you know about Lord Jester Gutter?"

Colonel Rohn Evan startled so hard that it opened his expression completely. Those eyes, far too youthful and unclouded to be a colonel's eyes, betrayed complete innocence. "Nothing that isn't common knowledge."

Damnit all. If Gutter had done all this, what was the benefit? Why destroy so much, and for what? "I need my bag. I have to show you something." Maybe the signet ring and the book would help connect things somehow.

"I intend to discuss the contents of your bag as well, but we'll wait until you're sober." The colonel returned his gaze to the book, but he clearly wasn't reading. He kept flipping pages, his gaze focused somewhere beyond the spine.

It sounded as if the colonel had already searched through Mark's bag. The only thing that tempered Mark's indignation was the seriousness of accusing a man of the colonel's importance of doing something so unseemly. "Did you find what you were looking for?" Mark asked tightly.

The colonel's cheeks flushed. "It is within my rights to treat you as a prisoner until I determine whether or not you're a threat to justice and liberty."

"And you're willing to stoop to something so low—"

"I'm grateful that you naturally attribute noble qualities to me that I may not possess."

"I take it you don't require a jester because you're perfectly willing to do anything you deem necessary yourself."

"That is precisely the reason I despise anything having to do with jesters. It is a false removal of responsibility. But I will not be accused of wrongdoing in this matter. You may consider it a sin to rifle a potential spy's effects, but I read no such thing—"

"So you do hold to some standard, whichever one is most convenient to your purposes." Their mingled tempers intoxicated all of Mark's senses. He drank it in with more relish than gracian. The color in the colonel's face held more vivid ecstasy than a masterwork painting, and his voice inspired shivers more profound than any music he'd heard.

"You don't flinch from my accusation, I see," the colonel growled.

"That I'm a spy? Spying on what? That fleet of warships in the bay can be counted by any sailor coming and going from the docks, and with a better-trained eye."

"I will not be lured into defining a target for you."

"I am only delivering a message. Please, colonel." That came out slightly less polite than a curse. "Allow me to dispatch my errand so I can quit this room, quit this house and quit you." Of course now he wanted to do anything but quit the colonel. He'd never felt so alive or filled with power as he did at this very moment. His body began to shiver violently, but inside he felt as straight and tall and proud as Prathador Castle.

Baron Evan stood proudly too, gradually composing himself until his face cooled and his hands relaxed. He softly closed the book and set it aside. All that time while his temper had raged, he'd held the book gently open in his hand.

Was his anger an act, or did he really possess that much control? Either way he'd be a deadly opponent.

"Tomorrow," the colonel told him. "If you're strong enough."

Mark glanced toward the hated bed. He started to feel heavy and miserable and lightheaded but he'd been in bed so long he couldn't stand it anymore. He managed to make his way over to it and pulled the quilt with him to a stuffed chair. "May I have a book to read?"

"Do you have a preference as to subject?"

Would the colonel allow it? "Sacred poetry."

"I have none here and I won't leave you to fetch it."

Mark marveled a bit that the man appeared to have no servants at the moment. "What are my options?"

"Vale, Sutter, Olmsby, Mullerman ..." All poetry. "Two books on botany, one of which my father wrote." Probably instructive but dull. "The Night of Swords." The colonel touched the spine of the book he'd been paging through. Mark had that account of a particularly nightmarish caucus all but memorized.

The colonel dropped his hand and looked at Mark expectantly.

"There's one more on the shelf," Mark said.

"You wouldn't be interested." The colonel spoke a little too quickly.

"You desperately need a jester." He might be a fine military man, but he had no social ability. He should have known that such a statement would only make Mark more curious.

"I suppose you plan to volunteer."

"No. I just want a book to read and all you did was make me more curious about the one that's left. As if anything on that shelf could be more dull than botany."

The colonel's neck stiffened. "I'm rather fond of botany."

"What you're more likely fond of is a connection to your father's interests and what his notes reveal about the inner workings of his mind. May I please see the book?"

"It's personal."

Mark laughed. "It is not! It's probably something embarrassing like a tawdry romance."

The colonel blushed.

"It is! It's a romance." The hilarity of it helped distract him from the increasingly insistent tremors radiating out from his belly. "Let me see it. Please."

The colonel snatched it off the shelf and stalked over. Mark pulled it from the colonel's reluctant grip, opened the fanciful but wordless cover and read the title aloud.

"The HandMaiden's Cup: A novel of forbidden love. I've heard of books like this but I haven't read one before." He decided not to admit that he'd read the other sort to Lord Argenwain—men romping and conquering everything with two legs, and sometimes more. Lord Argenwain's favorite, and Mark's, was Barry's Barnyard Scandals. It was truly awful but wonderful at the same time, more of a comedy than erotica.

The colonel moved to take it away. Mark clutched it to his chest. "You've had your fun. That's enough," the colonel said.

"You think I'm teasing you, but I really want it. Some of these books are ridiculous. But this looks interesting." He glanced over the first page. "The prose is clean and direct, but not too spare. Do you mind?"

"Of course I mind."

"I've noticed you haven't tried to foist blame onto Miss Trudy or a woman friend."

The colonel scowled. "The book is mine."

"A gift, I'm guessing?"

"Stop it." The colonel didn't sound angry. Was that grief?

He'd taken his curiosity to softer places than he'd intended, and touched something very private. "I'm sorry. Please. May I read it?"

The colonel walked away, took up one of the other books, and settled down to read. Mark did his best to focus on the words on the first page.

Marielle first saw him from an upper window while she waited to hear if she would be forced to visit Duke Amsbury that night ....

"They forced themselves upon each other with savage desire," Colonel Evan read while Mark could barely draw in one breath after another. "But then Thomas gathered her close and kissed her. Her body deepened against him and they became one being, no longer alone or afraid. They moved like waves, not against each other but like love traveling through liquid joy."

Mark gripped the colonel's wrist. "Read that again."

The colonel smiled gently. "I'll read the entire passage, and then we'll go back and read it again if you're still inclined."

Something sharp cut through Mark from throat to belly and his body cramped around it. The pain didn't let him breathe, only writhe. He held on to the colonel's wrist, terrified to let go.

The pain ebbed away and Mark lay limp in the sweaty bed. The spasms were getting worse.

The colonel moved the ribbon marker into place and closed the book. "I think it's time. Dr. Berto told me if you appeared to be in danger, I should give you a quarter dose."

"No."

"I insist."

"I would rather die." It frightened him, but he refused to go back even one step. "I want to be done, one way or another. So please. Read to me."

"This is damned foolish. There's no need to endanger your life in this way."

"Yes there is. You don't understand."

"Then explain it to me."

"How can I explain years of yielding because it was easy, or wise, or necessary? I can't describe to you how it is to trust someone you know is using you, and making yourself blind to the shame and disgrace of it. I have to say no again and again until ...." He couldn't describe a state of being that his heart wanted more than anything, but for which he had no name.

"Until you're free." Those dark words seemed full of understanding and knowledge beyond Mark's own. "Not because someone released you, but because you fought, and you won." The colonel sat very still and very near, his dark suit and dark hair a blur against his olive-toned skin and the shadows of his dark brows and dark eyes.

Yes.

The colonel sat back and Mark's hand slipped from his wrist. "But then Thomas gathered her close and kissed her. Her body deepened upon him and they became one being, no longer alone or afraid. They moved like waves, not against each other but like love traveling through liquid joy ...."

Chapter Fifteen

Mark sat unsteadily at Colonel Evan's breakfast table in a large sunroom by himself the next morning. His head kept floating away and fine tremors still shivered through him, but he felt more sober than he had in a long time. Bright sunlight passed through a double-dozen tall, narrow window panes to light the cream and pale blue room, making it airy and pleasantly warm without overheating. Heavy white shutters waited by to seal out the afternoon heat without closing off the light.

He wondered if he'd dreamt the colonel reading to him late last night.

He'd seen the cook, briefly. The elderly, long-haired gentleman dusted in flour had brought him some fresh bread, butter and jam and left without saying a word.

Mark picked at his food. The cook brought in an opaque orange liquid. Mark sipped. Orange juice? He'd had oranges. Argenwain could afford them on a fairly regular basis, but it had been a long time. He liked them well enough, but this was the most delicious thing he'd ever tasted in his life.

The cook also left a small plate of thinly-sliced ham. The ham on bread with the juice ... what the captain had said about fresh food came back to mind.

But to sail ....

And selfishly risk *Dainty* because he'd fled his indenture. She traded between the mainland and the islands.

The Church will never give me up.

Unless he paid that indenture off somehow.

Never sell the masks, Gutter had told him, but Mark contemplated just that while he ate, barely pausing to catch a breath between hungry mouthfuls. Assuming it was possible, if any jesters heard of it, they might shun him. He didn't care if they did. Unless Gutter had a friend here he wouldn't hear of it, and he was the only jester whose opinion mattered to Mark one bit.

"Good morning." Colonel Evan wore matched slate clothing with a white, sparsely ruffled shirt and cravat, again with a matching hair ribbon. Was it style or a lack of imagination?

Mark had to take a moment to swallow. "Good morning. I wasn't sure you were coming, so I started without you." His hands shook and his wounds had begun to wake up from the gracian, but at least his hunger had eased. He couldn't remember the last time he'd had an actual meal.

Trudy came in carrying the bag and Mark's body tightened up so much he regretted drinking all that juice. She set it on the table at Mark's elbow and left.

The bag had become an ugly, battered thing, and not just because it had been dragged through snow.

"You sailed in on *Dainty*," Colonel Evan said. "Her captain and I had a few words, and he sent over some of your effects. Clothing, cloaks, shaving kit, et cetera." He sounded cold and annoyed.

"Thank you."

"There are two sets of colors. From two dead jesters, is my understanding. And two masks."

Telling him that one of the masks belonged to him wouldn't make things look any better.

"You've fled an indenture, according to Captain Shuller. An indentured jester. I've never heard of such a thing."

Mark was very tempted to embrace whatever assumption the colonel might make about him. He had no way of knowing whether his training had been a real jester's training anyway, and the letter could have been forged. He had no idea why Gutter would forge the letter when a letter of recommendation by his own hand could have served, but he might have.

"You're very quiet, Mr. Seaton. If that's your actual name."

"You want the truth? I'm only here to deliver a message."

Colonel Evan gave him a dark look. "Then deliver it."

Mark opened the bag. It took him a bit to find the book and the ring among the neatly-organized things, only because they'd been placed at the bottom when the colonel had repacked his bag. He stood up from his chair and moved to the table's side so he could place them within the baron's reach. "These are for you."

Nothing happened for several heartbeats. Finally the colonel picked up the code book and flipped through it. "I'm waiting."

"That's all I have. Obsidian, the jester who'd meant to bring these things to you, was killed retrieving the signet ring. I don't know if he knew any more than I do. I had hoped, actually, that you would have something for me."

The colonel impatiently tossed the code book onto the table with no indication that he cared that people had died because of it. "And what might that be?"

What he'd gathered of the colonel's reputation and what he'd seen of the man so far was compelling, but that alone wouldn't have convinced Mark to tell him anything. The cold truth was that Mark had no one else he could trust except for Gutter, and Obsidian had already begged Mark to avoid Gutter in this matter. He had to rely on a dead man's words, not just in the matter of the code book and ring, but in regard to Gutter, *Mairi*, Mark's parents ... all the mysteries that had brought him here. "I hope you'll forgive me if I ramble. There's no easy way to present all I know and suspect."

Mark began with Obsidian's arrival and the strange, urgent requests he made. He had to backtrack to explain about his indenture, and Gutter, and *Mairi*, and his mother's murder and his father's disappearance. He stood on shaky legs, feeling unnaturally calm as he related details of events that had sent him into fits of rage and grief only a very short time ago.

"I'm sorry," Mark concluded, "that I don't know anything more about this. I wish I did."

The colonel braced against one hand on the table, his fingers steepled over the surface. His other hand came to rest on his hip where a pistol would usually hang.

Mark tried to read the colonel's expression, but he couldn't detect anything beyond a deep and dark concentration. A seasoned soldier, a hero if what he'd seen so far was true, could condemn Mark to death without a flicker of emotion. Mark's heartbeats shortened and huddled together. He managed to stand straight, but only just. Without his story to carry him, his legs once more threatened to buckle under him.

At last the colonel straightened up. "Have a seat." The colonel didn't look at him as he passed by to the cook's door. "Norbert, I'll have my usual breakfast."

"Very good, sir."

The colonel settled at the table's end opposite Mark. "Your story confirms my suspicions."

At last.

"I learned at church that you claimed that you carried a message, and Captain Shuller also mentioned that you had an important message to deliver. He told me that you seemed like an honest and gentle-spirited young man caught in a very dangerous game. The captain spent quite a bit of time with you—somewhere about three or four weeks I gather—"

Mark nodded.

"—and he has a reputation as a capable and honorable man. On the islands, there is no higher compliment. He wondered if there might still be hope in employing you on his ship."

Mark's heart leapt.

"But from what you've told me, that would put Captain Shuller at great risk, a risk he shouldn't have to take. He has his share of runaways and defaulters on his ship. They're from a different time and different circumstances. Prize money has freed them from their continental requirements.

"There is no prize money to win these days." The colonel paused as Norbert brought in a sliced orange, orange juice, toasted bread and mustard drizzled over a hard-boiled egg chopped with ham.

Something about the colonel's tone calmed him, though he knew he had no reason to believe that he'd avoid arrest, deportation, or even summary execution as a spy. He felt hollow, and shaky. If he had a touch of gracian, just to ease his body enough so that he could think—

No, gracian wouldn't ease the real source of his pain.

He'd lost *Dainty*. He should have given up all thought of her by himself, and he'd been working his way in that direction anyway, but the colonel had essentially forbidden him from returning to her. Mark grasped at the possibility of getting a recommendation for another vessel that didn't traffic with the mainland, but it seemed unlikely anyone would take him after he'd killed two islanders and stood in court as a jester.

"No comment, master jester?"

Mark's head jerked up. "I—I'm not sure I can claim—"

"I am. Let me ask you this. What was the name of the judge who presided over the murder case where you sat as witness?"

"Judge Wellman."

"What is his natural hair color?"

Mark thought back to his eyebrows and the amber eyes and perhaps the slightest wisp at his ear that hadn't been covered by his wig. "A light brown."

"What color are the horses that draw my carriage?"

"You have a blood bay and a black." He saw where this was going. "Yes, I have a good memory."

"An exquisite memory. You notice details and retain them with uncanny clarity, despite the fact that you were very ill. What is the female jester's name?"

"I don't know."

The colonel smiled. "I thought you might have overheard it. She's often spoken of. Still, I don't feel my point is disproved. You have enough mathematics to attract employment to a line of work notorious for its difficult calculations. Your comment about botany gave away your studies in natural science. I'm sure the arts and history have been included in your education. You're very well groomed, polite, deferential, but not weak. And your character is forged well beyond the strength of steel. I've weathered gracian withdrawals myself. I would have been proud to acquit myself as well as you did when I offered you that quarter dose. Though I maintain you still chose foolishly."

Too many compliments with too much purpose. "Why are you saying these things to me?"

"I've rebuffed hundreds of offers." The colonel stood and wiped his mouth. "Letters, elaborate personal presentations and introductions, recommendations, invitations from the finest schools in the world. They came flooding in after the war made us a nation, and made me the son of Perida's governor. I refused because I believe a nobleman should have no need for a jester. If there is unpleasant work to be done, he should do it himself in as lawful and noble manner as possible."

Mark felt like he'd floated partway out of his own body. He wanted to stop the colonel before either of them said something stupid, but his mouth wouldn't work.

"The result, however, is that I have few allies and no political influence. I never thought I'd want any influence, but ... this." He picked up the little code book. "This is yet another sign of danger."

"War?" The word rasped out. Obsidian had feared war.

"War would be the preferable outcome, Lark."

Lark.

The jester's named invoked with the colonel's voice changed something inside Mark. His last shreds of freedom bled away, and in its place something new and heavy took its place, heavy but strong.

He didn't want it, but he realized that he could use it. Even if he'd sailed away on *Dainty*, he couldn't run away from Gutter and the church forever. But if he unraveled the secrets ... *Mairi's* loss, his parents, Obsidian's death, the book, the signet ring, everything ....

He could win his life back, but only as a jester. Only a jester could settle all those accounts with justice.

If Gutter wanted Lark, he'd have him, but on Mark's terms, under a lord and master's eternal protection. If Mark bonded his soul with this man, Gutter could never force him on whatever path he'd chosen.

No doubt he'd intended to bind Mark's soul to someone steeped in something terrible ....

Apparently the colonel had been lost in thought as well. When he spoke again, he kept his gaze low, emphasizing his long lashes. "I think Cathret is poised to retake the islands, and they won't need to send ships and soldiers this time. Vyenne, Hasla and Osia would give it a try if they thought they had a chance. I've been helpless. Servants and former soldiers, no matter how clever or brave, are ill-equipped to help me discover and counter whatever plots might be unfolding. Our government is young, fragile and untested. I don't think we'll survive an orchestrated political attack unless all of us who truly believe in freedom rally together. To discover who my true allies are, and join them against our enemies, I need a jester."

He did need a jester. The islands, to maintain their freedom, needed the famed colonel at his full powers.

Hells. Obsidian ... was Obsidian going to offer himself to the colonel? Was that why he didn't want Gutter to know that he had the book and the ring? Were they proof of something, or tools that the colonel would need to arm himself?

Did Obsidian mean to offer to me in his place if he died?

He'd never know. He could only decide for himself.

Mark stood as straight as he could, took a deep breath, and closed his eyes. *Father, forgive me.* "I accept."

Dressed in his best clothes, Mark used a borrowed cane to help him limp the length of the dock where *Dainty* was berthed. Clean-shaven, his hair not only brushed but curled, white gloves on his hands and bows covering the buckles on his shoes, lace starched to a bright white, he eventually made his way to her gangplank and waited for someone to notice him.

Mr. Johns saw him first, and looked away but not in time to hide a roll in his eyes. He turned back with a smile. "May I—" And then his eyes widened. "Mark? Or should I say, master jester!"

Mark smiled and climbed the plank, careful not to catch his heels on the strips of wood in the center. The slightest misstep and he'd be rolling down the plank in agony. "Mr. Johns." He gripped hard when Johns offered to shake hands. "It's good to see you." His arm wound had already begun to burn, but the pain was worth it to see Johns again.

"Captain Shuller is ashore."

"Oh." He tried not to let his smile fade.

"But come aboard! He's expected later this evening. You're just in time. We expect to leave tomorrow early. The hold is full and most everything is in order—"

"Mr. Johns." Mark hadn't expected anyone to be so happy to see him and it hurt him more than he'd braced for.

"I heard about the ambush. Four on one. It was in the papers and everything. I had, none of us had any idea. I could tell you were a sharp one, but—"

"Mr. Johns, I have business I have to attend to, so I can't stay." Colonel Evan might or might not be watching him, but Mark felt the pressure of his stare like a heavy hand ready to pull him back to his future master's elbow.

Mark wanted to remove a hat to show added respect to the first mate, but he didn't have one yet. The one he owned was in no shape to wear except as a joke.

I don't know what's in worse shape—my hat or my body.

"Are you all right?" Johns asked. "You look awfully pale."

"I'm fine, thank you. I just wanted to tell the captain, and you of course, that I won't be joining you."

Mr. Johns let out a short laugh. "We figured as much, but the captain had his hopes up. He was sure you'd decided to leave the life for ho—that is, more simple work."

"You can say honest. I won't be offended." He'd never seen Johns, who'd been reserved toward him, so openly friendly. Maybe he was just expressing his relief that Mark wouldn't come with them, being polite and kind now that he knew he wouldn't be saddled with Mark's presence. "And I had set my mind to it, but I—I can't."

"Why, master jester, don't tell me you're sorry we'll be sailing without you. I'm ashamed at what we all served you, and some of the things we'd said and done when you came aboard. I really mean it. Anyway you know you'll always be welcome."

"I'll miss you, but you shouldn't miss me. I could have brought you trouble, and I still might, so be careful if you return to Reffiel or go to Seven Churches by the Sea."

"I'll tell the captain if you're not able to warn him yourself. We're obliged. Me especially; I'm doubly obliged. For Mr. Roadman, master jester sir."

"What about Mr. Roadman?"

"He's my very good friend from before the war," Johns cried as if it was obvious. "Half the crew knows him. He's ... well, you know, the war. He hasn't really been himself since. Lost most of his family: both parents, his uncle, his brother, sister and three cousins. His aunts and cousins on his mother's side still give care to him I hear. Anyways, I knew him when we were fishermen. He still fishes, but the rest of us, we sought our fortunes on traders. I figured, since I learned the ropes, why not? But I couldn't convince him. He swore he'd never sail again. In fact, halfway through he transferred from the navy to the army. Fought under Colonel Rohn Evan himself. Never got no rank, but I've heard it said it was 'cause he turned it down."

"I had no idea."

"He's not much of a talker, not anymore."

Mark offered his hand and Johns shook it. "I really must go," Mark told him. He couldn't keep the colonel waiting, and he wasn't sure how much longer he could stay on his feet. "It may be that I might make it here again tonight, but I doubt it."

"Business." Johns nodded. "I'll let the captain know." He grinned, his teeth very bright against his dark skin. "Please come to dinner. It'll be roast pork, gooeymup and pineapple for the whole crew. A real treat. The cook's ashore minding the pit now. If you haven't had roast pork done the island way, master jester, you're missing something wonderful. Even the high horsemen are mad for it."

"Could I bring a friend or two?" Maybe if he invited the colonel and Mr. Roadman ...

"Hells yes."

"I'll do my best." Mark gave him a short bow, which made Mr. Johns blush, and limped down the center of the plank. Part of him was relieved to be away from the barrage of words and emotions and everything else. The other part got smaller and colder the farther he got from *Dainty*.

Mark stopped beside the colonel on the unimaginatively named Bay Street that curved along the docks. Their carriage waited across the way. As much as he longed to run back and sail away on *Dainty*, something about standing with the colonel felt natural and surprisingly good.

"You've said your goodbyes?" By the sound of his voice, time hadn't tempered the colonel's annoyance at what he no doubt considered a waste of time.

"We've been invited to dinner. Roast pork, pineapple, and gooeymup, whatever that is, done island-style in a pit."

The colonel paused as if he was actually considering it. "I think we ought to spend the evening at Hevether discussing our options."

"We're going to be bound for life. Marriages get a reception. Shouldn't we?"

"I've been told that traditionally we're to gather with our own kind for an evening of toasts, if the couple is so inclined," the colonel said dryly. "Either option is unwise. Your condition is too delicate."

A laugh burst past Mark's pain and bubbled out, washing away his sadness. "Am I your dainty little bride?"

"That's enough." He headed for the carriage.

Mark would have pressed it except that, much as he appeared to be irritated, the colonel seemed amused and it wouldn't do to spoil his humor now.

Something else suggested he let the moment pass.

If Gutter had asked, Mark would have told him he saw grief in the colonel's eyes just before he turned away.

Chapter Sixteen

As they rode the carriage toward the church, Mark's mind spun in circles. He'd teased the colonel about this amounting to a wedding, but in many ways it was far more serious a matter, assuming a person really believed in an afterlife, *allolai* and *morbai*. A marriage was a lifetime contract involving property and presumed offspring. A bonding wedded two souls not just in life but after death.

Mark had read a great deal of history, and he knew that on rare occasions bonding ceremonies proved fatal to one or both people. The most cynical part of him wondered if it wasn't murder arranged by the church that used superstition and mysticism to cover the crime. The part of him that believed as his father did, and sometimes heard voices in languages he couldn't recognize, the part that saw a practical ship's captain baldly declare that his ship called to runaway indentured servants and made them tell truths ... and Mark had spoken truths against his own best interest for no rational reason ....

He started to chew his lip and managed to stop himself. It was a childhood habit he'd long gotten rid of. It didn't do his nerves any good to have that habit resurface now.

Marriage negotiations often lasted months. Bonding negotiations commonly dragged on for a year or more. Sometimes they began while a jester was still in university, especially if he showed particular promise. Most of the time, though, jesters would court several potential masters in the best political and fiscal situations they dared to try, hoping that one would find them suitable.

And here I am, not just fleeing indenture and throwing away whatever plans Gutter had put in place for me without even knowing what they are, but jumping into bed with the first man who draws back the sheets for me.

What would happen ... should he tell the colonel that he was a staghorn, or hope that the matter straightened out? Maybe the colonel would either not notice or care. After all, unless Mark made a particularly unwise choice of bedfellows public, the matter shouldn't affect anything. Jesters weren't generally held to any moral standard at all.

He'd been on a ship full of men and not one had given him so much as a flirtatious glance. Men of his slant might be even more rare a bird than he'd feared. The matter might very well never come up simply because he'd have no one with which to be scandalous.

And was it really a sin? Not that it ought to matter if a jester was sinful or not. By definition of a jester's role, he was hired to sin.

But the colonel wanted Mark because Mark was different than other jesters, and he assumed that they would act in a noble and honorable fashion together.

You have no idea how different I am.

The colonel was different too. Mark had met many nobles over the years, all vying for either Lord Argenwain's favor, or Gutter's, or both. The two men carried His Royal Majesty King Michael's highest favor, even now during Lord Argenwain's decline. The colonel seemed more pure, somehow, than any or all of them. And when he'd read to Mark, and held his hand, and helped him sit on the chamberpot and all those things, his touch, and the way he'd read to Mark ....

If Gutter asked, Mark would have told him that the colonel might have looked at Mark in a way that made Mark notice his long, dark lashes, and right afterward the colonel's gaze had hardened into a well-practiced self-denial.

Whatever Mark thought he saw hidden behind those lashes might have contributed to this rash haste that hurled them both to church.

The colonel fidgeted in his seat. It made him seem younger and revealed an endearing insecurity.

"Are you having second thoughts?" Mark asked.

"Of course I am."

Mark started to chew his lip again and made himself stop.

"I would have never done something like this before the war," the colonel told him.

"But the war taught you that it's more important to make a decision and act on it quickly than to dither and try to find the right decision." He'd learned that from history.

The colonel nodded. "Because the right decision might not exist."

"I wouldn't go that far." Mark tried a smile.

The colonel played a hand up and down his coat collar. "In war you learn to sacrifice."

"So this is a sacrifice." That made Mark feel even more uneasy.

"We won't know until it's too late." The colonel's hand drifted down to his buttons as he gazed out at the trees and blooming shrubs and couples walking with their children dawdling behind.

"That sounds like another war lesson."

The colonel nodded. He was fidgeting with a button and the poor threads were starting to stretch.

Mark pulled his hand away. "Stop it."

A flash of anger lit the colonel's eyes, helped by a beam of sunlight that managed to clear the park trees. Mark smiled again, trying to hide his fear and awe of the man. The colonel ducked his head and closed his eyes, breathing with too-deliberate a pace.

"You can still change your mind," Mark told him.

"So can you."

Mark laughed softly through his nose. "I know. But I think I'd regret it for the rest of my life. I've caught the man who turned away over a hundred offers. What a fool I'd be to reject him, especially since he helped save my life."

"Don't tease me. I'm well aware that this may be an elaborate trap."

"You're joking." It wasn't funny. It was terrifying.

"I flatter myself by it. The world's most famous jester would find no advantage in pairing me with his creature. I'm already helpless."

"Looking at it from that perspective, you're right. It doesn't work." Mark hesitated. "There is no way that Gutter could have predicted ...."

"What?"

"It's a little insane."

Colonel Evan gripped his arm. "What."

Mark tried to twist free but it only hurt more. "You're going to tear the sutures."

The colonel eased his hold but he didn't let go.

Mark's mind still had a few more calculations to make. "Gutter would have had to make sure Obsidian wouldn't come to him directly with the message. That could be done easily enough. Ensuring he would come to me ... harder, but possible." He spoke softly, so softly he wasn't sure the baron could hear him. It didn't matter if he did. "Arranging for Obsidian to come to me that day would have relied on Gutter or his agent encouraging Lake to act within a narrow period of time. Still possible. It's all possible. There are major weak points. Gutter couldn't just manipulate Obsidian into coming to me. Obsidian had to ask me to make the delivery in his place, and then I had to deliver it successfully."

"I'm not sure I follow."

"Gutter may have directed Obsidian, or he may have manipulated Obsidian. The end result is the same, though I find it unlikely that Obsidian would involve himself in a plan where he'd die. But if Obsidian wasn't a knowing participant in the plan, it's less likely that Gutter could have arranged everything to turn out the way it did. And there's another weakness. One person would have to know both of us well enough to predict that we would jump in together. Obsidian doesn't know me that well."

"It does seem far-fetched that such a person exists."

"Extremely," Mark agreed.

"The few men who know me well would not believe I would ask you to be my jester." The colonel smoothed his hand over his waistcoat. "But you're nervous."

Mark nodded. "Gutter sometimes travels in disguise."

The colonel shook his head. "I haven't made a close friendship since the war, and before the war, I wasn't important."

"I'm somewhat reassured." Mark resisted chewing his lip.

"It must have been very strange growing up in a household with someone so famously intelligent, cunning and ruthless."

"Stranger to love him," Mark murmured. "To worship him, and then suspect that he destroyed everything I loved so that I had nothing left but him. And it terrifies me that *Mairi's* loss may have been my fault. It may not have happened because of a grand, well-considered and long-planned calculation. I fear I may have caused him to burn with rage." Perhaps even a jealous rage.

"You argued?"

"No. But—he flinched." It was impossible to explain the significance of such a slight gesture to someone who didn't know Gutter. "I've never seen him flinch before," Mark added. "Not that I can remember anyway."

"If you don't remember it, it didn't happen."

"No." Mark spoke more sharply than he meant to. He tried to soften his voice. "Don't ever have that kind of faith in me. My memory isn't perfect. It's trained. There's an important difference. I do, and will make mistakes, and I won't see or remember things that may turn out to be critical. If we're going to work as partners, you can't—" He couldn't put it into words.

"I understand. But I will expect a great deal from you, and I will depend on what you tell me."

"I'll try not to disappoint you."

"Why?"

That one word had countless facets, and Mark couldn't begin to answer any of them. The colonel had revealed his true cleverness by asking it, and that was part of one answer. "I didn't want to be a cold, political monstrosity. But I used to be jealous of what Lord Argenwain and Gutter had. And now it's clear. Becoming a lord's jester is like falling in love. It's like meeting someone and in an hour knowing you'll be friends for the rest of your lives. I could walk away from this, and so could you, but it wouldn't change what we feel."

"You presume much."

"Am I wrong?"

The colonel's lashes lowered, but it didn't hide the pain there. "No. You're not wrong."

What had hurt him so badly?

Passers-by had collected into small groups on the sidewalk in front of the church to gawk. Colonel Evan ran his hand over his rapier—they had to leave their weapons in the carriage because apparently the ceremony forbade weapons. Mark wasn't used to wearing a rapier every time he went out into public, but he felt a little qualm too that Obsidian's blade might be stolen while they were inside. It had helped keep him alive that day near the docks, and he wanted it close-at-hand.

Colonel Evan climbed out first while the driver, Philip, stood by doing a fair job of looking dressy and formal despite being a former pig farmer and common soldier. Philip offered a hand and Mark took it when he stepped down. It made him look weak, but he was weak at the moment and it looked less ridiculous than crying out in pain and falling on his face.

Perida Church wasn't as grand as the church near Argenwain's manor, but it was still a thing of great beauty. Apparently they couldn't find or ship in enough white stone, so they employed a pale gray stone streaked and bubbled with red and white. The lantern at the top of the dome was the purest white marble, as were some of the rails. They were no doubt imported at great expense. She had only two galleries arrayed from the central edifice, but two arcades bending off the galleries enclosed a vast courtyard with lemon and orange trees and blossoming vines throughout. The garden's architecture rivaled that of any building Mark had seen in grace and beauty.

As they crossed the courtyard, a strange bird let out a cry like music bubbling underwater and flew across the courtyard in front of them. It had an ungainly tail shaped like a lyre and flashed with gem-like sapphire, gold and ruby tones, a remarkable display that surely no hawk or owl could ever miss.

"They're sacred." Colonel Evan had hidden himself behind his implacable and controlled exterior. "It's worth a man's life if he shoots one, and I won't protect you if you do."

"I wouldn't want to." Mark wished they would halt a moment but the colonel kept walking. He wondered if the pain from his leg wound would get much worse than this. He hoped not. His arm had started to gnaw at him too.

"They're a nuisance, actually. But by protecting them in this way, only their shed feathers can be gathered, increasing their value. A single tail feather will sell for twenty ar or more—a great economic boon for the island and its people. I will protect anything that helps the islands survive, sacred or no, including those infernal feathered vermin."

Mark chuckled. "I think Lord Argenwain has a spray of those feathers in one of his hats."

Colonel Evan sniffed and held himself proudly, as if his vanity was any less than the ancient peacock's. "I have no doubt of it."

"Why do you hate them so much?"

"Come spring you'll know."

They entered the building, and Mark stepped inside a church for the first time in his life. His gaze immediately flew upward to smooth ribs that graced the ceiling. Rafters formed a fan pattern at each corner whose intersections made complex geometric coffers. The center opened into a domed painting of glass and gilding and tile. Even the colonel stopped to gaze upward for a moment before he left Mark behind to stride across the entry toward an older gentleman and his even older jester companion. Aside from a young priest sweeping the vast floor, they were the only people in the room.

"General," the colonel said formally, extending his hand. The men shook warmly. "Jog." He only nodded to the jester, who smiled and nodded back.

Mark limped over to join them. They waited patiently in silence until he got there. Mark bowed.

"This is Lark." Colonel Evan sounded pensive. "Lark, this is my very good friend General Amery Glassfield."

The general nodded politely and offered his hand, so Mark shook, first with him and then with his firm-handed jester. "He's short. I think my wife is taller. How tall are you?"

Colonel Evan's cheeks flushed, but Mark didn't mind. "Five foot six, sir. And, before you ask, I'm nearly twenty."

"In three or four years?"

"Less than a year, on the 26th of Brusque, sir." Mark offered a smile, and the general smiled back. Mark dared venture a look at Jog. The jester didn't seem extraordinary. He wore a modern set of colors—mostly navy, with hints of a little of everything and not a lot of anything else. In Seven Churches and among the higher-ranked jesters, old and highly visible heraldic selections were preferred, but those color combinations were also jealousy hoarded using social rules and traditional conventions so that it required quite a bit of maneuvering to wear, for example blue, black and white in nearly equal proportions.

Jog kept his leather mask, dyed navy and decorated with a beautiful feathery pattern in white with hints of many other colors, in his pocket. The only paint he wore circled his eyes, lines of black interspersed with white and navy feathers and whorls. He had a matching sword, but the hilt was very worn and the decorated sheath battered by hard use. He had a scar on the back of his hand.

Mark measured that all in a moment, and he wished he had time to take in more but he didn't want the conversation to pause too long. "But I'm still young in my heart."

Jog chuckled at that. "So you two are determined. I know it seems like forever, but perhaps you might wait until tomorrow, so that we may discuss this. Perhaps over dinner?"

"Have you told your father?" the general added.

"If either of you have qualms about seconding—" Colonel Evan began.

"No. Of course not," the general told him broadly. Jog cast him a not-very-subtle look, and the general yielded to him.

"Why now?" Jog asked. "If there's a matter of urgency, let us help you. There's no need to rush into something that ought not to be rushed, and for good reason. At least live with the fellow a while."

"Thank you, but the help I require is a matter of insufficient service, not any given task. And I see no reason to delay when I know I will not change my mind in six months or ten years." Colonel Evan lifted his chin, his expression so sure and firm that he looked like an entirely different person than the one who'd nearly torn a button from his sleeve in the carriage earlier.

Mark was proud of him, as if he had any right of pride in this situation.

"Your father." Jog left the two words hanging.

The colonel refused to acknowledge the words.

"If I disgrace the colonel he can just chop my head off and get someone else," Mark reminded them.

Jog recoiled in shock. Even the colonel looked surprised, as if it was never done.

"Well it's true. And he won't be any worse off than he was on his own. I'm well-connected, though some may consider that more of a problem than a virtue, myself especially. I'm young, I learn quickly, I don't think too much of myself, and I trust him." He hadn't thought of it much before, but the strength of commitment jesters made in these bargains, not just after death but in life, seemed unfair. No chopping off of heads for lords who shame their jesters.

"And I trust him," the colonel said.

Mark tried not to preen at the praise.

The general and Jog exchanged looks. "I've used my influence to convince Dellai Bertram to perform the ceremony."

"Thank you." The colonel closed his eyes, took a deep breath, and let it out slowly. "I'm ready."

"Jog," the general said.

Jog nodded. "I'll fetch the dellai." The jester left the church, presumably to go next door to the court.

A dellai. He would be head of the Church of Meridua. Mark wondered if the man was recognized on the mainland as a dellai, not that it mattered. He had real power here, and he could end all chances of their bonding if he wanted.

Which might be a relief.

No. We're doing this, Gutter, generals, plots and dellai be damned.

Like the colonel said, this might be a sacrifice …

It would be worth it, if he could find justice for his parents, keep the islands free, keep people like Grant safe, and do things that mattered.

And admit it: deny Gutter, escape Lord Argenwain and spit in the face of mainland politics.

Not just deny Gutter, but punish him if for no other reason than because he bought an innocent boy lost in grief and put his small hand into the hands of a man like Argenwain.

He didn't dodge his emotions about it this time. He accepted them. Suspicions and fears aside, he'd finally distanced himself enough from Gutter's charm and grace and everything else to really feel angry at him.

It felt good to be angry at him. Gutter hadn't done anything wrong by introducing Mark into Lord Argenwain's household, at least according to church law, but Mark had suffered and he knew Gutter had been morally wrong to do it.

The general finally addressed Mark. "Has the colonel introduced you to his father?"

"Not yet," Colonel Evan answered for him. "After the ceremony we plan to visit my father."

We do?

"And then we've been invited to a celebratory dinner. Private, I'm afraid."

We have?

Did he just lie to his friend or decide that we're actually going to have some fun tonight?

"Excellent. I'd feared you would retreat into your fortress and begin outlining your strategy for an assault on island society. I hope you will allow me to arrange something for tomorrow," the general said. "Mostly military, of course, your old friends from the war. We never see you anymore."

"I would be delighted." The colonel looked sincerely pleased.

"Be prepared for a great many more invitations, of course. We'll do something of a brunch in anticipation of a dinner invitation from the mayor. Now, don't give me that look. Your jester will support me in this."

Mark nodded. Assuming the mayor, or rather his jesteress, arranged something, they would have to go. It would be Mark's first and best look at what they would be dealing with. "We'll talk," Mark promised both of them.

Lark hadn't even officially debuted here.

That's what comes from rushing.

"Do you have any advice?" Colonel Evan asked. "As far as the ceremony."

"Keep a cool head." The general's gaze flicked to Mark. "Both of you. And listen to Dellai Bertram. He'll guide you through safely."

They didn't have to wait much longer before Jog returned with the priest.

Mark had to fight not to stare in shock.

The dellai had tattoos on his face.

The priest wore his order's distinctive white and red robes with that ridiculous but intimidating winged hat. The dellai's hat had a cut in the center exposing crimson cloth. The white gloves with red palms, uncut beard bleached white, and uncut bleached hair declared him the head of the Church of State. All usual stuff. But those tattoos .... Had the islands reverted to some pagan practice unmentioned in secular history?

The priest looked like a stern man of ill humor. He nodded to both of them. "You are ready to be tested and bound?"

"Yes, dellai," the colonel said immediately.

"Yes, dellai," Mark answered after, partly because he wasn't sure the form of response and honorific would be the same as it was on the mainland, and partly because the tattoos fascinated him and he had to spend all his effort not to follow the lines snaking around the priest's face.

"Follow me, all of you."

The general and Jog allowed the colonel and Mark to follow first. Unfortunately they didn't go into the main chamber, where lords and their jesters gathered to do mysterious things and to listen to choirs and such. They went to the left into one of the galleries, which Mark imagined would be far less interesting.

He was wrong.

The long hall had arched windows that came to sharp points more than fifty feet above their heads. The rafters echoed the form and intertwined into a massive weave of structural art. But this time Mark's gaze wasn't drawn and held up, but to either side.

Books. Endless lines of them, and art, and sheets of music, and maps and scrolls .... Between each window stood a room of white stone with straight walls and a curved roof, like a lantern but long so that it projected nearly to the center of the gallery. Through the open doorways he saw treasures held safe from the brilliant light that came in through the windows. Every window had seats and tables where at least a dozen people could sit comfortably and study. And so did the priests and their students and young nobles study, usually in groups less than four, or alone. They wore gloves to protect the materials, and sat on the shaded side of the building so that the sunlight wouldn't bleach the treasures they held in their hands.

Mark wanted to dart into every room and see everything in it. The larger church in Seven Churches ... if he'd known what existed inside those galleries they would have never been able to keep him out. Perhaps the gallery on the other side had something else even more spectacular, but he couldn't imagine anything more wonderful than this. He didn't mind his pain so much, but he didn't pick up his pace so he could linger as long as possible.

"Why aren't there any jesters here?" Mark asked.

"They come from time to time. Perhaps they're busy." Dellai Betram's sarcasm lacked both subtlety and humor.

They reached the end too soon to suit Mark's curiosity. Dellai Betram stopped in front of a door on the left that led into the final lantern room. He drew keys from somewhere within his robe sleeve, most likely a belt that hung over his shoulder beneath his robes, and unlocked the door.

It opened to a stairway down. Mark's heart started to pound. Unusual carvings lined the walls. Feathery, scrolled or somewhat floral, they mingled in a way that wasn't particularly attractive, just strange. Some of them hadn't been completed, existing just as charcoal lines on flat stone.

The only light came through openings in the ceiling of the lantern room. The stairs were iron grate and let light pass on for some distance, but not far enough. It was pitch black below.

The stairway began to spiral tightly. Mark decided to go ahead of Colonel Evan when the colonel hesitated. "Are you all right?" Poised beneath him on the first spiral stair looking up, Mark felt even smaller and more frail than usual.

The colonel looked pale. "Yes."

Mark took a step down but the colonel didn't follow. Mark offered his hand.

"I'm all right." The colonel finally took the first step onto the spiral, and they made their way down step by painful step into deepening darkness.

"Try to keep up," Dellai Betram grumbled. "Feel your way along the walls when it becomes necessary. The hall opens to your left. Always travel to the left when you're going down."

"Is there anything to the right?" Mark asked.

"The way out, if you change your mind. But you can't come back that way. Once that door closes, it won't open to you again."

They still had enough light to see by at the bottom of the stairs, but only just. To the left opened a darkness even deeper than the court, completely unlit even by the smallest candle. He guessed, based on the opening, that the hall was about two armspans wide and as high. Dellai Betram walked down it as if he could see, though he measured his paces carefully. Mark listened. "Take my hand," he told the colonel.

"That's not necessary."

"Trust me."

Their gloved hands clasped. Mark pulled him along trying to match the stride that the priest used, his mind still counting the dellai's paces while counting his own. It stretched his leg wound. He gritted his teeth and pressed onward. The priest stopped and turned on his heel very deliberately. When Mark got to twenty five paces he did the same.

The priest used his keys, clicked open a door, and went inside. By the time Mark and the colonel caught up with him, the dellai had lit an elegant silver lamp with a silver striker. Mahogany furnishings adorned the small but well-appointed room. A narrow table of black stone with two chairs on one side and one on the other dominated the center. Four cushioned chairs waited on the sides, two and two, and behind the single chair at the table stood a narrow desk. The walls, ceiling and floor were blacker than night and perfectly smooth but with a dull finish that reflected no light.

Dellai Bertram fetched some paperwork from the desk drawer and a writing box. He opened it and the ink jar within. It held seven pens.

Unlucky seven.

"One last chance to change your minds. All of you." Dellai Betram looked at each of them. When his gaze settled on Mark, Mark felt pressure in his head like the start of a headache. "Very well." The dellai sorted through the paperwork for the next hour. It was both eerie and tedious work. If something happened to the colonel, the general would see to his affairs. In the case of infirmity of the brain, the general would see to the colonel's general care. The colonel had to outline what he wanted done in various situations, such as if he lost all powers of communication with the outside world and showed no improvement after a number of years of his choosing.

Since technically Mark had no one present to second him except Jog, and Jog was at best a disinterested stranger, Mark had to provide a list of people to which he would entrust various duties. *My effects, except for the masks, may be sold for best profit and the proceeds used for expenses related to my care. In the event of my death those proceeds should be evenly divided between Captain Shuller of the trade ship* Dainty *and Mr. Grant Roadman of Perida.* Mark wrote fairly fast, but the speed of his hand couldn't compare to Dellai Betram's. He wrote nearly as quickly as Mark spoke, and neatly enough to read. *If I die, I would additionally like Lord Jester Jog, if he's willing, to write Lord Argenwain and Lord Jester Gutter of the circumstances.*

"Now wait a moment." Jog, who'd been reading over Mark's shoulder, gave Colonel Evan a hard look. "Did you know about this?"

"What?" The general asked.

"He's connected to Lord Jester Gutter."

"Yes." Colonel Evan gazed at Jog as if Jog were stupid.

The general sighed. "I hope you know what you're doing."

"Well connected," Jog growled. "Was that a poor attempt at a joke?"

"Jog." The general's voice held a note of warning. "I don't want word of this to get out. Do you understand me."

"I wouldn't dare. It might get Rohn killed, and I love him just as much as you do." Jog covered his face with his hands a moment, then seemed to calm down. He let out a little laugh. "Hells, boy, you waited for a fair wind and got yourself a hurricane."

"There will be no mention of those places here," Dellai Betram said in a warning tone, and Jog sobered. "Now, Lark, in the circumstance that you become infirm of the mind, all decision as to what will be done will fall to Colonel Rohn Evan, a baron of Perida. That can't be changed. Do you accept that term?"

"Yes." He couldn't think of anyone better anyway.

Did you see that? The whispery voice sounded clear and close.

"But if something happens to the colonel as well, you have some choice. How long would you wish to be allowed to live in such a state, assuming you couldn't communicate your wishes in a sane and rational manner? A year? Five? As long as you may live? Or would you prefer someone make a judgment based on the circumstance, what they know of you, and the prognosis?"

He could ask to be shipped off to Cathret. Maybe Gutter would take care of him, maybe not ... would he want Gutter to do that? It might be his only hope, if he had any at all. But then he'd never be free again, and he'd be in Lord Argenwain's reach.

He could ask to be put out of his misery.

"Is there an asylum on the island that isn't controlled by the Church?" Mark asked.

What, who is that? A different voice whispered while the three men protested at once. Mark waited until they calmed down a little so he could be overheard. "I'd like to be under a doctor's care. If a doctor can't make me better after three months, I'd like to be sent to Cathret. To Gutter. If he'll still have me. If not, I best be sent to find out what the afterlife is really like."

He can hear you.

"Wouldn't family, even distant relations, be better?" The colonel asked it so gently it made Mark smile despite the unnerving voices.

"The church couldn't find anyone. My parents never mentioned a single relative to me or anyone. They eloped." The pressure in his head eased a little and he let out a sigh of relief, though he anticipated more voices with trepidation.

"Allow me to employ mine. I have a sister. She's well off. It wouldn't be a burden to see after you if the asylum—" The colonel winced. "—does you no good. And she's a strong enough person to let you go if your suffering seems too great."

"It's not about suffering. It's about getting better or moving on. I don't want to linger forever, a hopeless case. I would hate that." Mark crossed his arms. It helped him feel sheltered against everyone's scrutiny. They probably all thought he was pathetic and alone in the world. After his time walking through the snow, he knew this was nothing like being alone.

The colonel took a spare sheet of paper from the many strewn in front of them. "Write a letter to be delivered to her with your wishes. I promise you, she is a good woman. If you trust me, you will love her. I swear it."

The oath made him shiver. Mark took up a pen and wrote to her. He wanted her to know about his suspicions about Gutter, as well as the fact that in spite of it all, it wouldn't be so bad to be in his care if Gutter pulled the matter out of her hands. It took a long time to explain everything.

"My estate," the colonel began, distracting Mark from his writing though he forced himself to continue, "is all in order, only now I would like something to go to Lark if he survives me. Something substantial."

"The garden?" the general suggested.

"I don't think anyone but an islander could manage it," the colonel said. "It's too complex. Perhaps half the fleet?"

Mark had to lift his pen to keep from marring the letter.

"That is more than an adequate living."

"And Hevether," the colonel added. "My sister would have little use for it, and her living is such that she won't need the income from its sale."

He has a fleet?

When Mark was finished with his letter, he had to make a list of his effects. That, at least, took very little time. He hesitated, and then forced himself to write the amount of indenture, and what it weighed against. Part of *Mairi's* profits went into a hull fund in case of a catastrophic event. Most of it would go to pay the widows and orphans and any remainder would pay into his indenture. In the event of a positive balance, though, it would be an asset for someone to claim.

Like Captain Shuller, or Grant, or the colonel who had a fleet of some sort of ships, though he hardly needed it.

Mark gave the dellai his list.

And then there were the masks.

"The masks I want sent to Gutter." Gutter would know what to do with Obsidian's mask, and the one he meant for Mark should have stayed in his possession in the first place. "Lord Jester Jog, will you see to it please?"

"Yes. And by the way, since I serve as your second for the estate, we can dispense with the formality, Lark."

The priest made a note, then stood. "Thank you, general, for your perseverance." The general and Jog stood, and the general and the priest shook hands.

"Good luck." The general shook the colonel's hand.

Jog gave Mark a dark, sidelong look. "Well-connected indeed," he grumbled. "Next you'll tell us you have the Gelantyne Mask." But then he relented and offered his hand. They shook briefly. "Take good care of him. You're not worthy, you know. No one could be worthy of him, but you least of all. Runty mainland fop. You're kitten for a lion's paw."

"Jog," the general said in a warning tone.

The jester smiled and followed his master out. They shut the door.

All at once it was very quiet. Mark hadn't realized how even at Hevether Hall the constant symphony of ocean, conversation, working people, wind and birds had kept him company until they were all gone.

Dellai Bertram took an incense box and powdered incense from the desk. Within the box was a burner with an indented spiral pattern. He filled the spiral, lit the end and closed the box. "What happens in this room is not only sacred, but secret. You may discuss it between you, but it's very important you don't speak of it, or write of it, or hint of it to anyone else or the *morbai* may destroy your minds. Rohn, I've known you all your life. You'll be sensible about this. As for you, boy, it doesn't matter what you believe as far as the afterlife or spirits or what is or isn't sacred or what does or does not have a soul. The consequences are real."

Mark had nothing to say to that.

"Rohn, I know you have questions about sin. You may find some answers. They may not be answers to the questions that you most want to know about. I hope they are. I know you're also afraid. You have good reason to be. Regardless of the answer, however, I insist that you consider carefully before you act on what you discover. No one is free of sin. And no one may act without regard for what our society believes is sinful."

The colonel's eyes widened. "Are you saying—"

"No! Even if someone does know, they have to keep it to themselves, even here. The poetry is all we've ever had."

"Written by people going mad," the colonel said bitterly. "Written by people who might have already been mad in no way connected to revealing the truth of what is beyond mortal life."

"There always has been, and always will be, a barrier between us and the truth. That's also true for our everyday lives." Bertram moved toward the door. "No one can really know what's true. But they can believe in some things. They may even be able to count on those beliefs to guide them to a better life."

"Will you answer one question for me?" Mark asked. He doubted the priest would answer, but he was desperate to know.

"Yes?"

"If I die before the colonel, what happens to my soul? Will he still protect me, even though he's alive and I'll be elsewhere?"

"The sacred poetry teaches us that yes, you will be protected. You will be a part of him forever. Even if he decides to lop your fool head off. But I wouldn't test him, boy. It's his choice to protect you. He can always choose not to once he reaches the afterlife himself, if you go wrong." With that, the priest blew out the lantern. "Take the cushions off the chairs, and kneel on them." While Mark and the colonel did as he instructed, the dellai began to chant in an eerie whisper.

Mark couldn't bend his leg far enough to sit on his heels without tearing out his sutures, so he knelt straight. Even that hurt quite a bit. He hoped they wouldn't have to kneel for long.

The chant Bertram began to intone was in Hasle, but Mark couldn't speak it as well as he read it, and the words didn't quite match up with the phonetic pronunciation his instructor used to teach it to him. The cadence suggested music. It wasn't quite the same as the language the voices spoke, but it was close enough that it made him nervous.

Mark tried to memorize the words at the same time that he tried to translate, using the few words he recognized as a guide. Music would make it easier. Nervously, he murmur-sung under his breath along with the priest. At first he made quite a few mistakes, but by his sixth repetition he owned it.

The priest stopped chanting.

The door opened, then shut and locked.

They should have been, but Mark had a terrible feeling that they weren't alone.

Chapter Seventeen

It was so dark, the incense seemed bright by comparison. That glow didn't carry far enough to reveal even a tiny bit of the mahogany desk that the burner rested on. Mark shivered with fear. Even his breath trembled. He wanted to joke, to ask if all they had to do was kneel in the dark for a while to be bonded, but he didn't dare disturb the thing or things in the room with them. The incense made his skull feel like it had been lined with wool.

The room seemed to vanish except for that little glow. He reached out and felt the stone table, but when he drew his hand away again the room might as well not have existed, save for the resinous, phenolic smoke.

His heart tried to pound its way out of his chest. He tried to control his breath, but it rose and fell in desperate waves. The pressure on his leg wound grew until Mark had to stretch it out. It relieved the worst of the pain, but then when he knelt again it hurt even more.

He couldn't hear Colonel Evan—not a breath or a rustle. Mark reached and found his shoulder. His hand slid down the colonel's arm and probed for his hand. The colonel slid his hand together with Mark's and squeezed. He was trembling too.

The colonel released his hand after a few short breaths.

Mark's pain faded and he couldn't hear himself breathing anymore. It felt like he didn't need to breathe, couldn't breathe—it panicked him. He had to breathe. He felt lightheaded. He groped for the solidity of the table and found nothing. The glow from the incense faded.

Whatever it was in the room came closer. It felt like light on his face, not the warmth of sunlight but a similar glow like when he closed his eyes in summertime against the intense brilliance, but this was a faded blue in tone rather than the familiar orange glow. He strained to see it, his right hand searching for the colonel. There, but what he touched instead of a shoulder was something soft and delicate, like silk floating on water. "Colonel?" A ghost of phantom blue light lit and died away, as if his voice had somehow revealed it.

No answer. Mark drew his hand away, terrified of what he'd touched, fearing that it wasn't human. "Please say something," Mark whispered.

The wan blue glow brightened a little when he spoke. He didn't know if it was a good or bad thing, but he had to see. "Hello?"

It definitely brightened, and moved closer. He'd attracted whatever it was. And had something green moved over in the corner across the table from the baron?

E'emahl tro phani soll ....

You know what to do, it had said, but not with voice. It whispered in his mind like a memory of someone breathing the words into his ear.

Mark did know, but he was afraid to. He sang because he was more afraid of what might happen to them in the dark than of what he might see.

You walked alone across the land
You walked along the moonlit strand
You walked into the wide gray sea
Why did you go, my love a' lee

The music curled like whorls of light around him and traveled in undulating and spinning ribbons where they touched on ... he'd seen flowers like that before, but not in the world. He'd seen them in carvings on the church walls. They had throats that glowed like old embers and petals that spread into ragged fans of luminous blue. They had no stems or leaves. They just floated in gently undulating drifts within forests of feathery tree-sized forms. Mark floated in a bizarre forest through which jewel-colored orbs bobbed, pastel silken ribbons edged in diamond swam, and translucent bubbles moved within unseen currents. The blooms and feather trees in silver, pale greens and soft blues spanned acres. Something like glimmering sand flowed among them, teeming with minute living things, or so they seemed to be alive though he couldn't make out any form to define each sparkle. They were so strange as to be frightening rather than beautiful.

He seemed to be able to see in all directions at once and it confused his mind. He had no way of orienting, especially since there seemed to be no ground or sky. He could have been prostrate, hanging upside down, even turning in place without knowing it.

He stopped singing and everything began to fade into darkness again. He lifted his voice, afraid of what might come upon him without him knowing.

The light from his music reached a clearing where a sapphire river flowed down in leaps and steps and then swooped upward. Something like branches on trees pierced through here and there, and the watery band glittered with inner lights. It was populated by dark and frightening forms with long, delicate teeth.

He didn't notice them at first, but he knew what the dozen or so graceful creatures among the flowing blossoms must be. Tall and slender, their only relationship to human form was in number of limbs. They shifted and blurred. From what little he could make out as the notes of music glanced over them, their heads had no eyes, but had something like ears, cupped and furred like a fox's. Those ears rippled and expanded and shrank with sensitivity to things he himself couldn't hear in this dark and silent world where his voice provided the only light and sound. Graceful cheeks helped balance the long but diminutive noses that ended in strangely flat nostrils. They had small mouths and sharp, delicate chins. Hair flowed freely around them in shades of silver and gold and copper and umber. The nearest had skin dappled with passionate ambers and reds. The clothes, or perhaps their bodies had skin and fur that fanned out into elaborate layers that looked like skirting and sleeve, flared and billowed like loose sails luffing in gentle breezes.

One of them floated closer. This one was a terrible green—a green that would cover over once-glorious civilizations and put moss on bones, the implacable green of life that had no respect for the art and soul and pain of flesh beings.

Mark's song kept traveling and carrying light off into the distance though fear had choked off his voice. The light touched on tree-sized vines that climbed on no visible support to incredible heights, their roots traveling through whatever translucent substance served as ground to them. The music revealed a flow of stars far below, moving as a river of rainbow-touched clouds that glowed with their own light.

Just as the light began to dim on the nearest things, the green being drew something out of its side, as if extracting a rib. A sword, thin and clear as glass but very obviously a weapon with a swept handguard.

Thir kra muomaveh.

It kills for pleasure.

At first Mark thought it meant him, but he realized it was looking where the colonel would be kneeling. The amber and red being drew a blade as well and charged. Mark only had time to reach out with his hand in hopes of diverting the strike. The blade pierced right through his palm.

Mark screamed in shock. Everything washed out in brilliant waves and ribbons of blinding light.

They are mine!

The memory/words split through his mind with such overwhelming force that Mark clutched his head trying to keep it from exploding apart. He curled—his head whacked the table—and cradled his hand. His palm burned and itched and sliced him with pain all at once. The pain traveled like hot worms cutting through him with thousands of razor fins up his arm. The worms branched from his shoulder into the depths of his body to all his limbs. He couldn't even scream anymore. All he could do was gasp.

Let me.

You're mad.

You don't know who this is. Now silence. I must concentrate.

I know who this is and he is not worthy.

We must trust him.

"Lark! Damn it." The colonel fumbled around in the room. A chair scraped, the table slid. The desk drawer opened and the colonel rattled around in it. The striker rasped several times, sparking too-bright in the darkness until finally the lamp lit, momentarily blinding Mark.

The colonel knelt beside him and grabbed him up. "What is it? Show me."

The pain had begun to fade though he shuddered from revulsion. Mark tore off his glove, afraid of what he'd find.

Just a scar on his palm. Small, red—it had a mate on the back of his hand. It was a strange thing without blood or a bruise or a rash. It looked rooted in his skin, with green tendrils that faded into the flesh underneath.

His leg didn't hurt. His arm didn't either but he didn't care. He felt poisoned by this horror on his hand—what had it done to him, and what was it doing?

The crawling throughout his body faded into minute spasms.

"What is that?" The colonel sounded afraid. "What happened?"

"Didn't you see?"

"No. I thought I heard you singing, but it was far away. I could feel things like I've seen in sacred artwork, but without touching or seeing, or as if they were a part of me. I can't explain it." The colonel kept a tight hold on Mark as if he might drown if he let go. "Something attacked me. I heard you scream and I returned." He eased his hold and moved so that he could take Mark by the wrist. "Can you flex your hand?"

Mark made a fist, and then opened his hand and hyper-extended his fingers. They wiggled easily. "Everything feels fine." A fresh shudder of revulsion raked through him. He didn't want to look at the scar but he didn't dare look away.

"Squeeze my fingers." He held out two. Mark gripped and the colonel winced. "You're stronger than you look."

Mark released him, his senses still so overwhelmed from what had happened that he couldn't perceive the room as anything more than an uninteresting gray place. His chest felt heavy.

I'm still alive. We're alive.

But are we sane?

"Are you all right?" Mark asked.

"Yes."

The lock on the door turned and the dellai looked in. "You've both had visions?"

"More than that, it seems." The colonel stood and brushed off his clothes. "Lark has a scar on his hand."

"It—"

"Don't talk about it to me!" The priest cut Mark's words short before he could even get started. "Didn't I explain it to you?" He grabbed Mark's hand impatiently, and then offered his hand to the colonel. The colonel accepted, and the priest placed the colonel's hand over Mark's scarred one, as if he knew. He began speaking in Hasle, but Mark was too distracted to try to translate the words.

The colonel's hand melted into his. In shock Mark tried to pull away but they were connected, and the priest's grip was as immovable as stone. The colonel's heartbeat and his own clashed in frantic rhythms that gradually began to combine. Their hearts still raced, but they raced as one. The heaviness in Mark's chest lifted at last.

The priest let them go and to Mark's surprise, his hand was still his own. It still had the scar on it, but the scar had darkened and was turning a dusky blue with black tendrils that faded to gray beneath his skin before they vanished into the depths of flesh and bone.

"You are bonded," the dellai told them. He went to the desk and fetched a small book out of one of the drawers. It had a plain leather cover with one of the floating flowers embossed on it. The artist had painted it in faded blue with a gilded center. Mark might have thought it was a beautiful design before he saw the luminescent glory of the real—

He had a hard time calling that place, that existence, real. He loathed the thought that it might be a part of the afterlife. It might have been glorious and wonderful if he'd trusted the rules of nature to apply, but it was so strange and chaotic he dreaded the thought of being plunged into that place forever after his death.

Maybe it was one of the hells. Please don't let that be the Glorious Garden.

"Your heartbeats will tend to match," the priest told them. "It's my understanding that it can be a little disconcerting at first, but I'm sure that is the least of your concerns at the moment." The dellai began putting away the incense. "Go home. You'll find the hall is lit. Take it past the stairs. The door will lead out into the gardens. A guard will have keys waiting for you. They're struck especially for you. Don't lose them, and don't loan them out. They'll give you admittance to the gardens at any hour you wish. Sometimes, when the memories of your visions become too burdensome, it helps to sit among those who have *glimpsed*, even if you can't discuss it."

Mark didn't want it to be real, not any of it. He wondered how much of what his mother had considered superstition might be ... as the dellai had hinted, if not the truth then at least something that could be counted on.

Was the Hunt real? Did *morbai* gather to hunt particular souls, souls that had done evil in life? And what about what the sailor had seen? Mark had feared it might have been Gutter, but if the sailor had in fact been Stricken, a Seer .... But *morbai* and *allolai* couldn't manifest in the living world, at least not according to any legend or superstition he'd heard. They could only affect the mind. But how could anyone really know if that was true?

"Lark?"

That was his master's voice now, the one who would protect his soul from *morbai* in the afterlife.

But I think I protected his soul. What does that mean?

"Lark?" The colonel had softened his voice.

Mark nodded and went to the door. He worked his glove back on. He almost forgot the cane. He didn't need it anymore.

But it might be to my advantage to pretend I need it, at least for a while.

"You said we would visit your father," Mark reminded him.

"I think he would have been much more pleased if I had eloped with a whore." The colonel's shoulders tightened and he looked a bit green as they stepped out into the hall. Incredible frescoes depicted fierce battles between jesters, *allolai*, *morbai*, and lords on the walls. The *allolai* and *morbai* were depicted as human beings, but with skin colored in amber, saffron, sap green, azure, burgundy and other strange colors. "I would rather we present ourselves promptly than to make it appear as if we're avoiding him," the colonel added. "I may be a sad excuse for a son, but I'm not a coward." The colonel's gaze traced down the hall but he didn't appear to react to the terrifying and sometimes pitiful scenes of death and destruction.

"How could anyone consider you—you're a hero."

"Not to him."

What kind of man could make the colonel feel so inadequate? "Let's get it over with, then."

The colonel nodded. "And then dinner."

"And which dinner might that be?"

The colonel's brows lifted and he gave Mark a puzzled glance. "Were we not invited to dine with _Dainty's_ crew?"

Mark couldn't remember ever feeling so grateful and happy, though he'd received countless precious gifts from Gutter and Lord Argenwain over the years. "We'd better send word to Mr. Roadman. I hope he doesn't have a previous engagement."

"It will be good to see him again." The colonel bowed his head. "He was a good man in the war. If he'd let me I would have advanced him well beyond sergeant. In so many words he told me that men need a semblance of noble authority in a leader, and that he didn't have it." Colonel Evan lifted his head and glanced over the shadowed battle on the wall beside him, where strange creatures tormented fallen lords, and jesters reached in despair for aid from their dying masters. "I maintain that a hundred men would have gladly followed him to their deaths if he'd asked it of them."

Mark wished he didn't have to wait to see Grant again. He wanted to rush to _Dainty_ and be with regular people for a while. Ceremony, priests, otherworldly danger—he'd had enough of it, and the colonel looked ready to wash his memories in wine as well.

"I'm going to start to limp when we go up the stairs," Mark warned him. "I don't know how well I'll maintain the façade, but I'll give it a try."

"I'm not clear on what happened to your wounds."

"I'm not either, and until I understand it I don't want anyone to realize I'm fit."

The colonel smiled. "You would have made a fair soldier, I think."

"Let's hope we never find out if that's true."

The colonel, as apparently was his habit, watched the terrain as the carriage carried them to a part of the island Mark hadn't been to before. Mark had seen the bay, the docks at the waterfront, and the baron's manor on a rocky point exposed to the prevailing weather and waves, but near a tiny inlet where small boats could reach and leave shore during ebb tides without wrecking. Now they traveled inland and upward as the carriage climbed what the baron had referred to as a mountain, but would be called a hill on the mainland.

Some of the land had been cleared for crops, mainly sugar cane, vines and shrubs that produced spices, and fruit orchards. The vast majority remained wild. Exotic trees grew to vast heights. Most of those giants had barely a limb on their enormous trunks below a hundred feet. Many of the smaller trees, forced to straggle and claw in darkness or race for supremacy wherever sunlight won through, grew fruit with which Mark was familiar but hadn't seen the source, such as bananas and limes. Some he'd never seen before, like cucumber-shaped purple fruits suspended from massive five-leaved vines. And the flowers—everything seemed to remain in constant bloom. Even many of the trees had blossoms, some as tall and broad as a man. Most of the flowers had an appealing jasmine or orange blossom scent, but a few had strange, not-always-pleasant odors and his senses were soon exhausted by the over-ripe sweetness of decaying perfumes.

Birds hurried and cried through all this. He caught sight of real, actual and wild monkeys. Duke Fellburn's pet monkey was much smaller, a little golden thing with eager eyes. These were large and dark and a little ominous with their fierce, hooded eyes and enormous fangs.

"What are those?" Mark asked, pointing to them.

The colonel glanced up as they passed. "Mellicant's monkeys."

"Are they dangerous?"

"Not generally, but they can be destructive. Everyone has to lock their refuse in metal bins, otherwise they forage for meat scraps in them and make an unbelievable mess, not to mention they have a nasty bite and will attack in force if you try to run them off from it. They're adept at stalking large birds, and they've been known to take an occasional piglet. The males can get quite large. During the first part of the war, my camp was continually harassed by a troupe of more than a hundred of the blamed creatures led by a male of at least one hundred pounds. I hated them then, but now I'm rather fond of them."

"What changed your mind?"

"They learn quickly, as quickly as men. One made off with a pistol and it went off. Frightened him to pieces, but several days later, after we'd suffered through a particularly brutal engagement with Cathretan forces, he returned and stole another pistol, pointed it toward my men, and tried to fire it. It wasn't loaded, so it didn't go off. He made off with it and we never found it again. I swear that given time and instruction, they could be taught to do a great many things. I often wonder if they have their own language, religious beliefs, jesters, nobles and so forth."

Mark couldn't see what the colonel had found so endearing about them from that story. "He might have killed someone."

"Considering how many of his kind were killed during the war, I don't blame him. I killed a lot of men with less provocation."

It kills for pleasure.

Had Gutter known what Lord Argenwain was before they were bonded?

Have I bonded myself to a murderer?

"Did ...." He couldn't bring himself to ask, so he tried another question. "Did the beings, *morbai* or whatever, tell you anything about me?"

"They spoke to you?" The colonel paled. "Did they say something about me?"

He should have foreseen that question. "Yes, they did. I'm not ready to talk about it." How did a jester ask his master if he maimed and tortured and killed people for entertainment?

"I'm sure my father will discuss my sins. Whether you or I want to or not, he will bare all my sins within earshot of every servant—not that they don't already know my flaws. I'm grateful that they've kept my secrets well, though of course any day that could change."

Mark felt like a young maid who, when presented with her wedding bed, started to shriek for an annulment. Of course there was no such thing for jesters except the axe. In the other world he'd reacted with instinct, without thinking through the consequences of saving the colonel from the *morbai's* attack. Even directly afterward he'd felt nothing but relief that it was over. Now he had an awful feeling in his gut that he'd just done something very stupid.

What if it was doing the right thing by cleansing the world of a bloodthirsty monster?

I slept in his house. He took excellent care of me, and stayed his hand when he could have shot me as a spy.

But what if he decides I'm too much trouble? I can't believe I remarked so casually that he could have me put to death. He'd probably do it himself, and take his time about it. No wonder Jog looked so shocked. He must know ....

"It's too late for second thoughts." The colonel turned his gaze back to the jungle.

"I still trust you." Unfortunately now he had to because he had no choice.

"What does it say that we both feel foolish for trusting one another, and yet we do so anyway?" The colonel's eyes lit with a smile that didn't reach his mouth. The tender expression helped ease Mark's misgivings.

They passed a few grand gateways, climbing higher until Philip turned the carriage onto a broad road framed by marble pillars topped with alabaster horse heads. The trees gave way to horses grazing on a broad pasture of at least twenty acres, along with a herd of tiny deer that nibbled nervously at the far edge. Oranges and lemons ringed the house. A large pond had a bronze fountain at its center—a dignified horse pawing the air with one hoof, neck arched while water flowed from its mane across its powerful body. A dark hedge with red-edged leaves walled off whatever property lay behind the house.

The carriage horses followed the road around a massive floral display where vines with white, trumpet-shaped blossoms as long as Mark's forearm crept up a dead tree. Philip stopped the carriage in front of the main doors. The covered entry stood on a level with the ground, but a water-filled moat required a bridge to cross over to the door. The house had all the elegance and amenities of a modern manor: broad framing with simple fluting, plaster painted a soft apricot, a generous number of lamps, and plenty of windows. The only nod toward fortification aside from the moat lay in the windows on the lower level—they were all tall, but very narrow, and divided by stone. He'd never seen such a design. It was interesting, but not interesting enough to distract him from what lay ahead.

Mark barely remembered to accept help and favor his leg when he stepped down. He limped with the colonel to his father's house, where a butler had already arrived to open the door.

Chapter Eighteen

"Young Master Evan," the butler declared, his joy barely disguised behind his formality. He wasn't yet fifty if Mark had to guess, ginger-haired, heavily freckled, and he had bright blue eyes. "You're a welcome sight, sir. Morgan has already run for your father. Will you take a meal?"

"No, thank you Thomas. This will be a brief visit."

Mark's pulse raised, and he felt it wasn't from his own anxiousness alone.

"Coffee, sir?"

The colonel took in a breath to answer, held it, and then released it with a sigh. "Yes, thank you."

The butler stood there expectantly. Mark felt a terrible discomfort that didn't just come from his nerves. The butler was almost bursting with a need to know, but the colonel hadn't acknowledged Mark. Instead the colonel stood there, smoothing his coat nervously. Finally he slipped his coat off and handed it over to the butler.

Mark lost his temper. "I'm—" *Lord now. Shit.* "Lord Jester Lark, in service to the colonel."

The butler almost dropped the colonel's coat along with his own jaw. He fumbled into a rigid posture in a bad recovery. "May I take your coat, lord jester?"

Mark remembered to ease it off as if it pained him. He wanted to storm away, but held himself in check. He knew it wasn't just anger that made him want to leave.

I'm not going to run like a coward or hide as if I'm ashamed of our bond.

The butler led them past the bright and open entryway directly to a neighboring salon. Most of the light came from upper windows in the vaulting. The floors were an unusual red wood with no knots to speak of, and the walls were a majestic blue gray that enhanced the red. White trim, window dressing and white furniture helped brighten the room. Whoever had put it together had a good eye, but Mark couldn't appreciate it. Instead he resented it, and the mucked up arrival at his master's father's house, and his own foolishness. He'd ruined his life. He could blame no one for it but himself. Whatever plans Gutter had made for him couldn't be worse than this.

"I hate this house," the colonel muttered after the butler left.

"Are you ashamed of me?" Mark didn't care if the colonel was ashamed. He wanted to pick a fight.

The colonel hesitated.

"Is this how I can expect to be presented in the future? Skulk in with no mention of me and no warning of our arrival, made to introduce myself to the shock of all, and then forced to recover your clumsiness?"

The colonel's head cocked dangerously and he strode over until he was close and tall and imposing. "Excuse me?"

Mark had dealt with taller men all his life. He wasn't intimidated. "No wonder you're pushing thirty and not married, or are you? Perhaps you've neglected to mention your bride the same way you neglected to mention me to, oh, I expect you haven't informed anyone."

"I hardly had time."

"To pen a note and send it?"

"How dare you speak to me this way." His dark eyes blazed with hot shadows. They frightened Mark, but he didn't care. His heart pounded with passion.

"How dare you bond with me and then treat me like a servant. Worse than a servant. You treat Trudy with more courtesy than you treated me just now."

"We will not have this discussion here."

Mark started to answer when he remembered that their hearts beat as one. The colonel was right. This wasn't the place for an argument, much as Mark wanted it. He didn't want an ordinary argument, either. He realized he craved the brutality he'd dreaded in Lord Argenwain's manor. How could he want that? It was more repulsive a desire than the tiny itch for gracian he felt now. He steadied his breaths, hoping it would calm his heart.

Gradually, too slow to suit him, his heart steadied. The colonel seemed to calm as well, though his cheeks were flushed and his eyes still held that shadowed anger.

A tall, thin jester, dressed in emerald green and bald as a child's lie, strode into the salon with a man that couldn't be anyone but the colonel's father. His hair had gone mostly white, and he wore a close-cut beard and mustache but the dark eyes, proud cheeks, dusky skin and broad shoulders were all akin. He looked hale for a man of perhaps sixty, and cut a clean figure in his tidy gold waistcoat and white breeches. He wore his hair shoulder-length and loose at the front with a ribboned tail in the fashion of perhaps a decade before. He wore ruffles rather than lace, and had three large rings on his hands—two on the left and one on the right.

This was also the governor of Perida, Mark remembered.

The governor stared at Mark while his jester stood by a moment, allowing his master to take Mark in before the jester spoke. "May I present my master General Holiver Evan, Governor and a baron of Perida."

The man seemed to command enormous power, far more than Mark had given him credit for based on his personal knowledge of governors and their usual importance in society.

"My good friend Lord Jester Fine," the governor said by way of a brief introduction before turning on his son. "What in the seven hells have you done?"

The colonel stood there like a man calmly resigned to death while a firing squad took aim.

"I thought you had given up your sinful ways, and now you present me with this feminine mockery of a man, like a coward, after the fact."

"Sir, if I may." Mark wasn't sure what he'd expected, but not this. His instincts urged him to stay out of what was clearly a family matter and one he had no knowledge of, but he wasn't about to stand around while the colonel suffered humiliation because of him. "You can't mean to accuse us of carnal familiarity before the coffee has arrived. Assuming we're still welcome in your house."

"I think it would be in all our best interests to have fruit and cheese with a bit of white wine," Fine said, matching Mark's overture. "That way if we fling things at each other they're less likely to cause permanent damage."

The governor led his jester by the elbow just outside the room where they exchanged quiet words.

The colonel hadn't moved. In spite of all his fears and doubts, Mark couldn't help but admire his stoic demeanor and calm. And the pain— Mark hadn't known him long at all, but even he could see the agony behind the colonel's cold expression. Mark refused to sympathize with his lord until he knew more. Still, he couldn't ignore everything that had first drawn him to the man. Elegance. Pride. Surprising gentleness, and carefully tempered passion.

The governor and his jester came back inside. "Have a seat," the governor said tightly.

The colonel chose a chair with its back to an inner wall. Mark moved a chair close by him, but not too close in consideration of the father's accusation. He remembered to wince a bit when he moved the chair, and again when he sat.

Lord Jester Fine stood beside his master. "Your father is mainly concerned about how this will appear to society," Fine began.

"You uprooted our family to get away from the scandal in Saphir," the governor growled. "Only to throw it away for this—" He bit off whatever slur he planned to use.

"I don't care how it appears to you or anyone else." The colonel spoke softly, but his gaze never wavered from his father's face. "My interest is in Meridua's future."

"A jester is supposed to elevate his master's status, not drag him down. You trust this painted fop with Meridua's future? He'll not just disappoint you. He'll ruin you."

Mark had a good idea of what they were discussing. He wasn't sure whether he wanted to laugh or leave. This was a waste of time and effort.

"Is that disregard in your eyes, lord jester?" the father asked.

Mark should have thought to control the expression on his own face instead of idly listening to the governor spew his disapproval with the subtlety of a rutting ox. "I don't know what happened in Saphir—"

"He didn't tell you? I wonder what else you don't know about my son. Did he tell you that when his degenerate of a friend died in the war, he told me he would marry and live a life free of sin. Eight years I've been worrying and waiting for him to fulfill his promise. He is the last of our line. It's not just his familial duty, but his spiritual duty as well. And what does he bring home? A sheep wife."

Mark had to grip the chair to keep himself from vaulting out of it and demanding an apology. He'd heard many slurs uttered in jest or feigned jest in Lord Argenwain's house, but no one had dared utter that one. If there were worse, he didn't know them. "I would answer that, my lord, but I wouldn't presume to know you well enough to insult you regardless of whether you extend that courtesy to me."

Fine looked like he wanted to say something, but the butler arrived with juice and a fruit and cheese plate. "Saved by afternoon refreshments," Fine said, and began doling out a plate for the governor.

The colonel stood. "I'm afraid we have another engagement this evening, and we must be off."

The butler paused mid-retreat.

"Sit back down," his father said.

"I'm not in love with Lark, father. I intend to keep my promise, and Lark will help me at the appropriate time—a time of my choosing, not yours. He is a jester, nothing more, and nothing less. Now if you will excuse us." He walked out. The butler hurried after him.

He wasn't just playing in Saphir. He had fallen in love, and his lover had died. Nothing else could explain the hurt, the accusations, the pain that had shattered this family.

Mark stood, dazed by the implications of everything he'd heard. "If you'll both excuse me ...."

"Of course," Fine said gently.

Mark bowed and limped after the colonel. He didn't hurry. He had too much to think about. Using his cane gave him an excuse to move slowly.

Was the loss of the colonel's lover related to the killing for pleasure that had so offended the *morbai*? Maybe it made no difference to them, but it seemed slightly better to imagine the colonel had taken pleasure in vengeance than fearing his lord and master had charged onto battlefields with the hateful joy of a hunting hound after a fox.

The butler waited by the door with Mark's coat. "Good day, lord jester," he said kindly while he helped Mark shrug it on.

"Thank you." Mark offered him a smile before he left.

The colonel stood beside the carriage. "I'm sorry. That proved to be considerably more unpleasant than I'd calculated."

"I'm sorry I embarrassed you." Mark climbed into the carriage.

The colonel sat across from him. "You don't embarrass me. In fact, you did remarkably well. I was pleased, and impressed by your restraint. There was only one moment that I feared my father would provoke you into something. I'm not sure I'd regret it if he had. But you remained composed." He rubbed a place over his heart under his coat. "I'm certain I made the right decision. I believe I chose well."

The carriage began to move.

"But you still have doubts," the colonel added.

"I think we've both had enough." Mark sat back with a sigh. "Let's celebrate our bonding. We can worry about how we're going to work together the day after tomorrow."

"I'd prefer to set a few things straight first," the colonel said.

"I'm sure you would, but we already have an invitation for an early meal, and I'm sure we'll have a dinner invitation waiting when we get home." Home. The word caught in his mind, and in his throat. The part of him that was still a little orphan boy felt pain and hope at the same time. The more cynical part of him felt trapped in what was still a stranger's household.

"We'll be out late tonight if I have any say in it, which means we'll sleep in."

"Not together. I meant what I told my father."

That bothered him, though he was willing to let it go for now. "I hadn't assumed that. I wasn't even sure ...." There wasn't anything left to say about it anyway, except to ask those questions about the colonel's lover that he wasn't prepared to ask yet. "Never mind."

"I tried not to assume about you either, not even when you asked me to read to you."

Mark smiled. "Thank you, but I'm afraid my bend, for whatever reason, is painfully obvious to everyone who meets me."

"You don't go to much effort to disguise it."

"I've never tried to. I doubt I could."

"Nonsense. If you wish it, you can study it and present yourself ... differently."

"Is that what you did?"

The colonel shook his head. "No. But I didn't need to. My mannerisms have never struck people as supple."

"I don't think clothes or wearing a beard or changing my walk will fool anyone. But I'll try if you want me to." Having to offer it made him feel desperately lonely.

"I don't think it will matter. You're charming. Likeable. You had no trouble on *Dainty*, and after the trial half the nobles on the island contacted me. They wanted to put you up in their households and made various pretty arguments trying to convince me it was to my advantage. Changing so much of who you are will serve no purpose."

Whereas denying everything the colonel was served many purposes. The colonel didn't have to say it. It was written into his heart. He wasn't just mourning for his lost love. He mourned the loss of who he'd been.

Mark had no doubt he was happy in Saphir, and that he hadn't been happy since.

Mark drew his rapier and traced a large letter G in the sand. Waves glowing with an exquisite aquamarine phosphorescence caressed the gentle slope. Behind Grant, sparks flew toward the stars, dying before they could even hope to meet them. "Now you try," Mark told him. He had to concentrate not to slur his words.

Grant drew his service blade, an inelegant thing no doubt forged in a rush, born to kill but never meant to really live.

It had been so long since Mark had learned to write that he had a hard time understanding why Grant hesitated. Then he remembered something. "Let's try it this way." He drew three guidelines through his G and extended beyond, giving Grant plenty of room. "Start just below the top line, make a broad parry this way, a little deflection here at the center line——"

Grant traced a curve with a lot of awkward bends. He managed a pretty flourish at the end.

"Perfect," Mark declared. "You've made your first letter."

Even in the firelit darkness Mark could see the blush burn up from Grant's throat into his handsome face. "I won't remember come morning."

"Practice." Mark extended the lines. "And the day after tomorrow I'll teach you the rest of your name."

The colonel walked from the fire to where they stood, taking slow, measured steps in an attempt to hide his own drunkenness. "What have we here? Ah, the letter G. Fine work, Mr. Roadman."

"Thank you, sir." Grant's blush deepened.

"Lark, it is time for us to retire." The colonel set his arm around Mark's shoulders. Mark flinched to avoid yielding to him like a wanton debutante. He yearned for touch so much he would have gladly flung himself into Lord Argenwain's bed tonight. And the colonel was so incredibly attractive ... but of course in the morning it would be a mess of angry accusations. Mark hardly knew the man but he could still hear his words. *How dare you seduce me after I explicitly*— "Sir, I would rather stay a while longer."

The colonel's arm slid away with excessive indifference. "I will not have my driver up all night waiting for you while you revel yourself into senselessness and fall asleep where the tide will wash you out to sea to drown, or be eaten by sharks, or wake up half-eaten by crabs."

Through his wine-fogged faculties Mark tried to figure out a line of clarity from what he'd said and laughed at the hopelessness of it. "Take Philip home. I'll find my own way."

"It's at least a ten mile walk from here and this isn't Sa—this isn't Seven Churches."

"I can bunk on *Dainty*," Mark told him, and then he remembered she would sail away before dawn. It gave him a terrible hollow feeling that hurt even past his numbed senses. "Wait, never mind. I'd forgotten. Anyway, there must be a room I can hire in town."

"You'll wake some poor soul in the dead of night and force them to make you coffee at an unholy hour——"

Mark failed to stifle his laughter. "Please, don't try to make a point again. I understand better with one example than a chain of badly connected ones." He'd begun to lean and had to put his hand on the colonel's chest to recover. That chest lifted in lordly indignation. "I have to see a tailor anyway, first thing in the morning. I have no proper clothes for tomorrow's events. I hope someone has something close to my size that can be adjusted in a pinch. Who do you use?"

"Excuse me?" The colonel's face turned pink.

Mark sputtered, trying not to collapse into a fit of unmanly giggles. "Who is your *tailor*."

"Lauderland on Halfrye Street, but you'll never find it."

"I'll get him there, sir." Grant tried to swig wine from his tankard and failed because it was empty. He looked baffled and tried again more forcefully.

"I don't want to hear of any untoward behavior unworthy of the idle gossip in the afternoon gazette, Lark." The colonel gave him a surprisingly effective warning look considering his inebriation. His words made sense to Mark's befuddled mind only because he had a good idea of what his master would want of him. With that the colonel strode off with grave dignity.

"He's pounded," Grant said, leaning on Mark. Mark almost crumpled under the weight. Grant smelled like fish and sweat, but it wasn't unpleasant. "I've never seen him pounded before. Pounded or not, I'd still follow him through the hells in front of a Hunt."

Mark smiled. "I just swore to do it. And I think I did right, but I'm afraid."

"You, afraid?"

Mark looked up at him in surprise. Grant appeared to be in earnest.

The firelight flared from an added log, illuminating half of Grant's face. They both had green eyes, but Mark's were muddy and Grant's were deep and clear, the kind of eyes that inspired insipid poetry. "Can I tell you something? Something you mustn't tell anyone."

Grant nodded. He probably wouldn't remember anyway.

"I'm afraid of him," Mark confessed. "I'm afraid of what he's done and what he'll ask me to do and I'm afraid I won't survive to see my twentieth birthday. Worse than that, I trust him, and I'm afraid I'm going to do some really awful things because I have faith in him. Does that make sense?"

Grant nodded heavily. "I have to wiss now." He pulled Mark along with him, using him as a wobbly crutch.

Grant's eyes had closed and he leaned on his massive hand, scarred and calloused from the line work he confessed to prefer over nets, though he used both methods to fish. There was barely room for all their elbows, the wine jug, two mugs and the lone candle at the table. The scent of fish in Grant's room brought back memories of a time when Mark still had parents, and friends, and a neighborhood with actual neighbors in it. Mark remembered opening the door first thing in the morning and there would be delivery boys with baked goods and fish and milk and all kinds of things already about, and fishermen looking for breakfast after spending the earliest hours out on the sea. Sometimes someone's butler would be waiting to buy wine.

"There was this lieutenant," Grant began suddenly just as Mark had begun to doze again. Grant's breath trailed away, his eyes still closed. "Got killed. They were best friends. What can you do? It happened all the time. Sometimes every day, sometimes a lot of best friends all in the same day for days and days. And then the fighting stops for a while and you grieve." Grant took in a long, shaky breath like he'd just come up from almost drowning. "The colonel—he wasn't a colonel then—did things after his friend died. You'll hear about 'em, I'm sure, but not from me. He was just—lost—for a while. The Morbai's Kiss—they were his men for a while, you know. Then that jester took 'em over and they went on and on. His father's doing." Mark could only halfway follow what Grant was trying to tell him. He wished he hadn't been drinking. He wanted desperately to understand, to catch even more of the nuances of pain and pride and darkness in Grant's voice. "The general took the colonel away from the fighting as much as he could. He took him away so he could wean him off like you'd wean a man off of gracian.

"He's weaned off the bloodlust," Grant murmured. "He's strong. He'll never go back to it. That was war, l'jeste. You don't know, but every islander who lived through it knows. They know he's a hero. And no one is free of sin, the priests say. Not even the nobles. So he, the colonel, though he did things, he's still a good man. I think he was good even while he did them. I guess that makes me a bad man for believing that."

"No." Mark gripped the slack hand Grant had resting on his rough little table. He kept the touch brief, like a sailor, like a soldier, like a man who didn't lean. "You're a good man. You're the best man I've met."

"I'm just a fisherman."

"And I'm just a boy."

Grant blearily opened his eyes. "You fight like a man. And your eyes—cold as death. Only an idiot would look at you and think you're a boy. Only a fool would think you're weak, l'jeste."

Mark folded his arms and rested his head in the linen and lace.

"Let's have none of that." Grant pushed himself up, nearly tipping the table over in the process. "I've fallen asleep at my share of tables and you don't wanna do it. Trust me." He hefted Mark up under the arms and Mark half-stumbled, half-allowed himself to be dragged to the bed. Mark flopped back onto the thin quilt. Grant pulled Mark's shoes off, then wrestled, grunting, with his fisherman's boots. Mark forced himself to sit up long enough to take off his belt with the rapier, followed by his waistcoat. He searched in vain for a place to hang them without having to get up before he gave up and dropped them on the floor. He wondered briefly where he'd left his coat before he sank back on the bed and closed his eyes.

Chapter Nineteen

Mark couldn't remember being this hung-over in his life. Ever. Not only did everything seem too bright and too loud, and not only did his head hurt and his mouth feel like he'd lined it with vellum, not only had he been sick twice that morning, but he couldn't remember much of the night before.

And now he had to wear a mask for the first time. He stared at the mirror trying to will his imagination into coming up with something brilliant, but nothing happened.

I swear I will never drink like that again.

The easy solution rested in a small drawer in what had become his vanity, in his dressing room, in his house. He had a household again, and not as a servant this time. He had what had been the Pheasant Suite, a set of rooms with largely green and white décor and cherry furniture complete with both a private sitting room and a reception room as well as a bed room and a dressing room with a green tiled area and a copper bath in one corner. The colonel had asked him if he wanted to select different furnishings, and Mark had gaped at him like a dead fish. Actually, a dead fish had far more intellectual capacity than Mark had at the moment.

He powdered his face and throat, assuming he'd have to do at least that much.

Just put on the mask Gutter found for you and be done.

Mark edged his eyes in black and darkened his lashes. He smudged the liner because he didn't feel like being a pretty, tidy little thing. That was another person a long time ago.

Lake's cloak, a clear blue against the bloodied snow ...

The blue makeup he applied to his cheek sank the memories of that night into his skin. He formed it into an uneven diamond with an elongated point down the left side of his face. It needed edging—silver, like the steel that had cut him down, like the dove gray and white lining on Lake's cloak. The right side of his face had to be black and edged in gold because Obsidian had led him here and money allowed him to make the journey. Both jesters had led him here—Lake unconsciously, Obsidian with a reason Mark had yet to learn.

He tried different colors on his mouth, but none of them worked for whatever he was looking for, though variations of half blue, half black all intrigued him. The color tended to stain and it was hard to rub off, making his mouth sore. He soothed it with cream ...

The pale on his mouth ...

His heart skipped beats as he applied white makeup, leaving as little pink showing as possible. He rubbed his fingers in the blue, mingled it with a little white, and carefully applied it to appear ...

Obsidian's skin had turned a dusky white and his mouth blushed not pink, but blue.

It needed a little pale rouge. The blue was too clear.

When he got the color on his mouth right something shuddered inside him and recognized itself in the mirror.

Lark took in several shivering breaths, reassuring himself that he was alive and awake and real. The hangover didn't bother him anymore. He had too many things to do.

In a rush he strapped on his sword, a pistol, and Lake's former purse. He put on gloves—a gentleman always wore gloves when going out—and a hat. This one was all wrong but it was the only one he had. And a cane to remind himself to limp. Lark hurried out through the upper gallery to the colonel's suite. He went through the servant's doors into the suite, walked to the end of the hall to the private room door, let himself in and opened the door into the bedroom without knocking. "I need a signed note to assure the tailors I can use your credit."

The colonel groaned and rolled over in his bed. He sat up in shock, groping for a firearm that sat on his nightstand.

Lark just held out his hand and the colonel paused. "Don't shoot, just write." His heart skipped up its pace and then settled. He wished he could feel fear, could feel anything other than the urgent need to make himself presentable.

"Lark?"

"Do you like it?" Lark turned himself around. "Because I don't. I have some things in my colors, but none of them fit and they've been so abused they've been reduced to rags. And I need a new hat. When I get back, I hope you can find something suitable to match. But don't match me too well. We're not a couple going to a ball. This is our political debut." Lark's gaze traced over the colonel's bare chest. He looked very fine draped in a pale sheet with his hair in disarray. The greenish upper lip didn't suit him, though. "I suggest coffee and a lot of water. You need to work yourself up to dry crackers by noon at the latest, and it's already ten in the morning."

The colonel eased out of his large oak and bronze bed. Sadly, he wore underbreeches. "Where were you last night? I waited until one in the morning."

Mr. Roadman. Lark's gaze flicked sideways and up to watch a bit of sweet memory of them cheering and clapping while Mr. Johns danced in a way he'd said was peculiar to his home county of Kolo in Osia, his feet punching into the sand and kicking it up, his hands held above his head, snapping and clapping while three crewmembers sang and played on rough instruments they'd carried from their various homelands. Mark couldn't remember it, but Lark could. He remembered the whole night with perfect clarity, though at a distance as if he were a member of an audience watching a delightful bit of theater. "I'll be two hours at least. May I use the carriage?"

"Yes. Go. Just go." The colonel waved him away.

Unfortunately going to town required all work and no play. As he made his way through town he watched constantly without allowing anyone to be aware that he was watching them, noting who stared, who pretended to ignore him, and who took exception to him.

He and Grant had forgotten all about directions to Halfrye Street.

No matter. He procured directions from a young gentleman who couldn't keep his mouth closed and found the short, narrow street was almost entirely populated by tailors, seamstresses, cloth merchants, lace makers and all other manner of people associated with clothing. Lauderland had his space upstairs, and proved to be one of three reputable tailors that dealt with barons who had a military history. Lark explained and Lauderland, along with two assistants, went to work. He didn't have time to be fussy. He chose a black coat of very light cloth to go over his waistcoat. They protested a little but he assured them it wouldn't look overly strange if the blue waistcoat ended mid-thigh rather than going down to the knee. It was the latest cut that had been shown in the Cathretan Royal Court, though he refused to tell them that. He kept his breeches of the same blue, and ordered blue ribbons to cover the buckles on his shoes. As for the shirt, he chose a black one with thick ruffles and asked that the ruffles be edged in white in whatever fashion could be completed the most quickly. He promised them they'd have more work tomorrow, if they had the time.

They would make the time, they assured him.

While they labored to adjust what they had to fit him and create what they didn't have, he went shopping for a hat. The closest he could find that would work was a plain black with a broad brim, though his eye edged in blue didn't care for the slight.

Never mind, he soothed his left eye, *just be patient.*

He found a sapphire hat pin and pinned the brim up on the left side. Then he found huge white plumes and iridescent blue wing feathers to tuck behind the pin.

His left eye was happy.

He stopped back at the tailors' to see if they needed him to check their work against his body. They did. Lark left them again to shop for better gloves. He found some black ones, and brought them to a seamstress so that she could edge the cuffs in white and silver trim. Later he would need black gloves with blue palms and white and silver edging, and he'd need a black neckerchief with gold and silver, and gold rings.

The tailors earned their reputation by having the work done by one o'clock. Lark thanked them with a tip from his purse and headed for home.

The carriage ride haunted him because he had nothing to do but to live with himself until the first party. He'd never felt such loneliness. Even the memories of walking in the snow seemed preferable to the emptiness gaping inside him like a wound. He wished he could visit Mr. Roadman, even for a moment, but he knew the man would be afraid of him if he saw him like this. If he thought Mark's eyes were cold, he would shrink back in horror from Lark.

And that was the core of his loneliness. He knew his body, his face, his clothes, everything was so artful and steeped in that awful night by the Swan Bridge it was inhuman. Lark would never know love. Mark might find it someday, but Lark would always be alone, a rare bird with no mate, a morbid painting standing beside his master for people to remark upon but never welcome, and never touch.

The carriage pulled up to the manor and Lark stepped out, relieved that he didn't have to limp anymore. He found the colonel in the breakfast room with coffee and crackers. The colonel was halfway presentable in all black with a white ruffled shirt and neckerchief. The color revealed that his hair wasn't quite purest black, but had hints of red mahogany. He glared at Lark and straightened up. "Surprisingly tasteful."

"The crackers or my fashion sense?" Lark leaned on his cane. "I know you don't like me like this, but we're meeting jesters today and I have to be fashionable and wary and I can't afford to be shy."

"How can you—" The colonel winced and softened his voice. "How can you change like that? It's like—"

"I'm one of them. And you hate them."

"I don't like it. Change back."

"No." It hurt to tell him no. He desperately wanted to be Mark again too. Maybe that was Lark's saving grace.

He walked over to the colonel and allowed himself to lightly brush his shoulder as if by accident on his way by. "Have you heard from the general?"

"We're expected at two."

"Then we'd better leave soon." Lark went out and waited for him by the door.

The moments stretched but all he could think to do was stare in the vague direction where the colonel would have to come from. He had no purpose but as a physical and intellectual adornment. Without the colonel he might as well have been empty clothes hanging by the door.

At last the colonel arrived, no gloves, no hat, but at least he had a dress rapier. Lark opened the door for him, and they waited on the step for Philip. The carriage was still up front.

"I thought only living masks changed men," the colonel remarked.

That wasn't worth answering. Obviously the mask had changed Mark. Lark just hoped it wasn't forever.

"I think that you'd do better without the mask."

Please, just leave it alone. "This isn't easy for me."

"Then why do it?"

"Because I don't know what I'll have to do tonight. Debuts are tests. There will be welcoming gifts, and many of them will be connected to intrigues. They'll test my skills, my knowledge, look for weak points, including my ability to wear a mask."

The colonel clasped his hands behind his back and rocked on his heels impatiently. "All right then. You have two masks. Why not wear one of those? At least you can remove those and wear them only when needed."

"For one thing, one is a death mask."

"You have a—"

"And," Lark said, loudly cutting him off, which made the colonel wince, "for all I know the mask that Gutter gave me could be worse." Philip finally approached from the back of the manor. "This comes from inside of me.

It's part of what I am. I'm sorry you don't like it but it will always be there even after the mask is gone. It was there before. You just didn't see it."

The colonel waited until they were inside the carriage and on their way before he spoke again. "I suppose I could have deduced that the mask you took from your friend would be a death mask, but I wish you'd shared that with me openly."

"It's supposed to help protect us from the sins we do." Obsidian had managed to spare his soul from murder, but he faced the *morbai* alone. Lark would have never left him to die alone like that. He wouldn't have allowed vain hopes of saving Obsidian's life distract him from what had to be done. It seemed so clear now. No wonder he hated himself.

His left eye reminded him that Obsidian had meant to murder Lake long before he went to the bridge. It wasn't as if he didn't deserve to have the *morbai* after him.

The colonel appeared lost in thought. Lark waited until his expression changed ever so slightly before he asked a question that should have been asked a long time ago. "Are you sure you've never met Obsidian?"

"Yes, I'm certain."

"You said you've been courted many times before. You don't remember a young man about five foot eleven, curly dark hair, dark clothes with gold, and this rapier?"

At least the colonel bothered to glance at it. "No."

It made no sense. Why would Obsidian trust a man he'd never met over what he'd implied would be Gutter's objection?

"Wait." The colonel sat up a little. "Sid. Obsidian. I remember someone from about two years ago. He didn't court me. He was visiting someone in Perida. He stayed with the mayor." The colonel's eyes narrowed, perhaps in puzzlement but it also might have been suspicion or an unpleasant memory. "I met him only in passing. I was in town to look at horses and Feather introduced us. She forced me to accept a dinner invitation. I couldn't have spent more than five or six hours in his presence."

"What did you talk about?"

"I don't have your memory, Lark. The only thing I recall about it now was how cruelly Feather teased me. I think she suspected. Men are so flattered and flustered by her ...."

"But you weren't interested, and she's either vain, or observant, or worst of all both, and she suspected that the only explanation for your indifference was that no woman has ever turned your head." That was important to know, especially if Lark met Feather tonight.

"She'd be wrong, though. There are women I admire and respect, women who I would consider marrying."

"Your passion overwhelms me," Lark said dryly.

A faint smile briefly lit the colonel's eyes. For that moment Lark's loneliness eased, but then the clouds covered the sun again.

They arrived at a manor not too far from the governor's estate. Uncomfortably the governor was there, but he let Fine manage his conversations and remained courteous to his son. Lark memorized the names of all the military men, only half of whom had jesters, and watched them interact. No conspiracies leapt out, at least not into the open. Aside from the governor's cold manner toward his son, everyone seemed to get along well. It made for a dull afternoon. He memorized the wives' names just in case he might need to ask about them later, including the ones not in attendance with their husbands. Lark smiled and joked and drank very little but behaved later in the day as if he'd kept pace with everyone. The colonel's discomfort eased and he even rewarded Lark with a few smiles.

Then a messenger arrived with two letters. One was a formal invitation to dinner written in simple handwriting on expensive paper. Baron Gareth Newell, 124 View Road, Perida, would be honored to host a celebration in honor of Colonel Rohn Evan's bonding to Lord Jester Lark at 6pm, dessert and a concert to follow. The second was a work of art—folded red paper adorned with gilding, dried and pressed flowers and feathers, embossing and ribbon. The script was written on white silk.

Welcome.

Eight P.M.

Feather's signature had sharp angles and edges and she'd drawn a plume from the base of the first letter.

They had to leave directly from the general's house to make it to the mayor's house on time. They said their goodbyes and settled back into the carriage.

"You surprised me," the colonel said. "You were very ... you're very graceful."

"Thank you." His gut had tied up into knots.

"But now you seem nervous."

Lark handed him the invitation from Feather. "Keep this for me. It may have a secret message in it and I don't have time to look at it between now and the party." He had little doubt that she'd planned it that way. "I'll be going to her salon partway through the dinner party. I don't expect to be back home until after dawn."

"Don't be ridiculous. I insist that you and I leave together at midnight. They'll know you have to abide by my wishes."

"Please don't." Lark appreciated the protectiveness, but he couldn't allow it to interfere with his work.

"You're exhausted. We're both exhausted."

"That's what they want. They'll test me tonight, and how well I perform will determine what I'll be capable of on your behalf. If you interfere, you will sabotage my ability to serve you, and the islands may be lost because of it."

"I'm concerned that you will make an error or even get yourself killed before we've even begun." His hangover must have eased because he raised his voice without flinching. "You're holding well, but it can't last. Not through to the dawn. You'll make up for anything that's lost in the days ahead. I see no benefit."

Lark wanted to slap him. "Every jester of note, enemy or ally, will be at that salon tonight. That won't happen again until another jester debuts. This may be my only chance to see them together. They'll tire out as well. When they do I hope to catch those little barbs and dark looks and nods and subtle smiles that will tell me more about the politics on this island than months of investigation. Yes, it's risky, but it's necessary. And by the way, no one is going to kill me tonight, or in the morning when I drag myself home with the last of my strength. Those with real power will not tolerate an assassination at or directly after a debut. As much as I want to learn about them, they want to know about me and what my arrival means not just to the islands but to the world. Even a young, new jester has connections and those connections must be unraveled far enough for them to determine if I'm a threat, a no one, or of help to their causes."

"You seem wise for someone who claimed to be reluctant to become a jester," the colonel said pointedly.

"It's all academic. I have a good memory. I've read about these things. I know what's expected," Lark reminded him.

"I'm somewhat reassured," the colonel grumbled. "But I hope you will bear in mind that things are different in Perida. Our religion isn't the only thing that differs from the mainland countries. You may find that our jesters will turn to killing more quickly than your mainland kin."

It was a good reminder, though foreknowledge wouldn't help.

The mayor lived in town. His primary residence sat close to his immediate neighbors except in the back, where he had enough cleared land for a modest garden and to pasture two horses. Brick walkways separated the sand street from the more civilized landscaping and allowed people to stroll without danger of being run over by a carriage, though there were very few horses and carriages on the island to fear. The house was built something like a cake with ornate rails on each level. The top two levels were reduced just enough to accommodate handsome balconies. The entrance was recessed between the two large front rooms. Lark could see through the windows of the one on the left, where people had already gathered. Music played on violins and a piano seeped through to the outside, familiar pieces he knew well enough to accompany with his voice if he had to.

The girl who'd played violin so well ... he missed her music, and the sense of peace he felt in Argenwain's garden while he listened to her play. He hoped she was all right.

The curtains were drawn in the other room.

The cane reminded him to hobble a bit as he stepped down from the carriage. The sun had begun to set.

The colonel paused outside the carriage and stared at the house with the same expression he wore when his father had so cruelly berated him, but tension around his nose signaled a tinge of disgust.

Lark took the lead and limped to the door. He didn't have to knock—it opened under his hand.

Feather, the mayor's jesteress, flashed a warm and disarmingly youthful smile that made him doubt that she could ever be anything but sweet and truthful.

She'd be very dangerous.

"Lark." She wore red, and the dress took advantage of her sleek figure. She had little adornment around her hips, just enough to conceal the edges of her corset. The dress lay open in the front to expose deep red skirts and a stunning bodice in a brocade of warm and cold reds that gave it a velvet vibrancy like a fine red rose. The colors made her very pale, but not unappealingly so.

Her mask dominated her. Fashioned like a noblewoman's disguise with soft leather and gems, decorated with an artful application of red feathers, it made her into a young lady going to a ball. He would swear, though he didn't know how he knew, that she'd made it with her own hands. Against his will he felt a kinship to her because of that. Many jesters used old masks or employed a maskmaker.

He bowed with a brief flourish and accepted her offered hand, lingering in his kiss. It wasn't difficult to pretend awe in the face of her beauty. She kept hold of his hand. "Feather. Thank you. I'm in awe. I have to apologize for the inconvenience. I know this is all extremely sudden, and I'm in your debt for all the trouble you must have gone through. And yet," he said, peering past her, "no one would know that you haven't spent months planning this."

"I had a feeling the first time I saw you that I'd have you in my salon for your debut," she said brightly, pulling him in. "Everyone, our guests of honor have arrived." She gracefully stepped past him to accompany the colonel to the entryway into the drawing room. Everyone stood and applauded, fans flashing, nearly forty faces smiling, a few masked, most natural and human and eager. A few seemed too eager and nervous.

The jester with the unpleasant whorled design on his face stood out. He raised his glass of red wine to Lark, and Lark nodded to him. He tried to convey friendliness, but he didn't trust that jester one bit.

Feather left the colonel in the care of the mayor and took Lark around the room. She walked arm in arm with him, her gaze constantly distracted and flitting. At times it seemed she looked away or past him for no discernable reason, and her breath often caught on the edge of laughter.

He allowed the names of guests to flow into his memory, bowing as necessary. The island convention made it easier in many ways. Everyone was referred to as baron or baroness, and all the jesters present had been bound, though after tonight he wouldn't have to use the formal address. He was one of them, and they would all be on jester name basis from now on.

"Baron Kilderkin," Feather said, finally coming to the trio Lark most wanted to meet. "Lady Winsome Kilderkin, and Lord Jester Juggler."

Baron Kilderkin looked like the sort who married late in life and drank too much wine, as evidenced by his thick body, folds of yellowed skin and bloodshot eyes. He appeared unrelated to the lovely but clearly athletic lady of about Lark's age with amber hair and blue-gray eyes. She'd dressed in a pale blue gown. He remembered her. She'd stood up during the trial and cried for a physician. Neither of them seemed to fit the whorled mask and wary, cat-like stare of Kilderkin's jester.

Lark bowed to them all. "Pleased to meet you." He gave more warmth to the inflection than he had to the others so far. He could only hope for two things—that he'd just identified his worst enemy, or had met his best potential ally. If Juggler wanted an alliance, it seemed he planned to make it very hard for Lark to earn their trust. Anything in between would end up as a long battle with nothing to gain from it but the usual social necessities.

"Are you recovering well?" Either Winsome didn't know that one wasn't supposed to interrupt when a jester was in the midst of a long stretch of interviews, or she didn't care.

It made Lark smile. "Yes, thank you."

Feather finished the introductions and then took him into the vast dining room, where two dozen more guests had already seated themselves at a few of the tables and were deep in conversation. She didn't interrupt them, as none were jesters and therefore didn't need to be formally introduced to him if they already knew the colonel. She murmured about them into Lark's ear, somehow maintaining that sense of innocence while being very intimate. The most interesting group consisted of a man who made his wealth in sugar, a Cathretan lord who immigrated shortly before the war and fought nobly to keep the islands free, an admiral, two captains, and two single ladies whose parents were in the other room, and one of the lady's brother.

Feather led him toward the back of the house to a sun room where a much smaller group sat in conversation—two families with three daughters and two sons between them, two more jesters one of which was attached to the admiral, a single gentleman visiting his cousin the captain, and the gentleman's best friend.

Feather gathered everyone up at the dinner tables and the servers began bringing in a fragrant cream soup apparently made from a root similar to parsnip that grew exclusively on the island. The cook had combined it with imported carrots—exotic here but a common enough winter vegetable for Lark. The tropical seasonings, sweet and hot, made it uncommonly good. While he ate and asked about island life, he memorized the seating order so that he could write it down later. Feather no doubt took great care in arranging who sat where, and it might help him unravel the island politics later. She placed Winsome at the colonel's right elbow, and she sat at Lark's left at the head of the table opposite the mayor.

So the mayor wasn't married. Even if he'd been married, Lark would have wondered if Feather adorned his bed most nights. If the mayor ever wanted to get married she might have serious problems enticing someone suitable to join the household. Few women would feel comfortable not just with having a beauty like her in the house, but the remarks people would make behind their backs about the mayor's relationship with his jesteress.

That problem might prove to be an opportunity for him to grow closer to the imposing, heavy-shouldered mayor and his unique partner.

Roasted beef proved to be another mundane winter dish made fresh by a sauce based on a number of mysterious fruits. Their bread surpassed anything he'd had on the mainland. They served it with a surprisingly mediocre fruity red wine that worked passably with the meat. His mother wouldn't have offered such a wine for a nobleman's table, never mind for a debut party. Lark took it as a sign of ongoing strained relations between Cathret, which made the best wine in the world, and Meridua, rather than a comment on the butler's taste and skill.

"What school did you attend?" Juggler asked.

"Tells and Keener." Mark would have cringed but Lark didn't hesitate. He had no other answer and wasn't particularly ashamed of it.

"I've never heard of that school."

"It's a tutelage system."

Juggler's eyes narrowed. "I'm not certain I understand."

"I'm afraid everyone would be bored if I went into detail. I can sum up by saying that it takes a little less than a decade to complete studies."

"Is it something one does on one's own?" Juggler asked.

"Not at all. A master instructor selects the individual tutors, and guides the overall study." Lark knew what question would have to come next. "But that is something I'm not permitted to discuss openly. I could hint at why something like that would need to be kept secret. Unfortunately such hints would only inspire conjecture or doubts which aren't suitable for a debut."

"I'm satisfied with his credentials." Those were the first words the colonel had ventured without having them forced out of him by social necessity. "And if I may add to the mystery, a colleague of his was a welcomed visitor to our island. It is through that person that we became acquainted. You should have no reservations in regard to his fitness."

Lark wished he hadn't said that. "And now it becomes a game. I apologize for that."

"Please don't apologize." Feather laid her hand over his. He forced himself to blush and briefly lowered his lashes. His mask carefully concealed some of his expressions, but a good jester would notice his eyes and the color at his throat and he had to respond to her touch. The last thing the colonel needed was anything that would arouse more suspicions as to his lean. "This is the most excitement we've had in years, and it'll give us all something to talk about besides the poverty of our wine cellars."

"The wine paired beautifully with the roast beef, by the way," Lark told her.

"You're being too kind." Her hand slipped away and he deepened the blush. He dabbed his mouth with a napkin and made a subtle show of composing himself.

The servants began to take the plates away. Feather stood and curtseyed. "I'm afraid I'm going to be horribly rude and steal our new jester away for the remainder of the evening. I hope you all will enjoy dessert."

The other jesters stood and Lark got up as well. The colonel gave him a stark look.

He doesn't want me to leave.

Some of the cold and loneliness eased inside him, but Lark couldn't afford to comfort him or even apologize. He certainly couldn't stay, though he desperately wanted to. He left the only person he cared about in the whole house behind and allowed Feather to take his arm. He escorted her to the salon on the other side of the house.

Heavy mahogany double doors, fully carved and lined to thwart eavesdroppers, opened into a paradise of books, musical instruments, a large parquet dance floor, card tables, games and a vast liquor cabinet glittering with crystal. At least thirty jesters waited within. A group of six played cards. One set aside his book and stood, and the jester seated at a harpsichord playing a soft minuet concluded mid-piece with a flourish. Three old jesters barely gave him a glance from where they smoked in a dark corner. They sat as if they ranked alongside kings. Vanilla scented the oil in the lamps, filling the room with its sweet, warm scent.

And whispers ... he hoped it was the jesters, or a trick of the room, but he thought he heard something more, things that might only be in his mind.

So many masks in one place. The weight of that much skill, wisdom, intelligence and craft dragged down Lark's carefully held calm. Giddy and terrified at once, he allowed himself to be introduced to the new jesters. She left the three elders for last.

"Onyx." The dark porcelain mask with inlaid pearl glimmered with brief interest before he returned to his introspection. "Mortify." Something like a silk scarf with rough holes for eyes and black lace edges dipped in acknowledgement. The mouth smiled. "Grin." Grin wore a painted death mask of delicate wood, animalistic with a toothy grin and wild eyes that had holes in the pupils to peer through. Lark's heart leapt in fear and he was grateful when Feather dropped a respectful curtsy to the three jesters and drew Lark toward the dance floor. "The worst is almost over," Feather promised. "We've all been through this. I botched mine, so don't crawl away never to come out again if something goes wrong. Promise me, Lark, that you'll remain in my salon after your performance?"

He laughed, because he knew now what he had to do. Poets bemoaned the fact that some of the greatest artistic triumphs of the human spirit happened behind closed doors at jesters' debuts. Most of the jesters joined him in a chuckle, no doubt remembering their own debuts. It didn't matter that some of them wished him well, while others wished him ill, or even dead. For now they would all welcome him into their family.

It was a good thing that Gutter wasn't there, because Lark didn't plan on doing anything to make him proud. He wanted to do something he hadn't done in a very long time.

He wanted to honor the boy that Gutter had destroyed piece by little piece until he'd become something Mark's father wouldn't have recognized.

Lark closed his eyes and took a breath of his past inside of himself. He smelled oak stained by dark wine, and fish, and baked bread and old cart horses and spilled beer. He smelled the piss, sweat and vinegar of the street where he'd grown up. He heard the endless crowds, the rattle of carts, cursing, singing, crying, laughing, and children.

He heard his own laughter echoing in his memory as he ran with childhood friends whose names he could barely remember. Jenny and

Mitchell he remembered, though time had smudged their faces. And he began to sing their favorite childhood chant that they always sang while playing stick-skip in the street. He added embellishments to it by the third verse. The song came alive and he mated it to a sea chant in the same key. He then altered it into classic aria form. His voice honored the beauty of that innocent boy's voice, spoiled by lessons as cruel as the task master that insisted upon them. The aria honored that cruelty as well, because without that hardship, the boy would have had no chance of becoming a man.

He sang that aria from on high to the boy, and then returned to the sea chantey because the boy loved them. At last his voice settled low on its heels and softly sang the stick-skip song with skill the boy would never dream he could achieve.

But you do achieve it, Mark. And you will survive. Don't let Gutter break you, and don't let your own fears stop you. Grow up and be your own person. It'll be worth it. I promise.

Lark opened his eyes. The masks stared back at him, expressions hidden, eyes unblinking. They seemed to take in a breath in unison, and then the applause came.

The applause converted to a rhythm. Jesters rushed to musical instruments and began to play.

And they began to dance.

"You'll never see me in the company of these mainland-loving cold bloods," Bell told Lark, dealing another hand of cards. "But I can't resist a debut. There's something about the beginning of things. It's a birth as profound as a child's."

"And who's the proud mother?" Juggler asked.

Lark laughed. "Oh, I'm an orphan."

"Why do I get the sense that that's true in more than one way?" Bell asked.

Lark didn't let his shiver show through. It was amazing what they drew out of him, but he learned just as much from them. No book could describe the sensation of being carried by a flooded river with the wreckage of a city he'd never seen. Every shard of conversation came from a foundation he could only deduce and whose history he might never know. "Secrets are so rude, but we can't live without them. They're our skin."

"So true."

"You didn't just deal him a new hand," Furnish protested, striding over from a tight and laughter-filled conversation. "I won't let you keep him. Burn! Take Lark's place at the table."

"Burn!" Bell called. "I'll yield him if you come over. We haven't spoken in weeks."

Lark left his cards face down—he hadn't even had a chance to look at them yet—and followed Furnish. Furnish didn't take him to the group, but led him to the three elder jesters and dragged over a chair for him. "Sit," Furnish told him. "Stay."

Lark quieted under the old men's long looks. One of them began to roll a fresh smoke. "Do you know who you remind me of?"

"No, lord jester."

"Onyx," he reminded him. Onyx drew out a case of dried leaves and carefully packed them into the paper. "You remind me of Gerson Habrick."

"I hear he's Dellai now," Mortify said.

"Really." Onyx delicately licked the paper and rolled it with practiced ease. Grin opened a lamp and held it for him so he could light it.

Onyx offered the smoke to Lark.

"No thank you."

"They say you had leaf before the trial," Onyx said. "And gracian for your cure."

Lark nodded. "If you please, I'd rather not repeat those experiences."

"It does not please me." He held out the smoldering smoke.

"It's a test," Mortify told him. "We all go through it."

"It seems to me I've already taken that test."

The rest of the room quieted.

"You can perform gracefully before some of the most jaded and critical minds in the world," Onyx said. "But you've yet to show us what your mind becomes when your skull is a sieve and your tongue is cut and your eyes see through the canvas that is this world into the place we all must go."

"Take it." Feather's voice had none of its girlish charm.

"Take it," Mortify told him, "or get out."

Lark got up and limped out. He was furious with them, and himself, and he hated everything. It wasn't even midnight. He let himself out the door and went out into the tropical night. The dark and stars and soft sea wind cooled his temper but deepened his despair.

They knew he'd refuse. They didn't want him, and he didn't want them. But at least he had Bell. He was sure he had Bell on his side.

Someone ran after him. Lark slowed down and glanced back.

And stopped.

Juggler slowed and stopped a few paces away. "Come back." His voice had no inflection in it.

"It's not just a test to me," Lark told him, his anger rushing back. He wanted to say that he didn't want to go back, but he did very much want to return to that magical place that the smoke promised to give him.

A place without pain.

"You made Onyx look like a fool."

I did?

"He's a dangerous enemy, but he's old and he matters less and less. Come on. Don't be such an obedient pup." Juggler turned to the side, inviting but still lacking in emotion. The only thing that betrayed any feeling was his rapier. Lark couldn't say for certain why the way that Juggler held the pommel to keep the blade in check with such familiar indifference betrayed the jester's loneliness. But it did. As lonely as Lark felt, it was a shallow and passing emotion compared to the depths in which Juggler seemed to be endlessly falling.

"You don't speak for the others, do you."

"Fuck them." A trace of smile appeared and vanished. "You showed a little strength back there. Now is your chance to really show them how strong you can be."

"By accepting an invitation from you as easily as I allowed them to pinch my temper?"

"You killed my men." Juggler turned back toward Lark and took a step closer. His hand tightened on the pommel. Lark had to focus all his control to keep himself from reaching for his own rapier. He trusted that Juggler couldn't draw using the pommel faster than he could reach and draw in an off-line retreat. "Now does my invitation seem too much like an alliance against the others? If you walk back with me, you will still be very much alone."

"So why are you asking me back?"

"Because if you walk away, you'll win. I want you in the contest. The islands didn't win the war, you know. Cathret sailed away and left us here to rot. We're nothing but sailors who claim to have conquered the sea, when all we did was survive a single crossing thanks to a little grace and a great deal of luck bought with barrels of blood."

If Juggler had understood that the colonel needed Lark solely to find a conspiracy that would give advantage to the mainland, he would have never given that away.

He had to become friends with this mask. "You're wrong. The islands soundly trounced the mainland. Their naval forces are still recovering from their losses, some of which are tied to your docks and many more which decay at the bottom of the sea, along with a horrific number of their men. But if that doesn't satisfy you, I suppose I'll have to do. I think I represent about all the might the mainland can muster. Five foot six, barely over a hundred pounds and expensive shoes likely to trip me up if I ever got in a fight."

That earned a smirk.

"Why did your men attack me?" Instinct drove him forward relentlessly, defying all reason.

"You would never understand. I could say it was your wealth that drew them. I would also be accurate if I implicated their hatred of everything from the mainland. I believe you made it easy for them to attack you. They may have even truly believed you posed a threat to the man you now serve. It would all be true, but none of it would be the real reason." He spoke with real emotion now, his eyes burning from behind his ugly mask. "When every hour of every day feels as if you're asleep, and the world expresses its derision with handsome words of praise, you crave the purity found a breath away from your last heartbeat. All they needed was an excuse, and you provided them with many."

Lark didn't have to ask if Juggler craved the same thing. It was in his voice. And he was right. Lark couldn't understand it. Every time he relived that fight in the street he hoped it would be the last time. "Thank you."

"In exchange for my candor, I will expect you to do something for me sometime. I believe you're the sort of person who will hold yourself to that."

"I won't disappoint you." It was his first open pact with a jester, and Gutter would have rightfully lashed out in rage at him for making one with such a dangerous mask when he knew so little.

Lark hoped he knew just enough.

Chapter Twenty

The jesters sang and played him a farewell song. It may have been traditional for debuts—he didn't know.

Feather walked him to the door. "Are you sure you won't accept my carriage?"

Her face was so close ....

Lark touched her mouth lightly with his lips. His tongue darted with the slightest flicker between her lips, making brief, intimate contact with the tip of her tongue. She seized his hands and nuzzled closer but he evaded her, keeping the contact fleeting and tantalizing the same way he wanted to kiss the colonel for the first time someday.

Someday will probably be never.

Lark drew away and avoided her gaze. After an entire evening of dancing about, her eyes finally focused on him and him alone. He worried about what she might see. "I'm sorry," he whispered. "It must bore you to have so many men in love with you, and jesters must be the worst. They're pretending it's a game, and you have to play and—"

She set her fingers over his mouth and he quieted. It made it easier to let her lead the way. "You're wise for one so young."

That made him smile. "You can't be much older than I am."

"You might be surprised," she whispered. "Anyway, it's not boring with you. You're different."

Not too different, he hoped. "Good night. And thank you."

"I'm glad you came back." She turned in a way that let her watch him watch her walk back to the house for a good distance. He lingered a little longer than he wanted to, then set off toward Grant's room.

He wasn't sure Grant would be awake. A slight glow under the door encouraged him to knock softly.

Heavy footsteps approached the door. "Who is it?"

"Lark. Your friend. The jester," he added when the door didn't budge on the first word.

Grant opened the door, his bulk silhouetted by a single candle. He seemed a foot taller than Lark remembered.

"I have something for you. I was going to slip it under the door, but I saw the light—"

Grant stepped aside. "You look different with the—you know."

Lark ventured inside, uncertain. "I know it's almost time to go out fishing. I won't keep you."

"How would someone like you know when it's time to fish?" Grant shut the door. It was more of a welcome than Lark had hoped for.

"I grew up three blocks from the sea. Sometimes the noise would wake me up and I'd look out and see the fishermen with their nets, and sailors leaving their wives or their whores, and all that sort of thing." Lark drew the borrowed paper from his waistcoat and set it on the rough little table. He wondered if he'd ever see the inside of this room again.

Grant strode over. "What's that?"

"The alphabet. Do you want to try?"

"If this is about me saving your life, don't worry about it. It just happened. I didn't even really mean to. Not that I didn't want to, don't get me wrong." Grant seemed to not want to look at him. He fussed with cleaning his lone, empty breakfast plate from the table. "I guess I'm just saying it's not worth you going out of your way. There's no lighted way I'd learn to write anyway, when I can't even read."

"They're intimately connected. That's clever of you to think of it. I don't think that it's necessarily obvious to someone who's illiterate." Grant ducked his head at the praise. "Would you mind if I washed my face?"

"Go ahead."

It took a lot more work than he expected. He had to use soap and water and oil and cheap brandy before he got his face clean. His skin burned, but he had himself back. Exhaustion dragged him down and bent his spine, and he wasn't sure—maybe Lark had seen the truth of things, that he had no friends, no one who cared about him or even liked him. At least without the mask he could entertain the possibility that Grant might permit him a few more minutes of his time.

Grant sat at the table staring at the letters. Mark limped over and stood beside him. He bent and braced against the table so he could trace over the letters at the bottom. "These letters are your name. You can learn the rest if you like, but if you have a moment I'll teach you how to draw this."

"I don't have anything to write with."

Of course he wouldn't. "We'll use wine." Mark fetched the bottle and a cup. He dipped his finger in. "Do you remember the G I showed you?" He traced it on the paper. It didn't leave much of an impression, but it didn't have to.

Grant attempted a G on his own. The paper moved around on him, frustrating his awkward attempt so Mark helped him hold it. At the end of three tries he had a pretty good one. It encouraged him to try the R. Mark pulled up the other chair and they filled the bottom of the page with GRs.

"Before you know it you'll be able to sign your name."

"That might come in handy," Grant admitted.

"If you want I can come back tonight, or tomorrow if that's too soon, with some paper and such."

"Don't you got jesterly things to do?" It could have been a rebuff, but Grant's tone was more puzzled than anything.

"Yes, I do. But it's work, just like fishing is work, or baking, or what have you. No one wants to work all day every day, and no one is entirely defined by what they do. And—" He remembered singing to the boy he'd been. Making friends came so much more naturally to him in those days. The shy overtures, followed by that wonderful feeling that the friendship had always existed and always would. "I'd like to think that we're friends."

It took a blink of Grant's eyes and a twitch on his cheek and it was done. Grant smiled and he outshone all the wonders Mark had witnessed at his debut. "Okay." He let out a breathy laugh. "Wow. Am I not supposed to tell anyone or anything like that?"

"I'll tell you what. I'll try not to come here in my costume so I don't embarrass you in front of your friends, and you can tell whomever you like."

Grant choked on a laugh. He looked at the dawn's light glowing on his threadbare, checked curtain.

"I'd better go." Mark braced up, grabbed his cane, and Grant walked with him to the door, down the long stairs, and part way down the street before Mark started to shiver. He didn't realize what it was at first until he recognized the intersection where Grant had led him to his room, bleeding.

"You want me to walk you to the parks?" Grant asked.

He knew. No derision, no pity, just a matter-of-fact question.

Mark gave him a matter-of-fact answer. "I'll be more careful this time."

"You'd better be." Grant waved as he walked away. "See you tonight?"

"I hope so."

Lark was stronger than him. He never flinched walking through this neighborhood, though it was dark and the remaining men, however many there might be, could easily use revenge as an excuse to try and feel alive again. Mark hated that about Lark, and the cold, and the loneliness, and the constant calculation. Lark even hated himself. He hated himself enough that he had to obliterate his own face to feel like someone worthy of friendship again.

Mark slowly limped toward the parks. The island might not have carriages for hire, but they'd have messengers. He'd hire one and wait for the colonel's carriage in the church garden rather than fake limping all the way home.

A carriage rolled up the street behind him. Mark turned to look in case it was one the jesters he'd met who might be willing to take him home.

Mark nearly collapsed in relief when he saw the gray-haired former-soldier. "Philip!" He waved but Philip had already seen him and drew the horses to a halt. "I hope you haven't been all over the city looking for me."

"The colonel said if you weren't at the mayor's to try at Mr. Roadman's. I wasn't quite sure where he was at but I saw 'im on the street and he said you were headed for the parks. And here we are."

Mark let himself in before Philip could step down to help. "If I fall asleep on the way just leave me in the carriage." He shut the door, the wheels began to roll easily on the sand, he leaned back in the seat, and sank into bliss.

The colonel roused him. His eyes were bloodshot and stormy. "I'm glad to see you home," he said curtly.

Mark's mind groped desperately for more sleep. It was almost, not quite but almost, as bad as his hangover—was that only yesterday morning?

"A letter arrived this morning," the colonel told him. "It's in a puzzle scroll. The key is waiting for you at the church."

That woke him up for all of a minute. When his thoughts couldn't settle on a theory about who might have sent it—it might not have even been someone he'd met yet—he lost the last of his will to stay awake. Philip, the colonel and Trudy all helped settle him into bed, and he sank into soft bliss once more.

Mark locked himself in his bedroom and cleared his desk of half-finished songs, writing samples and notes.

His first puzzle scroll. He put on the winter gloves he'd worn on his trek through the snow, though no gloves he'd heard of would resist the needles that would snap from the case into his flesh if he made a mistake.

He hoped the priest had given him the correct key, or the message would be ruined, or he'd be poisoned, or both. The puzzle scroll might not be loaded, but he'd been taught to always assume that they were.

He counted the cuts in the key and carefully slid it in. One. It only turned to the left. He flinched when it clicked. Two. It only turned to the left again. His mouth was so dry he couldn't swallow. Click. Three, right. Click. It would be better if it got stuck, as most mis-fit keys would, than to turn in the wrong direction as a bad copy might. Four, left. Click. Had the sender tested it for safety? Five, right. Click. Each turn released a section of the puzzle within. The last turn popped the case and Mark jerked his hands back. No moisture, no chemical scents, just sheaves of paper-thin metal opening as the puzzle scroll hinged open. Each nested layer contained a page of paper. The central chamber had a pouch.

The coded letters written in familiar script gripped his heart. Gutter. That code was the only one Gutter had taught him personally, a code just between the two of them. He'd known it so long and practiced it so often that he could read it native.

Mairi died because of sin; unworthy lovers did her in. Lost, but she still lives between a morning song and soul unseen. Love will never die or fail, though away from her we sail and lose ourselves to storm and sea pretending we are truly free. Love will once again belong to soul unseen and morning song, and they will name a child of sail who will upon the waves prevail.

I can only guess what drove you away. It could be the belief that I desired you to go, or that I forced you to go, or that you had to go for reasons of your own. My concern for your safety is rivaled only by the dread that you may have been wounded in body or soul and have gone to strangers to heal rather than trusting in me. Whatever the reason, please trust in my friendship and love as I trust in you. Perhaps you doubt my motives. What you can't know is what I haven't allowed you to remember, though it's in your mind waiting to help you understand.

Come home quickly. I have so much to tell you, and it will change everything.

Mark stood up and paced. His hands trembled and he thought he'd be sick.

Gutter didn't necessarily know Mark was here. He'd wait for confirmation of the scroll's delivery before he'd act one way or another. If Mark didn't go to him, either Gutter himself or someone on his behalf would come to bring Mark back.

Mark paced faster. He wanted to run, but he had nowhere to run to even if he could excuse himself from the colonel's side to deal with this. If Gutter had asked, Mark couldn't have even told him why he wanted to run. He just knew he felt trapped, hunted and ashamed.

That shame ate at his insides. He'd bound himself to someone of low consequence, at least from Gutter's perspective. Anger would be preferable to the disappointment Mark anticipated.

He'll learn of it soon enough. Best tell him myself.

Mark had no reason to believe Gutter would kill him, and killing the colonel would serve no purpose. Mark would still be bound to him. He doubted that Gutter would vent his anger that way knowing it would strand Mark politically forever.

He hoped that logic and reasoning could temper Gutter's reaction. If Gutter had burned *Mairi* and her crew alive, then no one could predict him, not using any reason or motive that could apply to a sane person.

The fragility of Mark's political situation might prevent the lord jester from coming and fetching Mark himself. Gutter arriving on the colonel's doorstep would be very much like the king himself stopping by for a nice month-long visit. Whatever opinions the islanders held about Colonel Evan would explode into a storm of lies and speculation.

That truth might sway Gutter from interfering if he wanted to keep Mark safe.

Gutter no doubt sent the puzzle scroll with instructions that it be returned along with the key if the messenger couldn't find ... had it been addressed to Lark, or Mark Seaton? That might hint at what Gutter had designed, or suspected, depending on whether he'd manipulated Mark or had tracked him down after a desperate search.

The only reason the sacred messenger had delivered the scroll to the colonel was the bond. Even a sacred bond wasn't strong enough to hand Colonel Evan both the key and the puzzle scroll to complete the delivery. Now that Mark had gotten the key from him, the messenger could leave.

The messenger would catch the next suitable ship back toward the mainland to report a successful delivery. Mark was running out of time to respond to Gutter before news, like a new bonding to one of the island's most famed men, would reach him.

He found some old stationary and a pen in his bedroom's desk and began to write.

I can't come home.

Mark stepped back from the desk and forced himself to consider those words and what might follow. Would Gutter trust his assessment or would he try to bring Mark back by force? He wished he understood the full meaning of Gutter's poem. Trying to guess the meaning was dangerous—it would be too easy to misinterpret, though he thought he had the gist of it.

Home. Calling Seven Churches home had already begun to feel like a lie, though Perida didn't quite feel like home yet.

Should he mention Obsidian?

No. That could bring him here in a shot for the book and the ring. Right now he can only guess that I might have them.

He envied the famed jesters of old. Their secret exchanges weren't just clever, but tightly framed so that intended correspondents couldn't mistake each others' meanings while those who intercepted the messages would be misled and lost.

That made him realized something. Gutter could have written that poem such that Mark couldn't mistake its meaning. He must have blurred it a little on purpose, probably to keep Mark uncertain so he would be afraid to do anything but what Gutter asked him to do.

The letter had come too late to prevent Mark from doing anything drastic, if that had been Gutter's hope. Mark exposed a fresh piece of paper, leaned on the desk and wrote his next line near the center of it.

I love you, and miss you.

Hopefully Gutter would read trust and care in those words.

Unfortunately those words didn't lie. Somehow he'd lost the certainty that Gutter had to be involved in all that destruction. The letter had moved him like a love song, and he had to admit that he felt lonely and afraid even with the colonel to protect him. He'd need to find his anger, or something just as strong, to protect him from Gutter's influence before they reunited.

I'm happy, sound and safe here. I'll come to you when I can, he wrote on a new page. That wasn't perfectly true, but true enough for his purposes.

He'd include the gazette with its torrid description of his and Colonel Evan's jesterly elopement so that Gutter couldn't escape the full meaning of those words.

One more page.

I'll present myself when I can, too soon and not soon enough for both of us. Please wait for me. I beg your patience and I hope you will extend the trust that you so passionately described to me.

He might write a completely different letter depending on what he found in the pouch. At least he'd set down his initial answer. It would be a good starting point.

The pouch held an extra key and a vial. He opened the vial carefully and waited for its scent to reach his face.

The cloying, over-strong scent, a little like bad figs and dull brandy, touched his memory to a lesson that went over some of the world's most deadly poisons, an exotic and little-known one from the Surmellidan. It made his skin prickle. He closed the vial and set it aside.

The last item was a small roll of velvet with a flat backing.

Four golden sol and a pair of matched diamonds. A small fortune, presumably so that he could buy clothes and live well until Gutter reached him, or perhaps a reminder of the wealth he'd left behind and that would be his again if he returned. His thoughts leapt to only one use. He had even less time to dwell on the letter than he'd guessed. He set the pages in, and coiled the gazette at the center. He didn't bother with refreshing the poison. Mark locked it, and hurried out with the puzzle scroll and the velvet roll held tightly in his hands. "Miss Trudy! Get Philip. I need the carriage again."

"Can you do it?" Mark's impatience made him more forceful than he meant to be.

Dellai Bertram stared at Mark for a long time, not so much at him as into him. It made Mark even more uncomfortable.

The Dellai had no furniture, or books, or statues, only carved stone that made the walls, columns and ceiling into a garden-like space of white marble. Despite its graceful lines, the dellai's meeting chamber was a dead, cold place. "I see the advantage to you. What would be the Church's advantage?" the dellai asked.

"I could pay you a fee."

"How much?"

"I would have to investigate. You remember the effects I listed?"

"Oh yes." The dellai set his hand high on a marble tree branch and gripped it. "But this isn't just a fiscal matter. I don't make a habit of assisting jesters. And if I assist one, why shouldn't I assist any other that comes to me?"

"You want some sort of assurance."

"I want something tangible of use to all that is good and just in the world. At the moment I have no way of knowing if helping you will be of general benefit to all, or if it will create problems. For all I know, you may already be acting in ways that your new master would not approve." The dellai let his hand slip back down to gesture broadly. "Some sort of direct benefit now will at least offset any future trouble you may cause."

The messenger might leave any moment.

Mark remembered the death mask. "There was something in particular on my list that might be of interest to you." He was fairly certain he shouldn't be doing this, but he never intended to use the mask, and it might be safer here regardless. "A certain mask."

The dellai's expression fixed in place for a moment before he relaxed into a false smile. "I remember."

"What do you suggest I do with it?"

"It's a living mask?"

Mark remembered how he felt it flinch under his hand and shivered. "Yes."

"Let me see it before I agree to anything."

Mark bit back a curse. "The messenger won't wait much longer. I won't offer anything to do with the death mask again. Accept or decline quickly, please, before it's too late."

The dellai ground his teeth. "There is something unrelated that I have a bit more interest in, having to do with you and your master." He hesitated. "If Baron Evan dies before you do, you will be at loose ends No one likes to see that sort of thing, most especially the Church. I will do this for you on one condition. You will offer your services to the Church here in Perida. You will swear to do this. We, of course, may decline your offer at the time, but you ought to prepare yourself for the possibility that we will accept."

He had a feeling that swearing an oath to a dellai would bind him as hard as he was bound to the baron. "Why would you want anything to do with me?"

"I thought you were in a hurry."

Mark bit his lip. "I don't trust the Church. I've seen it do terrible things when people get in the way of what it wants." He couldn't bring himself to actually accuse the dellai of arranging for the colonel's death. No, the Church couldn't want Mark that badly, though a part of him wondered what all this was about. The voices? Gutter? The mainland? The dellai's face had flushed pink and Mark had to offer something quickly before the dellai cut off all negotiations. "I ... will present myself. I won't offer myself to the Church blindly, but I will listen to the Church's case and give it serious consideration. If you knew me at all, dellai, you would understand the great concession I make by promising this."

The dellai sighed through his nose. He held out his hand. "Swear."

Mark didn't have time to hesitate. He shook the dellai's hand. "I swear."

"Bring in your messenger," the dellai snapped.

Mark dove for the door.

The messenger was still there.

"He'll see you," Mark told him.

It was hard not to regard the sacred messenger with some awe, knowing their remarkable history and heritage. They were as well-trained as jesters, though in a different direction. This messenger had carried the puzzle scroll all the way from Seven Churches by the Sea without a clear destination. Mark could only guess what kind of danger and obstacles he'd faced trying to find Mark and complete his delivery.

The messenger carried the puzzle scroll in a special satchel. Once over a year ago Professor Vinkin had somehow gotten a messenger's satchel and brought it for Mark to look over. Though it had some interesting pockets and traps, it didn't appear all that special.

This satchel, like Obsidian's death mask, seemed alive.

The messenger with his rough beard and long hair, tough clothing and battered weapons, appeared at ease aside from his impatience. "Dellai, my ship won't wait much longer," he said.

"I will send a guard to hold the ship," the dellai told him.

Rank and sacred credentials didn't appear to sway the messenger. "Dellai, we will miss the tide, and my instructions require me to return as soon as possible. I will not wait."

Dellai Betram gave Mark a long look. "Then I will accompany you personally." He held out his hand.

It took Mark a moment to realize what he wanted. Mark squeezed his hand around the money case, wondering if it might not be used for something better, but he relented and handed it over. It wasn't just handing over the money without any sort of receipt that made him uneasy.

"Seaton?" the dellai asked.

"Yes. Mark Seaton." Why would someone as important as the dellai go all the way to Seven Churches personally? He could send the fortune with the messenger and a sacred guard could receive instructions and go to the mainland on the dellai's behalf.

The dellai glanced at the sacred messenger. "You will bear witness. On behalf of Meridua's Church, I will negotiate for Mark Seaton's indenture to be transferred to us. If it is paid in full by this and his other assets, I will seize any positive balance and you will still owe me that oath. Do we understand each other?"

Mark nodded.

Dellai Bertram walked out, bellowing at various guards to attend to him.

Mark tugged on the messenger's elbow before he could follow. "Tell Gutter—" he began, a bit desperate to find words. Nothing he said could help. He didn't know why it scared him so much to sever this tie to Lord Argenwain and the Cathretan Church, but it did. For many years the debt connected him to Seven Churches like bloodlines tied a family together. After this and the bonding, would Gutter even acknowledge his existence? "Tell Gutter I'm well."

The sacred messenger gave a short nod and strode away. After a breath Mark chased after him. "The message—did he ask you to deliver it to Lark, or Mark Seaton?"

The messenger spared him a glance. "Is there a difference?"

"There is to me."

"I was given both names, and more."

"What other names?"

By this time, with long strides that kept Mark running alongside, his limp abandoned, the messenger reached his horse. "The list is too long to repeat. If we meet again, Lark, I will be glad to oblige you, with Gutter's permission of course." With that he rode away. The dellai stepped up into a carriage, still barking orders, and hurried after him.

Gutter is going to hate me forever. I've ruined everything.

But it was done and done. It had been done when he'd abandoned his indenture, but until now he hadn't appreciated the full consequences of his actions.

So this is freedom.

Mark returned to the carriage. "Thank you, Philip. Please take me home."

"Are you all right, sir?"

Mark smiled. His concern sounded genuine. "I'm fine, thank you."

The long ride seemed much shorter than usual. Hevether Hall, with its stark face, black arched entrance and largely empty rooms felt cold despite the tropical heat constantly wearing at them from the outside. Poetic. A direct opposite of his home in Lord Argenwain's house which had been garish, constantly full of servants and visitors, and in winter had been warm, even hot inside while the ice formed envious knives outside the windows.

He heard the colonel's footsteps coming from the sun room through the hall and the enormous columned gallery that teed with the grand entrance before the man himself appeared. Mark waited near the main sitting room for him. "Where have you been?" The colonel's calm tone couldn't hide his anger.

"On business."

"Our business. You haven't spent an hour here except to sleep, and I have no idea what you're doing. As of now I'm reining you in. You are not to leave this house without my permission."

Mark couldn't help it. The laughed welled up and escaped before he could contain it. "Whatever will please you, my lord and master."

"You find this amusing." His head jerked up and too far back like a horse in proud defiance.

"No one else would, I know. They'd have to have had the day I've had." Mark didn't know where to begin. "Dellai Bertram has run off to the mainland. I've sent a message to Gutter. And I remembered something on my way into town for which I have to apologize."

Colonel Evan's hands flexed open and he stiffened his spine as if bracing for gale winds.

"It's customary for jesters to give a gift shortly after the bonding." His good humor dissolved into shame. "I don't even know what to get you, and I've spent most of my money, so I couldn't—will you give me some time?"

"I had wondered." Wreathed in dignity, the colonel approached a pair of paces. "I also remembered about gifts this morning, and I knew immediately what I wanted to give you, but I was afraid you would hate it."

Mark grinned and a set of soft chuckles tickled out. "We're quite a pair." Was that a smile in the colonel's eyes? He couldn't tell for certain.

"Yes, we are."

Mark chewed his lip. "You have me, sir. Whatever will you do with me?"

The colonel gestured toward the breakfast room. "Let's begin with a discussion."

"About?"

"Everything."

"We had one very splendid Yule in particular. Our last all together." The colonel hopped from rock to rock while the waves crashed. Foam occasionally floated by with the thick spray. Sometimes Mark had a difficult time hearing him over the ocean's roar, and the gull cries, and the sharp peeps from strange birds with brilliant orange throats and flashy black and white wings sharp as knives. "My father, my fiancé, my sister and her family, then two sons, and her husband of course. Later she had two daughters. She had her family in the proper way. Boys first, then girls, and she started at the ideal age. Father was so proud of both of us. We'd made smart matches, and our future looked so promising. He didn't know it yet, but I'd fallen in love with someone unsuitable. But my engagement hadn't fallen apart yet. I was giddy with my secret love, too self-involved and selfish to care about what it meant and what it would do to all of us. I've been happier since then, but never again ... content. For those several days we were a good family in good standing, and our future seemed perfect."

"How old are your nephews and nieces now?" Mark hoped they'd all lived, though of course the odds were against that.

"Little Ricky turns thirteen in a pair of months. He's the eldest. Melissa is four. All four are doing well. Father forbid me from seeing them out of an ignorant fear that I'd do something awful to the boys, but my sister receives me when I visit and ... and we all pretend that I'm obedient and stay away out of concern that I might corrupt them or hurt them. I miss them terribly. I'd see them every day if I could. I'm their only uncle, so I can say I'm their favorite uncle. They do seem to delight in seeing me, if only because they know I'll always have something for them."

It broke Mark's heart to listen to him talking about it as if it were someone else's troubles. What he didn't talk about seemed even more pitiful. Mark didn't even know his lover's name, never mind their history.

"Publicly, of course, we are an unbreakable bastion of loyalty," the colonel continued. "If we see little of each other, it's because we're industrious, and stoic, and all that. And we gather for all the required holidays."

"Who else knows?" He wished he didn't have to ask.

"Amery. A few of my lieutenants. My household and my father's household, of course." The colonel turned briefly to gaze at his home. He never turned his back to the sea for more than a second. Mark followed his example, keeping watch over the waves.

"Speaking of your household, it's too small for a house so large." Mark told him. "What do you have, fifty rooms? And you'd have more if it wasn't built with such immense spaces in it. You're going to need more than Trudy, Philip and Norbert to keep it up."

"Like the hells I do." The colonel said it in a mild tone, but the words stood firm against argument.

"It's not fair to them. They're not just caring for you anymore. Also, I have messages that will need to be delivered. Are you going send Philip for that, and have him be my driver in addition to his duties to the horses and the exterior property ...."

"You need to put my horses to use and stop using that damned carriage so much," the colonel told him.

"I'm not a good rider."

The colonel gave him a sharp look that softened after a moment. "Then you'll learn."

"It's not just messages and travel. We're going to open up more of those rooms and you're going to entertain guests at Hevether."

"No."

"Yes." Mark leapt from rock to rock over streams of flooding seawater to get ahead of him and stand in his way. "You have friends. You need to have them come to visit you. It's the best way to learn what's happening out there. You can't perpetually send me on forays hoping someone will let something slip. I'm a stranger here. Until I can get a reasonable foothold, you have to let me reinforce your alliances and make some of my own through you. Besides, it's very unattractive, sulking out here. Some might consider it romantic, but you'll never be able to take advantage of it. From a political standpoint it's worse than useless. It looks weak."

That last part got his head up.

"Every summer," Mark continued, "we'd have party after party at Pickwelling. The expense was enormous, but the rewards far exceeded it. Lord Argenwain has over a hundred servants and he'd move some of them from his country house to Seven Churches during the peak social season. We needed every last hand that could be crammed into the servant quarters. Sometimes we'd have twenty suites filled with guests, and dances with over two hundred nobles and all their hangers-on in attendance every week. That required constant cooking, cleaning, shopping, arranging, decorating and running about. I'm asking for so much less. A stable boy so that if Philip is away there's someone to tend to a visitor's animals. An apprentice for Philip, and a scullery maid for Norbert. Trudy should have a parlor maid and a chamber maid helping her at the very least. And you should have a full-time laundry maid doing laundry here at Hevether rather than sending your laundry out whenever you run out of stocking and sheets so that we can put more of the rooms to use and have things like curtains and—"

"Stop." A huge wave sent cooling spray high over their heads. It rained down in a soft mist. Sunlight caught the drops in his dark hair. "Just ... stop." He looked stiff and miserable and chilled despite the heat.

"All right." Mark stepped back. "Let's go back to the house."

The colonel followed him obediently, most likely because he didn't know what Mark had planned. Mark herded him through the seaward entrance, up the stairs and back to the seaward and roadward side of the house to the master suite, but not the bedroom. The colonel would certainly throw him out the moment Mark touched him in such an intimate environment. "Have a seat."

The colonel gave Mark one of those now-familiar warning looks, but settled on the narrow chair near his window. Other than a few other matching chairs, a bookshelf and a desk, the large private room between the master bedroom and the lady's suite had little in it. It looked as if he'd been forced to sell all his prize possessions to cover a large debt.

Mark doubted that such a man as this with his frugal lifestyle, lack of bad habits such as drinking and gambling, and lack of friends with bad habits, had any debt that outweighed his assets. The colonel had simply neglected his house, just as he neglected himself. Mark set a firm hand on his shoulder and began to rub. Naturally the colonel flinched.

"What are you doing?"

"Relax."

"I'll have an answer or you will lose that hand."

Mark doubted he was bluffing. "I was servant to an old man with an old man's aches and pain and stiffness and suffering." He set his other hand on the other shoulder and kneaded hard, though not quite enough to penetrate the steel tension in those remarkable shoulders. "Relax. I'm not going to rape you."

The colonel grunted. Mark gripped and shook him gently. Finally the muscles yielded. The colonel groaned.

"Naturally everyone who dared assume anything about Lord Argenwain figured he rode me hard every night. In actuality I spent most of our time together helping him walk up and down the stairs, massaging his hands when they hurt after he wrote all those politically necessary letters, and I rubbed his scalp when he had headaches. I read to him every night." Mark worked his hands up to the colonel's neck and stair-cased his thumbs up along his spine and back down. The colonel had knots everywhere but Mark needed him to learn to trust before he could work those painful places the way they needed. "He didn't have much ardor left in him. Just now and then, and he was never cruel."

"It doesn't matter. He should have never—"

"I know. Relax. He won't touch me again. That part of my life is gone."

The colonel tightened up again. "You sound regretful."

"I'm not." Mark didn't dare admit that he cared about Lord Argenwain, and how he felt so terribly lonely here. It would be impossible to explain why he missed Pickwelling, because he couldn't even explain it to himself.

"The more I hear of your life there, the less impressed and the more disgusted I am with the both of them, but especially Lord Jester Gutter. He seems to me little better than beggar boy herder."

Mark's teeth ground together, but he resisted the urge to defend Gutter. He poured his confusion and anger into his hands.

"No answer?"

"He paints roses." Mark pulled the colonel's coat off his shoulders. The colonel didn't resist. "During the summer he sits in the garden for hours, very early in the morning when no possible duty could call him away. Sometimes he'd have no sleep but he'd sit and paint the morning light and the dew and soft petals. It isn't just the beauty and the presence of those paintings that draw people to his art. They remark at how real the blossoms are, how fresh, how you can almost smell them, touch them, how they seem more alive than the real blooms were. But what truly entices them, and what most of them can't explicate is the love. And he loved me that way. He painted a portrait of me once. I can't bear to look at it. It makes me want to cry. I realized that he knew my pain, and grief, and hope. It makes the thought of his betrayal almost impossible to believe, though the evidence was always there, haunting me."

"Describe it to me. Your portrait."

Mark closed his eyes and saw it in his mind. His chest ached and his throat tightened. "I was sixteen years old, sitting in a chair in the study looking outside. It was summer. He asked me to stay there, and he came back with his watercolors. For weeks he would ask me to sit there for a little bit at a time and he asked me questions, made me laugh, made me think. In the oil I have my chin resting on my arms and I'm sitting twisted in the chair gazing into that summer light. Like the love in the roses, you can see I'm an orphan who'd gladly trade his fine clothes for rags if he could see his parents, even just for one moment, see them alive and well. There's no grief except in a subtle way in one eye."

The same eye on the black side of the mask he'd painted on his face as his first mask.

"He made me beautiful, and young, and fragile, but there's strength in my hands from the fencing. I was prettier then. I didn't have to shave."

"You joke, but ...."

Mark understood. He opened his eyes and let the feelings slip away. "Take off your waistcoat. Might as well take off your shirt too."

"No, I think I've had enough."

Mark didn't let him stand up. "Will you stop being so worried about your virtue and let me do this for you? I promise I won't seduce you."

"I'm less concerned about that."

"Oh please. You're still in love with whatever his name is. Just think about dog shit and monkeys with firearms and you'll be fine." Mark set his hands on the back of the chair.

The colonel sniffed and worked his waistcoat off. "You certainly know how to manipulate my moods."

"It's not hard. I just have to be cruel and annoying and you trust me. Better, you trust yourself. I don't think you need to worry, though. You want a lover. I'm just a toy."

That declaration sat heavily in Mark's mind for far longer than he wanted to live with it. The colonel didn't venture to refute it. He just stripped off his shirt, revealing a strong back, a soldier's back, the straight spine and smooth skin of a nobleman who always went outdoors in proper clothes. The only scars Mark could see were on his arms, and he had plenty there.

The colonel wasn't just young and handsome. He was clean. Lord Argenwain was always well-washed, but time and hardship and the endless wine and smoke and food and travel and everything else that had aged him had stained his skin and nails and hair into materials as fragile and marked as old paper. By comparison the colonel was as pure as clear, cold water.

It took all of Mark's will to keep from tracing the colonel's fine skin with his fingers.

"Now lay down. The rug there, or your bed, it doesn't matter."

The colonel obeyed, leading Mark into his bedroom. A flash of memory came from Lark—that calculating lust that had no soul, that would seduce this man if he thought he could get away with it. Of course Lark wouldn't consider it worth the risk even if he didn't worry too much about the household political consequences of his conquest. Lark feared rejection worse than death.

Mark hated what the mask had thought and felt. The colonel wasn't someone to trifle with, and they both had fragile hearts that would be too easily shattered in Lark's cold grasp.

Mark worked that fine back until his hands ached and his shoulders burned, worked until the colonel winced and moaned in painful but exquisite protest, worked until the muscles had a smooth, almost liquid consistency. The colonel's scent ... that fine, smooth warmth parted Mark's lips and drew them, but he didn't dare touch his mouth to that radiant skin. The physical and spiritual power beneath that skin could destroy him with a single word.

He left the colonel in his languor and set off for his room, trembling with something deeper than lust. He needed to write a list of things he had to accomplish in the near future.

Or rather I need the distraction.

He refused to whittle his wish. If he got into the habit he would forever be dashing away for privacy whenever the colonel inspired his lust. He'd rather calm himself with intellectual things, and then visit Grant and be a human being with a friend, a bottle of wine and things of no importance to talk about. Everything here was too confusing, and deprived, and too full of longing and loss and danger and fearsome responsibility.

Technically he wasn't allowed to leave the house without permission. He suspected that if he asked right now, the colonel might be happy to be rid of his problematic, neglectful and sinful pet.

Maybe in an hour he'd dare ask.

An open window on the way to his room conveyed the urgent rhythm of a fast rider. By the time Mark made it to the entry hall, Trudy had opened the door to the knock and received a decorated wooden box about the size of a sword case. She offered Mark the case. It felt empty. The paper tied to the latch had the symbol of a feather embossed in gold leaf on black paper.

"Thank you," Mark told Trudy, and shut himself in his sitting room.

The first debut gift had arrived.

Chapter Twenty One

§ Mark opened the case, and to his surprise it really was a sword. Specifically, it was a small, light town sword, the sort of thing a gentleman would wear as part of his formal attire but could provide quick defense if he needed it. It wouldn't last through heavy fighting, but it wasn't meant to. It was more than dressy enough for anything short of royal court. Feather had engraved it with his name on the hand guard in an artful script with enough sharp corners to be masculine even though it had many flourishes.

Every nuance—from the freshly-painted design of black and blue diamonds edged in silver and gold on the scabbard to the engraving and the item itself—spoke to him. Unfortunately he didn't know very much of Feather's language yet. He didn't have to in order to read the warning, and the invitation. Come play, but be on your guard.

An ally? Was it because she liked him, wanted something from him or from the colonel, because she knew about his connections and had a purpose for or against them ... but he couldn't let himself puzzle about that too much. Usually there was more than one reason why a jester did anything, and those reasons blurred over time. Only time could reveal her true purpose, not just to him but to herself.

He had to read the gazette and learn about what mattered to the islanders. He had to start practicing his fencing again, and he had to stretch to maintain his flexibility, and write lyrics for the inevitable next event, and create calling cards. He needed more clothes.

I need to design a mask I can bear to wear or find a mask maker who can fit me.

He also needed to do something more than respond to Gutter's letter. Much as he wanted to simply react to whatever nudges Gutter might apply, he couldn't afford to hand over that much control.

Am I really considering playing Gutter as an equal?

The only thing that would keep him from being utterly crushed by that greatest of lord jesters would be whatever love might exist between them. As strained as Mark's feelings had been toward Gutter, he was sure Gutter's own feelings would not only be taxed but masked.

Trudy knocked. "A message for you, l'jeste."

"Thank you, Miss Trudy." He opened the door and accepted the strange envelope. It had no seal, and it was made from a scrap of paper. He shut the door before he opened the envelope.

Meet me at the Barway Shore near Gullet Creek in two hours.

The handwriting seemed feminine, but it wasn't Feather's. It could be anyone with any purpose, including an assassination attempt, though it seemed a bit early for that sort of thing.

I should be afraid.

He wasn't, though. The message excited him. He had to know.

He hunted out Trudy. "Who delivered this?"

"A young man, l'jeste." Her usual warm gaze flattened.

"Any young man in particular?"

She looked away. "L'jeste—"

"Please, I'm just Mark."

She sighed. "During the war, we didn't have enough messengers, so we sent messages about with whoever dared take 'em. He's one. He'll never tell who sent it, and if you go after him I promise you the colonel would never forgive it. It's the island way. You hurt a message boy, you hang slow from the Sufferin' Tree. Messengers, they take their chances but a message boy is special, like a first-born son."

Like messengers used to be in that possibly mythical past when messengers were always treated with respect and no one would dare impede them, back when jesters wore bells to warn nobles when they were near and priests stained their skin with red ink. "I can't even ask him who sent the message, or send one back with him?"

"No, l'jeste. They don't do that."

It should have discouraged him, but it only made him more curious. "Baron Evan is probably taking a nap. If he needs me, tell him I'm following his orders by learning to ride so I won't need the carriage so much." He went to his room long enough to strap on his rapier and pistol. He doubted he'd need them. If it was a trap, he'd either escape immediately or fall to overwhelming surprise and numbers. His gut clenched into a hard knot and his hands shook.

The fear didn't deter him. If anything it fed his desire. The attack near the docks—he didn't want that again, just as he didn't ever want Bainswell's hands around his throat. But he would prove to himself that no matter how great the danger, he would do the right thing. Though he felt ill and he stilled smelled the blood as fresh as if it pooled at his feet at this very moment, he was eager. More than eager. This time he trusted himself. He hoped he would discover that he'd been justified in that trust.

By not dying.

Mark pulled on gloves, grabbed his hat and purse, and dashed for the stables.

Philip had chosen a good horse for him. The young mare, Bindart, took an eager interest in everything. She listened to Mark when he checked her from dashing toward the next new and interesting thing, and she seemed fearless. No flashy bird, no rustling vine nor snake in the road would deter her from her explorations, though the snake certainly gave her pause. She skipped back a little at that one, and then decided to try and sniff it but Mark held her back.

He stopped at a cartographer's business and inquired after a map of the island and the city. Despite Mark's recent bonding to one of the most respected men in all the islands, the man hedged and tried to imply he would have to make a copy especially for him. Finally, though, he agreed to sell a rough map with most of the main streets and landmarks on it for two ar. Maybe he thought Mark could afford it. It had room for embellishment and it showed the beach he had to find, so Mark agreed and planned to improve it later on his own. No doubt the colonel had much better ones, but to ask for one would have led to questions, and Mark didn't want to disturb his nap.

Bindart had been waiting patiently for him, but she was eager to explore some more. It made him smile. Not only did she spare him from faking a light limp everywhere, but she was good company in her own quiet way.

The map led him through a modest neighborhood with sturdy plastered walls, decent windows and thatch roofs in good repair. They thatched with palm fronds, and though the effect was rougher and darker than mainland straw, they looked just as sturdy and dry. Children and dogs shadowed him. Bindart wasn't afraid of dogs just as she wasn't afraid of anything, and even touched noses with a huge brute who had to weigh two hundred pounds. The dog was one of the sailorly-breed, all black and long-haired and seemingly impervious to the heat despite his heavy coat. Only a glint of eye showed through. His pink tongue hung out in a way that seemed friendly and kind. The dog eventually let them pass and went back to hiding beneath a large shrub.

The road opened to a pass between two large properties. A line of manor houses with broad properties stretched along a long, curved beach with a short point at one end. If the bracing wind was a regular visitor, it would be easy for large sailing ships to approach but almost impossible for them to leave. Mark looked for signs of anyone, but there wasn't even a footprint on the sand. He'd hoped as much. He was very early.

He walked Bindart on the wet sand for a while, and then through the short, choppy surf to cool her feet a little, hoping that would be all right for her. She seemed to enjoy it. He dismounted and led her to a shady place, and sat in the sand. He took off his hat. This place was so peaceful. Out of sight of the manor houses, he felt alone and at ease. He sang softly with the wind, and drank in the air that tasted not at all of oil or humanity but living fishes and flowers and salt and spices.

Bindart stole his hat. He fetched it from her without too much trouble. She gave him an almost human, coy look and tucked her head for petting. Mark obliged, unable to resist a growing fondness for her.

She warned him by pricking her ears forward, her gaze intent and curious. He saw nothing on the beach until Bindart's head jerked under his hands. She snuffled the wind, but couldn't taste the scent of a young woman in a servant's white dress and scarf walking in their direction. An island messenger? It would make prudent sense to send a messenger to a secretive meeting in order to relocate into even greater privacy, though Trudy had implied that they were usually young men.

As precious as first sons.

Mark led Bindart, who happily was too polite to dash ahead of him, toward the young woman. He didn't trust that she might not be a lure for an assassin, or an assassin herself. After all, she wore a dagger with a long, sleek line that could travel entirely through someone slender like him. His heart quickened as he approached. At a safe range he called to her. "I'm here."

She finally acknowledged him and hurried over. He recognized her rich hair and fair face.

Winsome?

"I wasn't sure you'd come." She halted a few steps away, not at all out of breath. "I had to speak to you in private."

"Will we be noticed?" He gestured toward one of the manor houses.

"Perhaps by the servants, but they won't realize who I am." She started walking again, toward the waves. Mark fell into pace beside her. "Are you well?"

"Yes, thank you. I'm on the mend."

She nodded. "I—has anyone spoken to you of a conspiracy?"

He couldn't let himself assume anything about her, though his instincts demanded that he trust her. "There are conspiracies everywhere. I haven't noticed anything special. Is there one in particular that you wanted to warn me about?"

She bowed her head. "Yesterday, a young woman was shot. They thought she was me."

That brought Mark up short. "Are you all right?"

"Yes, I'm fine, thank you for asking." Her voice was quite refined, but an island lilt bled through and her eyes tightened against the heavy gloss of unshed tears. "It's getting worse. I need help. I need the colonel's help, but I can't approach him. Our families have had little contact, and he ..." She chewed her lip briefly.

"Yes. He never goes out. I'm going to change that."

"It doesn't matter. I only want him to pursue ... things."

Mark started to walk again, hoping the motion would help her words flow. "I know it's hard for you to trust me. I'm a stranger."

"Yes." She seemed to clutch at the reason.

"And from Cathret."

"I trust the colonel's bond. He wouldn't take a chance on you if he thought it would risk our freedom." Again, she seemed to welcome the reason, which meant it wasn't the real reason behind her hesitation. He guessed it was Juggler, though it seemed unlikely that he would do anything against the islands, considering how hard he had fought to keep them free. He certainly wouldn't try to assassinate his master's daughter.

I don't know him well enough to trust that, and he might be under orders. But her father? No. That doesn't feel right. It's something else.

"We have a constitution," she said brightly. "Have you heard?"

"I have. I find it curious that so much of what's different about life here seems to revolve around ancient, often forgotten niceties. I wonder if I might not be wearing bells in a year." The idea made him chuckle.

"Bells?"

He shook his head. "I'm guessing the problem with having a constitution combined with elections is that there's no real sense of authority. A document can be changed. That's a good, and a bad thing when a nation is so new. And with no stable leader ... forgive me, but there's a chance I've missed it. No one's mentioned—do you have a—what will that person be called again?"

"President. No, we have no president yet." She took a few shaky breaths before she continued. "The last island finally signed the constitution only six months ago. We've set our election dates. The votes will occur over the course of a week, and we estimate that they will require a month to properly count, confirm and record. The nominants will be announced in a week, and I'm hoping the colonel will be one of them because ...."

Her hesitation gave his mind time to whirl. He might be jester to a man who in essence would be king to a small but very important kingdom. His heart bounded in panic. Bindart picked up on his fear. She must have sensed it through the reins. He tried to soothe her by stroking her neck. It helped her, but not him at all. Could the colonel feel his heart racing?

"The wrong president could unmake us." She stared at Mark as if she hoped to see into his mind. "Our constitution will be a sham, we'll lose our Church, and our way of life. We fought so hard. I'm not sure I can make you understand how important it is for the colonel to try."

He knew without asking that she'd been in the thick of the fight somehow, and not as a nurse. Shipboard, or land? He looked for signs of lack of grace in her stride, of scars, and saw none except those written into her eyes. Her voice had broken, but those eyes were fierce and wild like that of a lioness, ready to claw apart any threat that might cage her.

She would be perfect for the colonel. How could that man have not done anything toward an engagement, and for both their sakes? He would have a strong wife, and she would have a partner to help her achieve what a daughter could not achieve alone.

She glared at him. "I know this doesn't matter to you."

"Actually, I love everything I've seen about the islands. That may seem strange considering my initial welcome, but even that—if you'll allow me to confess something in confidence, it might help you understand." An innocent little revelation would show how well he could trust her based on how quickly it returned to him, if at all. And if it did get around, maybe someone would be able to tell him something more about his father's fate.

"Of course." She was still a wreck but dutifully attended him.

"My mother died in my arms, a victim of murder—"

"I'm sorry—"

"—and the Church's response was to settle my family's accounts as quickly as possible." She'd expressed her sympathy with real compassion, though that sympathy was softened, no doubt by what she'd experienced during the war. That compassion combined with her intimacy with death soothed him, and Bindart walked close and more easily alongside him.

"Everyone was good to me, but I was alone in my grief, and alone in my anger. As far as I could tell they gave up any hope of finding her killer. Her death may have even been arranged, and justice cheated to pay someone's salary. I don't know. It was just so passionless. Just another tragedy to be borne and not made a fuss over, because fusses are dirty and dangerous and unseemly and childish. But here, I see you're moved by my loss and you don't even know me. You're heartbroken because a young woman died in your place. You're crushed between hope and fear for your country, fighting hard for your dreams and against your nightmares. I wish I was born here. My mother was famously kind and fair and respected. Yet no one shed a tear in my presence, and no one swore to find justice in her name. Except me. I'm still looking, hopelessly. I'm worn out, and the tracks have faded. And like a typical Cathretan I waste time trying to behave and be a good person when I want to cause trouble and make demands and force them to tell me what happened. But unlike a Cathretan I refuse to let it fade into the past entirely. I intend to behave more like an islander, and fight for what I believe in."

He let her walk in silence as long as she needed to. They made their way near the waves. She let them wash over her shoes and wet her skirts. The sand spackled the hems and the white linen shoes with pale brown.

"Please, urge the colonel to campaign," Winsome said at last. "If he shows no interest, there are many who would still vote for him, but some will not out of respect for his privacy, and he won't win. He must win. He is the one we can all trust."

He wondered under what circumstances the young lady was shot. He wondered what danger Winsome knew of that made her so sure that the islands would fall back into mainland control. She had to have more than a fearful inclination. He didn't think the person he saw was inclined to act with this not-quite-desperation for fear of vague threats. "Will you tell me who you think is the greatest threat to our freedom?"

Winsome closed up like a nightflower come morning. "I couldn't say." She turned away and walked up the beach. Mark started to follow her, and she stopped. "I'd rather go on alone, thank you."

"But—"

"Please." She went on alone, leaving him there in the sweet wind. An especially long wave washed over his boots. Mark hipped up onto Bindart and rode in a direction that kept Winsome in sight. Once in town he guessed her route and made his way toward the hill, listening for a scream, a shot, anything that might suggest that her would-be-killer might try again.

Brave girl.

He didn't want to go home, not yet. He had too much to consider, and he had a few questions to ask of a trusted friend.

He turned toward the docks when it seemed unlikely he'd find Winsome again even if she did get into trouble. On the way he stopped by a stationary merchant, an ink shop, and found a nice quill point that held the ink quite well.

And wine. They'd need wine, and bread, and fruit ....

He left Bindart with a public stablemaster, and knocked on Grant's door laden with packages. He hoped Grant was there.

Heavy steps came to the door, and it opened slowly. Grant peered out, sleep heavy in his eyes.

"I'm sorry, I woke you. I'll come back another time."

"It's good. Just had a nap." The warm, sensual scent of his bed wafted out the door. "Can I help you with something, l'jeste?"

"May I come in?" Mark held the basket with the food a little higher.

"Sure." Grant stifled a yawn and stretched as he went in, leaving the door ajar. Joints cracked with strength. As much as Mark admired Winsome, she couldn't make his belly go soft and make the rest of him tighten, and flush his skin with heat the way Grant could so unconsciously.

Mark started setting up the table, dropping packages on the chair and floor as he went. "I found some decent wine. I hope it won't upset your stomach or give you a headache. It's much stronger than you're used to, and it's heavy."

"You don't have to be so nice to me," Grant said.

Mark slowed his progress. "If this is uncomfortable for you, just say so and I'll help you with your letters this one more time and go. I know it's difficult to refuse, but I give you permission to do just that, if you think you need permission." It hurt but he couldn't force a friendship.

"Refuse? What'd I forget?"

"Well, I thought we, that you wouldn't mind being friends. And friends, well, they visit each other and—"

"Oh. Oh! Oh, yeah, sure. I just thought, you know. You were pretty drunk the other night and everyone's a friend when you're drunk and all. And—letters. Yeah. I've been practicing but I think I messed up and—yeah. Here." He let out a soft, endearing laugh under his breath and started to help set the table. "I'll get the cups."

Mark relaxed. It seemed his heart would forever be fragile around the big man. "How has fishing been?"

He shrugged. "It's work. I do all right. I've got my regulars and yesterday I got this really nice swordfish that Manny sold for me to someone on the hill. I spent some of it on Judith and some got me winnings in cards and I

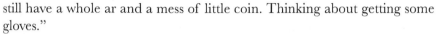

still have a whole ar and a mess of little coin. Thinking about getting some gloves."

He probably meant work gloves, Mark realized before he could open his mouth to make a recommendation. "You know the colonel likes you. You're more than welcome to come over to the house, if you don't mind the long walk."

"I've never been. Not sure I could find it."

"We're at the end of the Black Shore Road where the wind is just terrible. It's beautiful there, though. Wild. Miss Trudy told me that the whole manor shakes when there's a storm, and once during a storm the ocean came up high over the rocks and broke a window."

"A storm knocked down this whole place once," Grant told him. "Nothing left. Just a pile of sticks." He threw his arms open briefly before he settled by the table with cups and a corkscrew. "My boat? Belonged to a fisher who lost his life to that storm. My old boat, my dad's old boat, no one ever found it. It's probably at the bottom of the bay. Pieces of all kinds of stuff that used to be at the bottom of the bay came up on shore that day. A big chunk of ship with a cannon in it washed up, but my boat sank." He grinned and shook his head. "The sea." He pulled the cork. "The sea," he said again, softly, like a lovelorn fool with no hope of requite.

"Tell me again why don't you like sailing?"

"What? I got a sail. I'm not in some little rowboat, you know. I have a nice rig."

"I meant—I'd heard you had an offer to sail on a trader."

"Oh. That." He drew a knife to cut the pineapple up. Mark took it from him to clean it off first. Grant didn't seem to mind. "I just don't like it."

"Fair enough." Mark sliced up the pineapple himself. Strange how quickly he'd grown accustomed to such exotic fruit. At Hevether they always had a multitude of delicious and sometimes bizarre fruits every morning. Miss Trudy had mentioned that most of it came from the garden, using the same emphasis that he'd heard when he'd been bonded and implying it was separate from the small sheltered courtyard where they kept a few spindly citrus trees. It made him want to see this garden sometime soon.

"It's just ...." Grant popped the cork with effortless power. "I was on the gun deck. With the cannons, you know. During the war."

Mark could guess at the brutal conditions, but he couldn't pretend to understand the source of the darkness in Grant's voice. "I'm sorry."

"Can't bear to be belowdecks anywhere. It's funny, you know. I saw all kinds of things at the land battles. Men got killed by cannon all the time. And shot. Little holes that won't stop bleeding for money or mercy. People getting chopped up. Chopped up people dying slow, dragging parts that shouldn't be dragging. Broken faces are the worst, teeth everywhere but how they belong."

Mark wished he could take the man's hand and hold it, let him know somehow that he was here now, and safe, that he wasn't alone—something to comfort him.

Grant didn't seem to need comfort. He spoke of it with less emotion than he'd expressed about the mysterious sea. "Anyways," Grant continued, "there's something worse about being trapped below, and slipping in blood and oil and water all mixed, and the stench and the smoke and splinters, and the dark, and the noise making you deaf but not deaf enough to stopper the screaming—I have a horror of belowdecks even though it's not war no more." He poured the wine.

"Let's toast to lasting peace," Mark suggested.

"Lasting peace." They touched cups and drank. Mark watched Grant's expression while the first rush of fragrant richness unfolded into memories of summer—not just grapes but pears and currants and the flavors from perfumed fruits that didn't exist except in good wine. At first Grant just set the cup down, but then he cocked his head sideways like he was listening, and then he smiled. "That's good stuff."

"Thank you. My mother taught me about wine. Often people make do with something that's almost as good as a glass they had once that unveiled a kind of garden in their minds. I think that's how people develop preferences for a particular grape. One glass that gives you a perfect moment makes you crave the echoes of that moment. But there are many gardens to explore, and it's fun to discover them and appreciate them for what they are, instead of trying to recreate them, or putting up with a wasteland never knowing that gardens exist. If that makes sense."

"I guess, yeah. I get what you mean about the garden. I didn't know wine had, you know."

"Actually flavors that vary from vinegar and oak."

He chuckled. "Yeah."

"There's good vinegar too, you know. At Pickwelling the head cook had a passion for vinegars. That and good oil. He insisted that you couldn't cook anything worthwhile without using oils and vinegars good enough that you could enjoy them on their own. He used to drink half a glass of vinegar every morning. Tried to get me to do it for my health, but I couldn't bear it. But I had a sip now and then, especially in wintertime. I used to crave it during very warm weather. I'd feel thirsty and nothing but the vinegar would help."

"I get that!" He nearly reared up from his chair in his enthusiasm. "That thirsty feeling? It's weird. I never actually drank vinegar, though."

"Wine's better, but sometimes nothing but vinegar will do." Mark took another sip of wine. "Before we get too carried away with wine, let's practice some letters."

"You know, I saw a letter G on a sign the other day. It's stupid of me, but it made me happy. I read it. I read a letter G without you telling me that's what it was."

"You have every reason to be proud. I believe that your practice, and your ability to translate that practice to what you see outside these lessons, will allow you to read not just individual letters, but writing. I think by this time next year you'll be reading the gazette and writing messages to me when you want me to meet you at a pub somewhere so we can drink rum and have some good pit-baked pork."

"Ah, that was good pork that night."

"Yes, it truly was."

"What else you got there in that basket?"

"Ham, hard-boiled eggs, some sort of mustard sauce, limes, orange marmalade pastries ...."

Mark slunk in well after midnight. He hadn't meant to be gone so long. He forced himself to march upstairs, around the bend and down the hall that led to the colonel's suite. Though it was dark, he knew his way better than he expected after living at Hevether so short a time.

Mark made his way down the servant's hall to the colonel's suite and stood in front of the door, unwilling to knock, equally unwilling to walk away and hide in his room until morning. Finally he forced himself to raise his hand and relieve the worry and anger that no doubt had the colonel in fits. When no answer came, he knocked again more loudly, determined to go in and knock on the bedroom door if he had to.

Hurried steps approached and the door whipped open. The colonel looked wild even in the darkness with little more than a silhouette against the starlight to reveal his emotions. Mark didn't flinch back. It surprised him a little when no slap struck his face.

The colonel's posture tightened and cooled. "Where have you been?"

"I ...." He'd meant to use the excuse that he'd been out practicing riding, but the colonel deserved better. "I received a private message. I went to investigate."

"Trudy told me as much, but she didn't know where you'd gone, and she told me you didn't know who sent it." The anger in his voice made Mark tremble in anticipation. It was unbearable, expecting punishment to come at any moment and having it withheld ... he would rather have it over with in a flash, as sometimes happened in Pickwelling, than to wait for something more considered, and likely far more painful and lasting.

Mark doubted that the threat of lasting scars would prevent the colonel from striping his back.

And of course it would be too unseemly for the colonel to do it himself. He'd make Philip do it. It would all be very soldierly and demeaning and torture like Mark had never known.

"I demand an answer."

Mark stopped his tongue, though he wanted to point out that he hadn't exactly been asked a question. "In three days I'd like to host a party for you. At that time it might be a good idea to make public your interest in the presidency."

The force of the attack caught him off guard, as did the lack of tooth in it as the colonel slammed him into the hall wall beside the bath door with his hand twisted up in Mark's waistcoat. The colonel wasn't exactly in control of himself, but he clearly didn't mean to hurt Mark. At least not yet. "I will not. And if I'm nominated, I will withdraw, and if they elect me in spite of everything I will yield to whoever ranks beneath me." The colonel loomed close, his breath rich with wine. "You have manipulated me at every turn. You even pretended ... you have very skilled hands, and a keen mind, and I have no doubt that you have been truthful with me, at least as truthful as someone like you can be. But I will not be your plaything, and you will not ride me, not in my bed, and not up a social mountain where you can have your revenge against Gutter, or suit his purposes, or whatever it is you want. And you will never, ever ask Trudy or anyone in this household to lie for you again."

The roughness of that voice and his strength, so potent and so carefully held in check, excited Mark beyond any passion he thought he owned. It wouldn't take much to incite the colonel to more violence. Even a beating would be better than lingering here in an agony of need, but it wasn't worth it. He wished it was. He wished that they weren't bonded, and that he could struggle for something that would either beat him back to his senses or lavish him with rich sensations he'd only dreamt of.

Mark forced himself to do nothing, to wait and to let the man he longed for slip away. When the grip eased, Mark spoke softly and deferentially. "It was Winsome I spoke with. Until she told me, I didn't even know that nominations were pending. And I agree with her. If you truly fear for the islands and our freedom, you must at least consider protecting the constitution with your strength and the faith people have in you."

The colonel let go and his shoulders sagged. "You knew from the beginning that I might have a chance. That's why, the largest reason why, you accepted my offer. It's why you manipulated me into making an offer to you. Admit it."

"I can't admit it because it's not true. I know it seems incredible to you, but all I know of the islands is what my father told me and what I overheard by chance at parties. Lord Argenwain hates gazettes. He relies on Gutter and gossip to keep him apace of meaningful events. And I had no interest in island politics. Why should I? I wasn't allowed to be a part of the world. And I'm sorry to say but the islands didn't really matter to anyone I knew. They're a source of spice and sugar and expensive fruits. Lord Argenwain's friends care more about whether the Hasle Royals will invite His Royal Majesty King Michael to stay in Saphir for the holiest of days again than they do about island politics. The only place it would matter is in the king's court. Honestly I'd be terrified if you were made president. I don't have enough experience or strength or intelligence or anything that would help me. I, personally, could sink these islands and I don't want to be responsible for that. But I will take on that responsibility if I must."

"That's very generous of you." The colonel walked into his bedroom.

Mark followed him. "So you will leave the islands to the whim of politics because ... you're afraid? You think you're unworthy? You—"

"Yes. All of it. I'm not fit to be president in any way. They would run roughshod all over me. As would you. I would be helpless. I'd have no choice but to follow your advice at every turn. That isn't leadership. I'd be a doll propped up in a chair and fed tea that stains my teeth but can't sustain me."

Mark tried not to be distracted by that show of poetry. "You are a leader. You led in war."

"That was war."

"This too is war."

"My answer will not change."

When waiting in silence hurt too much, Mark moved toward the hall.

"It's all an act, isn't it."

Mark paused. "What?"

"You hated your duties. You learned how to act, how to please men, even seduce them but ...."

Let him believe what he wants. He'll believe it anyway.

Mark started to leave, but stopped. He couldn't let it stand. He couldn't allow a man he respected so much all but call him a whore and have the silence give credence to the lie. "The only reason you accuse me of that is so that you can pretend you'll never love again. You want to cram your soul back into the puzzle scroll where your father locked you up and be a husband and father. You might even find contentment like that. I hope you do. I hope you love again, man or woman, it doesn't matter. But don't you accuse me of deceit when the only person deceiving you is yourself."

"Stop confusing the question and answer me. Are you? Or do you despise that which you pretend to be?"

Do you want me to prove it to you?

Again, he couldn't expose himself to a violent rejection that might get him thrown out of the household he'd bound himself to, or yield to a passion that the colonel would later regret. The colonel still believed, after all, that his soul was in danger of destruction because of his bend. For all Mark knew it might be, though that wasn't the greatest threat to the colonel's soul. "I am. I have been in the presence of some of the world's most beautiful and seductive women, and I have to fake my blush every time."

"Do you feel anything for anyone?"

"Yes. I do."

"Who?"

Mark walked away.

The colonel followed him into the hall. "Who?"

"Have me flogged or leave me alone." Mark rushed through the gallery, shut his reception room door, locked it, and braced against it. Loneliness ate at his insides and raked out his heart. The colonel shouldn't have had to ask. Whether the colonel guessed Grant, or himself, or both, it was clear that Mark could have neither, none or anyone.

For a brief flash Mark thought about purchasing an entertainer. The only thing that stopped him was the fact that he couldn't ask around for a reputable one without exposing his lord and master to gossip and maybe even ridicule.

Someone like Grant could pay for a bit for pleasure without a thought or a single repercussion, while someone like Mark ... he wondered how Gutter managed to find comfort. Maybe he didn't, but more likely he took the time to make discreet and intelligent young women fall so much in love with him that they'd rather die than reveal the secret of their affair. He traveled so much, he could slip away into someone's arms for a month and no one would wonder where he was. They would always guess he had important, secret business to attend to, and his mail would await him at Pickwelling when he finally came home. He might even have children. Dozens. Dozens of happy families and wealthy mistresses that lived in manors who wore costly gowns and had smiles that hid a thousand mysteries.

Mark stripped, washed in cold water and went to bed, but didn't sleep for a long time. When he woke several more debut gifts waited.

Juggler had sent him a beautiful dagger. Unlike the sword, it didn't seem at all like a friendly gesture. Though it had no note, no inscription, and not a hint anywhere in or on the case or scabbard, the beautiful steel spoke to him. It said, plunge me into your own heart, or into mine, I don't care which.

Mark and the colonel ate dinner in silence, both picking at their food though the melon soup, bread with its exquisite crisp and delicate crust, and fish with deep pink meat, all tasted delicious. Every time Norbert came in, his clothes smelled of something sweet and chocolate, promising a wonderful dessert.

Mark set his fork aside. "This is ridiculous."

The colonel didn't say anything. He pushed flakes of buttery fish meat around his plate.

"Winsome knows something. She won't tell me but she might tell you. We have to arrange a socially acceptable meeting."

The colonel glanced up, then back down. He speared a tiny bit of meat and chewed on it excessively before he swallowed and spoke. "You have my permission to make such an arrangement. I'm sure you won't require my assistance for something so simple."

You really don't want to play this game with me.

Mark welcomed his temper, fanned it, then banked it carefully so he could relish it and employ it to its full extent. "I like her immensely." No response. That made it easier. "I can't imagine her as someone's wife. She's more than just another brave islander. She's an embodiment of freedom, and most marriages would destroy that." Mark paused so that the fatal blow would hit as deeply as possible. "She's more like a lieutenant."

The colonel flinched and Mark wished he could apologize. But just as fencing practice required a student to feel a good, solid hit and sometimes involved nasty injuries, the colonel needed this lesson.

He also needed a push off of a cliff, and Mark had just the cliff in mind. Unlike most of his ideas this one had been growing in bits and pieces from the moment he'd met Winsome on the beach. It completed itself as the colonel drained his glass of blush wine and stood. "Tell Norbert I'll have dessert later in my room," the colonel said.

"I have an idea that I think will suit everyone in regard to meeting with Winsome," Mark told him.

The colonel didn't deign to respond. It gave Mark courage to write the letter later that evening.

Dear Winsome,

Please excuse my boldness, especially since it is so out of my lord and master's character, but I must act quickly for the reasons we discussed earlier. The colonel and I would like to know when we may call upon you and your father to make arrangements for a formal courtship. Before you run too far away with your feelings in one direction or another, I hope you will consider the many conveniences this arrangement would afford to both households. Perhaps in time the courtship might afford you other, gentler comforts, but on that score I can't promise anything. On the one side I fear that the idea of a courtship from this quarter will leave you cold, while the other side, though sure that the colonel is of a passionate nature, is aware that he has boxed up that nature in his war chest and things are quite dusty and rusty in there. I pray you are not offended. I can only promise you that the colonel will not be insincere, and that he will remain on a proper course until you guide him in whatever direction your heart desires.

With great admiration, I am your devoted messenger.

lark

Before he could lose his nerve, he folded it up and went to the study where the colonel sat paging through old birding books. "I need your seal."

"It's in my office."

He almost leapt with joy. *Fuck you, and thank you, my lord and master. I love your cold and rusty, dusty heart.*

"That's the way, lord jester," Philip enthused as Mark backed Bindart into the shed. She'd resisted trusting him at first, but finally she relented. There was something magical about instructing her and having her yield though she was far stronger and larger and had a mind of her own. Mark gave her leave to exit. "Now give her a good pat," Philip told him.

Mark stroked her neck and murmured to her. "Good girl."

Bindart swung her head to the side, ears flattening briefly. At first he feared he'd offended her, but then he noticed a rider approaching at a trot. Juggler.

"I have to get back to the house." Mark swung off of Bindart and handed Philip her reins. "Thank you for the riding lesson." He hurried to Hevether Hall's side entrance. Philip looked confused until he noticed the rider as well, and went to meet the approaching jester to take his horse.

Mark rushed around until he found the colonel going through papers in his cramped and dark office near the base of the stairs. Why the colonel put up with such conditions was beyond Mark's comprehension. "Juggler is here. I'm guessing that he's responding to our letter on Baron Kilderkin's behalf."

"Good." The colonel continued fussing with figures. They looked like ship manifests.

Normally Mark would be beside himself with curiosity, but this was not the time for such. "There's something you should know. I—"

"I would prefer if you handled it."

In some ways it would make things so much easier. Much as Mark would enjoy watching the colonel plummet to his doom with taciturn detachment, it wasn't fair to Winsome. Besides, he'd had his fun. Now they had to be serious, both of them, and fully engaged. "Fine. But don't expect me to fuck her on your wedding night." Mark strode out.

The old chair scraped over the stone floor with a grinding screech. "Come back here. Now!"

Mark thought about forcing him to chase after him, but he stopped and turned and walked sedately back to the office doorway. "Juggler will be at the door at any moment."

"What have you done?"

"I have made the necessary arrangements. You will court Winsome. She will—"

"I'll what?"

"—give you whatever information she has in regard to Perida's political weaknesses. And if you're nice she might even let you kiss her hand."

The colonel turned pink, and then flushed red before he paled. In the distance the front door slid open.

"That will be Juggler." Mark bowed and took his leave. He'd expected a bit more rage, or more of a protest. Maybe this would work out better than he'd hoped.

Mark trotted down the stairs just as Trudy hurried up. "Oh. L'jeste." She curtseyed. "May I fetch something?"

"I doubt he'll be staying long, but maybe you can trouble Norbert for some juice and maybe those little sandwiches he makes. I would love to have some even if Juggler doesn't stay."

Trudy curtseyed again and kept going upstairs. He wondered if she was afraid.

Mark finished his journey down the stairs and bowed to Juggler. "It's good to see you."

Juggler had a dangerous glimmer in his eyes. "No mask today, Lark?"

He hadn't even thought about putting one on every morning like many jesters did. He didn't regret it. "Would you like to sit in the salon?"

Juggler made a show of looking around a bit at the paired columns and vast emptiness that teed on even more unused space with scarcely an urn to decorate it. "I've never been in Hevether Keep. It's ... interesting." He focused back on Mark's face, his expression probing and well-concealed behind his paint. "By all means."

Mark hadn't heard it called a keep before. It fit better than calling it a hall or a manor.

Mark was still in the process of arranging what had formerly been a echoing forty foot by forty foot room with no clear purpose into a proper salon. He could have easily spent a fortune just on games and musical instruments, but he felt uncomfortable dropping such a sum without being acquainted with the colonel's means, so he borrowed a little from the lean conservatory and equally lean gaming room. The fact that the colonel hadn't protested any of his expenses so far didn't really mean much. Too many lords lost their family fortunes simply by not paying attention to what sometimes seemed to them a limitless coffer.

Mark had rearranged the furniture and borrowed a cabinet from storage for liquors, but it still looked painfully bereft of comfort.

Juggler perused the room, walking slowly, his languorous gaze giving away neither disdain nor approval. "I have to admit the letter was quite a surprise to everyone in the household, except the lady. She seemed pleased."

"I'm glad that the letter wasn't unwelcome."

"Where is—"

"The colonel is very shy."

Juggler barked a startled laugh. He quickly reined it in.

"At least when it comes to this matter," Mark added.

Juggler drew a letter from his waistcoat. Mark accepted it without glancing at the seal. He'd have time to look it over later.

"What does Baron Kilderkin think of it?" Mark asked.

Juggler took a deliberate pace closer. Warning prickled over Mark's skin. "I'm very fond of my Lady Kilderkin." Juggler spoke softly and low. "This had better not be a game. Playing with young ladies may be a casual sport on the mainland, but here, a young woman's tears could easily inspire a duel."

Juggler had just said the wrong thing, and he had no idea. Or perhaps he did. Maybe Juggler guessed correctly that Mark found duels repulsive and barbaric, and wanted to see if the new jester was shy of them, even afraid. Or maybe Mark was missing something, his mind fogged by memories of a beautiful young man's pitiful death in the snow. Mark hated to admit it, but Lark would have been much better at this. "The colonel's intentions are honest and pure, though no one can guarantee the outcome."

"I'm not concerned about the colonel."

"You object to me in some way?"

Juggler took another pace forward. "The letter was in your hand, with your signature."

"Yes."

"I would have expected a young lady to have doubts when approached in such a manner without a prior basis for expectation, unless she recognized a subterfuge."

Mark's breath caught. Juggler knew about the meeting, and he opposed Winsome. Mark eased it in less than a blink, but Juggler noticed.

"You're charming," Juggler said, taking one more pace so that he stood at a pretty angle only a half pace from Mark's shoulder. "And handsome, in a dolly sort of way. I didn't notice any flirtation but you seemed excessively inattentive toward her at dinner the other night, which I've known men to employ in order to increase—"

"No." Mark realized what he thought. He couldn't let on any sign of relief. "I'm not making a play for her, Juggler. Please. I'm in complete earnest. I have to admit that she charmed me, and I'm flattered to think that some of my feelings might have been answered, but it's my hope that she and the colonel find happiness together. If you like, as an assurance, I will make myself unavailable as chaperone should they decide to meet."

Juggler's gaze measured Mark's face. He eased back a half pace and seemed reassured, though it could have easily been a ploy. "That won't be necessary."

"If her father approves, then I'd like to set a date to discuss terms, unless the family prefers a more informal courtship."

"I would think that the colonel would prefer a formal courtship himself."

"He will yield to the lady's preferences on all matters."

Juggler let out an impatient noise deep in his throat. "We will eagerly await the colonel's response." Juggler bowed.

"You're leaving?"

"I apologize. I have other matters to attend to today."

Mark walked him to the door, where Philip waited by. "You're welcome any time." He would have to be, if this courtship manifested. Mark wasn't entirely sorry for it. Though the strange jester intimidated him at times, Mark admired Juggler more than he wanted to.

"Thank you." Juggler gave Mark a long look before he turned and left.

Philip followed the jester out. Mark shut the door behind them. He drew the letter out and was tempted to open it, but it was addressed to the colonel and he was already in enough trouble.

The seal was a ring twined with flowers. It had to be Winsome's, though it suited her even less than her name, at least from what he'd seen of her so far. Mark carried the letter upstairs. He almost ran into the colonel, who stood skulking in the hallway like an eavesdropping servant rather than a master of his own household. Unlike a servant he remained there, his back braced against the wall at the banister's end. Mark offered him the letter. The colonel snatched it from his hands and bore it away into his office. He shut the door and locked it.

Mark lingered, waiting for a sound—cursing, pottery shattering, books slamming shut. Nothing. He'd just begun to retreat when a knock at the door below summoned him to the stairs again.

Trudy had also begun an approach. "I'll get the door. Thank you, Miss Trudy." She curtseyed and Mark opened the door. "Oh. You must be Mr. Leorliss. Please come in."

The young, noble-faced man with strong Hasle features didn't disappoint his heritage when he betrayed a thick, purring accent with his first words. "Yes. How did you know?" He stripped off his feathered straw hat hastily.

"The monogram on your case, and your name. Besides, I haven't invited anyone else of your profession. I'm hoping you will suit my needs." Mr. Leorliss looked very dashing in his pale blue and dove gray, and his eyes shone with inexperience and a trace of awe. Perfect. Mark almost asked if he wanted to shed his waistcoat, but just in time remembered he was no longer a servant required to take visitors' coats when needed. "Please follow me." He led the young invitation master to the breakfast nook. "Did you walk all the way here?"

"Yes."

"Next time I need you I'll send a carriage, assuming everything works out."

"Excuse me, but may I ask who recommended me?" Mr. Leorliss blushed, but Mark doubted that it was from any attraction. If anything he seemed uneasy.

"No one. I walked by your window and I liked your work." Or rather, Lark had. That cold and lonely mind had noticed everything that might be of use later. "Don't worry, I'm not going to ask for three hundred invitations in two days. What I have in mind will be public, to be posted about town. I'll take care of the personal invitations. Make yourself comfortable and set up any materials you'd like to present. I'll be right back."

Mark went out the side way through the servant's hall when he heard the too-calm but loud bellow. "Lark!"

The colonel's voice made him tingle and his toes curled. They really had to stop inciting each other like this before something gave way under the strain. He listened for the footsteps and backtracked toward the front of the house just as the colonel charged—not entirely calmly—down the stairs. He was about to call out again when he noticed Mark.

Mark braced as the colonel approached like a potent gust of wind. The power exhilarated him. "This," the colonel said, stopping short of striking Mark in the face with Winsome's letter, "is beyond cruel."

"What did she say?"

"Not her, you. You can't toy with people like this. I won't have it. I forbid it. Do you understand me?" The papers flashed near Mark's face again. He was a quick reader, but not quick enough to catch more than a couple of meaningless words. The colonel held the pages too far behind his leg for Mark to read any more.

Too late? Mark tried to compose an answer that wasn't flip.

"I will have an answer." The colonel's eyes blazed with darkness.

"I understand you. You're the one who doesn't understand. If she's sincere then at least try. And if it's all business then you have nothing to worry about."

"What about her reputation? If nothing comes of this she'll have been jilted yet again."

Mark hadn't considered that Winsome might have been jilted. It seemed incomprehensible that someone so fine would be pursued only to be abandoned. "I'll make it right. Don't worry."

"You have everything in hand, do you?"

His heartbeat lifted. He couldn't tell if it was the colonel's heart or his own temper starting to rise. "This is what comes of piling all your responsibilities on me."

"So you're punishing me?" The colonel loomed closer. "And using an innocent young woman as your weapon."

"I'm trying—never mind what I'm trying. I have business to attend to. Can we please discuss this at another time?"

"More business like what you've already arranged?" the colonel growled.

"Do you have better plans?" Mark took him by the arm and drew him to the main sitting room so that their voices wouldn't echo through the whole house. It surprised him a little that the colonel came along. He could have easily resisted. Mark shut the door. "Did you expect, with one look at me, that I could solve all your problems without inconveniencing you?"

"This is quite a lot more than inconvenience." The colonel kept crowding him. "There must be another way."

"Then inform me of this way. The presidency looms. Who would you have as president if not yourself?"

"Anyone but myself."

The stupidity behind that statement flabbergasted him. For a moment he couldn't even respond with a *ha*.

"Do you truly believe someone of your inexperience and my temperament would improve this nation's chances of survival? You're just a boy."

Mark flinched, and to his shame he had to fight tears. It was such a petty, silly slight. He couldn't account for why it hurt so badly. "And they're all corrupt, dirty old men, and Feather is a just a dress, and you're just a broken-hearted soldier. We're all merely something, but we all have power."

"I mustn't be given any power."

A shiver won past the hurt, dulling it. Would they talk about it at last? "Why anyone other than you? True, you have faults. Brutal honesty, self-denial, humility, pride, generosity, and overwhelming concern for everyone but yourself. All to a fault. Those happen to be the faults of some of the greatest men that have ever lived, including His Royal Majesty King Michael, who, had he not engaged in war to keep the islands, would likely still be admired here as much as he is on the mainland."

"You would change your mind if you knew me." The colonel walked to a window and looked out. His heart beat slowly, painfully. Mark could feel it because it beat exactly as his did. "I want war."

Mark's heart quickened against the colonel's powerful, slow pain. "No, you don't. You want a fight that you understand, something pure—"

"There's nothing pure about a battlefield." The colonel set Winsome's letter on a small side table.

"I came from a hard fight not too long ago," Mark reminded him. "And I don't want it back. Except ..." The colonel turned aside a little, but not far enough to really look at Mark. "I think you know what I mean. There's something important that comes from being overwhelmed and near death and understanding how short and fragile life really is. I'm living in that dark ... brightness. I want to do everything and anything, to risk it all. Not just because of the excitement in it. Not just because I want to succeed, or to fight for what I believe in. Because I have to know what I am. And because there's nothing better that we can hope for than to put ourselves between the good in this world and the things that want to tear it down." *At least, there's nothing better for us,* he thought. *Neither of us have a chance at love.* "We bonded in part because you knew you wouldn't change your mind in ten days or ten years. You trusted me. Please, trust me."

"Then trust me when I say I should not have the presidency."

Mark had to let the moment pass. If he brought up what the *morbai*, or whatever it was, had said, then the colonel would never go forward toward the elections. "Maybe not alone. But you won't be alone. You can lead in accordance with the common man's wishes rather than your own. You can employ a council of governors to help you make decisions. And you'll have me. You may even earn yourself a wife and family who will also guide you. I have put all this within your reach. You only have to stretch and take hold of it. Even if you don't succeed, you know better than I that if you don't even try, we'll lose everything. But if you try, even if you don't succeed, we may still win a little."

The colonel gripped the window sill in his hands, his arms spread as if he were hanging from chains, or ready to take flight. "This is the last thing you will do without consulting me."

"If you want me to be different from other jesters, you have to help me. You have to guide me. You have to do your part. Please. At least talk to me."

The colonel squeezed the sill hard, and then relaxed and let his arms slip down. His heart had quickened with Mark's. "I've wanted nothing but to talk to you since that day we walked on the rocks. You haven't been home."

Mark decided not to remind him that they had silent meals and many hours at opposite ends of the house. "Meet me at the breakfast nook and help me go over designs for the announcements. We're having a party. At that party, I hope you will announce your willingness to accept a nomination, if it's your honor to be nominated for the presidency."

"And if I will not?" The colonel turned and leaned against the wall beside the window, wreathed in shadow beside the hot, tropical sunlight slicing into the room.

"Then we'd better have another plan in place, because at this party, everyone will be expecting a grand surprise."

The colonel scowled, but Mark thought he detected a little bemusement lighting his eyes. That bemusement faded as he rifled through the pages. "The lady also sent me a page, without explanation, in code." He offered Mark the page.

Mark's heart skipped. "I'll be right back with the translation."

Chapter Twenty Two

He wasn't quick enough to translate in line. He had to write it out bit by bit. When he was finished decoding the page he went down the hall to the colonel's office, too puzzled to let himself leap to any conclusions, though what he'd gathered worried him.

The colonel turned away from his ship manifests when Mark settled in the doorway of his office. "Well?" the colonel asked.

"It's a ship manifest, written so that it appears to be a letter complete with return address on the exterior when it's folded along the lines," Mark told him. It was a clever device. That false return address listed the ship, its captain, the departure date and main cargoes in a place where it would be readily visible in a file.

"That's it?"

Mark nodded.

"Is it in the code you brought back from the mainland?"

Mark shook his head. "It's similar, but not identical. This one is an older, more primitive version. It must have been used between people who did business directly with each other with little fear of anyone intercepting the letters or taking them from storage. Winsome miscopied some of the symbols, but I worked it out." Or maybe that had been a deliberate ruse on the writer's part. Mark had a hard time imagining that she would make a mistake with something so important.

"Winsome copied it herself?"

That worried him too. "I don't know how she managed to get this, but she clearly had to copy it and put it back before it was missed."

The colonel stood up, agitated. "It can't be Juggler. I despise him, but I know him. He would never do it."

"What about her father?"

"Of course not. That makes even less sense. His wealth is tied to the islands—has been since his great-grandfather settled here."

"Who else could she have such ...." Her servant's disguise. She was quite certain of it.

"What?"

"I had Philip get me an old copy of the Wishful Moon Gazette. That servant girl who was shot for spying—Winsome was certain they thought it was her somehow."

The colonel paled and sat heavily, then stood up sharply once more. "Why didn't you tell me this before?"

"Because I don't know anything. I can only guess. You have to talk to her. She doesn't trust me, but she trusts you. At least, I hope she does. Even if she doesn't, we need more."

"Show me."

Mark handed him the manifest.

"Weapons and supplies."

Mark bit his lip. "And men."

"I don't recognize the ship."

"That's good. That means it's not one of yours."

The colonel grimaced and he leaned against his desk. "I wish I had your certainty. It could be a nickname. I'll ask my captains."

"Don't." Mark had a thought. "We have to be careful now. You can't appear suspicious."

"Suspicious? I want to find whoever is responsible and tear out their throats." The colonel's skin flushed with life and Mark saw for the first time that terrible blood lust he'd been dreading.

"What if it is one of your captains? What if several of them are involved?"

"Then I have all the power to end this without having to wade through political swill." The bright and eager look in his eyes would have given even Gutter pause.

"I'm still not certain what these supplies and men mean," Mark reminded him. "A military takeover? You honestly believe that's their intent? Perhaps guards after the fact, or security for the arrival of someone important. Have you forgotten that Dellai Bertram dashed to the mainland recently? That couldn't have been just on business of mine."

"He was on business of yours? I'd heard that he left."

"I told you he left. Don't you remember? We really must—never mind." Mark thought for a moment. "See if you can't get something more from Winsome. It may be too dangerous for her to copy more of these letters. Maybe I could go in her stead, if she's willing to tell us where she got this."

"I don't want her spying anymore, and I certainly don't want you spying either. Here, we execute spies, regardless of who they are and who they're spying on."

Would you really allow me to be executed as a spy? Mark feared he already knew the answer.

The colonel's shoulders settled. "If we're to have a party, we'll need more than three servants. But I don't want anyone that I don't trust in my house."

The change of topic suited Mark just fine. "We'll start with men you knew in the war, and their wives. Anyone you can think of that might appreciate three or four days of hard labor for a handsome wage."

"Three—what exactly do you have in mind?" No anger this time, or even irritation. If anything the colonel looked nervous. One of his hands trailed up to a button on his waistcoat.

Mark took a deep breath and finally asked. "Exactly how much can I spend on furnishings?"

"Why do you never answer my questions directly?"

Mark had to think about it. He could have come up with any number of clever excuses, but he realized the uncomfortable answer after only a few moments. "I'm afraid that if I try to explain everything you'll question every item or worse, argue against it and I'll realize I can't meet this or any other challenge and I'll fail. I don't let myself think about the future beyond a day or three." A cold shudder traveled down his spine into his belly. "Because then I realize it's inevitable that I'll be killed."

"Killed. By who?" Colonel Evan's demeanor gentled so much he was almost unrecognizable.

"Anyone. Everyone. I have disturbed the uneasy balance of power in Perida." Mark steadied himself by running his hand along the smooth surface of the colonel's lovely, red-toned desk. He didn't plan what to say for once. The words came without a clear idea behind them, in a mess, from the heart. "I'm especially afraid of what Gutter might do. What other messages might he have sent here along with the one to me? I just ... I want to accomplish as much as possible before it all ends."

"I've greatly endangered you through this bond."

"No. Not exactly. No. I chose this, and I chose to ignore the consequences. If anything, you're my best and only protection."

"I believe I understand." The colonel settled into his chair and pulled open a desk drawer. "Take this." He scribbled on several small pieces of paper. He handed five of them over.

Blank notes with his signature. Where was the joy? He only felt dread at this show of trust.

"Have no fear. I've had nothing to spend my fortune on. My hull accounts are full to bursting, the garden is doing well ... I only wish I could go with you into town, but I have a great deal of business to attend to."

"Thank you." The words caught in his throat.

"I won't let him hurt you again." The colonel reached, hesitated, then firmly settled his hand on Mark's arm. Warmth spread from his touch, like something sacred but so carnal and needy it seemed immoral to consider it something of the soul.

I won't let him hurt you again. Kind words with no hope of ever becoming a sound promise. They still inspired him to settle his hand on the colonel's shoulder in answer.

The moment his gloved hand settled on the rich, matte gray silk he knew he'd made a mistake, one he'd been longing to make ever since he saw the colonel for the first time at the trial. His hand smoothed down the colonel's chest. His heart thundered. He remembered that smooth skin, the scent of it, the glorious texture more fine than any fabric.

The colonel braced up from his chair and gently took Mark's wrist. A sensation like the pleasure of a luxurious stretch, but swift as a gasp, roared from below Mark's heart and spread down all the way to his knees.

"No." The colonel spoke the word under his breath. The heart that pounded in time with Mark's cried yes, but the colonel pressed past Mark and left him there with his notes and his yearning and a lot of work that had to be accomplished in a short amount of time.

"Can you help?" Mark asked.

"I'm in no ways good enough to be a servant in a fancy house." Grant put one foot up on his bed. His leg stretched easily long enough to reach from the table, where the remains of the wine and fruit and sausages Mark had brought were strewn like a badly-arranged still life.

"I have a hard time thinking of you as a servant too, but not because you're unsuitable. I think you'd do very well. I just would rather have you as a guest. In any case, I was hoping you could—" Mark's breath stopped as a terrible idea came to mind.

"What? Something wrong?"

"No." Mark forced the tension from his body. He still felt it, but he didn't have to let it show. "Can you handle horses?"

"I can't ride but I can boss pack horses around, and I can steer a wagon."

"I have a lot of deliveries that will come in over the next several days. I have too much work to look after them, so if you wouldn't mind directing the deliveries into the various rooms in the house, I'd be grateful. Also, at the party itself, I hope you'll help provide security. You can have charge of the front of the house, or the back. The colonel will give several men into your charge."

"I s'pose I could manage that. Doesn't sound so bad. But what's that got to do with horses?"

"Nothing. Never mind." The idea wouldn't go away. "I've had all the deliveries earmarked. I'll show you around the house, tomorrow if you have time, so you'll have an idea of where things go. By then we'll have a butler who can help you navigate." The idea still wouldn't go away. "You'll be paid for your time, of course. An ar a day."

"A whole bloody ar a day?" He exploded as if it were a pittance for a pound of sweat, but he went pale and then pink and clutched at his chest. His legs drew in.

"Are you all right?" Mark writhed between fear for his health and laughter.

"I'll quit fishing for that for sure."

"That seems unlikely, but thank you."

"What do you mean, clawing unlikely? I knew servants were full but fuck—pardon me, but fuck!" Uneasy laughter shuddered out of him.

"I thought you loved fishing. I didn't want to offend you by offering you servant's work."

"I could fish all I wanted after work without worrying 'bout storms and cuts and making rent."

"But you wouldn't be free, sailing across the water—"

"You sound like a sailor. I'm no sailor, remember? I fish. It's business. It's a damned sight better than some businesses, and sure I'm my own man, but it's not like I'd stop being my own man doing honest work in the colonel's house. But I'm clumsy and dumb and folk who do that sort of thing—"

"That's enough. If you want a permanent position I can get you one."

"Oh sure, and I'll be the one that needs looking after and being told what to do because I haven't any sense of it. I'm no beggar, and I wouldn't do you the disservice. But I'll do this delivery thing, and the security. I can do that."

"Maybe if you like it, you can stay, but it wouldn't be for an ar a day. You'll have a place in the household then, and food, and clothes. I wouldn't offer less than five ar a week, though. And you'd be paid more during events, and traditionally servants receive a Yule gift."

"And no rent. I could live better than happy on that. Is it true servants get days off?"

"A day off a week, and often they can get a morning or an afternoon here and there for the asking, or a week away if they want to visit a relative or some such. The days are very long, though, and the nights too short." The colonel didn't think about such things, of course. He didn't seem to pay any attention to his staff as human beings, though he treated them kindly enough. Because he was so short-handed, Trudy, Norbert and Philip never had any regular days off. No doubt the colonel assumed that because he didn't mind working every day and never socialized with anyone, that his servants were the same.

"If I stop fishing, I stop eating. Got hurt once, couldn't fish, starved for four days," Grant marveled. His crystalline green gaze had softened with fantasies of a lush life.

The idea nudged him again. Mark relented to it. "I ... there's something dangerous that ..."

Grant sat up with predatory intensity. "You got someone after you, I'll beat 'em down so hard there won't be pieces left to find of 'em."

Soldiers. He loved that purity and strength, though it made him feel small and weak. But not powerless. He could set Grant loose and it would be done.

He could ask, and part of him hoped that Grant would say no. He had to be careful with that for both of their sakes, but especially to protect Grant. "This would be more of a danger to you. I suppose it might work better if you stay close to home anyway, so never mind about riding out of town." Mark took a deep breath. "Do you think you could start a rumor?"

Grant shifted back and he looked uncertain. "Is it a lie?"

"Unfortunately, no, which is why it's dangerous. It's true, and the people who want it kept secret might hunt down its source."

"You."

"They'd first track it back to you. I have a feeling you'd do something awful like allow yourself to be tortured to death rather than give me up, but if they do find you, I want you tell them immediately. My fear is that they'd kill you anyway."

"Must be something really important."

He should consult the colonel first, but it would be better to start this as soon as possible, in case someone involved was a nominant. Taking a dangerous opponent out of the presidential elections before they'd even begun would spare them a lot of risk.

"I dunno. I might foul it up." Grant reached for his mug of wine, but seemed to think better of it. "What is it?"

"If you make it sound as if you'd heard it from somewhere else, that would help. Do you think you could do that?"

"What in the hells is it already?" Grant demanded nervously.

"There are shipments coming from the mainland. Men and weapons. Men with false names—each man on the manifest had two names listed, and a third name that may belong to a jester, or a lord, or a division—I couldn't tell. I think someone is gathering a small army on the island."

"You're humping me."

"No."

Grant lurched forward and covered his face in his hands.

"If word gets out, they'll have a harder time going about their business, and the captains will keep a closer eye on each other. It might be that this cargo is being transported unconsciously, and that worries me too. It could get ugly. Neighbors will start to suspect each other. People could die. Innocent people. If you don't think it's wise, I won't insist on this. I'm not entirely sure of it myself."

"No." Grant dragged his hands off his face and sat back. "No, it's gotta be done. I think I can do this. I'll do it. I even know where to start it."

Mark drew out his purse.

"What are you doing?"

"Get them drunk." Mark shook out the coins and sorted out the cupru. "Don't bring any ar with you if you still have some. Use more than one pocket, so it doesn't sound like you have a lot. No one will notice if you have to draw from more than one pocket in a given night. If they get drunk, they might even forget the rumor started with you."

"You do things like this all the time, don't you."

"No, I don't. I just know my history. This will actually be the first time I've attempted something like this." Mark put the ar away. "And I'm doing it backwards. In a lot of ways it's less dangerous and more profitable, and wiser to keep secrets. Revealing secrets, even an enemy's secret, can cause more problems than it solves. For example, you'll find that when a military secret is discovered it's not printed in the paper or spread among the ranks. Generals hold tight to them to control the situation as much as possible. They often don't want the enemy to know that they know. They'll spring it on them at an ideal time, when the force of it causes the most damage."

"So why are you doing it this way?"

"Partially because the colonel and I are isolated. We're alone, politically and socially. He can rally people around him, but it will take a lot of time, and the presidential nominations will soon be announced. There's no time to gather political strength."

"I think you're doing the right thing. People need to know. We didn't lose our friends just to get ambushed before we even get a president." Grant took a swig of wine from his mug. "By the which, I went to the postmaster and wrote my name, my whole name, in with a nomination."

That drew away the dark curtains from his mind and let in almost too much brightness to bear. "Really. Who did you nominate?"

"The rules say, I don't have to say." Grant's eyes sparkled with delight.

"Keep your secret, then." Grant's pleasure only warmed Mark's own.

"If they find out, what do you think they'd do to you?" Grant asked.

"That depends on when they find out, if they find out at all."

"But just supposin' they figure it out, say, before this grand party of yours."

"The damage will be done. If I were in their position, which is hard to imagine because I don't know their strength and numbers, but I think I would either try to win me over, try to turn the colonel, or if not him, the colonel's friends against me. That always steals the wind from a jester's abilities."

"But you wouldn't kill ... you."

"I have a hard time thinking that way, Grant. Blame it on my inexperience, my youth, my lack of determination—it doesn't matter." Mark drank more deeply into his cup than he had all night and filled it again. "I know they will consider it. I think it would depend on whether they predicted the colonel would be in a stronger or weaker position after my death. It will also depend on how much more trouble they think I could cause for them. With this act, I'm declaring myself direct, clumsy, and un-inclined to maintain control of the situation. From where I sit, it seems I'll be able to do little more damage to them unless the colonel is elected president, and he could do that without my help." Of course he probably wouldn't try without Mark. If anyone knew that, they'd certainly rid themselves of Mark if they could. "If anyone asks, tell them that as far as you know, the colonel wouldn't agree to be president."

"Why in the hells not?"

Mark's mind translated his words to say in the hell's knot, and it snapped him briefly into that confusion of vines and flowers. He shivered and took another swig of wine. "He doesn't want it." Mark guzzled from the cup and set it aside. That would be more than enough wine for now. "I happen to agree with you. He would do well. Not just because of his character. He's sturdy. You have him beaten in physical strength, but I've never met anyone with his spiritual strength. No bribe, no threat, no danger of failure will turn him aside from the right course."

"Here'n here." Grant raised his mug. Mark lifted his own, they clunked, and they drank to the future president, the people willing.

Mark rode home, or rather Bindart took him home, well after midnight. "I've got to stop drinking so much," he told her as he removed her tack. He rubbed her down a bit and walked unsteadily to the house. He stopped by the well pump near the stables on his way and drank until he felt overfull. He craved more wine but he dreaded waking with a headache again, which he'd have whether he drank more water or not.

"Damn I'm pounded." He chuckled, but then quieted as he opened the nearest rear door. This one let into the formal cloak and tack room. He took the way through the drawing room and up the back stairs. He staggered out into the open spaces in the central part of the upstairs toward his suite.

A band of light gleamed under the main doors leading to the colonel's suite. Maybe he'd left a candle burning. Mark carefully made his way over and cracked the door open. The bedroom door stood ajar.

The colonel sat on the floor. He leaned heavily on his window's broad sill, staring at something in his hand. It looked like something braided, maybe dark hair and a narrow ribbon.

Mark opened the door wider.

The colonel's gaze slid wearily to Mark before he shut his eyes. "Get out."

Mark stepped in and closed the door behind him. "Is it his, or hers?"

"I said get out." The words had no teeth among them.

His, then. "This isn't good for you." Mark went to help him up but the colonel surged to his feet.

"I shouldn't have to ask you twice." The colonel brushed his clothes straight. "If I have to ask a third time—"

"You'll have me flogged?"

"You wouldn't speak so lightly of it if you'd seen it done." The colonel stuck the braid in his waistcoat pocket.

"I'm sorry. I thought you'd be asleep by now. I just didn't want Hevether to burn down."

"No, of course this violation of my privacy is entirely altruistic." The colonel glanced outside at the stars. "Since you're determined to stay, perhaps you can explain why you were out so late." He drew the curtains shut.

"I was up to mischief, of course. Oh, and I've hired Grant to help us with the party." He tried to keep his tone light.

"Grant, is it? Mr. Roadman and you are close friends, then."

Something about the colonel's tone and the way Mark's heart ticked up its rhythm kept him from warming that jealousy with a little rubbing. "Not the sort of close friends you're implying. How could we be? He's more fond of women than wine. Besides, I thought you'd decided I was a liar and a whore." He shouldn't have said that last. It had to be the colonel's own heart working against them both.

"You're drunk."

"And you're jealous over nothing." He stopped himself in time, but he still thought it. *I would give you anything and everything if I thought you loved me.* "Now if you and Grant could be made into one man—"

Did I just say that aloud?

The colonel stalked over to him. "What was that?"

Maybe the colonel didn't hear every word. Mark set a hand on his chest to halt him. "Never mind. You're right. I'm drunk, and I'm going to bed."

"There is another, isn't there. You're seeing him in secret," he growled.

Ridiculous. "No." Mark backed away. Something about his manner made Mark uneasy. "I best leave. Forgive the intrusion—"

The colonel reached for Mark's arm but Mark eluded him, his wine-slowed mind finally perceiving danger.

"It's not enough to tease me like a cheap harlot, but then to humiliate me, publicly—" The colonel's voice murmured low with dangerous, sensuous tones. He put his hand on the door before Mark could escape.

"I think you're drunk." Mark spoke softly, a little breathless from fear. Unfortunately the colonel didn't smell drunk. Mark flinched as Hevether rumbled from a powerful wave slamming into the rocks. Fear started to mix with anger. "If you want me, you can have me. But you don't. Did you think I'd want to be alone and miserable for the rest of my life, just like you are?"

"I just want the truth."

Mark heard the pain this time. How could he have missed it? "Hush," he whispered. "It's all right." He expected something violent when he touched the colonel's face, but the colonel's lashes lowered and the stoic man's breath hitched. "It's all right." Stealing a kiss now would be a crime. Mark bit his lip. His heart pounded, but he felt a softer rhythm staggering, dragging broken across the shards of agony in the colonel's eyes. "It's all right." Mark slid his arms under the colonel's and drew him close.

The colonel barely yielded—just enough that he was warmer than stone to hold. Mark slowly dragged his hands along the colonel's tight spine. The colonel tucked his head and rested it near Mark's face and his arms looped loosely around Mark's body. Their hearts calmed.

Mark wished he could surge over the colonel like the waves on the rocks, but he had to go away. The colonel ... he'd say Mark was drunk, that it was a ploy. He'd say anything to keep from being hurt again. *Ha.* And the colonel had been so concerned about protecting Mark from further hurt. As if such lonely protection saved anyone from pain.

"While I'm here," Mark said softly, forcing a smile to warm his voice, "I should tell you that I have to move my room until the party is over. You don't have enough space downstairs. We'll keep this hall private. I'm blocking it off with an armoire and silk ropes."

"You shouldn't sleep in ... you shouldn't be next door." In what would be his future wife's quarters.

"I know. I thought I'd take the room next to Philip's downstairs."

The colonel's hands slid up Mark's back with unmistakable need. "That ...." He drew Mark up. Mark evaded his kiss and seized his lower lip in his mouth. He didn't resist the second kiss. His body arched and the colonel was at his throat, wrapping around him, tightening, grasping. Pleasure so strong it hurt tightened in his chest and Mark cried out.

The colonel covered his mouth with a hand and pressed him to the wall. "Hush," the colonel gasped, and slid his hand away. "Hush." He kissed Mark and worked at buttons. Mark's hands trembled too much to help much with the colonel's clothes. The colonel, Rohn, was steady though, steady and sure and potent. His breath and his racing heart betrayed his eagerness. Rohn traced an uneven trail down Mark's bared chest, around his ribs, teasing while he worked at Mark's belt.

Something like panic rushed through Mark until lips and hands played over him. He arched into the wall, a strangled, animal cry caught in his throat. Hands and lips coursed up his body. They freed each other of anything hampering—clothes, fears, doubt. That painful pleasure peaked in Rohn's strong grip and Mark fell into ripples and waves, washing endlessly in languor. His hands poured down clean skin, hardly distinguishing his lover's body from his own. Every breath, every touch radiated delight. One part of them struggled while the other urged and urged until Rohn grabbed Mark's hair fiercely and arched with grace and power. In that moment all that self-denial unmade itself, and Rohn was free.

Mark's strength slipped and he eased himself down the wall. Rohn knelt before Mark, his hands held flat together and trapped between his own thighs, head bowed, still panting, sweating. Sweat traced its way along

Mark's face and down his chest. He would have opened a window to let the sea air in, but it seemed better to swelter in luxury.

The heart of what they'd done began to falter in its aftermath. They exchanged glances.

Rohn stared at the polished wood floor between them.

So different, in every way, from Lord Argenwain who would often hold Mark in his luxurious bed until morning. Mark wanted to say something, but he had no words, not of comfort, or assurance, or apology. He stood and kissed the top of Rohn's head, gathered his breeches back up to his waist, and went to the door.

"I'm sorry."

Mark stopped, wounded to the spine. "You ought to be. Not for giving in, but for apologizing. You had love, and a lover. I never have, not like that. Your shame is my only treasure. If you're sorry for yourself, then be sorry, but don't you force your shame on me."

He walked out into the hall, disheveled and proud and confused and sorry too, but not for what happened. He was sorry they'd argued, and that he was drunk, and that Rohn was ashamed.

Thankfully they hadn't woken anyone. He saw no hint of Philip or Norbert when he passed the top of the stairs, nor any light at the end of his hallway where Trudy slept. The only thing that smothered the silence was the constant sea. He let himself into his room and found his bed in the dark. Mark crawled onto it and lay shipwrecked there until sleep dragged him down.

A knock woke him to bright daylight. He couldn't remember the last time he'd slept so soundly and dreamlessly. Mark sat up. "Yes?"

Trudy opened the door, squeaked and shut it again. "Excuse me, l'jeste. Grant Roadman is here, and there's a delivery of furniture waiting in the entry. I'm very sorry to wake you, sir."

"It's all right. Please see if Mr. Roadman wants any refreshments and tell everyone I'll be there in a half hour at most." Poor Trudy. Lord Argenwain's maids weren't in any way shy, and they had more reason to be, considering some of the things they'd stumbled into seeing. He hadn't even considered Trudy might be modest.

"Would you like some hot water, sir?"

"Yes, thank you, Miss Trudy. I'm putting on a robe right now." He had to laugh. Despite everything he felt wonderful, alive, and beyond happy.

Today would be a beautiful day.

Chapter Twenty Three

Every window in Hevether had been braced wide open, but even the strong sea winds barely penetrated the dense garden of humanity filling every open room in the house. Outside, half of Perida's commoners, and a good number of folk that had traveled from other parts of the island, as well as from some of the nearest islands, reveled in the courtyard and on the road leading to the manor. Torches and lamps and bonfires blazed, lighting fantastic costumes.

They expected one more grand entrance on this, the holiest of days, the first of Sooner.

Rohn Evan's and Lark's.

Mark ran his fingers over the mask that Gutter had given him. Every mask he thought to paint he'd halted midway through the process. He didn't want the blue and black diamonds again. He'd had no luck in town with any of the mask makers—there were only three and none of them suited him, even if they could create and fit a design in the short time he'd given them.

Rohn came into the bedroom again and stood beside the vanity. "They're getting impatient."

"No they're not. They're bursting with anticipation. They'll wait." It didn't help that he had to dress himself in Rohn's bedroom with the door closed while Rohn dressed in his sitting room, as if they hadn't shared ....

"It's not a very attractive mask," Rohn said, "but I think it will suit you. More importantly, I like it better than that other mask, the one you painted."

"Honestly?"

Rohn looked offended at the suggestion that he'd be anything but honest. "If I hate it I'll just remove it."

"Don't. Don't ever take off a jester's mask, especially a living mask."

Rohn's eyes tightened and narrowed. "Is it dangerous?"

"It can cause shock, like being plunged into ice water or seeing a dead child." Mark traced the mask's tears with a finger, took a deep breath, and raised it to his face. He closed his eyes. The lining felt silken and conformed to his face, warm as living skin. He tied it, and then he opened his eyes. For a moment he saw only himself in the mirror, his muddy green eyes too wide, his lips parted, and then something small seized the back of his neck at the base of his skull in a firm grip. His mind slipped sideways. He was losing, dying, losing his mind, slipping—

Easy.

"Easy," he said gently, and let out a sighing breath. He stood and set a hand on Rohn's shoulder. "It's going to be all right."

"Lark?"

"We're all right." He'd never felt so calm, or so sensitive to Rohn's fears, or to the graceful house his master had taken such pains to keep from accepting as his own home. He wanted so much to talk with Rohn but they didn't have time. "Look at me. Please." Rohn obeyed, braced like frightened horse cornered in a strange paddock. "I'm not a stranger. You know me. You've met this part of me before, and this part of me would never hurt you, not in anger, not in fear, not for fun, and not to punish. Never to punish. I'm your friend. I'm the one who kissed the top of your head, and the one who held your hand and led you through the darkness. Remember me?"

Rohn turned his head a little.

Lark offered his hand. Rohn bravely took it. Lark just stood there a moment, holding him, letting the calm of his own heartbeat soothe his master until he felt his friend the colonel relax. Lark let go.

Rohn let out a little laugh and ducked his head like a shy youth. He closed his hand into a loose fist, then worked the fingers like they'd been cold and had finally warmed.

"May I lead the way?" Lark asked.

Rohn gestured, and Lark went out into the hall. He paused at the top of the stairs. A noble couple passing by on the way to the private party rooms upstairs stopped. The woman curtsied and the gentleman bowed before he offered his hand. "Ah, Lord Jester Lark and Baron Evan! What a wonderful evening my Barbara and I have been having."

"Baron Wollard," Rohn said by way of introduction.

Applause began to ripple through the crowd, and a few cheers raised. Lark slowly descended with Rohn close behind so that they could greet each person as they went.

And so they went very slowly through the close crowds. Lark had never seen so many nervous, eager, excited and uncertain people in his life. Even Lord Argenwain might be jealous of this much elegance and so many fluttering fans. He danced one dance with a sweet debutante but that was all he had time for—the evening was passing too swiftly to linger. By the time they negotiated their way outside the bonfires glowed with a forge-like heat at their centers. The crowds of commoners outside let out a roaring cheer. Of course he had to sing, and encouraged them to sing along. Once he got them started they couldn't stop. He shook as many hands as he could.

How Rohn loved it once they were outside. Former soldiers gathered around him, delighted to see their colonel again. Beneath his smiling but formal exterior Lark could see the verge of joyful tears. Rohn had missed them all terribly.

Lark left him to his adoring men and went back into the house.

"Lark!" Feather walked gracefully toward him without impinging on anyone's conversation—a marvelous feat. She'd painted her mask this night, red feathers with gold edging, and her eyes were bright and brave.

"Feather." He kissed her hand. "Thank you again for your gift."

"I see you're wearing it."

"How could I not? It's perfect."

She blushed. "Thank you for your kind letter. You didn't have to go through so much trouble. You must have had dozens of thank yous to write." Her gaze drifted for a moment—not because something caught her attention or because of deceit or thought. It looked as if she'd lost herself a moment.

Lark couldn't let her know he'd seen her slip. "I didn't see you before now."

"We'd just arrived. The mayor's health doesn't allow him to linger as long as we'd like, and we'd rather stay late than leave early."

"I understand." He took her hand again, worried that she might slip once more. Something about the crowd overwhelmed her control. He didn't think it was the mask doing it. If anything, he would have guessed that the mask helped steady her. "Would you favor me with a dance later on?"

"I'd love to."

He bowed and moved onward because he had to.

He'd finally found Winsome.

She cowered in a corner, outwardly strong but ready to bolt. She looked stunning in a deep blue gown, her hair piled in dark curls, pearls and diamonds adorning her throat. He picked up a glass of punch made from various dark fruits and a hint of wine and brought it to her. "Lady Kilderkin." He offered his hand and she accepted it gratefully for his kiss. He gave her the punch and she sipped delicately. "Baron Evan is outside. Or do you think of him more as the colonel?"

She lowered her lashes and blushed at him. "Either."

Oh no.

It would be impossible to fix this problem tonight. He refused to hurt her even slightly. He'd let Mark talk to her some other time. He'd be better suited to gently guide her heart away from him, with his awkwardness and painful sincerity. "I'm pleased you're here. I'll be sure to let the baron know. He'll want to dance with you at least once, though with so many clamoring for his attention—this is what comes from being reclusive." He chuckled and she laughed softly. She had a sweet laugh, very kindly. "Is your father here as well?"

"And Juggler." She lowered her lashes again, but this time she tried to conceal her discomfort. Still hiding things. No doubt Juggler got in the way of her spying. If he found out he would put a swift end to it, and to what little freedom she enjoyed now. But she didn't seem to be afraid of him. Lark hoped that as a soldier and a woman she'd instinctively know if she ought to be afraid of him. "Everything is so beautiful," she added. "I had no idea. What little I've heard of Hevether—well, it was supposed to be—"

"Dreary. It isn't. It's strong, and serious, but it has a good heart that welcomes and protects those who need it the most. Like its lord."

"Like you."

"Oh, I'm not serious at all, or strong." Sadness colored his calm. "And I don't think I could protect anyone from anything no matter how hard I tried. But I would try."

She slipped her hand around his arm. "Gentleness is not weakness."

He set his hand over hers, briefly, trying to ease any sense of rejection as he pulled away, bowed, and kissed her hand. "I have to fetch the baron. We have an announcement to make and I think most everyone has finally arrived. I'll come back and talk to you again. Please don't leave."

She looked so forlorn. Hardly anyone paid attention to her.

He couldn't stand it. He offered her a smile. "Unless I can convince you to join us in that announcement?" He offered her his hand again.

She accepted, of course. He felt better about leading her through the masses than leaving her, though it would expose her to public scrutiny. Everyone would watch and make assumptions and take notes that they would later embellish in one of the three gazettes printed on the island. He supposed it was better for her to be perceived as someone desirable than a cast-off. At least Winsome didn't seem overly uncomfortable about the attention.

She'd probably regret it later, but he couldn't do anything about it.

Lark took her outside and she relaxed considerably. A large group of naval officers started to pounce her and Lark thought about leaving her in their care, but he'd already invited her to the announcement. He stopped long enough to allow her to introduce him to them and let her exchange heartfelt pleasure at meeting with them again before he took her to where the baron held court with a variety of officers and common soldiers.

"It's time," Lark told him gently.

Rohn's back tensed up straight. He excused himself formally and then bowed to Winsome. "Lady Kilderkin."

She curtseyed, and to Lark's relief her throat flushed. At least she found Rohn attractive.

He couldn't deny that it hurt, but it was for the best. He and Rohn could not be lovers and live forever after in exile with no heirs and a bitter father mourning the son he could never openly love again. Besides, Rohn would make a wonderful father, with Winsome's moderating influence.

Winsome took Rohn's arm, and not entirely to maintain a façade. She was nervous and smitten and they looked perfect together.

It took the three of them over half an hour to make their way to the front balcony. Lark began with a song. The guests inside came out to listen. He'd written it the day before but he knew it as if he'd sung it all his life. He sang of needing a home, and running from fire, running from death, held by promises like chains around his throat until they broke. It was his journey, but it was their journey too, and when the chains that bound them to Cathret broke, that was just the beginning. They struggled through war as he'd struggled through the snow, and now they all faced the same fears and hopes for the future.

The song held no answers, and no ending. When I come home, the chorus said. When I come home, he sang at the end.

The only sound afterward came from the sea and the fires.

"I have an announcement," Rohn said. Winsome gripped his arm, her face turned away as she held a handkerchief to her face. Lark hadn't meant to make her cry. "I long maintained that I would make a poor leader. It began during the war, but I led nonetheless out of necessity. Later I securely housed and guarded the governors and the best of our officers and citizens while they composed what is now our constitution. I signed with the others in support of that document which I will gladly risk my life to support. I still feel that I have been given too much credit in that regard, but I will not dishonor those who have faith not only in me but in all of those who labored to write our constitution. It was not the work of one, but many, and I will not appear to distance myself, as if I feared any flaws it might have would reflect on me. I stand by it, as I stand by Perida and the Meriduan Islands."

Lark had to force himself to look away and observe the crowd. They knew, but they could hardly believe what they were hearing.

"My closest friends have heard me say that I would never accept a nomination for president, and if forced, I would yield—" Rohn faltered and Winsome set her hand on his shoulder to steady him. It worked. "I would yield to another man. I understand now that it was cowardice, not modesty that moved me. I feared I would disappoint, that I would lead our new nation to ruin, that I wasn't strong enough, or brave enough, or wise enough. But I would challenge anyone who would dare to suggest that my friend Mr. Roadman would not suffice, or Captain Trellior, or Lady Kilderkin—that any one of us would fail. None of us would fail. We won the war. We are free because of the strength in each and every one of us, and it is cowardice to exclude myself from your ranks. The only ones that would lead us to ruin are those traitors who wished and still wish we were chained to Cathret."

Lark's breath caught. Unwittingly, the rumors he'd begun had come home. Rohn had insisted that he would speak extemporaneously, and he'd spoken very well, but their enemies would not take his open words lightly.

"A president is not a king. He does not stand alone, and he does not decide alone. I have nothing to fear of a nomination, because if I am nominated I will not be alone. But even if I was alone I could not shirk my duty. I would be honored, and duty-bound to accept. I will support whoever is voted into the presidency, for I trust in who we are, and what we've become. I trust in democracy because I trust in my fellows." It wasn't quite done, but Rohn faltered again, perhaps in part overcome by his decision, and by his promise, perhaps in part hunting for the best conclusion while under the weight of thousands of people whose numbers stretched long down the road. "Whatever you decide, I will abide, and I will not dishonor you again."

They applauded, and the applause began to roar until it drowned out the sea. As news traveled back to those too far back to hear directly, cheers began to resound.

Lark drew Rohn and Winsome off the balcony. "Now we have to make the rounds again," he said.

Rohn looked exhausted but he nodded. "Now that they've heard me speak I have little fear that I will have to bear that station."

"You think they'll be jaded and hear your words as manipulation and false modesty?" Lark had to laugh. "If it were any other, perhaps, but I'm afraid they know you too well to suspect subterfuge. You are right, though. No one else could have said those things and be believed."

It took a long time but they made their way down the stairs and into each room, leaving the salon-turned-dance-hall for last. There Lark maneuvered Winsome and Rohn to the floor so that he and Feather could finally share a dance.

"Did you write those words for him?" Feather asked as they swept together and apart and circled.

Lark didn't know the dance well, but he'd seen it earlier and it didn't require his concentration. "No. They came from his heart, on the spot."

"He certainly struck my heart." Her expression softened and grew ethereal. "Forgive me. Too much wine."

It was a lie. She could see something.

Lark's heart quickened. It made him think of Seers of old, though no one credible had claimed to be one in over a hundred years. Most of them were said to have gone mad before age fifteen, and more of them were women than men. Most were thought to be fakes whether they were mad or not. "I wonder if we have a few spiritual observers tonight." There might have been voices in his mind, but amid the cacophony, he couldn't tell.

Her expression didn't waver. "If Gutter were here, he would be pleased."

The mask gave him a little cover. "You're acquainted with that famed jester?"

"Aren't you?"

"Would it change your opinion of me if I wasn't?"

"Do you know my opinion of you?"

Lark laughed hard enough to miss a step. "I wonder how long we will go without a question answered."

"But they've all been answered. I knew you the moment I saw you, as you know me."

He couldn't let on that Gutter had never mentioned her. It might be too that she was trying to lure him into an admission on partial information. Or perhaps she meant to suggest that he knew she was a Seer? "You're too clever for me."

"And you're too bold for me. We are the ideal couple." She drew close with the dance and her mouth tickled his ear. "I know you, confidante."

She had him flustered and he couldn't let her notice. Lark led her out of the dance. There was nowhere private to speak with her, but he didn't need privacy. He wanted only to distract her and keep himself out of reach until he could gather himself. "I hope I can beg a favor of you." The strength of her attention on his every word unsettled him. "I would like to gather as many jesters as are so inclined to perform for at least one dance and at least one song tonight."

"You mentioned as much in the invitation."

"I think the time is drawing near, but I'm overdue in various places to check on the staff. If you wouldn't mind, could you collect them?"

"Not at all. Will a half hour suffice?" She smiled sweetly.

"I should be back by then." He took both her hands and kissed them soundly. He didn't have to fake gratitude. He honestly needed her help. "Thank you."

"You're most welcome." She vanished among the crowded silk gowns and fanciful hats.

Confidante. She had to mean Gutter's confidante, though Lark was far from it. The other possibility was more disturbing. He hadn't told anyone that he heard voices sometimes. Well, his parents, but they were ... gone.

And so what if he did hear voices? It could be his imagination, and those voices didn't tell him sacred secrets. Something else was at work, and he doubted it had anything to do with *allolai* and *morbai*.

You're lying to yourself.

Lark fled his fears to check in the kitchen. "Norbert, how are you managing?"

"Lord jester sir," he said shakily, surrounded by bustling help some of which seemed to hinder more than assist, "they keep bringing things in to plate from the pits but there's no room, and I tried to tell them to set a table in my room for that use but they can't find any."

Lark took him by the arm, concerned that the old man might collapse. "I'm sorry I didn't step in sooner. Come this way. Have some fresh air. It's sweltering in here."

"I don't mind," Norbert protested. "It's bound to be hot with all three ovens at full roar baking fowl."

Lark drew him outside. "You there, young man, go fetch me some water please."

"Now lord jester, please don't fuss," Norbert protested.

"Won't you sit here with me. I could use the rest myself." The estate's rock foundation sat on native stone. In many places near the manor, the stables and the service building, the builders had artfully cut out the natural rise and fall into benches, among other things. Norbert settled down and Lark sat beside him. The water arrived and Lark gave the boy a cupru. "Thank you. I have a more important errand, if you're able."

"Yes sir, l'jeste!"

"At the front of the house there are soldiers in fine uniforms standing watch. Tell the one with the white hat and shawl that we need a large table brought here. Tell them Lark sent you."

"Yes sir, l'jeste!" The boy dashed off.

"Thank you, lord jester." Norbert leaned heavily on his knees.

"I have to see how Trudy and Philip are doing. Please wait outside until the table gets here. On my way I'll stop and make certain that Gregor keeps a close watch on things." Lark stood and brushed himself off.

"Don't let him leave those birds in until they're falling apart, or the flesh will end up in the fire." Norbert started to rise but Lark settled him again.

"I promise, the birds will come out all right." Lark hurried back inside and found Gregor, the most adept of Norbert's new assistants, laboring over soup. "Set someone else to this task. Norbert is worrying about the birds."

"Yes, l'jeste."

Lark took the back stairs and caught Trudy carrying a heavy load of cut fruit. "Miss Trudy." He took one side of the enormous plate. "Where are the girls?"

"Thank you. They're downstairs helping serve, l'jeste."

"They were supposed to help you."

"Well Delia said she was overrun trying to keep the sideboards stocked. There's not as much to do upstairs, especially since they're helping themselves to drinks in the billiards room."

"There are four hundred people upstairs, if not more." They eased past the armoire and maneuvered around guests into Lark's suite, where everything had been cleared to the walls to serve as a chat room for their more distinguished guests. Juggler was there, and Onyx and the other elders as well as a number of nobles. Lark quickly memorized who stood close to who and decided to look into the other rooms as soon as possible. "I'll get at least one girl back up here. Delia will have to manage without her."

"Thank you, l'jeste."

Lark helped her set the plate and clear some old ones before he offered his hand to Juggler. Juggler shook with a short bow. "I have to admit I'm impressed," Juggler said.

"Thank you." Juggler's cold façade seemed thinner than usual. Behind it Lark glimpsed a hurt, wounded thing painfully hoping for a friend to lend a hand. There was something else there, too. A mistrust he hadn't seen before.

Juggler cocked his head as if trying to see behind the mask. "You make me curious as to how many masks you have."

"Just the one," Lark said with a smile, and Juggler surprised him by smiling back.

"You haven't met Gerson Wilden," Juggler said, leading the way. "Gerson, our newest friend, Lord Jester Lark."

The constabulary priest had the look of a well-aged craftsman, with large, calloused hands and rough skin on his face. The chain around his neck wasn't the only adornment he wore. He had a choker featuring a large, uncut ruby. Lark bowed, uncertain. The gerson nodded in answer. "Are you a friend to the church, young man?" the gerson asked.

"Since I've come here the church has been a friend to me. How the church regards me, I wouldn't presume to say." Juggler might have caught the slight hesitation but hopefully the gerson didn't.

The gerson's eyes narrowed in contrast to his smile. "The church here is different than it is in Cathret."

"Much to my delight," Lark assured him.

"You were at odds?"

"No, gerson. And I'm sorry but I can't comment on their treatment of me, as it would be unfair. There is no one here to defend the Cathretan priests, and I must admit that there must have been a great many misunderstandings, all on my part, as far as what transpired in my past. I hope to leave all that behind."

"Your mask—it is an older one, is it not? It seems familiar to me."

"It's new and unfamiliar to me. If you want to ask after it's history, you're much better off with your memory than any guesses I might make." Lark had to get out of this before the gerson inevitably asked where Lark got it. "If you'll excuse me, I have a few more things to look after, and an event I must organize. I hope you'll both attend the performance. Juggler, I hope you've decided to join us."

"I do intend to." Something had hurt him in the conversation.

Lark didn't have time to try and speak to him about it. He bowed to them and hurried out. He had to stop and talk to Bell. It took Bell several minutes to decline a hand of cards in Trudy's made-into-yet-another-card-room. After assuring Bell's attendance Mark slid past the armoire and took the back stairs down, and fled out to the stables.

Philip sat by with a tall cup of punch. He stood as Lark approached. "Lark, sir."

"How goes it?" Lark asked.

"I have more help than I need. The horses are all getting along for the most part."

"Good to hear it. Send word if that changes. I'll shuffle people around."

"As you like, sir."

Lark caught a server rounding the long way outside from the kitchen toward the front. He grabbed two cups of punch—a sip revealed that this one was made with brandy—and carried them to the rear of the house.

It was quiet here. Just a few people strolling in the dark, talking softly, the guards, and Grant. Lark could barely make out his form on the back step, one long leg stretched out. Even his shadowed outline seemed handsome in his new uniform.

"Hey," Lark said, approaching. "I brought you some punch."

Grant rose and stalked over. Lark hesitated for a critical moment. He barely dodged Grant's shove. "Get out of here," he growled.

Lark couldn't let him do this, not in sight of anyone. "Come over to the stables," he urged. "If you want to fight, fine but—."

"Fight? I'll wring your neck."

Lark kept moving backward and Grant finally stopped. "Just tell me what's wrong."

"You're wrong," he said in a harsh whisper. "You slept in my bed. I trusted you. I'll do my duty for the colonel's sake but after tonight I'm done, done with you, done with all of it."

He couldn't mean it. Any of it.

"Tell me it's not true," Grant demanded.

Lark had to fight to keep Mark from surfacing past the mask and falling apart. "Of what am I accused?"

"Tell me you're not."

The only reason Mark didn't immediately realize what Grant meant was because he thought Grant already knew, like everyone seemed to know. His belly went cold. "I didn't mean to keep anything secret from you. Grant, I didn't intend—I didn't take advantage—" He had to stop himself from blundering on because nothing he could say along those lines would help. He wished he knew exactly what had set him off, and hoped that Grant didn't represent a general hatred among islanders for staghorns. "If you hate me, and you want to go, then go. I'll consider your duty fulfilled, and I'll tell to the colonel that you had leave for personal reasons."

"You'd make your gruelly excuses in my name?"

Lark parried the sword attack before he fully comprehended that Grant had drawn. One cup of punch flew aside, the other struck Grant in the face. The giant man tried again.

Lark's swift defensive instincts nearly cut Grant's throat. Mark flinched in time but it cost him the line and Grant's sword slapped above his ear. Luckily he hit flat and didn't cut right into the skull. Mark's ear rang and the thud knocked him hard but he recovered and rushed inside Grant's range. Grant fell hard. It gave the mask time to gather up Mark's scattered senses and subdue his bearer. Lark stepped on Grant's sword and he lost the weapon. Lark picked it up and faced both points toward him. "Go home," he said loudly. "She's not worth it, Grant. I swear I didn't know she meant so much to you."

"She?" Grant's initial confusion gave way to understanding. "It don't take anything for you to come up with a quick lie, does it." Grant spat and stormed off.

Lark touched above his ear. The skin was broken and bleeding, but there was only a slight dent in the bone.

He had to clean up and return to the damned party. "You," he said, gesturing to one of Grant's men. "You're in charge." The man met him halfway and accepted Grant's sword. "Are you one of his friends?"

"No, lord jester."

"Then return his sword to me tomorrow morning. I'll have it delivered."

"Yes sir, er, lord jester."

Lark took the back way up to Rohn's sitting room. It had a good full-length mirror thanks to one of his shopping expeditions. His hands shook but his heart stayed calm, drawing on Rohn's steady and mellow mood from wherever the man was enjoying himself. The mask had done this before—used a jester's master's heart to steady its wearer. Lark could tell by the familiarity of the action despite it being the first time he'd done it.

Blood had stained his hair, and it showed the most in the lighter hair on top, though the darker curls near his neck dripped with it. Blood had gotten on his neckerchief, and his new coat.

He slipped the neckerchief and staunched the bleeding before he shrugged the coat off. He stripped carefully to the waist and washed out his hair as best he could. It wouldn't stop bleeding. He needed flour. Lark rang for Trudy.

It took her a few minutes, but she finally arrived and fetched the flour without hesitation or questions, though she blanched when she saw him. She helped him apply it. A scarf went over the bandage, and a new hat went over the scarf, a hat to match a new coat. He didn't like it as well as the one he'd been wearing, but it would have to do. He tied on a new neckerchief, a black one with gold and blue edging, and all was well with the world though the world seemed to have ended.

"You'll be all right, l'jeste?" Trudy asked.

"Yes, thank you. You may take a few minutes leisure if you like. The performance will begin soon, and there will be fewer things to attend to."

"May I watch it, sir?"

Lark smiled in spite of everything. "Of course."

He made his way down the stairs. Part of him feared that news of the fight would spread rapidly, but he realized that his was only a minor altercation among what had to be dozens by now. Men, especially young men, and drinking, and women dressed to best advantage ... it always led to fights.

Rational, yes, but it had been so much more than a fight to him.

He contrived smiles and everyone made way for him. Feather had done her part, and the jesters were waiting at their instruments.

Juggler led with a beautiful solo on a viola, defining the dance. It was an old and well-loved dance arranged in four lines, and partners hastened to their places. Winsome caught his gaze and he went to her, offering his hand. He needed a friend for this dance.

She seemed to respond to the hurt hidden behind his carefully crafted rapture as they bathed in exquisite music. Her touch was light, her demeanor undemanding and gentle. She didn't venture conversation. She eased his loneliness with a perfect understanding, though she knew nothing of what had happened. For that he adored her, and wished. Just wished.

The dance ended and it was his turn to perform. Feather joined him along with half a dozen other jesters, one of which he hadn't met. Feather quickly introduced them while the audience filled in where the dance had been. It was very crowded. Lord Argenwain's hall had been twice as broad, half-again as long and would have felt crowded with half the people. The heat began to get to him again. Feather noticed and fanned him. "Thank you." He had to stay calm, keep his heart calm, or he might faint.

A lady did faint not far from them. Two men nearby caught her and removed her to fresh air. She wasn't the first and wouldn't be last to faint tonight.

"Let's do Ciarrellos," Bell suggested.

It had been a long time, but Lark remembered it. "There are six of us. We can turn each verse into a solo."

"Then you have to go last," Feather said.

"I volunteer to go first," Bell said. They hashed out the order and agreed on the key of G minor.

It almost didn't feel like performing. Lark soon forgot that he had an audience. His voice played just as one instrument among the others. The dying knight in the song mourned his regrets and clung to his victories with more passion than Lark had ever heard before, even more beautifully than the Zhever Troupe that had moved him so deeply when they came to perform for Lord Argenwain three years ago. He forgot all his hurt until the song ended. He felt as if this night had been like the knight's death, full of wonders and sorrows that would soon culminate in the loss of all. He dreaded the morning when he'd go and return Grant's sword. He feared it would be the end of their friendship forever.

The jesters skilled at instruments struck up a lively song and the dancers with stamina leapt to it again. Lark retreated toward the front of the house.

Feather stopped him. "Oh no you don't."

"I need to get out of the heat," Lark told her.

"May I come with you?" She took his arm.

"How can I say no?"

"You can't." She walked with him through the front and out to the road. There was Rohn by a bonfire listening to a soldier go on about a dog that got into a mess tent. He was laughing, so happy. It healed Lark to see him like that.

"I was in love with him for a while," Feather said, encouraging Lark to keep walking. "And I loved Gutter too. Madly. No wonder I'm drawn to you as well."

"But we cannot be." He felt sorry for it.

"Your honesty astounds me, considering your teacher."

"You're beautiful, but you're not that beautiful."

She laughed, and then her attention faded. "They're watching us," she breathed, and her hand gripped his arm with hard claws.

"Who is?" he asked gently. Maybe she was mad and just hid it well.

"I needed you to know. It's all right. I can't say anymore but I can say that much." Her hand relaxed. "I should hate you, but I can't. I will miss you."

Though her voice moved in ways that didn't babble, her words certainly made no sense. "Miss me?"

She kissed his cheek and left him on the road to join up with an admiral or some similar naval person at another bonfire. He couldn't make out the insignia in the uneven light.

Lark walked back to the manor, uneasy. Perhaps she'd risked her mind to let him know what the beings in the afterworld were doing. Did she mean that the *morbai* and *allolai* had gathered to watch this event, or that they'd come for him in some way ... is that why she'd miss him?

Will they drive me mad tonight for some offense ... because of what Rohn and I shared?

Or maybe she meant something is happening here, tonight, or in Perida—

He thought immediately of ships burning in the bay, but that was just an echo of his own losses. He couldn't afford to leave the party to find out if something was amiss in Perida. Just in case he sent one of the private guards they'd hired to go to town and see if anything was amiss.

The house wasn't as stifling as it had been. People were starting to retire, drunk and sated and beyond exhausted. Lark selected a pretty young lady for the next dance. She proved a fine partner for a brilliant *stirrah*. The quick pace and galloping music soon made him laugh. He couldn't stay serious and worried and sad in the midst of so much joy. Before he knew it he was chatting about dogs—so many of the island's notables were obsessed with dogs, either hating or adoring them—with Bell, Jog, Fine, General Glassfield, Governor Evan, and a mix of other gentlemen and ladies. Lark posed ridiculous questions about dogs and they all tried to answer with facts while inserting things that would make each of them sound as knowledgeable as possible about the animals.

Someone brought him a fresh glass of punch. He'd barely sipped it when a new dance started up. "There—Marjorie. I promised her a dance and it will be this one. Drave, hold this will you?"

Drave accepted the glass and Lark hunted out Marjorie. The sharp, heavy spice from the punch was too cloying. No doubt this late the cooks were getting clumsy.

Marjorie preened and batted her eyes and Lark flirted just a bit while they turned endlessly through the *vellawei*. The hearty dance stole his breath and he couldn't quite catch it. "I'm sorry, I have to stop." He slipped out of the line, gulping for air, his heart staggering. It wasn't getting better, and that frightened him. He went to a window.

"Lord jester, you're flushed. Sara! Sara? Come here, lend him your fan." Lady Sara's husband Roth brought him a chair and Lark sat gratefully.

Someone screamed from across the room and Sara stopped fanning him. Lark felt so hot—and suddenly went cold with sweat. His stomach rebelled. He managed to get sick out the window. He smelled blood, tasted it in his mouth.

"Roth!"

"You, find Baron Evan and bring him here immediately," Roth barked. "Is there a doctor in the room!"

"There is," said Jog, rushing over, "but he's with Drave. It's poison. It must have been in the glass."

Lark struggled to remember who gave him the glass, but he couldn't remember. "Did you see? Did you see who?"

"It was a servant."

Lark barely managed to hold his stomach. "Find him, Jog. Please find him."

Jog rushed off.

Lark lost control and was sick again. It was almost all blood, warm blood. Roth let out an oath but Sara knelt beside him. "There's has to be something we can do. Tell me what to do."

Lark didn't know this poison. "Water."

"Fetch some water!" she cried.

Lark's heart staggered. He had to survive. He had to find the secrets, had to find his mother's killer, had to find out why *Mairi* burned. He'd momentarily lost his desire for justice and now everything would remain undone. Had Feather told him she would miss him because she poisoned him?

Juggler suddenly appeared. "I know what this is." His voice was hushed and full of pain. "I can smell it."

"The spice," Lark whispered, gasping for air. He shivered, cold to the bone.

"Fetch me a pistol. We can't leave him like this."

"Oh please no," Sara pleaded.

Lark arched into darkness and saw the *allolai* and *morbai* in the deep black, their clothes alive with teeth, blades drawn, flowers writhing all around them, their faces opening to reveal green and gold fire within while they waited for him. "I see them," he gasped, and his words pulled him back into the room. He'd fallen to the floor.

Rohn crouched beside him. "Where is that milk?"

"You can't leave him like this," Juggler protested.

"Stay with me," Rohn pleaded softly. "Please stay with me. Please don't leave me."

He had to survive. He had to get the mask off. The mask had to survive. He remembered how Obsidian had clawed for his mask, and everything made dark and terrible sense. If the mask remained on his face when he died, it might lose that which made it alive, and it had no soul. It would perish forever, a tragedy far more immense than one boy's life.

Rohn didn't understand and tried to prevent him from tearing it off, to prevent shock.

"Help him," Juggler snarled. "For pity's sake!"

Rohn hesitated. Lark dragged his fingers up and finally pulled the mask, scarf, hat, everything from his head.

The darkness swept in and the *allolai* and *morbai* reached for him. He screamed and the world blazed with light as if under a summer sun.

Mark lurched awake in Rohn's washroom, soaking wet, naked, wrapped in towels dripping with water and blood. His heart leapt painfully in off rhythms. His breath came in short, shuddering gasps. Rohn rubbed his back while the doctor measured something into a cup of milk.

"I think he's conscious," Rohn gasped.

"Sit him up." The doctor came over with the cup. Rohn pulled Mark up against his chest and the doctor tried to pour milk into Mark's mouth. Mark's throat burned and his stomach felt like it was full of razors. "If he can't keep this down, the pistol might be kinder."

Mark remembered the scent of Rohn's skin, and the kisses that had torn though him with ecstasy, and Gutter's letter, and diamonds sparkling, and Rohn's voice as he read that awful, wonderful romance. He forced himself to drink. The milk tasted beyond sour, and it burned into him. His belly tightened until it felt like his flesh had torn inside him.

Walking on the beach stroking Bindart, talking with Winsome.

Sitting with Grant—

No, that hurt too much, but he needed it.

Sitting with Grant, working on his letters, the pride so bright but so shy in Grant's eyes.

Rohn cupped Mark's head in his hands and held his face close to his cheek. "I'm sorry. I'm so sorry." A hand worked through Mark's hair, passionate, his touch hard with longing and desperation.

Trudy drew in close and wove her hand with Rohn's, gentling his touch. A man nearby wept.

Mark's heart steadied. His breath slowed.

"Stand him up," the doctor ordered.

Rohn and Trudy pulled him up.

"Walk him."

Mark tried to move his feet. At first he couldn't, but then a leg twitched in answer to his will, and again, and he limped along. Sleepiness tried to drag him down past the pain.

"Stop for a moment." The doctor set his head against Mark's chest. For several breaths he listened, and then eased away. "He's out of danger for the moment. Keep him moving."

Mark noticed everything in sharp patches connected by blurs of lost time. Philip stood by, eyes red. Norbert came in with hot water and Philip helped him fill the bath. Norbert came in again with more water. They bathed him. They dressed him in a nightshirt. They walked him up and down the hall. They forced water and milk into him, though he kept little of it down for long. The blurs between grew shorter.

The doctor listened to his chest again. "You can put him to bed."

"My bed," Rohn told them, and they walked Mark to the master bed. Trudy and Philip helped settle him in. Mark's eyes closed and everything went a frightening black.

"I'm sorry but I doubt he'll last a week," the doctor said somewhere in the distance. "Most patients die of dehydration or during a convulsion. Still, he might fool us. He's surprised me before." The silence behind those words filled with wind and the sound of the sea through the open windows. "By the way, I couldn't help but notice—he should have had terrible scars—"

"It's a sacred matter. That's all I can say," Rohn told him.

"I should document—"

"I wouldn't advise it."

The doctor sighed. "A shame, really, to be forced into ignorance when we could all be enlightened with so little."

Chapter Twenty-Four

Mark sat in the sun in the breakfast room, paper strewn on the table, sketching, his gaze occasionally lifting look over the jagged, bleak rocks. Beyond them the land rose into a long, sharp hill with black edges, as if it were parts of a notched sword peaking through a rotted scabbard of green.

Rohn came in and settled nearby. "How are you this morning?"

Mark felt his strength ebbing with every breath, but he said, "I feel stronger." He pushed the paper toward Rohn. "What do you think?"

Rohn gazed at it. "A garden."

"Just a little one. An acre or so. A wall, trees in pots, vines on the wall, benches, and flowerbeds with those knee-high things with blue flowers that seem to do well growing in sand near the surf."

"What's this?"

"A gazebo with a pool at its center and a small fountain. A horse fountain, naturally. You remind me of a horse sometimes, lost and trapped but bravely trying to trust any hand offered no matter how many times he's betrayed." Mark let out a sigh.

"You have a visitor." Rohn spoke so gently to him now, as if a hard word might break him.

He didn't want visitors, and Rohn knew it. Mark had heard coaches and riders come and go for a week and no one had disturbed him. Rohn wouldn't bother him with it unless it was important. "All right."

Rohn left, and a moment later heavy footsteps approached.

Mark's heart staggered and his breath hitched. He knew those footfalls. He didn't dare look in the doorway for fear of being wrong. At the same time he wanted to be wrong, because this would likely be the last time.

"Hey," Grant said.

"Hey." He barely made a sound, and he doubted Grant heard him. "Hey," he said a little more firmly. "Please, have a seat."

"I shouldn't stay. I just wanted, you know. To say I'm sorry."

"I have one more lesson for you if you'll sit." Mark gestured to a chair.

For a moment nothing happened, and then Grant walked into view, dressed in his new shirt and a halfway decent pair of trousers and a new pair of boots. He even wore a waistcoat, though it wasn't fitted very well to him. He sat and sank, all the strength sapped from his spine.

Mark wrote his name in a simple, even hand. "Mister Grant Roadman of Perida." Mark pressed the paper to him. "Upstairs there's a children's book. Rohn said you can have it. On each page there's an object, a common object. The first sound is the same sound as the letter on the page. You can teach yourself to read from that, but it would take a long time. It would go a lot faster if you let me tutor you, but you would have to come every day and work at least an hour at a time at it."

"Didn't they tell you?"

"That I'm dying?" Mark chuckled. "I'll be all right."

Grant ducked his head. "You haven't seen this poison work," he muttered.

"No, I haven't. But it's been eight days, and the doctor said I wouldn't last a week. I'm eating, and I'm keeping the food down. I can drink water. I just have to eat and drink more than I've managed to so far."

"You're eating?" He sounded almost offended by the idea.

"Bread and milk." Mark pawed the hair that had fallen into his face. His wrist brushed the first bristles of a beard. He hated it. It itched. He'd shave as soon as Grant left.

"About what I did—"

"It's all right."

"It isn't. You've been nothing but good to me. I listened to those idiots and got mad at you for them making fun of me. I got home and wished I'd flattened 'em all twice over. And I knew then I had to come back here and make things right and let 'em sneer. Because they don't care about me. Next week they'll be ribbing some other man about his woman, and the next about another man's crippled son. I shouldn't have cared what they said in the first place. I should have laughed. But I fought 'em, and I fought you, and when I came to say I was sorry they said—" Grant swallowed noisily. His breath shivered out in a shaky sigh, and he gazed at the paper with his name on it. "I figure whoever poisoned you'll try for you again. And this time I'll stop 'em."

Mark reached for his hand, but the big man flinched back. That would never go away. Mark acted as if he was only drawing another piece of paper closer to himself. "So, are you willing to work at Hevether?"

"I won't be no servant to you, but the colonel said I could work here if it's all right with you."

Mark drew up a contract and read it to him. "If you agree to the terms, then sign and you and Philip can start moving your possessions into the house. There's an unused room in the house I think you'll like. It's next to Norbert's."

"My thanks." Grant labored over his signature, copying it with far more ease than how he'd begun not so long ago with a G in the sand.

"You're welcome."

"I forgive you," Grant said. "But I won't forget. You took advantage, with your money and your goodness and your jester's sway. I figure you didn't mean to harm me, but it wasn't fair to call me a friend when all you wanted was to touch—" He almost choked. "—touch me now and then and maybe hope one night I'd be drunk enough. I done it with women. I know. It wasn't fair to them neither, though they said they didn't mind."

"I never hoped. I swear."

Grant's face, already held low, turned away. "Sorry, but I can't trust that."

Grant left. A short time after Rohn came in. "You've been up a long time. You should get some rest."

Before lunch. Mark's belly ached at the thought of it, both with hunger and revulsion. "I'm all right. Besides, it's time to invite ourselves over to Winsome's for a visit." It wasn't just a distraction. Even more than before, he felt time slipping away from him, and he had work to complete.

"No." Rohn spoke the word with a tortured gentleness.

"Please."

"You are not going to linger just long enough to see me married and then die. It's you, or no one."

"Actually, I plan to live." He was proud of Rohn for figuring out what drove him to stay alive this long.

"Then what is your flogging plan?"

The raised voice was so much better than the endless guilty gentleness. "Just, living." An unachievable goal, but living forever always was. "And working. I plan to work for you as long as I can. Stop trying to bury me. It's not going to get you out of the perfect match."

"Perfect? I don't even love her."

"You're a bad liar. The only reason you've fooled yourself this long is because you're gullible." Mark started writing.

"What are you doing?"

"Dear Winsome. I honestly do love breasts. Pay no mind to all those rumors about me liking the naughty parts of broad-shouldered men—"

Rohn tore the paper out from under Mark's quill. He read and sat back, a smile easing his expression. "You're—you're insufferable."

"Remember, she's still in danger. She might even put herself in greater danger trying to discover who poisoned me. Help her. And for pity's sake let yourself admire her, and let her love you. Don't let what we had turn into another tragedy that buries your heart. I want you to love and be loved. Are you really so afraid to open your heart that you'd sacrifice not just your own future but hers and Meridua's as well? And to preserve what? Your own loneliness?"

"I could get her killed too."

Mark wondered if Rohn counted him among those he'd gotten killed. "She was already in danger. Get her out of her father's house and into this one. You can protect her better if she's here and I can help her so that she isn't working alone. Please."

"All right! All right."

"And you write her. I'm tired." Mark tossed his quill aside.

Rohn looked a long time at the quill before he left the room.

The bell rang, its sweet ring still new and relatively unfamiliar in the house. Philip had been amazed that Rohn agreed to have it installed, after adamantly resisting one for years. Mark found little pleasure in it. Rohn gave in to almost everything he asked these past few days.

Trudy bustled in. "It's here. They're both here at the same time."

"What?"

"Your gifts to each other."

"Stephen is here?" His heart plunged. "Oh. Is it wrapped?"

"Yes, yours is wrapped. The colonel's gift to you is not." She broke into a grin. "I have to go fetch the colonel." She darted down the back way.

Mark pressed himself up and grabbed his sword cane. He hated it, but it helped keep him steady as he shuffled toward the front door.

Please be a good likeness. Please. And please don't let Rohn fall apart.

Rohn trotted down the stairs, Trudy leading the way. Norbert came out as well. "Philip will be beside himself to miss this," Rohn declared. His hand worked at a waistcoat button. Mark walked over to him and drew Rohn's hand away from it before he could pull it off with his worrying.

Trudy opened the door with flair. There stood the painter dressed in his best uniform beside his shrouded painting, hat held over his chest.

An unbelievably enormous black dog watched over pale gray, cream and nearly white puppies, the smallest of which had to weigh no less than seventy five pounds. Their handler stood by in a sailor's shirt and trousers, his cap stuffed in his pocket.

"Stephen? What are you doing here?" Rohn asked the painter.

"I'll wait after the dogs if you don't mind, sir," Stephen said.

"Very well." Rohn took a long look at the shrouded painting, and then turned to Mark. "One of the puppies is yours, if any suit you, and if you suit it." Rohn's hand found another button to worry.

Mark knelt, more than a little uncertain until they all trotted over to investigate. Their mother watched with proud detachment, her handler by her side. The man didn't have to bend or stoop to rest a hand on her back.

The puppies felt so unbelievably soft. Unlike most dogs their scent wasn't offensive at all. It was like clean silk and milk, or rather his memories of milk from before the poison did its work and spoiled his sense of taste. They had clean breath, a little on the milky side as well. One pounced up and licked his face. It tickled. He started to giggle. He couldn't help it. They grew bolder and swarmed him in gentleness, their eyes bright and eager to be loved, a little shy, not at all overbearing except the one that kept pouncing him for kisses. "You little rogues," Mark admonished them, running his hands over them as they tumbled over each other and put their broad feet on him.

"They're all of fine temperament. Anyone of them would be a fine choice," the handler told him.

A mid-sized pup of purest white with a faint ginger mask had nestled beside Mark's leg on the left, patiently waiting for Mark's hand. Mark wrapped an arm over it and it flopped its weight down, exposing the belly. Its short, feathered tail wagged. Two of the other puppies came over to snuffle it. It allowed them to for a little but then it rolled back up and placed one leg on Mark's, spine tightening, tail raised to form a curve, and the hair fluffed up. Her lip lifted into a sneer.

"That's Gale," the handler told him. "She'll be smaller than the boys when she's grown, but she has the heart of a soldier."

"How much smaller?" Rohn asked.

"She's big for a girl but it's hard to say. She might top two hundred like her mother."

"Are you going to be a big girl?" Mark asked her, rubbing her chest, her ears—she seemed to love it all.

"Well I hope he likes her 'cause she's picked him. If he wants any other he'll still have to keep her," the handler said.

"How about it?" Rohn asked.

Mark hugged her. "Just her."

"She'll keep you safe," Rohn told him.

"You're obsessed," Mark whispered into her fur. "He's obsessed with my safety, Gale. You'll have to help me keep him in his place." He never thought he'd think it of a dog, but she smelled good. Yes, like a dog, but that milk scent, and little like the sea.

"I'll be going, then," the handler said, and Rohn shook hands with him.

"Thank you," Rohn said.

"Won't she miss her family?" Mark asked.

"You're her family now. She's chosen you." The handler smiled secretively, donned his sailor's cap, and walked off. Sure to his word Gale didn't venture to follow. Instead she started to explore.

Stephen took a breath. "I have my doubts about this, sir, but it's what the l'jeste asked for. Me and the others, we've been working on it together, but I can't swear as to how well we did. Now if you don't mind, I'll take my leave." He bowed and started to go, but then he stopped. "Sir, it was an honor to serve with you in the war. All through the war. You needn't feel uneasy about what anyone thought. None of us ventured an untoward thought to it. We was all brothers, and we loved him too."

Rohn gasped and put a fist to his mouth. His breath shuddered. Mark started to tremble too. Stephen put on his soldier's cap and fled.

"You didn't." Rohn approached the painting breathlessly. Mark's heart hammered hard against his ribs. Rohn touched the shroud, caressed the soft cloth. Tears blurred Mark's sight. Rohn drew the shroud off, and Mark saw for the first time the proud young man with dark, Hasle curls and dark, earthy eyes. He seemed tall in the portrait, a hint of gentle mischief in his gaze and the turn of his mouth, but he seemed very serious as well. Driven. Passionate. Wise.

Unbelievably handsome. Slender but broad of shoulder, he looked classic and fine in his lieutenant's uniform of black and gray, the island's officer colors.

Rohn just stood and stared.

"I knew it would hurt," Mark told him. "But I began to think about how much I wanted to see ... I can hardly remember my parents anymore. My father never had a portrait done. He had a small portrait of my mother that he took with him everywhere. It vanished with him. I'd hoped there would be a painter among the ranks. I was surprised to find one that knew you both well. Is it a good likeness?"

Rohn reached but didn't quite touch the face. "Yes."

Gale dashed over to Mark and sat beside him. Mark hugged her close. She seemed to know that he needed someone to hold. He stood and left

Rohn with the portrait. Gale got a little underfoot but she didn't trip him as he shuffled toward his room. It seemed he needed a nap after all. He was so exhausted he could barely put one foot in front of the other.

"Lark."

Mark kept walking. "Yes?"

"Thank you."

Mark smiled. "You're welcome."

Lark and Rohn rode to the Kilderkin estate, Gale riding in the saddle draped over Lark's lap. The Kilderkin family had a house in town, but for whatever reason they wanted a more private visit. Lark had little doubt that it had something to do with Rohn's cold courtship and Lark's perhaps overly friendly regard for this prominent, if somewhat socially shunned young gentlewoman of Perida.

"She actually fought in the war?" Lark asked.

"Hmm? Oh, yes." Rohn lifted his head and his classic, broad-shouldered chestnut gelding arched his neck proudly. Bindart hurried up as she often had to do to keep up with the big horse. "She served on *The Hellardian.*"

"The flagship." Mark had had plenty of time for reading, so he'd learned many of the names surrounding the war, and finally had the beginnings of a sense of who comprised the heart of Perida.

"She was a sharpshooter. She shot more enemy officers than I did. After the war she never quite fit into society again. She wasn't the only woman who served, but she was the only one who killed so deliberately and so often."

"I would have never guessed. I thought such a duty would make a person cold." He had a hard time imagining that gentle-hearted creature shooting anyone except perhaps at a last defense.

"Like me?"

Lark smiled. "When I first met you I would have said yes."

They rode the last stretch in silence, enjoying the heavy, warm air of the thick woods, the strange birdcalls and flashes of brilliant color in the trees. Unfortunately the scent of fruit, no matter how temptingly sweet, made Lark's belly uneasy.

Juggler met them at the door. "Welcome."

Did you do it? Am I inconveniently alive, Juggler? I remember how quickly you called for a pistol to end my agony. Mark would have been nervous, angry, and upset but Lark knew at his heart that even if Juggler had done it, he wouldn't have wanted to. In a strange way they'd become friends. "Thank you for having us," Lark told him while Gale investigated the jester. "It's always a pleasure to see you."

"And who is this?" Juggler crouched to run his hands over Gale.

"Gale."

"She's beautiful. How old?"

"Four months." Amazing how quickly Lark had taken pride in her, though they barely knew each other. She behaved as if she'd known Lark all her life.

"She's going to be a brute. Heart of a marine." Juggler straightened up. "They're waiting in the library." He led the way to where Baron Kilderkin with his wine-sotted features and the young Lady Winsome posed like dolls in neighboring chairs. Juggler took the chair beside his master, and Rohn shook Lord Kilderkin's hand before he took the chair beside Winsome.

Winsome broke from her pale nervousness to smile at Gale. The dog investigated her first and allowed a petting, gave a sniff toward Baron Kilderkin, and returned to Lark. She flopped onto his feet so he couldn't move even if he'd wanted to.

"You're looking very well," Winsome told Lark.

"You don't have to say that." He knew his skin had begun to turn yellow and his cheeks had started to sink.

Her chin peaked under her lip. She bit her lip but not in time to hide a tremble.

"That was quite a party," Baron Kilderkin declared.

"Thank you." Rohn bowed his head briefly. "But I'm glad it's over, for now I may turn my attention to more important engagements."

The word engagements made everyone shift, Lark least of all though he suspected that he felt it more. Until this morning he'd allowed himself the luxury of not thinking about losing Rohn to a woman. They would still be living in close proximity until Lark eventually died, of course, but it wouldn't be the same. They'd had one moment, and that would be their only moment of intimacy. From here on she would be between them whether she was physically present in the house or not. Rohn would insist on faithfulness, and Lark doubly so. He wouldn't betray Winsome's trust any more than Rohn would.

"For someone who has declared an interest, so far you've shown my daughter little enough attention," Baron Kilderkin declared. He glanced over at Lark. "And she has not mentioned you overmuch, though another is often spoken of. I will not have a ruse. I won't accept it from any of you, especially my daughter."

"Father—"

"I know that part of my daughter's many charms is her bravery and her willingness to ignore society's opinion of her in order to follow her heart. But in this I will not yield. I approve of Baron Evan wholeheartedly, but I do not extend those feelings to that blond rat."

Lark and Winsome both set hands on Rohn's arms in time to keep him from vaulting out of the chair.

"Father," Winsome protested sharply. Juggler's expression had closed so much he seemed lifeless.

"I'm in no condition to court anyone," Lark reminded the baron gently. "Besides, I know you have few avenues of threat. Cutting off her wealth to make her seem less attractive will do no good. Our household has plenty." It started to dawn on him, but he had trouble believing it. "But I do believe your daughter loves you, and if you demand, she will obey. I will add this for your consideration. As soon as I'm strong enough I plan to sail for the mainland. I will be quite out of the way." Had the baron lost all care for his soul to protect his daughter, and arranged to poison Lark? He might have even done it himself.

Lark looked to Juggler. If so, had he done other things as well? Had he damned himself and his jester? If so, then the sense of kinship he felt toward Juggler made even more sense.

But this was all guessing. Just because it rang true, it didn't mean it was the answer.

Sometimes there's more than one answer. The memory of Gutter's voice comforted him at the same time that it reminded him.

Baron Kilderkin frowned under everyone's gazes for a long time before he spoke. "That is reassuring."

Rohn was trying to catch Lark's attention but Lark didn't let him. It would be for the best. Lark wanted to see Gutter again anyway. Whoever had poisoned him had done him a strange favor. Lark wasn't afraid anymore. He'd just ask Gutter directly about everything.

Juggler seemed to wake from death. "Perhaps Lark and I should leave you to continue your discussion in private." He stood and Lark followed his example. They bowed and Gale followed them out, up a narrow set of stairs, and into what Lark guessed was Juggler's sitting room. Juggler made the rounds lighting mismatched lamps until the room glowed with light. He could have more easily opened the dark curtains, but he didn't seem inclined to even brace one aside.

The room was crowded with old weapons, books, armor, musical instruments, bags, clothes hung and strewn everywhere—he couldn't possibly entertain anyone here. The clutter made it seem more intimate and private than any bedroom. And it revealed even more of Juggler's pain, but his love as well. He loved memories, and music, and dice and cards and games and gloves and weapons. He had some exquisite pistols, and his collection of daggers, though seemingly strewn with no care whatsoever, had no sign of dust or rust. Not even a stray fingerprint. Gale snuffled everything, and sneezed a few times.

"This is a beautiful piece," Lark told him, not daring to touch the gold and ebony pistol with blue abalone inlay. It was far closer to a work of art than a weapon.

Juggler picked it up brusquely and handed it to Lark handle-first. "Keep it."

"What?" It was loaded, and Lark didn't like the way it was pointed toward Juggler's chest. He accepted it just to point it somewhere safer.

"They're your colors. Keep it." He sat down at a small table and cleared it off with a sweep of his arm. "Cards?"

Lark set the pistol on the table with the muzzle pointed toward the thick outside wall. He found a small stool set askew in a corner and carried it to the table. "Yes. Thank you." He had to be careful of what he admired, it seemed. "You're too generous."

"Look at this." Juggler gestured around the room. "What am I going to do with it all? I've already given away a fortune to my men. I don't even remember who I killed for that anymore. It's another sign that it's time to give it away." He found a deck of cards within reach without having to hunt for them and began to shuffle. "Game?"

Gale returned to Lark and leaned carefully against his leg. "How about tellu?"

"I've never played."

"Excellent. I'd love to teach you."

Juggler rewarded him with a slight, brief smile. "I'd love to learn. Show me."

Lark dealt two hands face-up on the table and started going over the rules. Juggler caught on quickly, and recognized its relationship to the much more risky and famously bankrupting dukalt. In many ways it was a cleaner game, without dukalt's many traditional and quirky trumps and named hands introduced over hundreds of years by nobility and jesters in famous games. A keen mind could track the deck and better his chances of winning tellu. In dukalt, too much favor rested with the leader, and tracking the deck or studying odds gave little advantage. Players would often hold out longer than they ought to in dukalt, hoping that the lead advantage would help them win back their losses.

They played quietly for at least an hour without wagering, just counting points to declare a winner. Gale sat under the table, her head resting on one of her legs and one of Lark's feet. When Juggler finally won a hand he slapped the table and laughed. It startled Gale, but she set her head down again. "I finally got you."

"You did." It was a pleasure playing with someone who could keep track of points without paper or even a comment. They both simply knew each others' scores.

Juggler's pleasure faded. "Feather is quite taken by you."

Lark's skin prickled with warning. "Are you in love with her?" Gale lifted her head.

"Isn't everyone?" He chuckled softly, his gaze down-turned Lark sensed something there, something important. Juggler had yielded something to her, and he hadn't wanted to. "No, I don't love her. Far from it. We played a while. No, I love an entirely different sort of woman. I haven't seen her in weeks. You've been quite disruptive."

"I'm sorry I took you away from her."

Juggler stood and fetched a small vial from an elaborately carved wooden case full of vials. Opened it.

The scent of that spice made Lark's stomach lurch. He surged off the stool, nearly tripping over it in his haste. Gale hurried to the door and gazed at Lark anxiously.

"You ought to know its history, and how it's made," Juggler told him. Lark fought to hold on to the colonel's calm heartbeat, but he'd startled Rohn and now his heart lurched drunkenly between outright fear and the colonel's growing uneasiness. He hoped Rohn wouldn't come upstairs to check on them. He wanted to hear what Juggler had to say.

Gale came back to him and put herself solidly between him and Juggler.

"There's a rare flower known as *deatlall*, a nasty thing with a deep gullet full of liquid. Insects are drawn to it, crawl inside the flower, slip on this stuff, and drown in the gullet. The liquid has a scent very much like fresh blood, but it's not the liquid that's deadly to human beings. It's the slippery lining. It's deadly to pigs too. The flower grows in treacherous, swampy land but in a drought the pigs suddenly have access to it, eat it and die. It's so toxic that eating the flesh of a poisoned pig also kills. You'll find rotten pigs and dead gulls and dead rats all laying about, contorted by agony. The man who drank your punch after you did died very quickly in convulsions, but those thirty seconds or so must have lasted an eternity to him."

Lark forced himself to sit. He didn't have the strength to stand much longer and his trembling didn't help steady his legs. Gale braced against his knees.

"The poison's potency doesn't last, though. It took a lot of alchemy to develop it into this syrup. Just knowing the recipe is considered a sin." Juggler closed the vial. The scent permeated the room, rich and cloying. The jester went to the window and cracked it open. "Boiling it destroys it utterly, but it can be reduced with sugar in clear water very carefully on bright days in a cup resting in black sand. It takes a long time to make just a little amount. I renew my supply every six months or so, when I suspect the potency is ebbing. It's most destructive when ingested, but it can also do quite a lot of harm when painted on bullets, blades, and of course on puzzle scrolls." He offered it to Mark. "Take it."

"Why are you giving me this?"

"A little of the islands to take with you to the mainland. That is, if you really intend to go. More than one jester has seemed to sail away, only to be let off by long boat in a remote part of the island to return in disguise and hide in a baron's house, or a shack by the sea, or in the jungle, or near the swamps where few dare to go but a handful of hardy families who make their living in happy seclusion."

"I truly mean to go."

Juggler seemed relieved, but his expression lost its life. He sat heavily in the chair. The tension Lark felt in Gale's body through his knees ebbed.

"I'll miss you." Lark meant it, though part of him felt a relief that mirrored Juggler's. He'd be away from whoever had tried to assassinate him. He hoped so, anyway. "I will come back as quickly as I can, though." *If I live long enough.* "I have to help the colonel."

"Will he actually campaign?" There. Hostility, but it didn't seem to be directed at Rohn, or Lark. Someone Rohn was connected to?

"I don't know," Lark answered carefully.

Juggler smiled faintly. "He'll have plenty of barons campaigning for him." Sorrow, or maybe just fond memories that hurt only because they'd fallen into the past, gentled his gaze. The two strong emotions made no sense so close together, discussing the same person. There had to be a third party Juggler hated. It couldn't be Feather, could it?

"Rohn told me he knew you."

"He mentioned me?" Juggler shouldn't have been surprised, but his voice gave him away.

Lark nodded.

"I thought he'd put me out of his mind as much as possible. Or did he warn you about me? That would be closer to what I would expect." He tried to sound self-effacing, but the last word had a well-honed edge to it.

"He spoke gently of you. You are a hero, no less than him." Lark shuffled the cards, trying not to reveal how closely he watched Juggler.

"Ha."

"You both know what heroes do to win wars. I didn't mean hero in the bland way that history declares it."

Gale heard the footsteps on the stairs and the short way down the hall, her ears pricked, eyes bright. A knock sounded. Juggler rolled his eyes and went to the door. He opened it impatiently. "What."

"Pardon me, lord jester, but the baron is on his way out and requests that Lord Jester Lark accompany him home."

Not now. Damn him. Lark braced up using the table and his cane. Gale got out of his way, though she stayed close. He'd started to hunger anyway. Hunger no longer meant an uncomfortable yearning. It meant rising pain that quickly peaked into agony if he ignored it too long. He took up the pistol with some trepidation and thrust it through the back of his belt. It made a tight and uncomfortable fit beside his spine. "I would stay, but—"

"No need to make excuses. It's time." Juggler followed after them down the stairs. "Come visit one more time before you go. I'd like to play tellu again."

"I'll try. And you're always welcome to visit me." Lark offered his hand and Juggler grasped it firmly, not shaking, just holding with both hands.

"Be careful." Juggler seemed to be trying to warn him.

Lark hoped he'd elaborate, but he didn't. "You too."

Rohn waited outside already astride his horse. One of the Kilderkin servants held Bindart's reins, and another stood by. The young man helped Lark up into the saddle, and then lifted Gale expertly by tucking one arm under her chest and another behind her legs. Lark felt a lump under the saddle, but he ignored it and tried not to let his expression change as he helped Gale settle in front of him. Winsome was nowhere to be seen, nor was her father.

Lark waved goodbye to Juggler, and they started homeward. "How did it go?" Lark asked.

"Much better once you were out of the room." Rohn gave him a long look. "You're pale. Is the pain, or something more?"

"I don't know where to begin." Bindart chose her footing very carefully. It almost seemed as if she were afraid she'd drop him. He stroked her neck affectionately.

"Nice pistol," Rohn remarked dryly. "Now what's this about you going to the mainland?"

"I think it'll be best. Besides, I have a lot of business to attend to."

"I forbid it."

"We're together on borrowed time anyway. Please let me do some good while I can."

"You're my jester, and my friend, and I will not watch you sail off knowing I'll never see you again. If you go I'm going with you."

Lark closed his eyes and let go. Mark slipped the mask off. It took him a few moments to feel more like himself—afraid, ill, but able to nurture and protect a fragile humanity that Lark so often lacked. "I need to talk to Gutter alone. And as much danger as I'm in here, you'll be in ten times or more on the mainland. Besides, you have a campaign. And I won't be gone forever. Six months at most."

"The doctor gave you less than a month. What makes you think you'll even reach the mainland?"

"Dr. Berto also gave me a week, and I bet he didn't think I'd make it through the night when he first examined me. He's been wrong every time. I'll live like anyone else. I'll live until I die, and I'm not dead yet. I would like to settle a few debts, though. Gutter will answer my questions now." Mark stroked Gale's head, and then Bindart's neck. "I'll have Gale with me. It'll be all right."

"You keep saying that it will be all right, but it won't. I lost—I won't lose you." The rough, low words rekindled Mark's fears.

"You can't lose me. We're bonded." He had to change the subject or he'd start to dwell on the terrors that awaited him. "So. Are you courting her or not?"

Rohn ducked his head. "I am."

"Good."

"You give up so easily." Rohn's expression tightened and he galloped off. Mark trusted Bindart with him, but he was certain Gale would fall and he was worried that whatever was under the saddle might hurt Bindart or be lost if he tried to catch up.

It's for the best. I just have to keep imagining him with Winsome and a house full of children, all blissfully happy.

By the time he reached the house it was getting on toward sunset. Philip met him outside. He helped Gale down, and then Mark.

"There's something under the saddle," Mark warned him. "Let's get her in. I don't want any of the new servants to see."

Philip took her into the stable, Gale roaming around them and the horse all the way. When they got Bindart in her stall Mark flipped up the saddle. It was a thin leather case carefully tucked between the saddle and blanket with ties draped under the saddle's frame to help hold the case in place. Mark took off his waistcoat and draped it over his arm so that it hid the case where he nestled it under his elbow. He walked to the house, Gale trotting after him with her tongue lolling. He was careful not to hurry, and took the back way up to his room.

The case held several pages and envelopes. He drew one out.

The broken seal ... RT—

His eyes rolled back and he smelled the spice. He'd been poisoned, dying. His head cracked on something and he was drowning in a stream of luminous sand that glowed an ugly yellow brown. He couldn't scream, or move, or breathe—

Mark gasped in a hard breath that seared him more than his burning belly. He was on the floor and Gale was whining, rushing between licking his face and scratching at his door. He'd pissed himself and all he could smell was that poison. He was so weak he couldn't even move.

Trudy knocked. "L'jeste? Is everything all right?"

Gale clawed frantically at the door and her whine turned to keening. Trudy opened the door and shrieked. Gale bolted out and then back in. Trudy collapsed beside him and stroked his face. "You'll be all right. I'm right here. You'll be all right." She rubbed his back.

Rohn charged in. "What happened?"

"He had another seizure."

Another. He didn't remember having any others, but he knew he'd missed a great deal during the worst part right after he'd been poisoned.

Rohn drew him up into his lap. "Trudy, get Philip and then start a bath." Rohn held him close. All Mark could do was rest in his arms. "You'll be all right."

Mark found the strength to speak. "I told you."

Rohn let out a pained laugh. It felt good to hear it so close and drumming at his ear through Rohn's chest. Gale climbed onto him and licked his face. "No," Rohn told her sharply. "Off."

She sat back, apparently understanding the command. Rohn had told him that the puppies had been partly trained, but they hadn't had time to go over anything except a few simple commands like sit, stay and heel. He suspected it would be a lot more complicated than directing a horse.

"Don't." Mark had to gather his breath. "Touch. The papers."

"All right. They're all over the floor, though."

"Leave them." He'd had gloves on. Even if they were poisoned, it wouldn't have touched his hands. It was random chance that he'd had seizure just then. But it didn't feel random. He had to be careful. He wanted to be sure before anyone else got hurt.

His eyes managed to focus on one of the pages. He'd caught a glimpse just before everything went black, but he didn't fully comprehend it.

They were written in the code he'd learned from the book, the book that came with the signet ring whose stamp was in the cracked seal. None of it was in Winsome's hand. They were all original. He was within an arm's length of knowing but he couldn't reach it.

"Shh," Rohn breathed in his ear. "Just rest."

"There's no time."

"We'll wash you, and feed you, and then if you're strong enough you can start translating all that gibberish."

"The seal."

"I see it. Is it the one taken from Obsidian?"

"Yes."

Rohn held him closer. "Those papers have traveled over water. I can smell it." He pulled the ribbon free from Mark's hair and stroked the locks until he'd pulled all the loose ends away from Mark's face. "I can translate it while you recover."

"No. Don't touch them."

"I can wear gloves as well as anyone."

As his senses returned he realized more and more. "There's no time. You have to get Winsome out of that house."

"What are you talking about?"

"Those came from the Kilderkin house. They might be her father's, or Juggler's—if anyone realizes they're missing she'll be in danger."

"No. No. You're confused. She must have gotten them from somewhere else. If if she hadn't, her father wouldn't harm her. Juggler wouldn't harm her. No."

"I think the papers did come from her house. It explains so much." It explained why she didn't come out and tell them what she knew, and why she was so reluctant to name allies and enemies. "I don't know what they'd do to her, but we'll never see her again, that much I know. No one will ever see her again." His strength was starting to come back.

Philip hurried in. "Is he all right?"

"Philip, help Lark undress and get him cleaned up. And don't touch those papers. I'm going back to the Kilderkin estate. If I'm not back in two hours, I want you and Grant to bring all the servants into the manor and secure every door with a lock on it in the house. All the new servants will stay downstairs, and you and Trudy and Norbert are to remain here with Lark. I want Grant on guard at the main stairway. Understand?"

"Yes, sir."

Rohn transferred Mark into Philip's arms and stalked out.

"Now now, sir," Philip soothed. "You let me do the work. We all got practiced at this while you were at your worst. Norbert's already making you a meal. You'll feel better after."

"Cover those papers with something, please."

"I'll do that in a moment."

"And I don't want any of the new servants anywhere near this hall." The idea that Rohn might not make it back home started to grow, and he realized how little merit he'd given to Rohn's fears. He wanted to use his lord and master's same words, but Rohn had already left.

Please don't leave me. Don't leave me here alone.

As if she'd heard him, Gale came close again and licked his face. Disgusting, but she loved him and that made it all right.

"That's enough of that, doggie," Philip told her fondly, and began helping Mark take off his waistcoat.

Chapter Twenty Five

Every time Gale went to the open window, Mark paused in his labors. It was well after dark, long past two hours, and they were all under Grant's careful watch. She looked out a while, then returned to him. He stroked her fur. They'd both eaten as well as they could—she on exotic rices and ground goat mixed with herbs Norbert swore were healthful, Mark on a half slice of bread and a half glass of milk. It took an hour for the pain in his belly to subside. His work helped distract him.

Trudy had fallen asleep in a chair by his hearth. The hearth's presence always amused him. As far as he knew a fire had never burned in it. It was always too warm for that amount of heat. They burned candles within it instead, now held on an elegant framework he'd purchased not long ago.

The firm light of a lamp lit his papers. The letters mentioned the star, the moon, the cup, the face and the blade quite often. By context, though he didn't want it to be true, he was certain Baron Kilderkin was the cup, and the baron was deep in some sort of conspiracy to cover the face.

He'd translated them out of order, and it wasn't clear what order they were supposed to lay in. Maybe Winsome had them in order initially, but he'd ruined that when his body seized up. One thing for certain, the blade was angry about revealing the face too soon. Without dates ... but these letters appeared to be months, maybe years old, too old to refer to Mark. Still, the covering of a face seemed ominous, and there were many parallels he could draw between his journey and the veiled events unfolding here.

Obsidian had preceded him. In what role? Why had he come here?

He'd so hoped to find the answers plain and clear, but the letters only raised more questions.

At least the manifests were of some use. They named the captains, and those captains were well aware of their role. Two of them were Rohn's.

Gale went to the window again. Mark listened, but didn't hear a horse. He made notes on the side paper and set a letter between two others where it seemed most likely to belong.

No, there was a horse.

Mark got up and looked. His heart leapt. They were both home. "Philip." Mark went to the door, keeping his voice low. "It's them. Let them in the back way. Let Grant know they're here."

"Yes, sir." Philip trotted off.

Mark took a sip of water and let it roll around in his mouth. It hurt less to drink in little bits too small to swallow. He wet his mouth often though his thirst often urged him to gulp it down. He'd done it more than once, and paid in pain.

The door opened downstairs. Gale hurried out into the hall and he soon heard her pattering down the stairs, panting. Human footfalls followed her back up.

Rohn stepped into Mark's room and Mark hugged him hard. He kept it brief, and they both stepped back to let Winsome in. She was shaking. "Philip, get her a blanket, please."

Trudy stirred and made a soft sound. Winsome's gaze stopped on Trudy, then fell and her already solemn mouth softened with hurt.

It would be better not to tell her the truth if she suspected that Mark and Trudy had an understanding.

Trudy sat up. "Colonel!"

"Hush. I told Grant to send all the new servants home. I don't know how long it will be before the Kilderkin household realizes Winsome is gone, and I have no idea what they'll do. They will come here first, however." Rohn kept a protective arm around her. "Have a seat." He helped her settle into the other chair by the hearth, then went to Mark's desk. "How goes it?"

"Slowly. But you should see this." Mark showed him the damning manifests.

"Oh no." Rohn took them in hand, his gaze sweeping the pages over and over. "Could this be a lie?"

"No," Winsome said. "So ... you deciphered it?"

Mark shook his head when Rohn opened his mouth to speak. "Where did you get these letters?" Rohn asked.

Winsome's eyes brightened. "Let him go. As soon as he realizes what's happened he'll run, and he'll take Juggler with him. Just let them go."

"Who else?" Rohn demanded.

Too sharp. Mark wanted to elbow him but Rohn stood just out of reach.

"I don't know." Winsome drew the blanket closer about her shoulders.

"Why didn't you come to me sooner?" Rohn snapped.

"I—believed. But then I started to have doubts and—"

"You were involved?" Rohn spoke Mark's own shock.

"My father didn't want me to be involved, but I found out. I didn't realize how deep it went, what it truly entailed, until six months ago."

Mark kept his voice as calm and gentle as possible. "What's really involved, Winsome?"

"I thought it was the Church, but it's ... it's a conspiracy against His Majesty Michael of Cathret."

Her misery kept Mark from assaulting with her wild questions. "Which side is Gutter on?"

"Gutter?"

It seemed impossible that she didn't recognize the name. She was in shock. "The King's favorite, Lord Argenwain's jester. Is he for or against the king?" He wished he could believe with absolute certainty that Gutter would never harm His Majesty, but he couldn't.

"I don't know."

"What about Obsidian?"

"I don't know that name. I'm sorry."

Which side was Obsidian on? What had he done by coming here with this code? If Gutter was rightfully by the King, then Obsidian was against
....

He couldn't even think. His mind whirled in panic. "I have to get on board a ship as soon as possible."

"You are not sailing into the thick of this alone," Rohn growled.

"I have to. It's never just about one man, though His Majesty is far beyond a man. His whole family may be in danger. The queens, his children, his last living brother."

"For all you know one of his own family members may be at the heart of it."

"I'll forgive you that because you were at war with Cathret, but that family is sacred in its deepest sense. They can't be assassinated because they are protected. Anyone with ill intent that goes near them goes mad. You've seen now. We've both seen now what is beyond this life. You know that protection like that would not be extended to anyone unworthy." He shouldn't have had to explain it. His irritation eased when he remembered how Grant had blushed to hear Mark speak ill of island ways.

That seemed like a long time ago.

"What can you do in any case? Expose these to your mainland friends?" Rohn waved the letters in his face.

"I can't expose anyone mentioned in those letters, not without knowing more. The letters, the manifests, everything has to remain absolutely secret, and Baron Kilderkin and Juggler must be put in doubt as to whether we have them. They may hope that even if we do, we can't decipher them." That gave him an idea. "Winsome, I want you to write a letter. I want you to be truthful except in one regard. I want you tell them that you've hidden those papers, and that you'll show them to a certain friend you've made unless the baron leaves with Juggler for the mainland, never to return. Can you do that?"

She nodded.

"I'll ask one more question, and I hope you trust me enough tell me the truth. Do you know anyone with a seal like this?" He held up one of the envelopes.

"No."

"You've never seen it anywhere else?"

"No."

"Thank you." He wished he could believe her. For now he would only allow that she was likely telling them the truth. "Trudy, can you put her in the guest room across from your room please?"

"Yes, sir." Trudy curtseyed and hurried to her work.

"Philip, can you find me a place on a ship bound for Seven Churches by the Sea?"

Philip looked to Rohn. Rohn stood tall and silent and too much like the man Mark had first met. "Do it," Rohn said softly.

Mark went out into the hallway for some privacy, only to see Grant sitting at the top of the stairs, a sword in one hand, a pistol in the other. Rohn stepped out into the hall as well. "I'll make doubly sure of the locks," Rohn told Grant. "You're relieved."

"I'm all right, sir," Grant told him. He had a grim, tight look in his eyes and he hunched with weariness.

"That's an order."

"Yes, sir. Thank you, sir." Grant stood and went downstairs, his heavy steps sounding every crack and squeak in the staircase on the way.

Gale came out and sat anxiously beside Mark, tail wagging, panting, her bright eyes not quite hidden by what would soon be long bangs.

Rohn bent his face to Mark's and kissed his cheek. Mark longed for so much more. How could they live in the same house and never be together again?

By stepping back. Mark edged away, though he allowed himself to touch Rohn's face. "Give her a chance," Mark whispered.

"Are you leaving because of what you've found, or because of her?" Rohn whispered back.

"All of it. And more." He wanted to stay more than anything, but he didn't dare admit it. It would make it too easy for Rohn to convince him to stay.

"You must come back."

"I know." Mark took his hand and kissed it. "I waited for you to come back and it ... I won't leave you waiting forever. I'll come back."

"You swear?"

Rohn had him there. The poison could still claim his life, or any number of accidents. "I'll write you every day."

"The post from Seven Churches only reaches us twice a month."

"Then you'll have a lot of letters at once. I promise I'll send any urgent news by sacred messenger." That would still be at least three weeks delay. Mark almost went to him again, but something warned him, perhaps a slight squeak in the floor. "I have work. Check the doors and windows, and then get some rest. It's been a long night."

"Lock your door," Rohn told him.

Sure enough Winsome stood just inside the door, listening. He doubted that she'd heard much. "Have you started your letter?" Mark asked her.

"I'll write it in my room."

He understood her need for privacy. "Here." He fetched her everything she'd need and carried it down the hall for her so she wouldn't get ink on her hands. Trudy had done an admirable job of preparing the way, including some food and a pitcher of fresh water. "Lock the door. Ring the bell if you need anything."

"Don't leave us. You should wait. My father may have already secretly engaged the next outgoing vessel, and I dread to think what might happen if you sailed on the same ship. Or what if the captain is part of the conspiracy that tried to end your life? You'll be helpless."

"Help Rohn while I'm away. He doesn't do well alone." Mark left her before she could become even more overwrought. She'd probably still imagine the worst that might happen, but at least she wouldn't feel compelled to create potential disasters that would make even the most seasoned soldier hesitate, never mind a boy out of his depth.

Mark leafed through his notes before he set his mind to reading the letters again. Before long his head drooped and he braced it on his arms, just for a moment.

Gale's pacing woke him. She needed to be let out. He pushed up, his stomach pinched and burning, his throat raw.

The lock turned on its own so slowly that at first Mark didn't perceive the motion. He tried to make no sound as he crossed to the pistol he'd set carelessly on the table beside the door.

The door swung wide and Mark dove for the weapon. The masked creature fired. The sound seemed to shatter the room. The mask drew a rapier as Mark put his hand on the pistol.

He knew he was too late. He brought the pistol to bear and threw himself to the side—

Gale grabbed the mask's sleeve—

—the rapier point stabbed the floor by Mark's chest as he cocked the mechanism—

—the pistol fired what seemed like an eternity after his finger squeezed the trigger.

The mask thrust. Mark parried with his gloved hand. He heard a muffled voice somewhere in the house cry his name.

The mask staggered. Mark caught the blade but didn't manage to pull the rapier free of its hand. The whole face was covered with the death mask, but he knew who wore it.

Blood splattered on the floor.

Mark scrambled for Obsidian's pistol and his rapier. The mask pursued him. Mark cocked the pistol as he turned and fired. He had to drop Obsidian's pistol immediately to defend himself. The mask fought hard, as if it hadn't been wounded twice, but it moved more laboriously as it engaged his blade. Nightmarish, the gorgeous stripes of emerald, ruby and sapphire revealed no mouth and the eyes were hidden by copper silk. Gale attacked it again, distracting it for the slightest instant. Mark forced the opportunity with a sharp deflection and thrust hard.

The arms spread and then contracted around the blade where it penetrated high in the chest just below the throat. Mark tore his rapier free.

The masked thing fell, lifeless. Mark yanked off the death mask and began to sing as he reloaded Obsidian's pistol. He hoped his voice would help Juggler somehow.

The whole house vibrated with subtle but terrible sounds. A pounding on a door, footsteps hurrying, men muttering to each other, someone on the main stairs.

He'd barely finished reloading when a Morbai's Kiss in a deep red uniform appeared, his face painted with smears of blood and ash. Mark fired and the Morbai's Kiss flopped down bonelessly, an ugly red cavity where the point of his nose used to be. Mark sheathed his rapier and reloaded both pistols. His heart thundered but he felt only two things: a cold, unfeeling requirement to protect his fragile body, and deep concentration as his mind swept through countless calculations. He concluded his song and listened a moment. He couldn't make out much. His ears had numbed somewhat from the sharp pounding they'd gotten when the pistols went off.

He couldn't feel Rohn's heartbeat.

A glance out the door one way revealed four of the blood-painted soldiers, two at the far doorway into the master suite, and two at the top of the stairs. A glance the other way—no one, but both Trudy and Winsome's doors were open. He dashed toward the women first. One of the Morbai's Kiss fired at him. He ducked in Winsome's room, Gale on his heels.

Winsome was gone. He ran across to Trudy's. Blood everywhere, and Trudy had crumpled where her bed and the wall made a corner.

He left Trudy. He'd been moving too quickly for any emotions to catch up. Something broke inside him and all emotion fell away into the dark crevasse beside Trudy's body.

The intensity of his hunt carried on without his heart. Two shots missed him on the way to his room. Mark readied himself by the door.

"Get him," one of the men said.

That would make the hunt easier. He had to be careful, though. These men were experienced hunters themselves.

"Sit," Mark whispered firmly to Gale. "Stay." Rohn's heartbeat suddenly came to life within his chest, running faster than a gallop, but Mark kept his own breaths steady.

At least he knew Rohn was still alive.

He heard two approaching.

Mark turned into the hall and fired both pistols. One man fell partway down the stairs, the other dropped and fired back. Mark ducked back into his room and reloaded. The man who'd dropped got to his feet and advanced. Two others joined him, their presence betrayed by the bare floor.

Mark didn't finish reloading in time. His hands didn't shake but his fingers had gone clumsy. He dropped the pistol and grabbed the first man who came in the door. He pressed his rapier against the man's neck and shoved with a slicing motion. The blade bit deeply, and the hot blood jetted out—

The colonel's door burst open. The remaining two in the hall fled for the little-used staircase beside Trudy's room. Rohn took the main staircase down and Mark followed them down the back staircase. "Rohn, don't!"

But Rohn did. The men managed to make the bottom of the staircase, but then they cried out, fighting for their lives in a room in which there had once been food and dancing and laughter and wine. Their feet scrambled on the floor slick from blood. By the time Mark managed to make the bottom of the stairs, his legs wobbling, one lay dead and the colonel had a dagger shoved up so deep inside the other that his fist was buried inside the man's gut.

"Rohn." Mark staggered to him. "Rohn, it's over. Rohn. Rohn, Winsome is missing."

That finally got Rohn's attention. The satisfied, predatory look on his face ebbed away to be replaced with open fear. "Missing?"

"I hope she left before it started but they might have taken her somewhere. And Trudy ...."

Grant.

Mark stumbled toward the lower servant's rooms, his legs barely able to carry him, all his cold calculations fracturing into panic. Norbert's, Philip's and Grant's rooms were all open. He half-fell, half-leapt into the doorway.

Grant lay on the floor on a rug soaked in blood, his throat gaping, white showing amid the red. That exposed throat was an architectural marvel, a graceful, open arch filled with crimson. Mark fell beside him and covered the wound. Grant was still warm. The *morbai—*

He wouldn't let them have him. "You can't have him!" he screamed. He wouldn't let Grant go into that horrible darkness alone.

A crushing pain filled his chest. Mark grabbed the fishing knife Grant always kept at his belt. "I won't let you have him!"

Strong arms grabbed him. "No, Lark. No. You have to stay with me. You can't help him." Rohn crushed him until his ribs flexed and he could barely breathe.

"He needs me! The *morbai* can't have him he needs me. Please. Please oh please, help me." He needed to sing, he had to sing, but he couldn't catch his breath. He had to stop gasping, stop the pain ....

It was too late. Grant was already gone. How long had he been gone? He'd died while Mark was sleeping ....

"He was a good man. It has to be enough. You can't help him. Please." Rohn tucked his head close against Mark's. "You promised yourself to me. Please. I need you, Lark. I need you."

Grant lay there, still handsome, the fall of his hair marred by blood, his broad shoulders slack, those clear, green eyes as lifeless as glass.

Mark dropped the knife.

Rohn relaxed his hold and drew Mark closer. "Don't look." He tried covering Mark's eyes but Mark pushed his hand away.

Grant is dead.

Gone forever. Fodder for the *morbai*, the Cathretan Church claimed. He didn't want to believe it. He wanted to believe as the islanders believed but he feared the Cathretan Church was right. He hated it; he couldn't bear it. He wished he could die. He should have died. Then none of this would have happened.

Mark finally looked away. He could see Grant in his mind, sitting at that rough table, drinking bad wine from a mug. He had such a beautiful smile. "He was a good man."

"I know."

The mad moment had passed. He knew he had to stay. "Let go," he whispered. Rohn's hold on him eased a little more, but he didn't let go.

He couldn't touch Grant's face. The big man wouldn't like it. He'd flinch away if he could. Mark touched his sleeve instead.

Grant had just learned to read small words. Mop. Spot. Lip. Man. He'd been so rightfully proud of that achievement.

Rohn hoisted him to his feet, gasping, on the edge of sobs. "We have to find the others. Norbert?"

Dead in his room as well, though he'd killed one. Philip had been stabbed through the heart in his bed. Rohn carefully checked them for any hope of life while Mark stood in the doorway both times, watching, nose and eyes running but too numb to weep.

They went upstairs back to Trudy's room. Rohn felt at her throat, and then gasped. "She's alive."

The words shocked Mark back to life. "I'll get the doctor." Mark stumbled back downstairs, out to the stables, and saddled and bridled Bindart as quickly as he could manage. He felt little on the hard ride to the doctor's house, and told the doctor to rush ahead of him as he couldn't possibly keep up.

He'd noticed something in the stables and he didn't dare think too deeply upon that together with the possibility that Trudy would be dead by the time he got back.

Winsome's horse was missing.

When he got home, Mark put Bindart back in her stall and sat heavily on the rock bench outside the stable door where Philip used to sit. In time a mist came in and the sun rose behind it. The gulls began to cry themselves awake.

Rohn left the house, his shoulders bent and his clothes streaked with blood, Gale following close behind. The dog saw Mark and bounded to him.

Rohn sat down on the bench just within easy reach. Gale sniffed at them and then roamed about.

"Is Trudy alive?" Mark asked, too weak and too grieved to dare hope.

"The doctor said she'll survive."

He should have been overjoyed.

The sea pounded on the rocks. Mark felt it through the bench. His hands were cold and his belly was filled with knives but he didn't want to eat. He would rather starve.

"Where do you think she is?" Rohn asked.

It took Mark a moment to realize that he'd meant Winsome. "I don't think they took her. I think she went to deliver the message to whoever was helping her at the house. I think it was that young man that helped me into the saddle. Maybe she wanted to bring him back here with her, so that he'd be safe."

"Do you think they caught her?"

Mark jerked himself away from visions of Grant laying with his throat open. His skin had been so white. "It would explain the quiet attack in the middle of the night. If she'd been at Hevether they couldn't risk her getting hurt. If they have her, they'll have put her on one of the traitor ships by now."

Gale returned and settled on Mark's feet.

"Gale saved my life." Mark stroked her leg. "More than once. More than I noticed, I'm sure."

Rohn took in a harsh breath. "Why did they do this? And why spare me? They had me around the throat." He shuddered. "They could have killed me but they fought to restrain me instead, and I managed to break free."

"The blood and ash gives it away. The old ways. This came from the Church. You're noble. They couldn't kill you because you're of noble blood, and therefore sacred. But they could destroy everyone around you."

"To stop me from becoming president? For all they knew I would fight for it just to fuck them." He hissed the last words, and his hands scraped the rocks.

"Maybe they didn't believe you could win, with me gone, with everyone you trusted gone. You'd be alone with the dellai, or whoever is behind this."

"Not the dellai."

"We didn't think it was Kilderkin either," Mark reminded him.

That quieted him. "But he was away. Dellai Bertram was away. It had to be Kilderkin. It was Juggler. It had to be them."

"Juggler made a point of introducing me to Gerson Wilden. It might have been him. And Dellai Betram may have left instructions. We don't know anything. If we assume it's over, we'll be vulnerable."

Rohn took in another sharp breath, as if he'd stopped breathing and his body forced him to. "We have to fight back."

Mark agreed, but it wasn't clear how. "We need to get Winsome back."

"I don't trust her anymore."

Mark could imagine her screaming in rage and fear, pounding on a door or on a crate or wherever they had her confined.

Assuming they let her live. If this was the Church, they could have forced Juggler to do far more than he'd be willing to do for even his master. Maybe it would be because of his master. Maybe they promised to save his soul. If his master had become a monster, there'd be no other hope for his soul. They could make an ugly argument that Winsome was no longer a noble in soul either, that she was too scarred from the war and in bed with their enemies. The Church always found some excuse in their fucking sacred poetry. "So you'll leave her to whatever fate they have planned for her."

"If she wasn't in on it from the beginning."

"You don't believe that. I won't let you push her away, not when you should be charging in to her rescue."

"She never needed rescuing. She rescued others." Rohn put his head in his hands. Mark rubbed his back. "I'm so tired." The colonel's words verged on weeping, expressing a trace of the grief that threatened to overwhelm them both.

Mark slumped over his strong back and held him, breathing in his scent all mingled with blood, ignoring the pain in his heart and in his gut, pretending that as long as they were together it would be all right. The sacred guard would be here soon, and jesters and barons and their servants, an army of gawkers ....

Three riders galloped toward them. A beautiful young woman in an islander's gray and black uniform, fashioned to fit a woman, led the way, followed by two servants. Winsome threw herself off her horse. "What happened? Are you hurt?" She knelt in front of the colonel and took his hands in hers. "Are you hurt?" she whispered. "Give me your orders, sir. I'll do what has to be done." When Rohn said nothing she stood, and her voice rang with a gentle but potent command. "Nils, go to the governor's house and tell him to send every servant to Hevether Hall immediately. Tell him it's an emergency. Barry, go in the house and see what aid you can lend." She knelt in front of the colonel again. "Come to the pump," she said softly. "Let's wash off this blood."

They told Mark that he sang beautifully at Grant's funeral. Mark couldn't remember what song he'd sung until he read it in the gazette. They'd printed the lyrics.

It would be the last island gazette he'd read for a long time. For the past two weeks there had been little news, or so it seemed since the Massacre at Hevether. Two children had been born, Bell was suspected of having a new lover, and a fisherman caught a sunken figurehead in his nets. He'd sold it to a shipyard, which hoped to restore it.

Mark got up with the help of the table and his cane. Some days he felt stronger, but today the oldest of men could have outpaced him.

Gale stayed close. In the last two weeks she hadn't only grown visibly larger, but more somber.

"May I help you, lord jester?" Richard, the governor's butler, along with several other servants from the elder Evan household, had come over to clean up after the dead and help around the house. Richard left the doorway and walked alongside Mark on the side opposite of Gale.

"No thank you." Mark paused at the threshold. "If Gutter should arrive, there's a letter waiting for him. Rohn knows where it is."

"I'm sure the famed jester will be sorry he missed you."

No sign of Winsome or Rohn. "All right, then." Mark made his way down the steps. Gale stayed with him, though she loved carriage rides and usually ran ahead to leap in. "Tell—"

He sensed Rohn's quickening heartbeat and stopped. Rohn caught up with him. For a moment he faced Mark, tall and sober, and then he hugged him close.

Mark sank against him. Rohn pulled Mark's hat off and kissed his forehead, his cheek, his nose, and then they kissed with such sweet, painful brevity Mark almost changed his mind about going back to Seven Churches by the Sea. He felt vulnerable, exposed, and so in love ....

He couldn't stay. "Don't sit in front of that portrait all day," Mark admonished him. "And don't have one done of me, either. I don't want to have to worry about you. I can't have the distraction. I need to know you'll be working, and visiting with your friends, and meeting people. And I want you to—"

"I know." Rohn kissed his forehead again. Mark took his hat back and played with the brim. "But I don't think it will ever be. She's not you."

"That's a good thing." Mark touched Rohn's face one last time, and then stepped up into the carriage. Gale bumbled up behind him and hopped up on the seat across from him. "I'll write every day."

"I don't care if you write. I just want you to come back home before it's too late." Rohn shut the door and their new driver took Mark away from love.

He never wanted to see Pickwelling again. He didn't want to face Gutter anymore. He just wanted to stay home.

He turned his gaze away and closed his eyes. Gale hopped down from the seat and settled on his feet, pinning his legs.

He stroked her soft ears. She was just a dog, but she made him feel as if he wasn't completely alone.

At the dock most of the island jesters had gathered. He moved down the line, shaking hands, saying goodbye knowing he wouldn't miss a single one of them. Feather was gone, as was the mayor.

And I killed Juggler. I cared about him, and I still killed him.

They'd found a set of duplicate keys to Hevether just inside Mark's room, the means for the deadly surprise that Juggler and his men had sprung upon them. Rather than risk the chance of another set's existence they'd changed the locks throughout the house. It didn't make Mark feel any safer there, but safety didn't matter so much as that sense of home, and belonging, and longing that he'd grown to accept whenever Rohn was within reach.

Fine stopped him. "He'll still be here, and he'll be safe when you get back. My master and I will see to it personally."

Jog shook his hand hard. "I'll go with you if you want."

"Thank you for the offer, but no." Jog found the servant who'd given Mark the poison, or rather he found his corpse. "I'll keep looking," Jog told him. Someone had to see something."

"Thank you."

"Sorry about your friend. We'll look after the colonel while you're gone."

It seemed everyone would look out for Rohn. It didn't reassure him.

Mark climbed on board *Dainty*. Captain Shuller shook his hand vigorously. "I was wrong about you," the captain told him. "It's a sure sign of a sailor when he grows thin rather than fat on island fare. We'll soon put some meat on your bones with honest cooking."

"Thank you, captain."

The captain's smile faded. "I'm sorry to hear about Mr. Roadman. He was a good man."

"Yes, he was." Mark had taught himself various responses so that he didn't have to think or feel when he said them, but somehow Captain Shuller made his heart ache with fresh pain.

The jesters began to sing and the sailors threw off the ropes that bound *Dainty* to the dock. Rowers pulled her around and out, and the sails went up. Mark leaned against the rail, listening to the farewell song, wishing. Just wishing. Gale watched the retreating bay with alarm. She paced back and forth and whined. Mark stroked her head and she settled, sitting heavily on his foot.

Someone joined him. He jumped with shock when he realized who it was. "Winsome?"

She smiled wanly. "I'll help you find him, but I won't let you kill him."

She thought he was hunting her father. "Winsome, go home."

"It's too late."

"Winsome—Captain—"

"I'm paying my own way, and the captain won't throw me off at the nearest island no matter how much you beg or threaten him. He remembers me from the war." She leaned on the rail and closed her eyes. "I've missed this."

She'd sailed more than Mark ever would. He leaned on the rail again, her hair tickling his face. "I'm not going after your father."

"You'll have to. You have to follow him to find the ones who started this."

"Why can't I follow Feather and the mayor?" he argued. He didn't want her to know about Gutter. For the first time in his life, he felt ashamed of his association with that great jester. He didn't like the feeling. He preferred to be afraid, or wary, or proud. And Lord Argenwain ... what would she think when she found out what sort of services Mark performed for him?

Maybe she wouldn't find out. Or if she did, maybe she wouldn't tell anyone. After all, it might reflect poorly on her future husband's choice of jester.

She scowled and knitted her fingers together. "You'll need my help."

"I have Gale," he pointed out.

That made Winsome smile, though it faded fast.

"And your reputation?" he pressed.

She sheltered her gaze with her lashes. "Even if I cared, there's nothing I can do to change anyone's opinion of me for better or worse. Besides, it might be best if the colonel keeps his distance from me, at least until the situation with my family sorts itself out."

Would she kill her father? He wished he could say no for certain. "What about Colonel Evan's heart?" Mark asked gently.

She shook her head. "He doesn't love me."

"He loves you," Mark assured her. He touched his lip, remembering their short kiss, their last in the living world. "He just doesn't know how."

emprazeman.livejournal.com

What can I say about E.M. Prazeman?

Well, for starters, it's a pseudonym. The artist known as E.M. lives and loves and sometimes brawls in the Pacific Northwest, a big change from being an illegal alien refugee from the old Eastern Bloc.

Fully naturalized now, E.M. writes and gardens and raises livestock. Has a fondness for swords and history. Is a better shot with a bow than with a gun, but isn't too bad with a .45.

In the last year the Prazeman household has hosted Kurdish expatriates, SWAT medics, former special operations soldiers, (ostensibly reformed) criminals, Finnish martial artists and the occasional author or school teacher from a remote village. These people come to E.M. to decompress and think.

I know. I'm one of them.

Rory Miller
Author of "Facing Violence"

Mark is dying.

Meridua's fragile hold on freedom
is slipping ...

... and Gutter has plans for him.

But Gutter isn't the only one with plans.

Confidante
A song will transform love into war

VIOLENCE

A Writer's Guide
Second Edition

"... a superb resource ... written by a man who knows his stuff" -- Barry Eisler, NYT best seller

"... as a long-time martial artist and a writer ... I can tell you, it's the real deal ..."
-- Steve Perry, NYT best seller

RORY MILLER

Best Selling Author of *Facing Violence*

Click through the Wyrd Goat Press website
and buy your copy today
wyrdgoat.com

What could be more fun
    than chasing goats around the orchard?

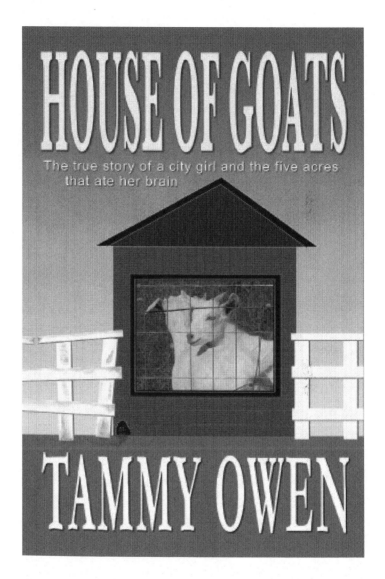

Reading about someone else doing it.

Click through wyrdgoat.com and enjoy the disaster.

Confidante

BOOK TWO OF THE LORD JESTER'S LEGACY

is now available at Amazon, Smashwords, Barnes & Noble, CreateSpace and other fine retailers You can also order Confidante and other great books through Wyrd Goat Press
www.wyrdgoat.com

An excerpt from Confidante:

He rang the bell. So familiar, that fine chord, like a velvet hammer striking piano wires. Most house bells just rang something between a dinner bell and a cow bell.

A boy answered and Mark stepped back in shock.

It could have been Mark himself standing there, though the young man was maybe sixteen, and prettier, and of course he would be taller later though now they were about a height. Blond, like Mark, but without the darker hair at his neck and behind his ears. He wore Mark's old clothes. Was it because they suited him, or because he didn't warrant a separate identity?

The boy drew himself up a little taller and his ice blue eyes stared boldly at Mark for a moment before he dropped his gaze, as he must to someone who was theoretically his better. "Welcome to Pickwelling. May I ask who is calling?" His voice had little refinement, and a bit of a dockside swagger to it.

"Lark." But it wasn't Lark who stepped inside the house as the boy reluctantly backed out of his way. He should have worn his mask, protected himself from this. There was the hated statue of the boy reclining alongside the fawn. And there, the stairs that would lead him to Lord Argenwain's bedchamber. That familiar route. To the left, the study where he'd spent hours with tutors.

"Master jester." He sounded as if he didn't believe Mark could be one. "May I—are you here to see someone?" the boy asked, sounding ruffled.

"Is Gutter home?"

The boy tensed. "No." He said it as if he was glad, and offended, and afraid. "Master jester," he added belatedly. "Would you—"

Mark handed him the card he'd made. "Is he in town?"

"I'm not sure I should tell you that." The boy stomped over to the butlers bell and rang it. "Would you like to wait for the butler in our sitting room? It's right over—"

"No, thank you. And I know where it is."

The boy started to gasp and his body shook. "You're him. You're Mark."

Mark wanted to grab him and take him away from the house, and he wanted to slap him, and he wanted Gutter to be here and he wanted to run.

Lord Argenwain. He couldn't face him.

Mark went out the door. "I'll return," Mark called over his shoulder. "Tonight. And if Gutter is not in town then I would like to know so that I don't waste any more of my time."

The boy ran after him. "Master jester—"

"Lord jester," Mark corrected him.

Made in the USA
Charleston, SC
05 December 2015